THE WHITE COCKADE

THE WHITE COCKADE

by

JULIET DYMOKE

London

DENNIS DOBSON

First published in Great Britain in 1979
by Dobson Books Ltd, 80 Kensington Church Street, London W.8
Typeset by Computacomp (UK) Ltd., Fort William,
and Printed by Billing & Sons Limited,
Guildford, London and Worcester

ISBN 0 234 72044 1

' ... Let him never come back to us,
There would be doubt, hesitation, and pain,
Forced praise on our part, the glimmer of twilight,
Never glad confident morning again.'

The Lost Leader. Robert Browning.

Prologue

November 1745–June 1746

The grey dawn of a November morning had barely broken the darkness when Donald Fraser went quietly into his sister's bedroom. She was still sleeping, her dark hair spreading from under the white nightcap tied beneath her chin, one arm stretched across the pillow. She looked so young in sleep and she had been so late to bed last night, but he must wake her, and leaning down he touched her shoulder.

"Bab," he said urgently. "Wake up, child. We will be away in half an hour and if you are wishing to see us go—"

She opened her eyes and then sat up at once, sleep banished. "Donald! Is it morning already?"

He sat down beside her. "Aye, and a cold one too. The men are beginning to assemble, but we've time for a bite. Aunt Jean has set it out in the parlour—will you come down?"

"Of course." Already she had her feet out of bed, searching for her slippers. "I'm sorry I was not waking sooner, but after last night—I had no desire then for my bed at all."

He nodded, watching her as she put a dressing robe about her shoulders, and hastily taking off her nightcap brushed her hair before tying it back with a ribbon. For all she was only fourteen years old and ten years younger than himself there was a deep bond of affection and understanding between them. She looked a child this morning, but last night, he thought, with her hair dressed and powdered and in her ball gown she had looked a grown woman. "Did you enjoy your first ball?"

She turned from the mirror, her eyes bright with the memory of it. "Oh indeed I did—the music and the dancing, all those hundreds of candles and the dresses—but I wish the Prince had danced. Why did he not dance, Donald? Every woman in the ballroom wanted to dance with him. And he looked so grave."

"He has grave matters on his mind. To be setting out to march into England, to fight for the crown for his father King James—God save him—is no light affair."

"I know, I know," she said, momentarily sobered, "but I shall never forget how he looked last night, so handsome in the tartan and wearing his garter star, and when I think he came with only seven men, that he trusted himself to us—oh, you are fortunate to be going with him."

Her brother smiled. "I know, *m'eudail,* that you would give your soul to be marching with us. I am thinking the Good Being was mistaken when He gave you the body of a woman."

"So do I," she agreed, and then as he stood up in readiness to go downstairs she came to him, laying her hands on his chest, her face glowing again. "I shall be so hungry for news. Did you ever believe that it would really happen, that Prince Tearlach would come? We have hoped for it and prayed for it as long as I can remember and now that he is here understanding is not on me that every man in Scotland has not drawn the sword for him."

"There are some who fear for their skins—and their property," he said scathingly. "They will only come out when we are at Whitehall. And by then the work will have been done by more eager hands."

"How I wish I might be there to see it. You beat General Cope so easily and if the rest of the enemy are as frightened of our Highlandmen—"

"I doubt they will be," he broke in. "The Campbells—may they be cursed—and the lowland Whig clans will not be scared of our pipes and our wild clansmen. And we will have to face General Wade and the Duke of Cumberland too with more men at their back than Johnny Cope had. Nor are they likely to repeat his mistake—" he saw the doubt on her face and added, "but if we can hold our Highlanders we will beat them. Only the clansmen don't like going too far from home."

"But this is different. We are fighting for Scotland. Oh why didn't Macshimi call all our clan out? Why does he hold back?"

"Our Chief has his reasons, I suppose," he answered, but he was as distressed as she was that Simon Fraser, the aged Lord Lovat, had not yet responded to his Prince's call. That wily old man preferred for the moment to sit on the fence, talking politely to Lord President Forbes of his loyalty to King George while at the same time encouraging his son, the Master of Lovat, to be busy among the Frasers so that they were in readiness to rise when he chose to call them. Nor had he refused the request of Donald's father to bring out the Frasers of Duirdre to join their Mackenzie cousins and neighbours. They had marched from Duirdre to join Prince Charles Edward in Edinburgh, sharing the high hopes, the enthusiasm for the man who was the son of their rightful King. The fact that the Prince had come without any of the promised French help was soon forgotten as he won over Chief after Chief; in the Highlands nearly all the clans were 'out'— repressed, burdened with taxation, hedged in with petty restrictions they did not hesitate to dig out their hidden weapons from peat and thatch and turn on the foreigners who had invaded their glens in an endeavour to root out their culture, their way of life.

With the defeat of Cope at Prestonpans John Fraser sent for his wife and daughter to join him in Edinburgh and attend the Prince's court at Holyrood House, the palace of his Stuart ancestors. Aware of the stigma that no other Frasers were present, he bore with fortitude the Prince's "Well doubtless we shall see Lord Lovat when all is won." Donald's own face had burned at the reproach, but knowing the Master well and his Fraser cousins of Inverallochie and Froyers and the rest, he guessed they must be straining to join them, to take part in the campaign.

"They will come out," he said confidently, "and soon. Are you ready to come down, child?"

She nodded and picking up the flat blue bonnet he had laid on the table when he came in she fingered the white cockade, that symbol of the Jacobite cause, that she had sewn there herself. "I'm afraid my stitches are not very good. Mama would have done it better."

"I wanted you to be after making it for me." He took it from her, glancing down at the inexpert knot of ribbon. It was so typical of Bab's efforts, for she had never cared for such occupations, preferring to hitch up her skirts and go to the loch with him when he fished, or to climb the slopes of Lurg Mhór, their own mountain, gathering blossoms in the spring, or blaeberries in the autumn, the sun touching lights in her dark hair, her eyes always bright for him as they were today. Above all she was at her best on her rough Highland shelty and could stay in the saddle all day and never tire. A girl for life, Bab!

"It will remind me of you," he said, teasing her, but he added more gravely, "If it pleases God, I shall march into London with it in my bonnet."

"It will be so strange," she said suddenly, "if it is there that we shall be meeting again."

An odd little silence fell. His grip on her hand tightened and he was aware of a strange certainty that it would be so, yet it was not a certainty that seemed part of the present hopes. He looked over her head to the window where the light was growing. Sometimes it was as if 'the knowing' was on him, as if a curtain was drawn aside only to fall again as quickly, yet leaving behind something that could not be erased from the memory. Then the moment was gone, the excitement rose again, and he bent to kiss her forehead. "Come, for I must break my fast and you'll not have us late on such a day?"

Together they ran down the stairs of the tall house in the Canongate which belonged to their aunt and uncle. In the first floor parlour candles had been lit against the bleak morning and hot bannocks and mulled ale set out on the table. John Fraser and his younger brother William were eating standing, both dressed in tartan trews and plaid, armed with broadswords and pistols, the white cockade in both their bonnets, the eagle's feather of the chief in that of the elder. William's wife Jean was attending to their needs and when her nephew came in she handed him a pot of ale and a bannock with the injunction to eat quickly.

"Break your fast," she said, smiling up at him, for she was very fond of him. "I'd like fine to know where ye'll tak' it tomorrow."

He took the bannock. It was hot and the butter melting, the taste of it good in his mouth. "I'll wager, aunt, you made these yourself. You've servants below, I know, but no one bakes a bannock as you do, and to eat it standing is to signify a hasty journey and a good end."

She gave him one of her rare smiles. She was a Lowland woman, without the Celtic love of poems and omens, nor did she set much store by the prophecies of their bards but she was at one with them on this day.

"Maybe. Twill be a cauld march, I'm thinking."

Donald had one arm about his sister as he ate. "We'll not be minding the cold today, with Tearlach to lead us." He swallowed the last mouthful and took a pot of ale, warm and spiced, glancing at his mother.

She was the only one seated, such was the air of urgency in this room, but she was also the only one who was not Scottish born. Twenty-seven years ago as Lady Caroline Denby, the younger daughter of the English Earl of Harlesdon, she had visited Paris and there met a Highland student, falling deeply in love with him, a love the young John Fraser returned in equal measure, but it was only after two years pleading that she persuaded her father to agree to the match. Fortunately, despite his misgivings, the Earl had liked John Fraser. The marriage would mean that his daughter would be living in a remote part of Scotland, west of the Great Glen, but at the same time he saw that Fraser was a gentleman, well educated, that he had means and would be able to support his wife in a comfortable home, and eventually he agreed. It had been a happy marriage, but Lady Caroline had never really adapted herself to Highland life, had never understood nor accepted the outlandish ways she had not anticipated, nor had she learned more than the few Gaelic words necessary to communicate with her servants, and now the prospect that a Highland army was about to march into England, to attack London itself, terrified her. She wished that the young Prince had not come, that her husband and this tall son of hers had not taken up arms for him, and she sat in her chair, her hands clasped tightly together, watching them as they ate.

Bab was on fire with eagerness for them share the Prince's triumph, she thought, but Bab was all Highland and her mother had never understood the wild spirit that sent her daughter headlong from the ladylike accomplishments she wished her to possess to chase after Donald in pursuits, in her opinion, wholly unsuited to a girl. But they were all content enough at Duirdre and Lady Caroline could not repress a little shiver as she recalled that night when a wild kilted figure had come knocking at their door crying out that the Prince had landed.

William Fraser was stuffing the last of his bannock into his mouth. "It's time we were away. By God, John, you are fortunate to have your son to march beside you."

His wife glanced at him, as if she wished he had not spoken the thought that was uppermost in their minds. "Aye," she said in a low voice. "Shame is on me that our son should not be with you, Mac Domhnull Àrd. I'd gie him a piece o' ma mind if he was here."

"William was never a fighting man," her brother-in-law said. "You can't be changing the lad, he always had his head in his books. Well, Caroline, will you and Bab be at the window to see us pass?"

She rose from her chair and came to him, her eyes brimming. "Take care, John. Oh pray, take care."

He laughed. "I doubt if we will have time to think of caring for ourselves. But don't fash yourself."

"How can I help it—when you are marching against my countrymen?"

"Caroline!" Jean Fraser was made of sterner stuff than her sister-in-law. "We have talked of this before and you said you would not—"

"No, no—" Lady Caroline forced back the tears. "Oh my dear husband, I cannot say I am glad, I cannot feel as Jean does, but I will pray for your safety. I will not think of—of what may happen."

"We will win through," he told her cheerfully and led her away to the window. There he lowered his voice. "But if aught should go wrong promise me you will take Bab to your father. Promise me, Caroline. If we should fail the English vengeance will be fearful."

"John!" she clutched at his coat. "I can see you are not as hopeful as you let others think."

"Perhaps I am afraid the disagreements among ourselves will be more·danger to us than ever the redcoat soldiers will."

"I wish—I know I should not say it—but how I wish *he* had not come at all."

"My dear," his voice hardened, "I do not like to hear you speak so. You know we have waited years for this, you know the provocation we have suffered, and you knew I would never hold back. I told you that before ever we were wed, I told you I was 'out' in the 'Fifteen and would go out again."

"I know, I know," she agreed helplessly, "and indeed I am proud of you, but I cannot forget that I am English."

"But a Highland wife," he added. He was still a fine looking man, and though his thick black hair was streaked with grey his figure was still upright and spare for he had never indulged himself at the table, and spent his days out in his glen, hunting with his people, riding up the mountain to the shielings, riding to meet with his neighbours, attending firelit *Ceilidhs* by night, an active man and still the same man with whom she had fallen in love so long ago. With his arms about her she plucked up the courage to respond. "Yes, John, I am, and we will wait here with Jean to hear of your victories. Forgive me if I am a little fearful for your safety."

He smiled down at her. "If you were not I would be thinking your love for me a passing thing—which it is not, heart of my heart. You will have enough to do keeping our wild girl from dressing as a boy and being after coming with us!" He took her chin in his hand and bent to kiss her, adding gravely, "But promise me you will remember what I have said—if things go against us."

She gave her promise and somehow summoned up a smile, reflecting the genuine sweetness of her nature that had won him to her so long ago in Paris. "You will be angry with me," she added with a little laugh, "if I say I wish we were all at home. I have been so happy at Duirdre. But I only want what you want, my dearest."

"Then that is enough," he said and glanced over her head to where his son and daughter stood together, their hands tightly clasped. They were very alike, he thought, the same almost black hair of the Duirdre Frasers, the same greenish eyes under straight dark brows. Donald was exceptionally tall and Bab seemed likely to be above the average height for a woman, a pair to be proud of it seemed to him, and releasing his wife he went over to his daughter and kissed her forehead.

"Watch over your mother for me, and perhaps while we're away your aunt Jean will be teaching you to sew a straight seam." It was an old joke between them for in fact he too was happier to see her riding the mare he had given her, than to have her sit primly with some embroidery in her lap.

The last of that snatched breakfast was eaten, and then as a sound reached them from far away in the distance, Bab cried out, "Listen! It is the pipes! The march must be starting."

The last embraces were given and for a moment she clung to her brother, fastening a button of his coat, smoothing his plaid and then he was gone down the stair after his father and uncle, his long legs, bare under his kilt, covering three steps at a time.

Left alone the three women looked at the remains of the breakfast in a forlorn silence. Then Jean Fraser said briskly, "Come, we must dress if we are tae be at the window tae see them pass. Bab, child, stop dreaming and be after finding your clothes."

Five minutes later, a tartan shawl about her head and shoulders, Bab stood with her mother and aunt, the sash thrown up regardless of the cold of the morning. The street below was lined with people now, faces at every window, all eager to see the fighting men, for the Prince had chosen to lead his army from Holyrood where they were assembling, back into the city by the Canongate and through the streets before leaving it, one section to go west towards Carlisle, the Prince's division to head south.

After a little breathless waiting the first of the long columns came into sight led by a pair of Cameron pipers and some two dozen Cameron Highlanders. And then behind them came the man that every head craned to see—his royal highness Prince Charles Edward Stuart, already Bonnie Tearlach to his followers. He was astride a fine grey horse, clad from head to foot in the tartan, an eagle's feather in his bonnet; perhaps the best looking of all the Stuarts he stared straight ahead of him out of large and expressive brown eyes, only occasionally turning his head to incline it to a group of cheering people, or to glance up at a window with a smile, as always, for the ladies who embraced his cause as strongly as their menfolk.

"Oh," Bab exclaimed, "if only it was summer and we had white roses to throw at his feet."

17

"Mayhap 'twill be summer when the lad rides home again," her aunt Jean said, "but this morn is as guid as a summer's day for Scotland."

Behind the Prince came his Lieutenant General, Lord George Murray, and the other Scottish lords, followed by Donald Cameron of Locheil, his brother Dr. Archibald and the rest of the clansmen. Next came the men of Clan Donald led by Keppoch, Glengarry and Glencoe, the Stewarts of Appin, the Mackenzies, including John Fraser's nephew, Fergus, who waved up at the window of the tall house to his aunts and his cousin. And then at last a piper led the next contingent below them; he was playing 'Lovat's march' and he was followed by a young clansman carrying the Fraser banner with its Gaelic motto *'Neoni mur maille Dia'*. Behind them rode their Chief, his son marching beside him, his 'tail' following and consisting of his hanchman, his bard Aileen Dru, his tacksman Fraser of Achnahoy and some thirty men from Glen Duirdre, marching in kilt and plaid, their targes slung on their shoulders, and on their long hair blue bonnets carrying the white cockade and their clan badge of a sprig of yew. Some had muskets and fowling pieces but most only carried broadswords and dirks and each man had a pouch for what food he could carry.

"Wailiedragles indeed!" Jean said fiercely. "Some fule may ha' called them that, but they're a bonny sight the morn."

Bab's eyes were only for her brother, the pride in her scarcely contained. Her voice was exultant as she called out in their native tongue, "God go with you, Mac Domhnull Og!" He turned, lifted his bonnet and waved it and she clutched at the window ledge, longing to be down there with him, knowing that the heart of her marched with him.

Slowly the files of men passed, the music of the pipes died away, the street emptied. Windows were closing but as she still leaned out to see the last final glimpse of them Bab exclaimed, her face still alight with excitement, "Oh, how shall we wait? It is hard to be a woman."

"Losh," Jean said. "I'll be after finding work for ye, ma girl— mayhap y'll be a laird's wife one day, but 'tis nae harm to be a guid cook forbye. Come in, ma lass, or ye'll be falling into the 'gate."

Bab withdrew reluctantly and Jean pulled down the sash. Watching them, Lady Caroline cried out suddenly, "You do not know, any of you, what you are about! I tell you they cannot beat the whole of England—it is to their deaths they have gone." And she burst into helpless tears.

18

Eight months later, in contrast to the joy of that dank November day, on a warm June night brilliant with stars, Donald and his father stumbled home to Glen Duirdre. Wounded, dirty, with empty stomachs, their clothes torn and bedraggled, they reached the shelter of their own house and now slept on top of the coverlet of the bed in the main bedroom just as they had thrown themselves last night, in utter exhaustion.

John Fraser's coat bore a dark brown stain around the shoulder and his trews were in shreds at the knees, a blood-stained bandage about one thigh. His face was drawn, dark shadows beneath the eyes, and even in sleep there was a cleft of pain between his brows. Donald lay with his long limbs sprawled, his kilt twisted about muddied knees, a half healed sabre cut seaming one cheek. He had kicked off his shoes but his right hand had remained closed on the dirk lying between them. Then as his eyes opened in startled recollection, he sat up, listening intently.

Only a faint gleam of light came through the closed shutters, but it was clearly morning and with one glance at his father he slid off the bed and went to the window. He did not open the shutter at first but peered through. There was nothing to be seen outside but the loch lying still and smooth in the morning sunshine, the mountain reflected in the blue water, the familiar rowan tree springing from a shaft of rock and hanging crazily over to gaze at its own image. There were no soldiers, no redcoats marching in a file down the rough road that led through the glen, and he heaved another sigh. Evidently they had given the patrol the slip the night before and unless the English officer knew of this remote place in the wild country between Loch Monar and Attadale they were probably safe for a while.

He opened one of the shutters a few inches and then coming back to the bed stood looking down at his father. It was seven weeks since that awful April day when in biting wind and sleet the Jacobite cause had gone down into the mud of Drumossie moor, seven weeks since the last stand at Culloden when he had seen the men around him slaughtered by English guns and English swords, the clans mown down, all their hopes gone.

Moments remained vivid—one when an English dragoon had ridden at him, the gleam of a sabre swinging downwards and the shock of pain as the blade slit his cheek open; others as, with blood blinding him, he saw his father's piper fall, blown apart by a cannon ball, and the young clansman who had carried their banner trampled to death in the mêlée. And it was all over so quickly, barely an hour sufficing the Duke of Cumberland to defeat the Highland army, the white cockades trodden into bloodied ground.

Not long before the end his father, already wounded in the shoulder, had received a musket ball in the thigh, and Aileen Dru had at once leapt over his Chief's fallen body and stood over it until Donald had fought his way through. Between them they dragged John Fraser clear, over the dead and the dying, away from the surging English dragoons that faced them. By now the Highland army was routed and scattering and somehow in the hideous confusion they got their burden safely away into the now welcome mist and rain.

They fled to the west, escaping into familiar hills, where they had been forced to lie up in a cave for some weeks, for by then the wounded man was in a high fever. Eventually they moved on again, hiding by day and travelling by night, always towards Glen Duirdre. Two nights ago they had stumbled wearily into a shelter of rocks and trees on a hillside and Donald had sent Aileen Dru to see if he could find a crofter who would give them some food, and that was the last he had seen of him. During the dark hours he heard a shot which had warned him of the proximity of a patrol and he could only hope that somehow Aileen Dru had evaded it.

During the next day he and his father stayed hidden in the shelter, but when darkness came he helped him away, half carrying him, a slow stumbling progress, until at last they had reached their own house, half expecting it to be burned. He reached out one hand to touch the bed post. It still seemed a miracle that the house was here, that no soldiers had found this remote glen, that last night Duirdre House stood, as it had done for two hundred years, a stone building of moderate size where the Frasers of Duirdre had lived among their tacksmen and crofters for far longer than this present house had sheltered them, descendents of the first Mac Domhnull Ard, Donald the Tall. But it was the first time, he thought, that his father had come home without his 'tail', that retinue without which no chief ever travelled.

He turned towards the door and it was then that he heard his father stir. "Donald?"

He came back to the bed. "I was going to see if I could find something for breakfast. God knows where Morag is or Angus Coll, but there are some more of those oatcakes in the kitchen and we didn't finish the whisky last night."

"I am not hungry."

He laid his hand on his father's forehead. "You will be having the

20

fever again, but you must try to eat a little. I might even be able to make some porridge," he added with a faint smile. "I watched Morag do it often enough when I was a boy."

He went away down the stairs, and the thought came to him how short a time ago it was that this house was a place of warmth and light, graced by the presence of his mother and his sister's vibrant lively presence. He had not seen them since the army had marched out of Edinburgh, and his mouth drew down into a thin line, pulling at the scar on his cheek, as he wondered what had become of them, whether they were still at his aunt's house, what his mother had done when she had heard of the tragedy. He thought she would be lost without his father's strength.

He opened the door of the parlour and then looked into the dining room. Everything seemed normal, unchanged, as if waiting for the family to assemble there once more. He turned away, not going in. This was no time for memory, nor for looking to what was gone. He had the responsibility of getting his father to safety and when this old house would see them all again was a question for the nebulous future.

He passed through the library and went down the steps to the small back hall and then into the kitchen, and there a sudden sound and a shadow startled him.

His own presence had no less effect on the woman who stood by the hearth, a broom in her hand. She gave a little shriek and cried out in Gaelic.

"Morag!" he said swiftly and spoke in the same tongue, for she had no English. "I did not hear you come. I was thinking you must have gone home to your father."

She came forward, staring at him. "Is it yourself, Mac Domhnull Og? Dear Saints be praised, you are alive! But your poor face! And Duirdre himself? You'll not be telling me——"

"He is upstairs, but he's badly hurt and he has a fever."

"Ah——" She clasped her hands about the broom handle, a comely woman of middle years, and he was glad suddenly that she had no man, that he had not to give her the news he would have to take to some others in the clachans, but it was still bad enough. He looked at her rosy face beneath the white curch. "You heard what happened to us?"

"Aye, Seumas my cousin sent his boy to be telling us. And Callum has come back, sore wounded as he is." She laid the broom by the hearth, slow tears trickling down her face. "I'm thinking Duirdre must wonder why he took our men to die. There's none but old ones and bairns in the glen now."

21

Donald reached out for her hands but for a moment he could not speak, the holocaust that had enveloped them all too appalling for mere words. He had picked up scraps of news on the flight west; a wounded Cameron had told him that the Prince was in hiding with a price on his head, somewhere with Cluny Macpherson, he thought, while a woman who had sheltered Donald and his father for a night, told them that she had heard that Locheil had escaped into Lochaber with young Clanranald. But he had no news of his Chief, Lord Lovat, who had finally called out the whole clan in the desperate months of the new year, nor of Simon Fraser the younger, the Master of Lovat, who had not reached the battlefield with his Fraser contingent in time to take part. Yet they would all have died for the Prince, as he would have done if it had so fallen out, as he would still do if his body could shield him from Cumberland's vengeance.

He looked down at Morag. "You know why we went. I think Achnahoy got away and I saw my cousin Fergus not long before the end, but whether he lives or not I can't tell."

She put up a hand to wipe her cheeks. "And the two of you boys together and so wild, the pair of you. I pray God will send him home. Were you seeing Aileen Dru at all?"

"He helped me bring my father out, but we lost him on the slopes of Creag Dhubh. I'm fearing he was shot for we heard firing." There was a moment's silence, the weight of sorrow heavy on them both. "At least you've not had the soldiers here," he said at last but did not add 'yet' though he knew their coming must be inevitable. One night he had doubled back on his tracks in search of food, and had come in the darkness upon a burning croft, seen a woman bayoneted with her child still at her breast. Later he had seen an old man and a boy, lying in their own blood beside their plough in a field, and neither could have been involved in the battle. The expression on his face made Morag reach up to touch his cheek.

"*Mo chridhe*, the wounds will heal."

"Will they?" he asked wrily. "I doubt it, Morag."

She understood him. "And that young man, that all this was for— what of him?"

"He is in hiding somewhere and please God will be got safe away. There are French ships off the coast somewhere and I must try and get my father to the sea. But I don't like to leave you all here. Some of the men may yet come back for we were scattered all over the hills after the fight and if the English come—"

"There's naught for them here," she retorted sturdily, "but my

22

father still has an old musket and if they should set foot in our glen—"

"Oh, Morag," he said and sighed. "I fear you do not understand."

"I understand I must be about caring for the laird." She jerked her head toward the ceiling. "What can I be doing for himself? I know something of tending wounds."

"A fresh dressing would be a comfort to him, but for the moment our pressing need is for food. We found a few oatcakes last night, but we've had naught more solid since two days ago when a woman at a croft gave us some meal and we made a poor enough mess with it."

"My grief," she said, "I'll have a hot breakfast for you before I look to the Laird's wounds."

She began to bustle about, lighting the fire and lifting down a heavy pan from its hook, and watching her Donald found a swift comfort in the warmth of the old kitchen and the familiar figure who had been there as long as he could remember.

When she had set two bowls on a tray she momentarily laid both hands on his sleeve, touching his torn shirt. "My bairnie," she said for all as if he did not tower over her, "I never thought to see you so." Her eyes filled again and then she braced herself. "But I'm an old fool standing here when Mac Domhnull Àrd needs to break his fast. Up with you and I'll bring a dram for you both."

"I found a bottle last night," Donald said, "there's plenty left."

They went upstairs together. Morag took one anguished look at her wounded master and set about lifting him higher on to the pillows; she would have fed him herself if he had not assured her he was able to do that office for himself, and the food and the whisky seemed to revive him.

She dressed his wounds, muttering Gaelic curses under her breath directed at the English in general and that foreign man in London who had no right to set his will over Scotland. John Fraser smiled a little in a tired manner and when she had gone back to the kitchen glanced up at his son.

"I fear Morag's curses will not make our own glen safe for us. Are you going to try to find old Malcolm?"

"I thought so. If no one else has his boat he will take us off to the islands, and he'll know if the French ships have been seen."

The wounded man shifted, an expression of deep despair on his face. "We are come to a sad pass, are we not? That I should have to abandon my own people! If I stay—"

Donald came over to the bed and sat down upon the edge of it. "Father, you cannot stay. You and Macshimi will be hunted down—

you know it—with Locheil and Cluny and the rest. It will not serve our tacksmen and crofters, those that are left, if you are found here. If we are gone, it may be better for Morag and old Dougal and the bairns."

"I suppose you are right. It seems we must depend on the French." The old indignation rose in Donald. "If only they had kept their promises to the Prince! With a French army at his back we'd be in London today." He was silent for a moment. Even without the French, if they had not turned back at Derby, if the Prince's staff officers had not quarrelled at that fatal council meeting, who was to say that 'Bonnie Tearlach' would not be in Whitehall at this moment?

"Instead we are fugitives in our own home," his father finished his thoughts for him. "The cause is lost for the moment and we can only thank God the Prince was not taken on the field, and pray that he will get safe to France. No man in the Highlands would betray him, whatever price they set on his head."

"No indeed," Donald agreed, but the price, he thought, would be paid by ordinary men and women in blood and fire and destruction. All that was left for the leaders was escape, a life of exile—or the rope or the firing squad.

He straightened his back and stood up. "I'll be away then, and with a better will now that Morag is here to care for you. I should be to Sheldaig and back long before nightfall." He glanced down at the worn face. "We ought to be gone in the dark hours if you're strong enough."

His father nodded. "A day's rest will suffice me. At least we must thank God your mother and sister are not here—the redcoats have little respect for the women of—rebels." He broke off, a frown on his forehead. "I hope they are with your grandfather and when we are settled in France they will be able to join us there—if indeed it pleases God to bring us over the water."

"I wish I had not to be leaving you, but I'll be back as soon as I can. I want to go up the glen. There's little enough we can do for our people, but at least I can talk to those who have no men to come back."

"There's a chest locked in my cupboard." John Fraser tried to raise himself. "Give the widows some silver."

"I'll see to it." Donald paused by the door, an odd uneasiness making him reluctant to go. Of what use to tell his father not to be anxious when half their clan lay dead at Culloden, the men that lived hunted through the hills, Fraser women ravished, children slain—when their Chief, Macshimi, was in hiding somewhere with a price on his head no doubt, and young Fraser of Inverallochie who had led the clan into battle lying with those that had fallen, thrown probably into a common grave on that ghastly field? Donald had seen two of his cousins fall and his uncle William, though he had dragged himself away, had been too badly wounded to have survived. Of what use to say 'rest' when such horror lay on their minds, when their last memory of their Prince had been of a man with a ravaged, tear-stained face giving the *sauve qui peut* to his last remaining troops.

Donald leaned down and took his father's hand in both his. "Try to sleep while I am gone."

John Fraser smiled up at his son. "*Beanachd leibh, Mac Domhnull Og.*"

Donald gave him one last glance that said all that needed to be said between them, his father's soft voice, carrying its customary blessing, following him as he left the room. He paused only to change into a clean shirt and a strong pair of brogues and then went down the stairs and out by the kitchen door, leaving Morag to watch over the sick man.

All that June day he walked, by little known tracks familiar to him since boyhood, skirting the northern slopes of Lurg Mhór, passing under Sgùrr na Feataig and crossing the Achnasheen road and the river where it was shallow enough to wade. The road itself had been empty save for a man driving a small cart. By mid-day he could see the heights of Ben Eighe and Liathach, their strange white shale giving them a bleak and forbidding look. There he turned left along the track by Upper Torridon loch, the water blue and still. One or two fishing boats were out as usual, undisturbed by the holocaust of the last weeks.

At last he came down among the fishing crofts at Sheildaig where Loch Torridon went out to the sea and cormorants clustered on a group of tiny islands. There luck was with him for old Malcolm Mackenzie was mending a net, his gnarled fingers weaving with a skill acquired long ago. He nodded when Donald made his request, the lines on his face deepening as he heard more details of the defeat than had yet reached this remote place. He agreed to ferry Duirdre and his son down the loch to the sea and land them in the region of Ob Lusa on Skye. Donald talked with him a while, rested his long limbs on the sand and ate some of Malcolm's bread and cheese before starting on the journey home.

The sun sparkled on the gentle water, the June day so warm, the prospect so peaceful, that suddenly he found it more than he could bear and getting to his feet turned his face from it to the long walk back to Duirdre. Now that his mind was free of the reason for his journey he slackened his furious pace a little, taking in every detail of mountain and water, of young green fern and heather not yet in bloom. It would be dark when they came this way tonight for there would not be a moon and after that—when would he see these hills again and his own glen? When would he see the forest about Loch Monar, visit his Chief at Castle Dounie, go fishing in Beauly river with the young Master of Lovat? Never perhaps, for it needed little imagination to visualize what the soldiers were about, wreaking the Duke of Cumberland's vengeance on the 'rebels'. The little he had seen had shown him they could expect no mercy.

About four o'clock he stopped to drink from a burn for the sun was hot. He took off his bonnet with its tattered white cockade, soaking his face in the cool running water, and then lay back on the tough heather stalks, loving the warm earth with the passion of one saying farewell. Yet surely they would come back, they *must* come back!

He shut his eyes, breathing the smell of the earth, of peat, of the young growth all around him. And then because youth was also strong in him, he sprang to his feet, setting his face to what had to be done. He walked on, pausing only at a croft to accept a cup of milk and talk briefly to a woman with a couple of shy children clinging to her skirts, but he could give her no news of her Mackenzie man.

At last in the late afternoon he reached the slopes that hid Duirdre from sight and deciding to enter the glen from the far end to visit the outlying crofts of Achnahoy, he took the old track to the north of Lurg Mhór. But even as he began to climb the soft breeze brought a different scent. He paused, his head lifted, catching the acrid smell of burning, and if any doubt of imminent danger lingered, a pistol shot shattered it.

He began to run frantically, knowing the path so well that he was as sure-footed as the deer that followed it and a great deal swifter than the cattle the herdsmen drove that way. And as he came round the side of the mountain the glen, as he had dreaded in nightmare, opened up before him. He threw himself down on the track and stared, transfixed.

The place was teeming with redcoats. They were everywhere, setting light to crofts, the dry thatch burning fiercely in the summer heat, thick dark smoke swirling upward in the breeze. The glen he had left in peace that morning, sweet and fresh in the June dawn, had become filled with horror, with a cruel vengeance brought down on the innocent. He could see old Dougal lying sprawled before his croft, an ancient and useless fowling piece beside him; women and children were shrieking, running from their burning houses, and he saw one woman—it must be Dougal's daughter—rush at a soldier with a knife. She was bayoneted and a boy screamed. The soldier turned on him and he too fell, over the body of his mother. By another house the soldiers had dragged out a young man. Donald raised both clenched fists to his face. Dear God, it was Callum! The lad could hardly stand, his leg bandaged, one arm hanging loose, but the soldiers set him against his own wall and shot him.

They had an officer with them who was directing the search for rebels and weapons, and some of the soldiers had been sent to round up what cattle they could find.

Donald sprang up, regardless of the target he made. The desire to go down, to send at least that damned officer in his scarlet coat and gold lace straight to hell before they despatched him, was overwhelming, but he had only his claymore with him and a *sgian dhub,* no pistol— and what could one man do against a column of armed men? And there was his father and Duirdre House. What was happening there? He could not see for the trees below and bending almost double he began to run along the ridge as he had never run before, but there was little hope in him that the soldiers had not reached the house. Yet it was possible that warning might have come, that Morag might have got her master away into hiding in time.

He plunged half way down the slope and there reached a small spinney of silver birches, leaping over fallen logs, his feet crunching on the old dead twigs of last year, until he came to the far side. He was sweating and there was a sickness of fear in his stomach that had not been there even in the worst moments on Drumossie Moor.

And then he saw the house. It was already beginning to burn. Some of the men had set faggots by the front door and the ground floor windows had caught alight, the shutters burning brightly. On the path before the door the body of Angus Coll lay sprawled. Donald leaned against a tree, watching in impotent anguish, his mind casting about wildly for some way to reach his father, but before he had time to think he saw Morag run from the kitchen. She was shouting in Gaelic, a heavy griddle in her hand, a sight that would have been humorous if it had not been set in tragedy. One of the soldiers caught hold of her and Donald stood rigid, but the sergeant not understanding her merely thrust her aside impatiently and sent men to guard the kitchen door. The officer rode up towards the main door and called out something Donald could not hear.

God in heaven, what was he to do? Had his father had been warned, had he slipped out before the soldiers came? Hope rose. Mac Domhnull Àrd might even now be out on the hill behind the house and, thinking of his father's wounds, his fever and exhaustion, Donald was beginning to grapple with the problem of how to cross the glen unseen and reach the far slopes when, with a crash, the door fell in.

There was a moment's pause, an imperceptible halt in time, the officer watching, the soldiers with their muskets levelled. Then, over the burning wood, stepped Duirdre himself, his face blackened by smoke, a bare dirk in his hand.

The officer called out again, and above the sudden roar behind him as the flames seized the woodwork in the hall, Donald heard his father's voice, carried on the wind. "Never! God save King James!"

In the copse above his son stood in an agony of indecision. Every instinct, tribal, filial, urged him to leap down the four hundred yards that separated them, to get to his father's side and die with him. Yet even his small experience of battle told him that he would be shot or bayoneted before he could reach him. He clutched at his tree, turning his head from side to side, hot tears scalding his eyes, the fire seeming to burn him though he could not feel the flames up here. To throw his life away in one gesture—it would avail his father nothing, and beyond all doubt he knew it would not be his wish, for he had a mother and a sister and a duty to them. Oh God, why had he gone to Shieldaig this morning? Why had he not stayed, kept watch, got his father away?

All this flashed in a brief instant through his mind as he stared blindly at the scene below. And then, equally swiftly, it was all over.

The officer beckoned two of his troopers forward, but even as John Fraser braced himself, prepared to sell his life at least at the expense of some English blood, one of the troopers, over-excited, his finger on the trigger, discharged his musket. The Highlander fell, sprawled before his own doorway, the dirk spinning from his hand.

"Damn you, who told you to shoot?" the officer shouted. "I wanted him alive. He might have known where—" he broke off and, dismounting, went over to the fallen man, turning him over. Then with a shrug he turned away from the heat of the burning house, remounted and rode back into the heart of the glen, ordering his men to begin driving off any cattle and stock they could find.

In the copse above Donald slid to his knees and then on to his face among the tiny birch cones. He no longer cared whether the soldiers found him or not. He was aware of nothing but that his father whom he loved lay dead below and he had done nothing to save him, that he had witnessed something that, though he was powerless to prevent it, he would rather have been sharing. Duirdre had been destroyed in blood and fire by that officer in a scarlet coat now riding so unconcernedly away, and his loathing and shame bereft him for a while of his senses.

How long he lay there he did not know. The afternoon faded into evening, the sun went down behind Lurg Mhór, the wind dying with the sunset, and it grew cooler in the copse. At last, drained of emotion, chilled and empty, he dragged himself to his feet. In the twilight he saw that the glen was empty. The crofts still burned, the corpses lay where they had fallen. Any left alive had fled into the hills. The soldiers were gone, their work done.

He came down, crossed the little burn and went up the path to the house, to where his father lay, left as far as the English officer was concerned, to lie unburied until he rotted. John Fraser lay on his back, his eyes staring sightlessly at the first stars, the neat hole where the musket ball had passed through the breast of his coat barely bloodied. Death had been swift.

With a sudden low cry Donald knelt and gathered the body into his arms, drawing down the lids, holding the dead man close. Hardly knowing what he was doing, he rocked to and fro until his eyes caught sight of the abandoned dirk which the soldiers had forgotten to remove. He picked it up with one hand and put the iron to his lips, a wordless oath torn from him in his grief and misery.

The late summer darkness fell, a clear still night, the mountain and the stars watching over the Glen of Duirdre as they had always done, cool and remote, unmoved by what had been done there this day.

Chapter 1

A group of officers stood by the doorway of Lady Denby's ballroom surveying the brilliant scene as the dancers moved through a quadrille, a little orchestra in a gallery above, a hundred candles set in crystal chandeliers lighting the scene. The officers were scarcely less brilliant themselves in their scarlet coats with gold lacing, elaborate cuffs, and white buckskin breeches. They were of His Majesty's Second Troop of Grenadier Guards and considered themselves the élite of the army.

One, a very young lieutenant, remarked that though there was no doubt a card room he proposed to stay in the ball room.

"I'm not surprised," said a middle-aged man with the insignia of a captain. "You burned your fingers at White's this afternoon. It's too high for you there, pup."

The lieutenant flushed. "Oh, I can stand my losses—I think," he added with a sudden rueful grin. "But I have not Major Astley's luck."

The major gave him a sardonic glance. "If you think it is luck then you are more naïve than I suspected. Harry, do you dance? I shall find my cousin Georgiana and see if there are any new beauties come to town."

Captain Lord Harry Cavendish leaned his generous bulk against the door. "We all know you take first pick! I shall be content if Miss Georgiana will dance with me, and a fig for Philip Denby."

"If you think to filch my cousin from him let me tell you that the chit seems to be very much attached to him, though quite why I'm not sure. Denby is a nice enough fellow but dull. However, I suppose Georgy has enough spirits for both." Major Astley surveyed the room. "An hour or so here will suffice. After that I'm off."

"You are on duty? I thought—"

"His Majesty cancelled the lévée for tonight. He was—unwell."

Lieutenant Chambers gave an indiscreet laugh, and Harry put in smoothly, "I heard he and the Prince of Wales had words this morning. Was Cumberland involved in it?"

"No, thank God he was not," the older captain lowered his voice.

"The Prince is at loggerheads with the Duke too. I really believe he would have liked to see his brother beaten at Culloden."

Major Astley gave a snort. "Cumberland has his faults but he would not have tolerated this morning's argument. His Majesty took to his room and so I was released from attending him. I'm due back at White's in an hour. Do you come with me, Harry?"

Lord Harry laughed. "To see you fleece Everard again? I wouldn't miss it for the world."

Captain Brooks, whose whole air proclaimed a life lived in the army, yet without achieving a higher rank than that of Lord Harry so many years his junior, said laconically, "Sir Laurence Everard is a bad loser. He must be in debt to you for an inordinate amount, Rupert."

Major Astley shrugged. "Large enough. But if he wants the chance to win it back, who am I to deny him?"

"They say he owes all over London," Harry said. "I doubt you'll get your money."

"I'll get it," Rupert Astley answered, "one way or another. I do not like unpaid debts."

Lieutenant Chambers glanced at him and was rather glad that it was not he who was on the receiving end of that remark. He stood somewhat in awe of his senior officer. Rupert Astley was of medium height with a thin strong body; his cropped hair was hidden beneath a white wig tied at the back with black ribbon but sandy eyebrows and a freckled skin betrayed his colouring and his eyes were an exceptionally vivid blue. He had a nose slightly too large for his face and a mouth that might have been pleasant had it not had a rather hard twist to it. It was only when he smiled that his charm became apparent and then it was such that he drew friends to himself with no apparent effort and which he accepted in a casual manner that the young lieutenant envied. Despite having received the sharp end of his major's tongue on several occasions, he never lost the opportunity to be among his social circle.

At that moment a fair girl in a soft pink gown, a pink rose in her powdered hair, came hurrying across to him. "Dearest Rupert, you have come. I did so hope you would."

He kissed her hand and then her cheek. "I promised you, Georgy, and I don't break promises. Is Philip here?"

"Yes, indeed. There, in a green coat, dancing with—"

Rupert's hand tightened on hers. "Who is that girl with him? I've not seen her before."

Georgiana glanced towards the dancers. "That is Miss Barbara

Fraser. You will not know her as she is only just come to London. She's Phil's cousin. Is she not a lovely creature?"

The major was watching her intently. He saw a girl, slender and a little taller than average, dressed in a yellow gown, her hair powdered and piled high on her head, with an oval face, a mobile smiling mouth. At that moment in the dance she turned and chanced to look in his direction. Seeing his gaze fixed on her she returned it with one equally speculative until the dance led her away again. He made a sudden involuntary movement and then dropped his cousin's hand. "Present me, Georgy."

Lord Harry Cavendish gave an exaggerated sigh. "Curse you, Rupert. I met her last night at the Ormondes' supper party and she's promised to ride with me. Must you cast your eyes on every girl I like?"

"I do not know that I shall like her. Tell me about her, Georgy."

"Well, she and Phil had the same grandfather—the Earl of Harlesdon. I expect you remember him? He was very wealthy and although, when he died a few years ago, the estate was entailed and both Harlesdon Hall and title went to his male heir, his cousin George, he left his other house, Wilde End, to Phil and his fortune equally between his two sisters' children, Phil and Bab." Georgy paused and sent Rupert a swift upward glance. "So Bab is something of an heiress."

Lord Harry scratched his head, setting his wig askew. "It's damned hot in here. Of course I knew Lady Denby was the Earl's daughter and I seem to recall her sister marrying Laurence Everard some time ago, but before that—she'd not been in England for some time, surely?"

"No. Lady Caroline's first husband was a Scottish gentleman. Bab told me Lord Harlesdon had not liked the match very much and she had only come to England once before as a little girl, but during the rebellion four years ago her mother brought her south to stay with her grandfather."

"Very wise," Major Astley commented, but his remark scarcely interrupted the flow of his cousin's information.

"Bab's father had an estate somewhere in the Highlands but as he fought with his clan and was killed, neither Lady Caroline nor Bab went back."

"Oh?" A slight frown crossed Rupert Astley's face. "Miss Fraser's father was a rebel then?"

"Yes, and her brother too, but he escaped and went abroad."

"I see." He was still staring at the dancers. "So now she is Laurence Everard's stepdaughter."

"I don't envy her that," Captain Brooks said rather sourly. "Everard is one of the least acceptable members of White's."

"He can be pleasant when he chooses," Georgy said, "or I suppose Lady Caroline would not have married him."

"No doubt," Rupert's smile was rather cynical, "she was glad enough to find an English husband after what happened in Scotland. And probably Everard thought he was marrying an heiress. He must have been considerably put out when he discovered it was Mistress Barbara and not her mother who shared Harlesdon's wealth with your betrothed."

Georgy tapped his arm with her fan. "Now you are being disagreeable, Rupert. Is my uncle here?"

"No, the gout keeps him at Astley House, and he has not been well for some time. Ah, the dance is over. Now, if you please, Georgy—"

"Oh, very well." She tucked her hand into his arm and led him across the floor where the dancers were moving off. "Bab, here is my cousin, Major Astley, who wishes to be presented to you. Rupert, Miss Barbara Fraser."

He bowed. Under that powder her hair must be very dark, he thought, and her eyes were a greenish hazel set wide apart with black brows. As Georgy had said she was indeed lovely, with a clear pale skin and finely moulded features. He put her hand to his lips. "Perhaps, Miss Fraser, I may be fortunate enough to secure a dance?"

She smiled at him but shook her head. "I'm afraid, sir, I am spoken for all evening. Lieutenant Chambers has this minuet."

"Rank carries some privileges," Major Astley said. "He will not argue with me."

"Oh, that is too bad." Georgy shook a finger at her cousin. "If you will release me, Phil, I'll go and console him."

Mr. Denby, a quietly dressed young man, bowed to his former partner and was beginning a polite remark to Major Astley when the music began again and the Major appeared not to have heard him. Georgy whisked him away and Rupert Astley held out his arm. Miss Fraser accepted it and they took their places.

For a few moments neither spoke, moving through the measured steps, and then she asked if his regiment was stationed in London.

"I am in the Life Guards," he told her, "we attend His Majesty."

"I should have known perhaps, but I do not understand your uniforms and what signifies."

"How should you?" he countered. "You are from Scotland, are you not?"

A little warmth crept into her face. "I am Highland born, sir."

And proud of it, he thought amusedly, despite her English mother and grandfather. "Georgy has told me a little. I gather you have lived in England since the late reb—rising," he changed the word hastily, "and your mother is Lady Caroline Everard. Everard's estate is near St. Albans, I believe—do you like it there?"

"It is pleasant enough. I am able to ride a great deal and I like that."

"Do you not ride in London?"

"Yes, on most mornings with Georgy and my cousin Philip, but the park is no exchange for the countryside in Hertfordshire."

His eyes gave a practised sweep over her figure. Yes, she would sit a horse well. "Perhaps I may join you one morning?" But it was hardly a question and she merely inclined her head.

When the dance ended he escorted her to the room where refreshments were being served and procured two glasses of madeira, finding an alcove where they might sit together.

She sipped a little and then asked if he had seen much service.

"I was at Dettingen and at Fontenoy where the French trounced us and my lord Duke of Cumberland conducted the most masterly retreat I've ever encountered," he said smiling, and then asked if this was her first visit to London.

"I came last year, but my mother was unwell and we did not mix in society."

"And are you enjoying it now?"

"Very much. Georgy has been so kind."

"She's a good girl," Rupert agreed absently, "at least when she holds her tongue still." Barbara Fraser, he thought, was not of the usual stamp of butterfly to be found in London ballrooms. Since the day he had left Eton girls had come easily to him. He had had several mistresses, one or two affairs that had caused scandal, in particular that relating to a certain Mrs. Walters which resulted in a duel with the irate husband, but all this lent him an experienced air which in no way deterred match-making mamas from bringing their daughters to his attention. His father told him in no uncertain terms that it was time and more that Rawdon had an heir, but though he might have had the pick of the year's eligible young ladies, none of them attracted him for that role nor had he met one with the calmly appraising look of this girl with her total lack of fashionable coquetry.

He leaned back against the velvet seat and regarded her with

34

interest. "I believe you have a brother?"

"Yes, but I have not seen him these four years. He lives in Paris."

Her eyes were shadowed, her head half turned from him and he found himself looking at her profile. Something made him continue to probe. "I hope your family did not suffer greatly in the troubles in Scotland?"

"I'm sure Georgy has told you, sir," she said with quiet dignity, "that my father died for that cause. I lost cousins and an uncle and our Chief, Lord Lovat—" the green eyes became suddenly bright with suppressed feeling, "you must know that he was sent, an old man near eighty, to his death on Tower Hill."

So she had fire too! He inclined his head. "We had better not argue the rights of it—it has all been over these four years and there has been a general pardon for those concerned."

"A pardon, yes, but the terms of it!" She broke off sharply.

"Harsh perhaps, but necessary for the nation's peace," he said without pretence. "Why does your brother not return?"

"My father was attainted, sir, and his estates forfeit." And then she shut her lips firmly. Her colour deepened and she said, "I beg your pardon. I should not have—"

"It is I who should not have asked—here at least," he answered, and to change the subject spoke of her grandfather. "My father knew him well. In fact Lord Harlesdon often dined at Astley House before his health began to fail and he retired to Wilde End."

At once the stormy look went out of her face. "He was such a dear old man, and I was devoted to him, except when—" she broke off and only when he prompted her did she go on. "—when he and Donald quarrelled. But this is of no interest to you, sir. Suffice it to say I was very sad that he died so soon after we came to live with him." She paused, looking round the room. "Tell me, Major,—I know so few people in London—who is that distinguished-looking man talking to those people over by that pillar?"

He wondered what she had been going to say, but he followed her gaze. "Why that's David Garrick, the actor. He is enthralling everybody with his King Lear at the moment, though I find the piece too gloomy for my taste. Have you been to the theatre yet?"

"No, but Georgy's father has promised to take us tomorrow afternoon."

"My uncle and aunt have a passion for the theatre so I don't suppose it will be your only visit. You would find Congreve's plays more entertaining. And do you see that middle-aged man in a brown periwig talking to one of our chief ministers, Mr. Pelham? That is Mr. Fielding, the lawyer who is the author of *Tom Jones*."

"Oh," she said delightedly, "I am reading his book just now. Georgy lent it to me and I am enjoying it excessively."

He was amused. "I rather imagine you would do so. Squire Weston puts me in mind of the gentleman whose estates border ours at Rawdon!"

"That is your country home?"

"Yes, in Berkshire. It is—" he paused, "it is a fine house and there is a large park, and the village is considered one of the most beautiful in the county. I should like you to see it some day." He stopped abruptly and she glanced keenly at him.

"I can see that you are very attached to it. I should like to see it very much."

"Yes," he said and then, hardly knowing why he was telling her so much he added, "but we have not been there a great deal since my mother died, many years ago. My father prefers Astley House and the company of his London friends."

An odd little silence fell and a moment later a young beau in blue satin came to claim her hand and the Major had perforce to let her go. "But I shall see you again," he said, "in the park."

She gave a sudden smile, the whole of her face lighting up. "If you can catch me, sir!" And then she disappeared into the set already forming for a quadrille.

He stood watching her. The last sudden flash of humour, the boyish challenge, attracted him further to her and there was a faint smile on his face also as he made his way back to the entrance hall. There he found Harry Cavendish talking to a tall dark man with a keenly intelligent expression on a face that might otherwise have been ugly.

"Good evening, Simon. I did not know you were coming here tonight."

"My dear Rupert, you did not trouble yourself to ask me this morning or I would have told you. What, are you going?"

"Yes, to White's. I have an appointment there."

"To fleece Laurence Everard," Harry grinned at him, but Simon Ravenslow said without amusement, "I heard about your play this afternoon. Don't you know the man's in debt all over town and at Newmarket too?"

The Major shrugged. "I merely offer him the chance to reverse his losses."

"Which he won't," Harry put in. "You're too good for him, Rupert."

"You play too high," Mr. Ravenslow added. "It's foolish."

"I agree." Harry spoke in a heartfelt voice. "Damme, I can't afford to play with him, Simon."

Astley shrugged. "Where is the interest if the stake is not high?"

"Oh, in my league we play to amuse ourselves, not to fleece our friends."

"You are extraordinarily dense. I merely wish to rid White's of Laurence Everard's obnoxious company. At least," a sudden odd frown crossed the sandy brows, "that was my intention."

"To force him out?" Harry whistled. "Well, there I'm with you, Rupert, but it's a risky business—he has some acquaintances who'd not like it. And I'd not play with you in this mood."

"But then," the Major said softly, "as you say, you only play among friends. Everard is not numbered among mine—and if you and Simon are determined to censure me you will not remain among that august circle either."

Harry burst out laughing and even Simon Ravenslow's lips twitched. "Go and play then," he said in his deep voice and Lord Harry added, "I grant you Everard is a tiresome fellow, but what do you think of his stepdaughter?"

Rupert glanced towards the ballroom. "Five minutes in a minuet is hardly enough time to form an opinion."

Harry shook his head at such caution. "I needed less than that to see she is out of the usual run. Here's Georgy—we are saying what a pleasant addition to London society your Miss Fraser is."

"Of course she is," Georgiana agreed, "and I am delighted she will be a marriage connection when I wed Phil. I hope she will come and stay with us often." "I must go," her cousin said. "I'll see you later, Harry. You too, Simon? Georgy, walk to the door with me." And when they were out of earshot he asked what time she rode in the park with her staid Mr. Denby.

"He is not staid, and you are very horrid about him sometimes. I may say I would rather marry Phil than a rakehell like you any day, whatever the gossips say."

"The gossips may have wished it, but I never asked you to marry me," he retorted. "You'd plague the life out of a man. Now, what time do you ride?"

"At eight. Rupert! Do you really like Bab? I thought you were taken up with Lady Mary Symonds."

"That little affair has become wearisome—and I like all heiresses," he told her coolly. "I live in the hope that I will find one who may be tolerable."

"Well, I don't like you in this mood. You don't have to marry for money."

"No, my dear, but neither do I have at my disposal the means I would like. My father keeps the purse strings a sight too close."

She pulled her hand from his arm. "Go to White's then and win a fortune if you can. But if you come riding tomorrow I hope you will be less acid."

He bent to kiss her cheek. "I am not acid, little cousin," he said in a more pleasant tone, "merely realistic. And still in that vein I suppose you realize Miss Fraser is a Jacobite—and somewhat too outspoken about it?"

Georgy gave a little shrug. "Of course I know it. And that there are houses in London where ladies sing Jacobite songs and toast the Young Pretender—Priscilla Cavendish told me about a certain Lady Primrose who holds such gatherings and wears a white rose in her dress—but it does not signify, does it?"

"No," he agreed, "I think that cause has out-run its day, but it is still treason, my dear."

"I would not have thought a few songs worth that name," Georgy answered with a faint smile. "It is rather romantic—do you know they actually hold their glasses over a jug of water when they drink to 'the King' and it is easy to see what that means."

"There was nothing romantic about the Rebellion of '45," he retorted, "and I doubt your friend Miss Fraser would thank you for thinking of it in those terms. She has not forgotten her father nor the rest of her relatives who died. I am surprised you should be so thoughtless, Georgy."

"I am not," she was stung into replying, "but it is all over now. And I am surprised you spoke of it at all."

"So am I," he said and he was frowning again. "I would be obliged—if she asks you—if you would not over-emphasize my service in that misguided country four years ago. After all, I was only seconded temporarily to Barrell's regiment and as you say there is no point in raking over old sores."

"Certainly I won't, if you don't wish it. And," she added with a return of her usual light-hearted manner, "she may not, sir, be interested enough to ask any questions about you at all."

38

"You are a minx," he said and laughed. "Did I tell you, you look very pretty tonight?"

And because they were really, beneath the banter, extremely fond of each other, she reached up and kissed him soundly. "You have always been able to twist me round your finger, haven't you, Rupert? Until tomorrow then."

Half an hour later he was at White's, seated in the card-room, facing a man of middle age with a florid face that had once been handsome. Several others had joined the table and for a while the play went back and forth until the pile of coins beside the Major's place began to grow. One or two gentleman fell out as midnight passed but Sir Laurence Everard and Major Astley remained facing each other. Everard called for another bottle of claret. He was already part drunk and was playing recklessly.

Lord Harry Cavendish had left the ball and now stood behind Rupert's chair watching admiringly. It was, he told Simon Ravenslow afterwards, rather like watching a skilled fisherman playing a salmon.

When the small clock on the mantleshelf struck one, not only had Everard's complete store of guineas crossed the table but several notes of hand as well—the sum involved amounting to several thousand pounds.

With considerable care Major Astley gathered up the cards. "I think, Sir Laurence, that will do. I hold other notes from you, do I not?"

Everard glowered at him, his wig crooked, his cravat fallen loose. "Oh aye, you don't need to remind me. But the night is young."

"As far as you and I are concerned, sir, the night is spent—as is your presence in this club."

A sudden silence fell. The few men left in the card-room came across to the table to see what was happening, for where Rupert Astley was there was invariably some sort of entertainment, if not outright scandal; the Major had a prickly pride and occasionally took violent dislikes, as he had done to Laurence Everard. The latter's neck had gone turkey red.

"Curse you, what do you mean? You have had the devil's own luck tonight, or—" he broke off for those hard blue eyes were fixed on him.

"Surely," the Major's voice was very soft, "Surely you were not going to accuse me of cheating?"

"No—no—" Everard blustered. He filled his glass and drank off the contents. "I assure you, Major—" but his voice was slurred and the words trailed away.

Rupert Astley was leaning back in his chair, the notes held between slack fingers, but his whole body reflected an underlying alertness. It was the older man who was much less in command of himself, shuffling in his chair, an unsteady hand still holding his empty glass. "I imagine," Rupert said, "you will not wish to mortgage your estate to pay me?"

"Mortgage my—Good God, sir, why should I do that? I shall certainly find other means to settle my account with you."

"He makes Rupert sound like a damned tradesman," Harry muttered under his breath, but Everard seemed not to have heard and went on, "If you will but wait a week or so—"

"I hear of other debts." The Major had not taken his eyes off his opponent's face. "That you dare not show your face at Newmarket, that your credit is no longer good at Vauxhall."

"Oh come!" Captain Brooks had joined them. "That's a bit strong, sir."

Rupert Astley gave him one brief glance. "This is not, I believe, your affair, Brooks."

The Captain subsided and Sir Laurence slammed his glass down on the table. "You're worse than the damned money-lenders. Between gentlemen—"

"Between gentlemen debts are paid." With great deliberation the major folded the notes and tucked them into one of his large scarlet pockets. "Yet I think—I think our affair may be settled another way. You see, I attended Lady Denby's ball tonight—but perhaps we had better continue this in private."

Everard stared at him, his face turning an even deeper shade of red, his mouth open. Those who were watching the little scene were intimates of Rupert Astley and were looking at him, half expecting a call to a meeting at Barn Elms. Only Lord Harry had an inspired inkling of what might be coming but he had the sense, half in disbelief, to keep quiet.

Chapter 2

On a mild afternoon, some two months after Lady Denby's ball, Donald Fraser was making his way across the Pont Noyal to the south bank of the Seine. It had been one of those brilliant days in April when the thick blosson of the cherry trees seemed all the brighter for the blue of a cloudless sky above them, and he paused on the bridge, leaning on the parapet. He had that afternoon made his way through a particularly noisome and narrow street in search of a certain bookshop and it was a relief afterwards to return to the Rue St. Honoré where the flower scented gardens of the Tuileries Palace dispelled the unpleasant odours of the meaner side of Paris.

A convent bell began to chime followed shortly by a carillon from another tower until it seemed as if all Paris was caught up in their music. He knew this city well for he had spent two years at the university here, and he had become fluent both in French and in Latin, but adapted as he was to the language and the people, no one could ever have mistaken him for a Frenchman. Presently he went on his way and turning into the Boulevard St. Germain he entered a small wine-shop, for it was warm and he was thirsty, and ordering a cheap wine he opened one of the books he carried.

Despite the noise and talk all round him he was soon absorbed, barely glancing up when the wine was placed in front of him but presently as he turned a page the bill of sale fell out and floated to the floor. He bent to pick it up and as he did so he saw the date '*le* 16 *Avril*, 1750' written at the top. He drew in his breath sharply. How could he have forgotten, not realized it was the anniversary of the battle at Culloden?

He folded the bill with care and put it in his pocket but he did not return to his reading. Instead he clasped his hands over the open book and sat staring down at them. The sight of that date wrenched him away from the café, away from Paris, back to a very different day and the sleet and the wind on Drumossie Moor, and once more he lived through that nightmare that had not ended when he had clambered over Fraser dead to drag his father away. Time had eased the burning anger, the savage grief of that last afternoon at Duirdre but there remained the memories and a deep-rooted desire to fulfil his oath of vengeance, sworn as his ancestors had always sworn, on the iron. He had not been near enough to recognize that particular English officer's face again but what matter? They were all equally responsible and his vengeance could fall where it might. His loyalty to the House of Stuart, and to the Prince himself, remained as strong, perhaps stronger than ever for he clung to it with all the obstinate tenacity of his race and his own nature. But there was no way now to express it. He was laird of a sequestered estate, forfeited by his father's inclusion, even though he was by that time dead, in the Act of Attainder, along with other Frasers—of Foyers, Gortuleg and Browick, all known to him. Duirdre was now administered by the Duke of Argyll, aged head of the hated Clan Campbell. He had heard that a few of the crofters remained in the glen, that the clansmen who had managed to return had been pardoned by the Act of Indemnity and he was thankful, but Duirdre was in the hands of enemies and the English had built a fort not far from Loch Monar.

He drank some of his wine, though he was hardly aware of doing so. Instead he was seeing Duirdre as it must be now, the house a mere shell, the servants, the horses, the cattle all gone. But at least his father rested there. He had buried him near the rowan tree by the loch, wrapped in his own plaid, and he had watched all night by the grave, twisting on his finger the ring he had taken from his father's hand. In the morning, emptied of all feeling, he had gone through the glen, helping those who came timidly down from the hills to bury the dead, but there was nothing now that they could do for him or he for them, and at last he left for Shieldaig where old Malcolm ferried him across to Skye.

There he had fallen in with Neil MacEchain and learned that the Prince himself was on the island. He joined him once more and Charles Edward's courage and cheerful acceptance of all privations drew an even greater admiration from him than he had given in the more hopeful days. But no one spoke of Culloden and once when someone mentioned Lord George Murray, also in hiding somewhere, a bitter anger had flashed across the Prince's face. "That man!" he had exclaimed, "I owe all my misfortune to him. If he had not forced me to turn back at Derby I doubt my poor fellows would lie dead on that dreadful moor." And he had walked away from them all, the tears streaming down his face.

It was unjust, Donald thought now. Lord George had been a

competent commander, and hardly to blame either for the miserable quarrels at Carlisle and Derby, or for the ultimate tragedy, but he had nothing but sympathy for the Prince's grief and remorse.

At last, after weeks on the move, dodging the English patrols, French ships had sailed into Loch Nan Uamh and taken them off. For a while he stayed with the Prince but it was stultifying existence and being without any personal means he took a commission in the Régiment d'Albanie, that Scottish bastion of the French army.

Exile was bad enough but it was made worse by the news of the miserable state of his poor country. The Duke of Cumberland's vengeance had torn the life out of the Highlands, releasing on innocent and guilty alike such men as General 'Hangman' Hawley and the sadistic Captain Caroline Scott. Encouraged by their officers the soldiers had indulged in blood and rape and plunder and not since medieval times, Donald thought, had such atrocities been perpetrated, such vengeance exacted; the stories that reached Paris were enough to rob all Jacobites there of peaceful sleep. He heard with revulsion of the treatment of his cousin Isabel Fraser, at whose wedding he had danced not long before the Rising, of how she had been raped by four soldiers in front of her captured husband and then forced to watch him hang. Yet there were odd gleams of compassion. A kinsman passing through Paris told him that Fraser of MacIver had been saved by a certain Lord Boyd, an officer in the English army, and how another officer had refused to pistol young Inverallochie when he lay wounded on the ground—though this deed was then done at General Hawley's command by a common soldier.

A letter arrived in answer to his own from his cousin William, informing him he would be wise not to try to return as yet. His aunt Jean, after the tragedy of Culloden, had gone to live with her son, for William had predictably remained safely at Inverness throughout, tending his law practice—a canny one, William, Donald thought with contempt—but of their own family they were the only two left and what affairs remained to be dealt with he had perforce to entrust to William.

Sitting here on this bright day he supposed he must be thankful for his life, his freedom—as indeed he was—but the scrap of paper reminded him of all those less fortunate than he who, if they survived the prison at Inverness and the journey to London in filthy hulks, had ended their days on the gallows, an object lesson for all who still dallied with the Jacobite Cause.

The greatest spectacle of all for the citizens had been the execution of his own Chief, Macshimi, and his face still burned as he thought of that old man—intelligent, humorous, admittedly crafty, with a past that did not bear scrutiny, a born plotter, going to his death with a joke on his lips. He had been caught hiding in a hollow tree and his heir, the Master of Lovat, was also caught and imprisoned in Edinburgh Castle to await the King's pleasure, which he was still doing four years later. The soldiers had razed Castle Dounie to the ground, destroyed Lord Lovat's salmon weirs, taken the contents of his house, including his wine cellar, all his goods and livestock, and left nothing but wreckage of a once great estate. At last the Government tired of persecution and the Act of Indemnity offered pardon to all who would submit and take the oath to King George.

And that Donald had not been able to bring himself to do. From being the son of a chieftain of a great clan, marching to war in kilt and bonnet with a sprig of yew fastened to his white cockade, he had become a disillusioned young man of twenty-eight in a shabby blue coat and brown breeches, an exile with an inner loneliness that nothing could dispel.

Quite suddenly the sound of that hereditary title he had rarely heard applied to himself since he had ceased to be Donald the Younger and in a language far removed from the talk around him, startled him to such an extent that he knocked over his glass and wine spilled over the pages of his book. For one brief instant he stared at it in horror for, perpetuating his thoughts of a moment ago, it seemed as if at the sound of his name a stain like blood was spreading over the table before him.

Then the slight dark man who had come over to his table repeated the greeting, both hands held out.

"Mac Domhnull Àrd! Is it possible?"

Donald rose, at the same time endeavouring to wipe the wine from his book before he dropped his reddened handkerchief and took the outstretched hands. "Neil MacEachain! Where have you come from? Have you been in Paris long? After you went to Avignon I heard that you had gone to Spain and then to Rome—even that you had journeyed to Sweden."

MacEachain sat down at the table, smiling in a rather melancholy fashion. "One question at a time if you please. Yes, we did go from Avignon to Spain but whoever mentioned Sweden on our travels was mistaken—nor has His Highness visited his father in Rome."

Donald sat down opposite him and called for more wine. "I'm more glad to see you than I can say but I could wish that you had not startled me so for I think this book is ruined."

MacEachain glanced casually at the open volume. "I am sorry—is it so precious?" Once a schoolmaster in the Highlands he was now a man with one purpose in his life and was inclined to be impatient with what he considered trivialities.

"I've had a journey across Paris to purchase it for my employer, but never mind that now. In truth, I was not reading it when you came, I was remembering what day it is."

Neil's face darkened. "I had not forgotten, nor has His Highness. This is the worst day in the year for him and I must not stay long away."

"He is here—in Paris?" Donald asked in surprise, and when Neil nodded, went on, "Tell me how he has been faring. I have been so hungry for news and I have heard nothing."

I will tell you it all but first, what are you doing? When we last heard of you, you were serving in the Régiment d'Albanie."

"I resigned my commission after that disgraceful business at the opera house. I had no desire to serve in an army that had made peace with England, nor under a Government that could treat our Prince so poorly."

"Yes, I might have guessed you would do that. What then?"

"For a while, nothing." Donald moved the book so that it could catch the sunshine to dry the pages. "You knew my sister and mother were in England?"

"Yes, I remember that. Your grandfather was an Englishman, wasn't he?"

Donald nodded again. "My mother has remarried, a Sir Laurence Everard, so there was no question of us returning as a family to Scotland."

Neil's brows shot up. "This marriage did not please you?"

"What do you think? But I cannot blame my mother for she is English. Only it grieves me that Bab is so far out of my reach."

"You have not been to England?"

"My dear Neil, until recently I have not had the means to get as far as Calais." But he said it with humour.

Neil was silent for a moment. The serving man had brought their wine and he was sipping it slowly. Then he said. "You have not thought of going home—to Duirdre? There are certain funds—"

"You are not thinking of the gold buried at Loch Arkaig? It came too late to help us when it was needed, and I'd not touch it now."

"All it can do now is to help our own people," Neil said. "Dr.

Cameron has been to Scotland distributing some of it. His brother Locheil's widow received a considerable sum, and rightly so. I'm sure that if—"

"No." Donald shook his head. Not long after the Act of Indemnity his grandfather had written to him offering to use his considerable influence on his grandson's behalf, to try to regain Duirdre for him, if he would return and qualify to the English Government, an offer which Donald, in the bitterness of defeat, refused; the old man sent an angry reply and that was the end of all communication between them. Yet Duirdre was still his inheritance and the longing to return to his own glen to see once more the rugged shape of Lurg Mhór and the loch below was always with him. Only the thought of what he would have to do in order to set foot there again always held him back. And it would be a maimed existence with his religion proscribed, his national dress forbidden, the carrying of arms made a matter of treason so that he could not even hunt his own game.

He looked across at his companion. "Sometimes I think I ought to go back, but apart from the fact that my house is burned and every possession we had taken away, it is the swearing of the oath that holds me back. Could you take it?"

"Call down on myself the death of a coward and burial without prayer if I broke it? No, I'm not sure that I could," MacEachain agreed sombrely. "It seems to me the English Government had some understanding of our Highland ways to inflict such a swearing on us. Yet some have taken it and without dishonour."

"Perhaps they had more to go back to. I have neither house nor wife nor children," Donald said and his tone was a little short.

"Well, I have one piece of news you may not have heard. Your new Chief has been released from Edinburgh and is gone home to rebuild his house."

Donald's face lit. "Simon is free? That is good news indeed." His memory of the Master was of a dark eager youth, who must now be a man changed by years of imprisonment, but at least there was a MacShimi at Beauly again. "Now tell me of the Prince. I was horrified when I heard he had been arrested at the opera house."

"After the French signed the treaty of Aix-la-Chapelle we became an embarrassment to them but they did not keep us long at Avignon. We were free to go, but the truth is that the Prince is not wanted at any court. As you know, he and his father do not always see eye to eye and with his brother now a Cardinal, he refused to go to Rome. It would be—"Neil paused, "a final acknowledgment of defeat. In

46

truth, Duirdre, he is a broken man, and finds no peace anywhere."

Donald sighed. "He is not the only man whose life is broken. Rumour has it that he finds his solace in drink and women."

"I can't deny that, but whether he finds solace I can't tell. Only forgetfulness for a while, perhaps. He is haunted by dreams of his year in Scotland and what followed." Neil clenched his hands, his thin face taut. "And this I know—for the suffering the Rising caused he has paid. My God, he has paid!"

"We have all paid," Donald agreed grimly and MacEachain reached out to lay a hand on his arm.

"I know, *laochan*. God knows the Elector has bloodied his hands with his tyranny over us, but we've not bowed to him yet."

Donald gave a sudden rather harsh laugh. "With our strength buried on the moor and the rest of us living in exile or under wretched conditions at home, I am thinking that is an idle phrase."

"Idle phrase, is it?" Neil retorted. "Never! Not while there's a Highlander left. There's still a chance of achieving what we failed to do in '45."

"*Mo thruagh!*" Donald exclaimed, "you are not suggesting Scotland could sustain another rising. We are crippled enough and there would not be any support from the French now—and heaven knows they did little for us last time."

MacEachain leaned back, pushing away his empty glass, his eyes shadowed, but there was a tenseness about him that betrayed a smouldering eagerness within. "No, we all know that is impossible now. We have different lands."

Donald leaned forward. "You mean His Highness is to try some new venture? For God's sake, explain."

"There is nothing to tell yet, but if the chance came—would you be serving the Prince again?"

A surge of corresponding eagerness rose in Donald. "You do not need to ask that. You know the motto of my clan—and I would be ready. Yet I don't see what can be done—"

"Maybe not." Neil smiled briefly. "But there is hope. If there were not, I think the Prince would go out of his mind," he added. "Give me your direction and when our plans are a little more formed I will get in touch with you. By the way, you have not told me what you are doing now."

Donald pulled a notebook from his pocket, wrote on it and tore out the page. "I am to become a librarian, of all surprising things. Do you remember the Chevalier de la Rouelle who served our regiment for a time? No? Well, he owns an estate some miles out of Paris and I am in his employ, and likely to be so for some time. But if I should leave before I hear from you where may I find you?"

"A letter to the Convent of St. Joseph in the Rue Dominique will reach me. We are guests in the secular wing. The Princesse de Talmond is there, but this you understand is for your ears only."

"Of course." Donald had met the Princesse once, when she had first become Charles Edward's mistress, a beautiful woman who had fallen victim, as had so many, to the indefinable charm that had led both men and women to risk lives and honour and everything they had for him.

MacEachain rose. "I must get back to His Highness—I only came out to do a small commission for him and on this day of all days—" he broke off, slipping a hand in his pocket. "Would you like to have this?"

It was a small medal bearing a likeness of the Prince and the word *Revirescet*. "It will flourish again," Donald translated, looking at the engraving of a withered tree from which a vigorous new branch was emerging. "Please God. His hand has been heavy on us. Thank you for this, Neil. Which way do you go?"

"By the bridge. Will you walk with me?"

Donald nodded and after they had paid the reckoning they walked back the way he had come. Despite the fact they had been speaking in Erse, once they were free of the crowded shop, Neil seemed inclined to be a little more expansive.

"There is a great deal of unrest in London, you know. The scandals at court have shocked many people and the House of Hanover is none too popular. In fact it seems the Elector and his eldest son are hardly on speaking terms. The so-called Prince of Wales makes a point of keeping company with friends who are known to have Jacobite sympathies."

"That may be so, but drawing room politics generally achieve very little."

"And at Oxford," Neil went on as if he had not heard, "a certain Dr. King, one of our most ardent supporters, is speaking openly against the Government with no action taken against him. There are others like him. It is possible that a bold stroke, a political stroke, you understand, might meet with considerable support."

Donald walked a little way in silence. Neil MacEachain, the Prince's secretary and companion throughout all his wanderings, must surely know better than anyone what hopes there were for the eventual restoration of the House of Stuart, yet for a moment Donald did not know what to say. He had lived so long without any such hope that he was dubious of any unaided plan. Yet he wanted to hope. He thought of Charles Edward as he had been in the best days, presiding over a ball in his ancestral home at Holyrood House. "How is he?" he asked suddenly. "Is he well? Does he believe there is any chance he will go back—that any of us will go home?"

"Of course," Neil answered firmly. "Some days he is as you remember him. The old spirit rises in him again and—oh, indeed we have hope." Neil paused. "This is where our ways part, I think. When there is any news, or if we leave Paris, I will contrive to let you know."

"And tell His Highness he may count on me for any service I can still give."

"He will be knowing that," MacEachain gave him a sudden warm smile that lit his normally sombre face. "God keep you, Duirdre."

Donald watched him thread his way past the crowded booths of the professional letter-writers, past the stalls and the flower sellers, before turning away himself. But he did not go immediately to the inn where he had stabled his employer's horse. Instead he made his way to the little church of St. Germain des Prés, and walked down a side aisle to a tomb which was the reason why he came to this particular place, for within it lay the remains of a certain James Douglas who had died more than a hundred years ago. It was the knowledge that Scottish dust was here that had become a link with home and he sat down, his books on his knees, his hands clasped over them, his eyes on a pattern of sunlight on the floor, his mind going over all that Neil had said. It was like the first gleam of light on what had been a very dark road, for not even to Neil had he revealed the depths to which he had been reduced after he had resigned his commission.

He had moved into a cheap apartment in the poorest quarter of the city, and but for the kindness of the concierge he might have starved. He sold most of the few possessions he had brought away with him, including his father's watch, but not even when he was most hungry had he parted with the gold ring he had taken from his hand before he buried him that terrible night at Duirdre. His clothes grew threadbare and he himself so thin that they hung upon his large frame. Too proud to allow anyone to witness his poverty he had lost touch with most of his exiled countrymen and only the small sums of money his mother managed to send him from time to time and a short period as a tutor kept him from actual starvation. Bab wrote to him frequently but he had not let either her or his mother know the true situation. He thought of her constantly, wondering how she had changed, whether she was happy, wishing he had means to support her himself so that they might be together.

Alone, without friends or family and constantly hungry, even his superb physique and sane outlook were assailed and he was nearing desperation when a chance meeting with Armand de la Rouelle saved him. He literally bumped into the young Frenchman with whom he had but a slight acquaintance and they had stood for a while talking in the Rue St. Antoine. He was aware, with shame, of the Frenchman's alert eyes taking in his shabbiness, but he was astounded when La Rouelle explained that he had recently inherited his uncle's estate and that as the library was in a shocking condition and needed cataloguing, would M. Fraser be interested in such employment? Donald, too desperate to refuse, though he was aware the offer had been made on the spur of the moment, accepted it. It was not charity, he told himself, but honourable employment and he must see it as such.

Thus began an association that was extremely pleasant for it ripened into friendship between them. He enjoyed his work in the big library overlooking the terraced garden at Mentonnay and life in the château flowed smoothly. In a short while he regained his former robustness, bought himself a new coat, and refused to look further into the future than the span of his present work, hoarding the handsome salary the Chevalier paid him against future needs.

But now with Neil's words uppermost in his mind, he was shaken out of the quiet of the last few months. Was it all to begin again, the struggle, the hoping, the desire to rid his country of the domination of an unwanted foreign king and perhaps—once more—the anguish of broken dreams? He thought again of the moment of Neil's arrival, at the wine spreading its dark stain on the table. Was it an omen? The Celt was strong in him, and there was an uneasiness he could not entirely throw off, however nonsensical he told himself it was.

And suddenly all the old loneliness swept over him once again, the grief for his father, the longing to see his mother and Bab, a yearning for all that, in the spring of '45, had seemed so permanent. Oh God, would he never see Duirdre again? Was he condemned for the rest of his life to this cheerless exile? He raised both hands to his face, his mind in a tumult as Neil's words reached out to him.

The books on his lap, released, slid to the floor with a thud that disturbed the one or two worshippers waiting for Vespers to begin.

The sunlight had gone now and he glanced at the altar where a boy was reaching up with a taper to light the candles, wondering if he could begin to pray again for all that he had thought utterly lost. From his earliest years he could remember his father at family prayers, beseeching a blessing on the exiled House of Stuart, and he had only to close his eyes to see that familiar room, hear his father's voice and smell the peculiar odour of the old leather chair by which he always knelt. Now nothing remained of it but charred timber. Yet the words remained and became entwined with the new hope that Neil had raised today.

With one impassioned prayer for the Prince they both served he gathered up his books and went out, into the April sunset so far removed from the wind and rain of four years ago on Drumossie Moor. And there was now, for him, another small gleam of light, at Mentonnay.

Chapter 3

It was almost dark when he turned into the drive that led to the château; bordered by tall poplars it curved through parkland flanked by wide fields, and over to the left lay the village of Mentonnay. At the far end of the drive between the trees he could see the lights of the house extending a welcome that was a symbol, he thought, of the reception the family there had given him. In French custom there were numerous relatives living with the Chevalier de la Rouelle and his sister—Tante Clothilde, the widow of Sebastien de la Rouelle from whom he had inherited the estate; Tante Julie, an elderly cousin who had kept house for Clothilde and Sebastien and who continued to do so without consulting Armand as to whether he wished it, occupying the position with such tenacity that he told Donald he had not the temerity to suggest any change; and finally there was another cousin, Gaston de la Rouelle, who combined the duties of parish priest with those of family chaplain at the château.

In the cobbled stableyard a groom ran to take the reins and Donald slid rather wearily out of the saddle but it was not entirely physical tiredness that made him glad to be back at Mentonnay. He entered the house and was about to cross the hall to the library when the door of the salon opened and Armand de la Rouelle came out.

"Ah, *mon ami*, you are back at last."

Donald paused, the parcel of books under his arm. "I met an old friend and stayed talking longer than I meant to, that is why I am late. Unfortunately a glass of wine was spilled over one of the books, but I will try to replace it when I am next in Paris."

"It must have been something of a reunion," Armand suggested humorously, but seeing no response to this sally he merely took the book and examined it without any sign of annoyance. A quick inspection showed that only two pages retained a dark stain and he said firmly that it would be quite unnecessary to replace it. It was an expensive volume and he was well aware that his librarian's resources hardly ran to such luxuries. Donald however merely replied with finality that he would prefer to replace the book and Armand shrugged.

"As you will. You had no difficulty in finding the bookshop?"

After a brief conversation they parted, Donald to wash and change after his journey, and presently he joined the family for supper. This was served in the smaller room next to the salon, the two aunts appearing in rather out-of-date gowns, and both were more inclined to chatter round the small table than they were in the dining room with its wealth of silver and gilt and its high-backed chairs. Almost at once this evening Tante Clothilde paused over her soup to inquire whether M. Fraser had heard news of his family.

"Not recently," he told her, smiling a little. It did not cease to astonish him how any piece of information went round this house; no doubt they had all heard of the damaged book and his meeting with Neil. "My sister is not the best of correspondents. She was never one to be at indoor pursuits if she might be out walking or riding. I believe my stepfather's estate is in a very beautiful part of the country—though I do not know it."

Tante Julie glanced up, her close-set eyes regarding him curiously. "You do not visit her—nor your mother?"

"I have not been to England since our defeat, madame."

"It is a great misfortune for you to be so far from your family," she agreed. When she wanted to know something she asked it with French directness. "It is to be hoped that your sister finds her new father amiable. She has perhaps other kinsmen as well to accompany her when she—er—walks or rides?"

A corner of his mouth lifted. "She is, madame, a somewhat independent person." He was thinking of Bab's last letter and her remark that when she was unable to tolerate Sir Laurence any longer she could at least escape on horseback across the fields. "She prefers to ride alone, I believe."

"Alone?" Julie de la Rouelle could hardly bring out the word. "Do not tell me she is allowed to ride with no one in attendance?"

Tante Clothilde, busily crumbling bread, shook her head and was beginning, "Why, in our young days—" when her nephew interrupted her.

"My dear aunt, I have no doubt that when you were a girl you were brought up far more strictly, but things are a little different now. And I understand that in England, and I suppose in Scotland too, young ladies are allowed more latitude than here in France. Isn't that so, Monsieur Fraser?"

Donald swallowed the last of his soup. "At home we were so isolated that we had a great deal of freedom. I'm afraid that rather than occupations generally considered more suitable, my sister always preferred to share my pursuits—the fishing or the stalking or walking on the mountain."

"Fishing!" Tante Clothilde exclaimed in tones of horror. "And what is stalking? Bon Dieu, I do not understand the present generation."

Donald glanced across at Mademoiselle Marthe and saw that Armand's sister was smiling, her soft brown eyes alight with humour.

"I think I envy your sister," she said. "Here we are much more restricted."

"Nonsense," Tante Julie spoke sharply. "How can it be seemly to—"

The Curé, who had not spoken so far, leaned forward to address his elderly cousin. "In every generation, madame, the young seem to be viewed with disapproval—yet I think they do not want mere censure. Encouragement is more positive."

"Gaston, you are inclined to be sentimental," Tante Julie answered with asperity, but because in reality she always attended to what he said, she shrugged her shoulders in a typically French manner and began to talk of King Louis's latest love affair with a frankness that, when he first arrived at the house, had appalled Donald. Now he was used to such conversation but he thought amusedly that he would have liked to tell her that though Scottish girls might be allowed a wider choice of occupation they would never be permitted to hear the outspoken talk to which Marthe de la Rouelle was now listening without any apparent concern. The Curé had a slight frown on his face as he sat turning his wine-glass in his thin fingers, but even he did not interrupt to change the conversation.

Donald suppressed the desire to pay Tante Julie back in her own coin and after a while his thoughts returned to his meeting with Neil. He became silent and when later he joined the Curé for their usual game of chess he found it hard to concentrate.

Gaston de la Rouelle moved a pawn and glanced at his companion. "I think, monsieur, your mind is not on our chess board tonight."

Donald roused himself. "I'm sorry." He paused uncertainly, his hand on his knight for so long that the priest added, "I think—you will forgive me if I am impertinent? I think your meeting with your friend today has disturbed you. Armand told me about the accident to the book."

Donald stiffened. "I have said that I will replace it."

Gaston de la Rouelle shook his head with a faint smile on his intelligent face. "My dear Monsieur Fraser, do not misjudge my cousin. He is not in the least concerned about that. Only about you. We hope you did not hear unhappy news from your country?"

"No—that is—on the contrary. Yet in a way—" Donald stopped abruptly.

"A most ambiguous sentence." The priest was still smiling gently. "What am I to understand from that?"

"Nothing," Donald said and was aware of how churlish he sounded. "There are some things I am not free to discuss."

"Then the matter is closed." M. de la Rouelle's hand hovered over the chessmen. There was no trace of offence in his voice. "Checkmate, I think. You see, you are not playing with your usual skill. That was too easy a victory."

Something in the words caught at Donald's attention, though in a totally different context. Too easy a victory! Was that what they had allowed the Hanoverian? An hour on Drumossie Moor four years ago this day and it was all over. No, it could not be so and somewhere, somehow the White Cockade must be worn again.

The Curé, as always after their game, retired to his study and Donald, taking a book, went over to the window seat, but seeing he was not attempting to read it Marthe picked up her embroidery and came to sit beside him.

"I hope, monsieur," she asked in her low voice, "that my aunt did not offend you at supper. She is very outspoken."

He roused himself at once. "Not in the least, and I am sorry if I gave that impression. No, it was something quite different that—" he broke off. Was he really so transparent that they all read him so easily? If so, it was a tendency he must mend, especially with this girl beside him.

"Then you are troubled?" she was asking, and he looked down at her, seeing her slight, almost childlike figure in a pale blue gown trimmed with lace and little bows set against the dark red curtains. She reached, as no one else had done, behind the barrier he had erected over the years since he stepped aboard the ship in Loch nan Uamh. Yet he must not let it fall altogether and he braced himself.

"I assure you I am not in the least troubled, mademoiselle. It was only that my friend and I talked of home today and of—" he hesitated and finished rather lamely, "—of the past that is better forgotten."

She fingered the fringe of the curtain, knowing that was not what he intended to say. "You seldom speak of it," she said at last.

"No," he answered rather stiffly. How, after all, as a guest in this

55

house and in her country, could he speak of that strange year of triumph and disaster, of his resentment at the lack of French help for his desperate Prince. "There are some things I would rather not talk of even now."

"I think you have never ceased to want to return to your home, Monsieur Fraser."

"No," he repeated in a low voice, "though I doubt I will ever see it again."

"Oh come," she bent over her work, not looking at him, "is your exile so very hard?"

He looked sombrely over her head at the dark red of the damask curtains behind. "Every day of every week never ceases to be exile." He caught her hand almost violently, hardly aware that he had caused her to scratch it with her needle. "I have lost everything I cared for, my home is burned, many of my people killed or fled—nor can I go back except to a life hedged round with restrictions that might drive me to desperation—even if I could bring myself to ask for it. Yet I do not think I can support life in exile for the rest of my days. Do you wonder that I find it so hard?"

She lifted her head, her expressive face full of sympathy. "No, I do not wonder. But I thought that here—we have tried to make you welcome."

He saw at once that he had hurt her. He pulled out a handkerchief and dabbed at the blood on her finger. "Believe me, you have done so, no one could have been kinder. And I am sorry that I scratched your hand. You know I did not mean to do either."

"I am sure you did not." She smiled up at him, her face saddened. "Yet it is exile. Is there no chance that you may be able to go home one day?"

"Perhaps, but it would be at great cost." Would she understand if he told her, if he explained that he would have to beg his land from the English Government, take an oath that offended every belief he held? Even as he paused she seemed to sense what he was trying to say for she asked, "The cost would be sacrificing much that you would call honour?"

"Yes," he agreed, and for the first time wondered if he put too much upon that word. Aware that he was still holding her hand he released it. "You are very perceptive, mademoiselle. Forgive me if I have burdened you with my troubles. This is an anniversary that has brought them more to mind than usual."

"I wish that I could do something to help you." She sat looking down at the little red scratch. "Would it not be pleasant if we were to invite your sister here? She would be permitted a visit?"

"Would you do that?" He looked at her, more grateful than mere words could express, and he had a sudden desire to put her hand to his lips and kiss that scratch. Instead he said, "It would be a great kindness and a joy to us both if it could be arranged. I'm sure my mother would raise no objection."

"But do you not wish to see her also? If your stepfather could bring them—"

He shook his head. "I doubt that would be—" he broke off, biting back the words. "But I would very much like to see Bab."

"Then I shall speak to my brother about it."

At that moment Armand himself called across to her to give them some music and the rest of the evening passed pleasantly. Nevertheless later, in the privacy of his richly furnished bedroom, Donald did not go at once to bed but sat in the big chair by the fire, thinking over what had been said. Bab would come, he was sure of that, but quite how it could be arranged without their stepfather's escort he did not know and neither of them would wish for that. Perhaps his cousin Philip Denby would bring her. Bab's last letter had been full of a visit to London and of a certain Miss Georgiana Milne who was betrothed to Philip. He remembered him as a quiet studious boy of twelve whom he had seen on his only visit to his grandfather, but Bab seemed to have made a close friend of Philip's betrothed and she wrote of their rides in the park, of balls and routs—a world utterly remote from his own and far removed from the old life at Duirdre. He was glad for her, but he was more deeply hurt than he would admit, even to himself, that she had adapted herself so easily to English ways. Yet it was not her fault, for she had been little more than a child when it all began. She had seen none of the horror of the aftermath and he must be ever grateful that she had not suffered as many Highland girls, as their own cousin Isabel had done. And her letters, infrequent as they were, were full of her affection for him and her longing to see him.

Mademoiselle Marthe understood that. A little warmth that owed nothing to the fire crept into his face. Her kindness, her gentle ways, had reached out to him almost as soon as he had come, poor and proud and a little stiff in manner, to Mentonnay and now there was an unspoken sympathy between them. On his side, more than that. Her presence gave him a happiness he had never known before, yet there could be nothing between them—he knew that. He had nothing to offer her, or any woman, even if she cared for him in that way, and of that he was not sure. Probably she was merely kind. He was an impoverished foreigner from a cold and distant country and that was perhaps all she saw, her natural generosity responding to his need.

He must think no further on these lines, and getting up he began to undress. As he did so a hand in his breeches pocket encountered the medal Neil had given him. He pulled it out and stood looking at it as it lay in his palm, at the engraved word that meant so much. Would the Cause ever flourish again? Please God! He said the words aloud and then, opening a drawer, laid it beside the white cockade he had taken from his bonnet when he left Scotland—a scrap of ribbon, once bright and fresh, sewn into place by Bab's unskilled fingers but with loving care. Now it was torn and dirty yet he would keep it until, perhaps, Bab should make him a new one. Some day, somewhere he would wear the white ribbon again—but when that day was finally to come it was to be in a manner he could not have envisaged tonight. Tonight it was all that remained to him from 'the Prince's year' and he shut the drawer on it firmly.

But he was still restless and going to the window he drew the curtain. It was a clear night with a hint of a late frost, a full moon casting white light and dark shadows on the terrace below, the two stone effigies of the Mentonnay lions turned into gigantic monster-like shapes on the paving stones. Leaning his head against the window frame he thought of Duirdre and how the moonlight shimmered on the silver water of the loch, as perhaps it was shining tonight, the rowan tree springing from its rock, his father's grave nearby, as it would continue to shine when he too was gone.

He had all his race's awe and awareness of the dead and the life beyond the grave and he faced once again the onslaught of longing and loneliness, the knowledge that he might never have the happiness there had once been in Duirdre, certainly not with the French girl sleeping in the room along the corridor.

It was to the memory of his father that he turned and for an instant it was almost as if the spirit of John Fraser was in the room, imparting something of his courage and his strength to his son. At last Donald drew the curtain, shutting out the moonlight that only kept memory alive, and went to bed. But he was oddly comforted.

In the morning he wished he had not spoken so openly of his feelings. He wondered if he had sounded ungrateful and made up his mind to speak to Marthe when he might find the opportunity, to thank her for the possibility of a visit from Bab. However, Armand insisted on carrying him off to ride to an outlying farm and though he protested he should be at work in the library he was not sorry to be out in the spring sunshine.

As they rode down the drive he said,"This is very pleasant, Chevalier, but I am sure you do not employ me to ride with you."

La Rouelle laughed. "Perhaps I do! There are too many women in my house and a little male company is extremely welcome."

"But you have M. le Curé."

"True. Gaston is a good fellow, but," the Frenchman shrugged his shoulders, "he is a priest and I find that, cousin or no, priests will be priests. You understand that? Or perhaps you do not. Your priests are different, are they not? Married, for one thing?"

"Yes, I suppose you could say they are different," Donald said with a touch of amusement. "But most of my clan is Catholic, you know, so I was somewhat used to meeting Catholic priests before ever I came to France. My Chief is of your faith, though my own particular branch has always been attached to the Episcopal Church of Scotland."

"That is like the Church of England?"

The amusement faded from Donald's face. "Very like, except that we pray for one king, the English for another. Before the Rising in the Highlands at least, both Catholics and Episcopalians tolerated each other very well, but now the English authorities have forbidden our way of worship as well."

"I am sorry." Armand wore his own religion lightly but nonetheless sincerely for that. "At least here in France you are able to visit your own chapel—where is it?"

"Near the Faubourg Saint-Antoine."

"Then pray consider yourself free to attend it whenever you wish," Armand said with his usual thoughtfulness, "unless Gaston succeeds in converting you. I'm sure he has tried."

Donald smiled. "He has not, nor would he, as you very well know. He is a wise man, your cousin."

"I suppose so," Armand said resignedly. "Oh, indeed I have a great respect for him. He is as able as any man to understand the business of running an estate, which I myself am only learning, but he will break off a sensible conversation to remind me that I have not been shriven lately. Bon Dieu!" He made an expressive gesture. "As if I have time, here, for sin! Mind you, there is a girl in the village who accommodates me sometimes, but that is a man's way and hardly likely to send me to hell, *hein*?" He glanced at Donald, his mouth turned up at the corners, a quizzical look on his face, and had the satisfaction of seeing the Highlander laugh outright. "Life should be," he went on, "at least part pleasure, do you not think so? I am sure that is how the good God meant it to be. There is no harm in a little self-indulgence, accompanied of course by an equally small amount of repentance."

"A simple philosophy, Chevalier," Donald said. "What does your cousin think of it?"

"Oh, I do not discuss such matters with him if I can help it. But we have common ground in my tenants who are also his flock. He is very zealous, our Gaston, which is perhaps what I find trying. A little moderation is to be desired in all things."

"Perhaps." Donald had already begun to see that Armand's easy going ways were not always compatible with the priest's keen sense of duty. "It is not so easy to achieve when one is persecuted for one's faith, but then, monsieur, you do not know what that is like."

"Maybe I do not, but neither am I without imagination."

Donald inclined his head. They were riding slowly down a lane of trees, the hedgerows bursting into green, the sunlight dappled at their feet. "You have shown that," he said at last, "in your kindness to one exile."

Armand flung up his hand. "Do not mention it again, Monsieur Fraser. It is you who do a great service for me. Ah, here we are." And Donald wondered whether he referred to his work in the library or as a relief from priestly company. It was impossible not to be amused by the Chevalier de la Rouelle.

They did not return until the afternoon and it was nearly four o'clock when Donald looked up from his work in the library to see Mlle Marthe go down the garden with a basket over her arm. Quickly he pushed up the window and stepped over the low sill on to the terrace. He walked with the silent agility of a Highlander and she did not hear him until he was beside her.

"May I carry your basket?"

She handed it to him, smiling. "Thank you. I am just going down through the copse to pick the last of the daffodils. I'm afraid they are nearly over."

He looked keenly down at her as he fell into step beside her. She had been ill during the winter, coughing a great deal, so that in common with the rest of the household, and apart from his private feelings, he had come to share a concern for her health. But today there was some colour beneath the transparent whiteness of her skin and her soft brown hair had a sheen to it that caught the sun.

"You look much better," he said at last.

"Indeed I am. I am always well when the winter is over and it is so warm today."

They had reached the end of the formal gardens and Donald held open a small wicket gate for her to pass through.

"We can go through the copse or by the pool," she said. "Either way is very pretty."

He turned towards the trees and at once a familiar scent caught his attention. Silver birches! No, that was not the way he wanted to walk with her and he suggested they go by the lake. It was small and sparkling in the sunlight and on the far side was a mass of bright yellow daffodils.

Marthe paused by the water's edge. "It is very beautiful here, isn't it? I love to walk this way, especially on a spring day."

He nodded, glancing round the clearing. "I think you would love our lochs at home. We have firs there and tall pines and on the hillsides when the heather is out there are great splashes of purple as far as one can see. Our lochs are still, like that pool, but wide and very deep and in our northern light they look silver. I wish——" he broke off suddenly and laid the basket down on a fallen log. "But I did not come after you to talk about Scotland."

She sat down on the log. "No, monsieur?"

"No. I came to ask your pardon for what I said last night. It must have sounded very rude."

"We are getting used to your northern manners," she answered with a mischievous smile on her face and he was startled.

"Are they so very bad?"

"No," she shook her head. "I was only teasing you."

He sat down beside her, absentmindedly stripping the bark from a piece of stick. "I cannot tell you," he began, measuring his words with care, "how much your hospitality has meant to me, the kindness you have all shown me. I was unpardonably ungrateful if I made you believe anything else."

She was smiling at him as he covered the moss with strips of bark. "You have become one of our household."

He made a gesture with his stick. "Perhaps, but I have to remember that it is a business arrangement and as such will be terminated. I must not grow too fond of Mentonnay."

She was sitting very still now. "I know Armand is delighted to have you here."

"Nevertheless my work will be done in a month or two."

"What will you do then?"

He shrugged his shoulders. "I don't know. Perhaps your brother or M. le Curé might know of a family in need of a tutor—or a librarian."

"They might," she agreed, and then she added, "but I shall ask Armand to find you further work here."

"No," he broke in sharply, "I cannot let you do that. When the cataloguing is finished, I must go."

"But if your sister is to come—"

"Naturally we should enjoy that, but afterwards—" He had spoken more harshly than he intended, but he felt instinctively that for Marthe to interest herself too much on his behalf might not please his employer, nor would his own pride permit that she should ask favours for him. Then, aware that he had done again the very thing for which he had set out to apologize, he added, "It is very kind of you," and knew that the words sounded lame.

She shook her head. "It is not being kind at all. It is just that I do not want you to leave us."

There was silence by the water, the daffodils forgotten. A solitary moorhen, lulled by the stillness of the two who sat on the fallen log, emerged from the rushes and made its leisurely way to the far side. Donald watched it, yet aware of nothing but the girl who sat quietly beside him, her hands clasped in her lap, her white muslin dress seeming to add to her frailty. Yet she had an air of serenity, and that, coupled with the words she had just spoken caused him to make a sudden move as if to take those hands into his own. But almost immediately he checked it. Between them lay a great gulf and he had no right to try to bridge it. Afraid to trust himself further he got to his feet.

"The sun is going down," he said abruptly. "You will take cold if you stay out here any longer. Allow me to escort you back to the house." And he held out his hand to help her to her feet. The warmth of that contact, formal though it was, seemed to bring a little more colour to her cheeks, yet as she rose her face betrayed the hurt he had inflicted. He saw it but he turned away resolutely and picked up the basket. "I'm afraid it is too late for the daffodils," he said.

They walked back to the house in silence. Already the sun was sending long slanting shadows across the grass, the transient warmth of the April day gone.

Once she glanced up at him, but he did not meet her gaze, his face set, the line of his jaw stiff and unrelenting as he strode across the grass. He did not notice that she found it hard to keep up with him.

When they reached the house Armand was in the hall and Donald said at once that he had some work to finish, disappearing into the library, while Marthe told her brother she was tired and went upstairs to her room.

Armand stood where he was, watching her go. Neither her heightened colour, nor the neglected basket had escaped him.

Chapter 4

That evening Marthe did not come down to supper. Tante Clothilde said that she had a headache and was having some soup sent up to her room. Donald ate without noticing what was put in front of him and afterwards, excusing himself on the grounds that he wanted to write a letter, went up to his own room. There he sat down, drawing pen and paper towards him, but he got no further than 'My dearest sister,' before putting the pen down again to rest his chin on his clasped hands, his eyes brooding unseeingly on the points of candleflame in front of him.

He could not wrench his mind from that moment by the lake when Marthe had told him beyond all possible doubt that she cared for him sufficiently to want him to remain at Mentonnay. Whether she loved him as he now knew he loved her was a further question. Yet he was certain that if he wished to do so, he could win her love. And he had cruelly rebuffed her in such a way that it must have wounded her deeply.

He got up and began to pace up and down the room, his hands clasped behind his back, as if only some kind of action would help combat the turmoil in his mind. He wondered with amazement how he could have hurt her so much—yet it had to be done. Even had he still possessed Duirdre there would be considerable doubt as to whether Armand would consent or wish to see his sister transported to the wild country where Duirdre lay—in this milder air of Mentonnay she had poor enough health. As it was the question did not arise, but for a few brief and overwhelming moments he allowed himself to contemplate it. In the past when he had thought of marriage, of the day when sons of his own would roam the glen, assemble round the big table in the dining room, he had always assumed that his wife would be of his own race, used to the way of life in the Highlands. Never had he dreamed of falling in love with a girl whose whole upbringing was utterly remote from his, yet who had so captured his heart that he did not know how he was to endure life without her.

64

He sat down on the edge of the bed, his elbows on his knees, his head in his hands. He would never be able to ask her to marry him. Even if he qualified to the English Government, even in the unlikely event of Duirdre being returned to him, how could he take her, used as she was to this place, to the ruins of his house, to a land of mists and snow and bitter winters? He must put all thought of it from him, wrench her image from his brain and his heart. But it was hard, and he stayed for a long while, his head in his hands, while the candles guttered and his letter remained unwritten.

At last he was roused by a knock on the door and a footman entered to ask if he would spare a few moments for M.le Chevalier in the library. Rather dazedly he nodded, the struggle fought and won too recent for him to wonder what Armand wanted at this time of night. Consequently he was totally unprepared for the interview that followed.

La Rouelle was standing in front of the fire, an elegant figure in cherry-coloured satin and a white tie wig, his hands clasped behind his back and had Donald been as perceptive as usual, he would have noticed the absence of his host's usual genial expression. As it was he closed the door without more than a cursory glance and said, "You wished to see me?"

Armand nodded. "Yes, I wanted to——" he broke off and then appearing to change his approach asked how much longer the cataloguing would take.

Surprised, Donald replied that it should be finished in about two months.

After another short silence the Frenchman said, "I presume you will then be wanting other employment?"

Exactly what he was inferring by this question Donald was not sure. "Naturally I shall have to do so. Forgive me, Chevalier, but am I to understand that you wish to know when I shall be leaving Mentonnay?" It seemed extraordinary after their talk this morning and Donald stared at him, trying to read that mobile countenance.

Armand stopped prowling about the hearthrug and turned to face his companion. "I am sorry, *mon ami*," he began in a conciliatory tone. "it is not that I want you to leave. Far from it, as far as I am concerned, but—*mon Dieu*, this is very difficult—it is that I am coming to feel it might be better."

"I don't understand," Donald said stiffly. "Are you not satisfied with my work?"

"I am more than satisfied. It is not that."

"Then—what?" Donald had not moved from his place by the big desk. Some instinct warned him of where this conversation might be leading. He folded his arms across his chest and waited.

The Chevalier did not seem to want to come to the point. He poured out two glasses of wine, but he did not attempt to drink his while Donald ignored the gesture. At last Armand braced himself and looked across at the Highlander.

"It is simply, my dear Fraser—forgive me—that I have reason to think my sister is beginning to enjoy your company—too much. And that it is the same for you."

Donald did not move. "Indeed? Why should you think that?"

"I am not blind! I have suspected it for some time, but I thought as far as Marthe is concerned that it might merely be interest in someone who is a foreigner and a guest in our house, and," he smiled a little, "very definitely not like the men of her own society. This afternoon I was, however, disabused of that idea."

Donald lowered his eyes and stared at the carpet. "You honour me."

Armand glanced across at him curiously. "Are you going to tell me you did not know it?"

"I cannot possibly speak for Mlle Marthe's feelings in this matter."

"You have said nothing to her?"

Donald lifted his head. "What do you take me for? Of course I have not."

"Yet something happened this afternoon, something was said."

"Nothing of a direct nature, I assure you. Nor would I do so without your consent—even if I was in a position to ask it, which I am not."

"Then I am right in thinking that for your part you are not indifferent, that given other circumstances you would?"

Donald stalked away to the window where he stood staring out into the darkness. "Had my situation been otherwise," he said slowly, "but it is pointless to explain."

"Explain?" Armand queried, his voice soft.

Donald felt his temper rising. "My dear Chevalier," he retorted as if the words were being forced from him, "you know perfectly well, without submitting me to the indignity of having to explain my poverty, my difficulty in returning home, that I cannot support a wife—certainly not at present, possibly not at all."

Armand glanced at him, and then picked up his wine glass, gazing down at its contents. "I see. You understand also, that apart from that she could not be asked to live a life involving any sort of hardship, nor would I permit her to attempt it. Were you to wish her to share the life you have to lead—and I mean no disrespect to you for that—I should have to withold my consent."

Donald swung round. "No doubt," he retorted stung, "but that question does not arise since I have not asked, nor am I likely to ask for your permission. Believe me, I have too much concern for your sister's welfare for that."

Armand seemed relieved. "I am glad you see the position so clearly. I would like you to believe I have only her welfare at heart and I must ensure a suitable marriage for her. Hardship is not for Marthe."

Donald had a sudden picture of her sitting on the log, her hands folded, and for all her delicacy he saw, what apparently Armand did not see, a strength of character that might carry her over much that was difficult. "I think you misjudge her," he said at last.

Armand gave him a sharp look. "You are not after all suggesting—" and after a violent gesture from Donald, he went on, "no, I see that you are not. Permit me to decide what is best for her. Had things been otherwise, I think you know that my friendship would have extended to welcoming you into our family."

Donald inclined his head. "Thank you. I know you mean that. But you need not fear that I am unaware of the many barriers between myself and your sister. And if there should come a time, if my country should be restored to its rightful place with its rightful King—"

Armand glanced at him. "You mean you would return to fight if your little princeling demanded it?"

"Should my lawful sovereign demand it, yes."

"Even if you were married to Marthe?"

There was silence in the big room except for the crackling of the logs on the fire. It was as if Armand had probed almost unwittingly to the heart of the problem as Donald himself had not done in that struggle upstairs in his bedroom. He felt very cold. "Yes, even then. I have a duty to King James and to my country."

"*Dieu me damne*," Armand said in sudden irritation. "How concerned all you Scotsmen are with duty."

Donald felt the hot anger rising again. "If you wish to insult my race I will leave you to do it alone."

He turned towards the door, but before he could reach it Armand had crossed the room and caught his arm. "I intended no such thing. You must not take offence so easily." He picked up Donald's untouched glass and handed it to him. "Drink this and let us talk the matter over sensibly." He went on rather more carefully. "There is a further point which has to be considered. You are not a Catholic."

"I am aware of that obstacle but it has been overcome before now. A dispensation, I believe——"

Armand interrupted him. "Yes, it could be contrived but it would not make matters any easier for you or for Marthe. Neither Gaston nor my aunts would wish to see her married outside the Church, nor indeed would I—if it could be avoided."

"You think I would not respect her faith—as I am sure she would respect mine?" Donald queried and added in a more caustic tone, "Or do you have it in mind to ask your cousin to convert me—as you suggested he might this morning?"

"You had no need to say that," Armand answered curtly. "Naturally if you were of our faith it would ease the situation, but I would not suggest you abuse your conscience to do so, nor would Gaston. As it is, it need not concern us for it is not the only, nor indeed the main objection. I merely mentioned it to——"

"To add to my unsuitabilities which seem endless. It might have been better to forbear to do so and merely dismiss me for the servant I am."

Armand's eyebrows went up. "Now you are being ridiculous. You are not a servant nor would any librarian be so considered in this house. We all have a great regard for you and, for my part, a friendship which you seem determined to destroy." He began to twist the empty wine glass in his hand. "I regret the things I have had to say to you but my duty as Marthe's brother has forced me to it."

There was a short silence. Donald set his glass down on the small table where the decanter of wine stood on a silver tray. "I should have thought Mlle Marthe herself might be consulted where her own happiness is concerned."

Her brother shook his head. "I think not. That is not how things are done in my country. I do not mean that I would force her to wed against her will but she is young and emotion is not the best guide as far as marriage is concerned." He glanced at the rigid figure of the Highlander. "You see, do you not, why it might be better for you to leave us, before there is any deeper involvement on either side—much as I myself will personally regret it."

"I see that I should go as soon as my work is done and during that time I will undertake not to seek your sister alone as I did this afternoon. Will that suffice?" Was he foolish, Donald wondered, to try to cling to a few more weeks in which he might look at her, if nothing else.

The Chevalier sighed. "I doubt it. I know this is not easy for you but have you considered that to prolong your stay might be to fan what maybe she is not yet fully aware of?"

"You mean," Donald said deliberately, "that you fear she may indeed be on the point of loving a man whom it would be better for her not to love. Or have you discussed it with her since this afternoon and know it to be the truth?"

"No, I have not—naturally. I merely think that if you remain— forgive me again—I doubt if you are the man to disguise what you feel for her."

Donald stiffened. "If that is what you think I had indeed better leave in the morning. I have no desire to cause embarrassment to any one in this house."

"I am sure you have not. But you must see that to stay would be to encourage—" Armand saw the expression on his companion's face, but he went on, "to encourage what would be best left alone. I do not imagine," he added with a faint smile, "that you are made of stone." He was startled, practical man that he was, to see that face turn slowly pale with anger.

"How dare you?" The words were flung at him. "How dare you suggest—"

"I merely suggested one must be sensible," Armand interrupted hastily. "In France we talk of these things openly and I think—"

"I don't want to show what you think," Donald snapped. "You make me thank God I am a Scot. *Mo thruagh!*" The Gaelic expression slipped out. "Your attitude has changed since this morning. I will pack and be out of the house tomorrow."

Armand began to lose his own patience. "There is no need for such haste—that would indeed cause embarrassment. You are being singularly stiff-necked, Monsieur Fraser. I have done nothing more than to suggest you are as other men. But if you think I insulted you let me say only that I am speaking out of concern for Marthe. Surely you must see that I do not want her hurt or upset."

"That is the only consideration that carries any weight with me," Donald retorted, but he had himself in hand again as he turned away. "I will wait a day or two and then find the need to return to Paris."

Armand bowed formally. "That is indeed best—for both of you. Naturally I shall arrange that you receive your full salary before you go."

"I see you are determined to humiliate me. I shall not accept payment for work I have not done." Donald opened the door but before he could leave Armand, who had his back to him and was leaning one arm on the mantleshelf, picked up a letter which had been lying there unnoticed. Endeavouring to make his voice sound normal he said, "This came from England today. I should have given it to you earlier."

He held it out. Donald took it blindly and stuffing it into his pocket, went out of the room and out of the house, slamming the great door behind him.

Outside he stood on the terrace in the darkness, in the grip of such a towering rage that for a moment all his passionate nature rose in one mighty rebellion against all that had happened to him, against this land of exile, against all Frenchmen and Armand de la Rouelle in particular, until he felt as if it would choke him.

Then he strode across the flagged terrace and down the steps to the long gravel drive. Beneath the trees it was dark and a cool wind was blowing. He walked rapidly away from the house, hardly aware of his surroundings. It did not seem possible that so much had changed since yesterday evening when he had returned from Paris and thought how welcoming the château had looked. Now it would welcome him no more. And it had come about in such a manner that he would be quite unable to return as a guest of the family. It was damnable and he cursed Armand furiously. Yet he knew that Armand had not intended to imply the final insult, that he had acted only to avoid a situation that might become untenable. And in a sense the Frenchman was right.

At the thought of Marthe Donald felt a further wave of despair and frustration. Probably he would never see her again. He would return to the old wretched life in Paris and for one bleak instant wished he had left that distant birch wood and hurtled down the slope to die with his father. Bab did not need him now, for all her affection, neither did his mother, and he wondered for what purpose he had been saved.

By now he had reached the lodge gates and unless he roused the lodge keeper he would have to turn back. It would be rather foolish to wake the man at this hour and would look very odd as he had neither greatcoat nor baggage. He must return to the house and attempt to sleep. Then he could be closeted in the library before the family came down in the morning, make some excuse later in the day and be gone by the following morning—and had he but known it the letter which lay forgotten in his pocket would indeed have provided him with just such an excuse. But the farewells made necessary by sheer politeness would be hard, Marthe would be hurt and he did not think he could bear to see that desolate look on her face again. Despite their quarrel, it would be difficult to forget all Armand's former kindness, nor did he want to think he would not again talk with Gaston de la Rouelle for whom he had felt both friendship and respect. And he realized just how attached he had become to Mentonnay itself and its gracious way of life.

He walked quickly back up the drive and deciding it would be wiser to go in by the rear of the house, skirted it and went under the archway into the small courtyard flanked by stables, storehouses and outbuildings. Usually this was lit by lamps set in brackets on the walls, but tonight they were out and he was surprised. He paused for a moment to get used to the deeper darkness within the stone walls, and then, as he was about to grope his way to a door that led into a rear passage, some instinct warned him and he stayed where he was in the shadows, listening intently.

As he peered into the darkness he saw two darker shadows move. They seemed to be carrying some sacks towards the archway and for a moment he wondered if it could be two of the servants, almost immediately dismissing this idea for they would have had the lamps burning. These were men raiding one of the storehouses—but even though it had been a hard winter with much poverty in the countryside, Armand cared for his own tenants and he could not believe they could be from among them.

While he was wondering what to do, very much aware of the fact that he was unarmed, a light leapt in one of the buildings, flickering and fading and growing brighter with the orange brilliance of burning hay. At once he realized that, whether by accident or design, they had set the place on fire and the wind was blowing in the direction of the house.

In the split second that he watched it he remembered that there was a small bell tower in the archway, though he had never heard the bell rung; then he was pelting across the yard and fumbling wildly for the chain. It seemed an age before he found it and when he did it was rusty and resisted his tugging, but at last he wrenched it down and the harsh clanging of the clapper burst on the night silence. He pulled it furiously and then ran towards the burning building. At the same moment the two men, scared out of their wits, made for the gate. Donald ran at them and caught the first a blow on the jaw that sent him spinning; the second man sprang forward and they grappled together. Donald could feel gnarled hands grasping at his throat and tried to wrench them away, aware of hot breath on his face and the unpleasant odour of garlic and cheap liquor. They swayed backwards, locked together, and both lost their balance, falling across a mounting block. Forced to release his grip the man rolled on the cobbles and Donald staggered away from him, but before he could return to the attack, the other man recovered sufficiently to come at him again. He swung round, lunging forward with his right fist, but the man ducked—a knife flashed and Donald felt a searing pain in his side. He doubled up as the knife was wrenched free, and a stinging blow on the back of the neck sent him down without a sound. As he fell he struck his head on the corner of the mounting block and was lying there unconscious as doors opened, light streamed out, and both owner and staff of the château came running into the courtyard.

Chapter 5

Donald opened his eyes slowly. He had the sensation of returning from a long way off, but where he was and where he had been he did not know. He seemed to be in a room full of sunshine and as it hurt his eyes he closed them again. But after a moment he reopened them and turned his head on the pillow. He saw that he was in his room at Mentonnay and it was very quiet except for the sound of birds in the garden below. He looked towards the window and saw that someone was sitting there reading. It was Gaston de la Rouelle in his long black cassock, his breviary in his hand.

"M. le Curé," Donald said slowly and distinctly, as if to assure himself that he was not still dreaming. He seemed to have been dreaming a good deal just lately and it was hard to separate fact from fantasy.

The priest got up at once and came over to the bed, a pleased smile on his face. "My son, you are awake at last. God be praised."

Donald frowned. "I don't understand. Have I been asleep long? I can't remember."

The Curé pulled up a chair by the bed and sat down, his fingers on the pulse of Donald's right hand which lay limply on top of the coverlet. "You have been ill for quite a while. Do you not remember what happened?"

Donald put up the other hand to his head and felt the bandage, and the movement caused considerable pain in his side. Memory began to come back—the struggle with the thieves, the alarm bell ringing and before that the solitary walk and the quarrel with Armand. As the last incident became clear in his mind his expression changed abruptly.

The priest was watching him intently. "What is it, my son? You have much pain?"

Donald turned his head away. "Only a little—I remember now what happened. Those men—did they get away?"

"I'm afraid so. We were all so busy getting the fire out that they escaped in the darkness. But thanks to you the damage was small. How do you feel now?"

"I don't know. I don't seem to have much strength in me."

"You are weak from a fever; that knife wound caused considerable inflammation, and you cut your head when you fell on the mounting block, but that is healing up well though I've no doubt you still have a slight headache."

"I have indeed," Donald said and put up a hand to his head, aware of a dull throbbing.

A puzzled look came over his face. "I have not been conscious since that night—how long ago?"

"Nearly two weeks. At times I thought you were sensible, but more often you were delirious."

"Delirious?" Donald fixed his eyes on the face above him. "You mean I talked? What did I say? Who was here, who heard me?" For a moment he tried to struggle up, but the priest leaned over and gently eased him back on to the pillow.

"Calm yourself, my son. You rambled a little, that is all, and only to me as far as I know. I have been here most of the time. You see," he pointed across the room, "I have had a small bed put in here so that I could be with you. No one else has paid you more than a short visit— just to take my place while I said Mass."

"You mean you have spent all your time here, nursing me?"

Gaston de la Rouelle smiled. "In my calling we become used to sick-beds and I am considered a pretty fair nurse. Now you will need some nourishment. I will order you some soup. You have had nothing so far except some brandy and milk which Mlle Marthe or I fed you with a spoon."

"She—she has been here?"

"Yes," the priest answered quietly. "At first she was the only one who could make you swallow anything."

He went downstairs and Donald was left alone. He felt very tired, too tired to think clearly, except to hold on to the fact that she had been here while he had been, as it seemed to him now, very far away in some dark place. He closed his eyes and presently dozed off.

When he opened them again, Marthe herself was sitting by his bed while a manservant set a tray on a small table beside her.

"Ah, you are awake again," she said, smiling down at him. "My cousin has gone to see one of our tenants who is sick, so I have come to give you your soup. I am so very glad you are better." She tucked a napkin about his neck and then picked up the bowl, stirring its contents with a spoon, and from her whole manner Donald felt sure that Armand had said nothing of their quarrel.

"Thank you," he said at last. "I understand I have much to thank you for. M. le Curé says you have taken good care of me."

"Oh, it is he who has done that—I have only helped a little when he has had to be absent." She dipped the spoon into the soup and he tried to lift himself a little. "No, no, you must not do that. Let me put this pillow behind you and we will manage very well."

He obeyed her and submitted to being fed, mainly for the pleasure of being dependent on her for a little while. So skilfully did she manage that none of the soup was spilled and Donald felt considerably better when he had finished it. She went away then, but if he closed his eyes he could see her sitting there with her quiet smile and gentle hands, and he lay in a kind of peace that was disturbed neither by the memory of his bitter quarrel with her brother nor of the parting which full recovery must bring.

It was several days before the Chevalier de la Rouelle came to the sick room. By that time Donald was wondering whether he intended to come at all. He was wondering too if he was only in this bed on sufferance because he could not be moved and it was not a pleasant thought, but in his present state of physical weakness he found he cared less than he might otherwise have done. And the Curé was consideration itself. Whether he knew of the quarrel or not, Donald had no idea.

However on the fourth day after he had regained his senses, he was sitting propped up by pillows staring idly out into the garden, which was bright with spring sunshine, the scent of wallflowers coming in on the warm breeze, when the door opened and Armand walked in, so quickly and quietly that he was standing by the bed almost before its occupant was aware of his presence.

"My dear Fraser," he said at once, without the slightest sign of embarrassment, "I am delighted to hear you are better. Your excellent nurse tells me you are now improving rapidly."

Donald looked up at him and meeting the Frenchman's frank gaze took his cue from it, answering as if nothing unpleasant had ever occurred between them. "M. le Curé has been very kind. Indeed, I can't think why—"

"Our good Gaston is never slow in performing such works—he dreams of a martyr's crown I think." Armand paused, a slightly cynical smile on his lips. "But you gave us all a fright, you know. When the servants carried you in, we thought you were dead."

Donald was tempted to ask the Chevalier if he would have minded,

75

but he held his peace and Armand went on, "You threw my aunts into a state of frenzy. In a few minutes Tante Julie had the entire household running in circles—at least those who weren't fighting the fire—" He glanced humorously down at the sick man and then walked away to the window where he stood looking out, the smile gone from his eyes.

He was thinking of the cry Marthe had given when she had been the first downstairs to ask why the bell had been rung, only to find their guest's bloodstained body lying on a couch in the hall, and how he had held the distraught girl in his arms and tried to make her realize it was no corpse that lay there. Thereafter there had been no pretence between them, though nothing specific had been said. Armand occasionally cursed himself for having brought this impoverished Scot into the house, but when the latter's fever rose and it seemed as if he might die after all, he was unable to prevent Marthe having access to the sick room—nor, after one battle royal during which his sister's stubborn determination took him by surprise, did he attempt to do so. His genuinely sympathetic nature was roused by the sight of her small taut figure and pale face confronting him over the unoccupied desk in the library, and when Tante Julie expressed her disapproval, for once he rather sharply asked her to hold her tongue. Which reproof so astonished her that she obeyed him and did not mention the matter again.

He turned round and came back to the bed. "It seems I owe you a great debt," he said, "but for you I might have lost not only those buildings but Mentonnay itself and I need not tell you what that would have meant to me." He paused but Donald lay silent, staring at the bed post, so he went on, "Luckily only part of the north side of the courtyard was destroyed, mostly stores and harness." An amused glint came into his hazel eyes. "If you had not rung that bell and roused the household and, I might add, the entire village and every dog in the neighbourhood—"

"It was all that I could think of on the spur of the moment," Donald confessed, a reluctant smile on his own face.

"Thank God you did, though how you pulled that rusty chain that has not been touched for years, I don't know." Armand came back and seated himself on the bed, completely at ease. "At any rate it was most effective. The men who started the fire were not, I believe, any of my own tenants. I have questioned them all closely and satisfied myself on that score. I'm afraid the rascals got clean away. But if you had not come upon them and acted as you did, God knows what would have happened."

Donald looked at him rather sombrely. "I saw my own house burn. I would not have had the same happen to Mentonnay."

Armand answered simply, "And for that I can never repay you, *mon ami*."

Good God, Donald thought, does he think I did it to gain a bargaining point? "Please do not talk of debts," he said stiffly. "It is I who have been in yours ever since you brought me here—though I believe you think I repaid you very ill."

Armand clasped both hands about his knees. "I see we had better discuss this matter once and for all so that we may understand each other. I know that I owe you an apology. When we quarrelled that night we both said things we should not have said, and I want to ask your pardon for what you thought was an insult to your honour. I really did not mean to speak so baldly nor did I think you would ever so abuse our friendship—and I hope I may still call it that. If you have reconsidered the matter you will know what I did mean."

Donald began to pull at the fringed bed-cover. "Yes I do know—I knew that night when I was out in the drive. And—" he hesitated for a moment, "of course you were right. When I am well, I must go."

Armand stared down at his riding boots. "But I have reconsidered too. I should like you to remain here until your work in the library is finished, and of course you cannot resume that before you are quite well again. That will give us time to see what can be done about your future."

Donald, to his intense embarrassment, found the weak flush of illness creeping into his cheeks and he did not look at his companion. "What can I say? Your kindness is—" he did not finish the sentence. "Yet my situation remains the same, does it not?"

Armand got to his feet. "Perhaps. But I think we will not go into that now. Suffice it to say we understand each other somewhat better." And he added cheerfully, "You must concentrate on regaining your strength and as soon as your nurse allows it you must come down to the garden. This sunshine will do you good."

For a moment there was a silence. Then Donald raised his head, the hectic colour fading a little from his face. "Thank you," he said again, and hoped that Armand would know all that he wished those two words to convey. Then urged on by Armand's total change in attitude, he went on, albeit uncertainly, "Mademoiselle Marthe—I suppose you have not—you would rather I did not—nothing has really changed—"

Armand thrust his hands deep into his breeches' pockets. "I wish you had not asked me. I am no longer entirely sure what would be best for her." He hesitated, but he was determined not to tell his guest of that scene in the hall after the accident, and he said merely, "I would only ask you to give us time to talk further."

Donald relaxed against the pillows. "Willingly," he said in a low voice. He saw no immediate answer to the seemingly impossible barriers, yet Armand no longer totally rejected him, nor, against all odds, did he feel his love to be hopeless, and a curious languid happiness began to settle on him. He became aware that Armand was holding out his hand.

"Shall we consider our debts cancelled then?"

He took the proferred hand at once and Armand smiled down at him. "Good. Au revoir then, *mon cher*. Ah, here is your vigilant nurse," he added as the door opened and his cousin came in. "No doubt he has come to turn me out."

The priest nodded. "Yes, it is time I dressed the wound."

Armand went, shutting the door quietly behind him and as the Curé unwound the dressing from the wounded man's side he did not fail to notice the lessening of tension in his patient's face. After a few moments he said, "Armand did not come before because he felt, as I did, that you needed absolute quiet, but I think his visit has done you good."

Donald glanced up at the thin, alert face above him. He was certain now that the Chevalier had not spoken of their quarrel and he was immensely grateful. "You have all been very good to me," he said at last.

The priest's attention was on the wound and his careful bandaging. "It is part of my calling to care for the body as well as the soul."

"And my body is doing very well under your care. As for my soul," a faint smile crossed the patient's face, "I told M. de la Rouelle not so long ago that I thought you too wise to try to convert me."

Gaston straightened and laid the soiled bandage in a little bowl. "Did Armand think that I should? Monsieur Fraser, as a priest I would of course wish to see all men share my faith, but I have never believed in coercion whatever my cousin may, in his flippant way, have suggested to you. That does not produce faith. And," he added, an odd expression passing fleetingly over his face, "there are a few rare spirits who are in grace, by nature, and with those," he paused, "it is wiser not to interfere."

He gave Donald a sudden warm smile that lit his austere features and carried his bowl out of the room, leaving his patient gazing after him in some astonishment.

On a warm afternoon a week later Donald was allowed out into the garden for the first time and lay on a chaise longue under the mulberry tree on the lawn. Picot, Armand's dog, dozed at his feet, stirring only to snap at an insect, and Donald himself had some trouble in keeping awake. He lay back comfortably, his eyes on the distant woods, blue in the unexpected heat of this May day.

Since his talk with Armand, though nothing further had been said, he had felt oddly at peace. It was enough that he was here, that he still had what he had discovered he valued, Armand's friendship, that he might sit in this garden, watch Marthe as she walked among the lilacs, listen while she read to him. Though he was certain Armand had said nothing definite to her, there was an unspoken content between them. He had spent the long quiet days reading or dozing, talking with Armand or the Curé, occasionally playing chess with the latter, receiving a visit now and again, something of a state affair, from the two aunts. There was, it seemed to him, a subtle change in the entire household. He was accepted in a way he did not think had existed before. And there were the treasured moments when Marthe came into the room on some errand or other. He found himself telling her of the old days at Duirdre, of half forgotten incidents from his boyhood, as if he had shelved, at least for the time being, the difficulties that every day of returning health brought ominously nearer. It was a false peace, and he knew it, but as he lay here in the dappled shade of this tree, listening to the distant sound as she practised at her spinet all that mattered was the present moment.

He was just beginning to drowse when Armand came across the lawn with a letter in his hand. "For you," he said, holding it out. "I think it is from England. How are you feeling today?"

"Very well," Donald said, smiling. "I fear I am a fraud to be still accepting an invalid's privileges. I should like to get back to my work soon."

Armand lowered himself on to the grass and sat fondling his dog's silky ears. "You may do that when Gaston permits it, not before. Please read your letter if you wish to do so."

Donald broke the seal and then glanced up. "By the way I have been meaning to ask you—the night of the fire you gave me a letter, did you not?" And as Armand nodded, he went on, "I thought so. I put it in my pocket and never saw it again."

"Nor I," Armand told him. "We had to cut off your coat and it was so soaked with blood it had to be burned—I am afraid your letter must have gone with it."

"I suppose so," Donald said. "I was wondering where this coat came from."

"I had it made for you—and do not protest, my dear Fraser, for I simply will not listen to you. It was the least I could do."

"In that case I will say nothing but thank you. This letter is also from my sister so perhaps it will tell me any news I may have missed." He sat silently reading for a moment, and Armand lay back on the grass, gazing up at the sunlight filtering through the leaves of the mulberry tree until he was roused by a shocked exclamation in a language he did not understand.

"What is it, mon ami—bad news?"

Donald shook his head mutely and read again the first page of the letter. At last he said in a dazed voice, "My sister is apparently married."

"But that surely is good news. My felicitations. Are you acquainted with your new brother-in-law?"

"No," Donald said slowly, "and I do not think I wish to be." He turned the letter over and oblivious of the surprise on Armand's face, read on for a while. "She writes that she has married a gentleman by the name of," he consulted the closely written page, "Major Rupert Astley, the only son of a certain Lord Rawdon, whoever he may be."

"It sounds a suitable match."

"You do not understand. He is an officer in the English army, in the Life Guards, Bab says. I cannot—I *cannot* credit it. That she should accept such a man! It does not seem possible."

Armand pushed his over-affectionate dog aside and sat up. "I do not see why this should be so unpalatable to you, especially if she is happy in the match."

"How could she be?" Donald's voice was constricted. "Four years ago we were fighting that army. They defeated us on Drumossie Moor, as you know, and afterwards—My God!"

"But that is long past, and surely there is peace in Scotland now?"

"Peace?" Donald looked at him as if he had asked a singularly foolish question. "No Jacobite can be at peace with the Hanoverian usurper, nor a Whig, let alone the men who ravaged our country. Did you ever hear how they used us after the battle? But no, of course you did not, how should you?" He leaned forward, his eyes burning. "They shut our wounded in barns and burned the buildings over their heads, they hounded our women and children from their homes so that they died of the cold—it is cold in Scotland in April. They kept hundreds of our men, half clad and starving, battened down in ships that took weeks to reach London; they kept others in jail without sufficient food or water or medical supplies and even took away the few aids our surgeons still possessed. You know what was done to my own home and my own people. And my father was shot, unarmed, outside our door. Do you expect me to be glad that my sister has married an officer of that army?"

Shocked by the passion, the naked hatred that had burst forth, Armand began, "I had no idea——" and then changed his mind. This was a Donald Fraser he had never seen. "Even so," he said in a conciliatory tone, "you do not know that your sister's husband was in any way involved. Surely the entire British Army was not sent to fight in Scotland?"

Still in the grip of his revulsion, Donald nevertheless shook his head. "No, probably he was not, for I doubt that the Life Guards were involved——I believe they do not leave the country unless the King does so——but this is not the point. She has married a man who wears a uniform we loathe, and he belongs to those who destroyed everything we possessed. I cannot understand it. She was always so——so loyal. I wonder what pressure was put on her——" . He began to read again. "Yet she does not say it was so——"

Armand laid a hand on his arm. "*Mon cher*, do not distress yourself. Remember it is four years since the fighting ended, and you told me yourself that she had journeyed into England before that. And she is considerably younger than you, is she not? It will mean less to her than to you."

Donald looked at him in a strained manner. "Yes——yes, she is not yet twenty. You are right of course——I must not blame her——and until I know more of the circumstances——" he broke off and picking up the letter read on to the end. A little sigh escaped him and when he had finished he folded the sheets and put them in his pocket. "She did write to me of course, telling me of her betrothal, and that must have been the letter burned with my coat. I did not think she would have taken such a step without informing me——now she wonders why I did not come, nor write to her. The marriage was arranged quickly because Lord Rawdon was ill, and she is distressed at what must seem my lack of concern for her. Poor Bab." He leaned back in his chair and gazed down at Armand still sitting on the grass. Picot, realizing his master was no longer solely concerned with petting him, lay immobile, his head on Armand's thigh, his yellowish eyes fixed on Donald.

"She wants me to visit her. It seems they have a house in St.

James's Square and a family estate at Rawdon in Berkshire. But I do not know that I shall go."

"That would seem a little churlish, if you will forgive me for saying it. Unless your sister appears unhappy in the marriage, would it not be kinder to find out what manner of man she has taken for a husband before condemning him? You cannot mean to hate all Englishmen for the rest of your life."

Donald's mouth was set hard. Perhaps that was just what he did mean to do, yet Armand's words made sense, and in truth Bab's happiness meant even more to him. And he could go. There was nothing to keep him from doing so once he was well enough to travel, for he had managed to save most of the generous salary Armand paid him and poverty was no longer an excuse. Another more disturbing thought occurred to him. "This seems to be the answer, does it not?"

Armand did not raise his head and returned to caressing Picot. "The answer to what?"

"I think you know what I mean. Here is my reason for leaving. I must see my sister, if only to assure her I am not so lacking in affection as she seems to think. I could write of course, but as you say, I ought to see this man she has married and judge for myself whether the match is really for her happiness. I'll go as soon as I can and then your worries will be at an end." The words were hard to bring out and sounded harsher than he intended. So much so that Armand jumped to his feet, oblivious of tumbling the sleeping dog aside.

"I thought we had reached a better understanding," he said and stood staring down at Donald, his hands clasped behind his back. "Have I not shown you that you are welcome here, that I want to——" he broke off. "Your concern about your sister should make you more perceptive about my concern for Marthe."

Donald put up a hand to shield his eyes but dropped it almost immediately. "Forgive me. That was very unfair of me. But you see, even with this reason for going it will not be easy for me to do so."

Armand's annoyance evaporated instantly. "I know that." He gave a deep sigh. "If I could give Marthe to you without reserve I would. I have come to think there is no man I would rather have as my brother, but——"

"You need not say it," Donald broke in in a low voice. "I know it is out of the question at the moment and far better that I leave, but," he glanced up, "it is not only that I do not want to leave her." His eyes wandered from Armand's face across the lawns to the beautiful turreted house, the grey stone terrace, the beds of wallflowers, the distant trees and the miniature lake. "I have grown to love this place and I do not wish to say goodbye to any of you. M.le Curé's kindness I can never repay and," a slight smile crossed his face in an effort to relieve the tense moment, "I think I shall even miss your two estimable aunts."

"*Bon Dieu!*" Armand laughed. "Then you have indeed felt at home. But seriously, this is only a visit to your sister and I beg you most earnestly to come back here, or at least to let me know when you return to France." A sudden thought struck him and he added, "I trust that you are in no personal danger in England?"

"Not in the least," Donald answered without hesitation. "My father was listed in the Act of Attainder, but I was not, therefore I must be included in the general pardon of the Act of Indemnity. I may even wear a sword in England which I would not be permitted to do in my own country."

"*Quelle horreur*—to be without one's sword is to be half dressed. Well, I am relieved to hear you are not running a risk in journeying to England. How long will you stay?"

"Not very long, I should imagine. I cannot think I shall have much in common with my brother-in-law. I only want to see Bab and my mother too, then I shall return." He paused, staring down the length of the lawn to a tall cedar tree. "And perhaps it will be best if when I do I write to you from Paris. I am sorry the work in the library is not finished but I am sure you will find a competent librarian to do the work."

Armand brushed the thought aside. "I am not thinking of that wretched library." He hesitated, one hand on a branch of the mulberry tree, the other pulling at a young green leaf, tearing it slowly to pieces. "I wish I knew what to do."

"I am sorry," Armand could barely hear the words, "I did not intend to fall in love with your sister nor to make her care for me—if she does."

He did not answer that. Having covered the grass with torn leaves he turned back to face Donald. "Love is something we Frenchman know a great deal about," he said half sadly, half amusedly, "but we do not confuse it with the hard facts of marriage and settlements and the future of the family. *Peste*—it is nearly five o'clock and I have a letter that must catch the diligence as it passes through Mentonnay. I will see you at supper, *mon cher*."

He strolled away across the grass. Picot watched him, uncertain whether to follow his master in the hope that he might be going to ride in the park or to continue to lie in the sun. However, seeing Armand mount the steps of the terrace, he turned back and stretched out again beside the couch.

"You lazy animal," Donald said absently, but now he showed no disposition to follow the dog's example as he had done earlier in the afternoon. All drowsiness was dispelled by the letter and the subsequent conversation and he took the sheets out of his pocket to read them again. He could still hardly credit the contents nor believe that Bab—the sister who had scrambled over the hillsides with him at home, who was as Highland as he was—had married, seemingly willingly, an English officer. He read one particular sentence over and over again—'I do wish you to meet my dearest Rupert, and I beg you not to judge him until you have seen him.' And she clearly thought he disapproved so strongly that he had neither answered her letter nor come to attend the wedding. He must at least put that right, for he could not have her thinking him as heartless as that.

He folded the letter again, got to his feet and began to walk slowly back to the house. He must go, as soon as possible, but it was with revulsion that he contemplated staying under Major Astley's roof, for all it was Bab's roof as well. How could he accept the man's hospitality, eat his bread? An enemy was an enemy and in the Highlands, where there were such strong traditions of hospitality, there were equally rigid rules about one's dealings with those one was at war with—and though, as Armand said, the fighting was over, the enmity certainly was not, as far as he and many other Jacobites were concerned. What had possessed Bab? He smote one fist against the other. Great God, what had possessed her?

Chapter 6

With the time set for his departure taken out of his hands by this news, Donald made his arrangements for ten days ahead. Armand mentioned at supper that evening that M. Fraser had received news which necessitated his travelling to London; there were polite enquiries about his sister and her husband and after a few expressions of regret that he should be leaving, the matter passed off without further comment. Donald did not look directly at Marthe throughout the meal, and later in the salon she sat beside Tante Clothilde winding silks and there was no opportunity for anything but formal conversation. He did not know whether he was glad or sorry.

The next day when she spent a short while with him in the garden she said only that she was sorry he must go, and went on to ask him about Bab. Her eyes were shadowed, her face a little paler than usual, her delicacy emphasized, and he kept his tone light, answering her questions as best he could. This was the way it must be, and he did not think, when he returned to France, that he would come back to Mentonnay. To be constantly near her with no hope, to have to resist day by day the temptation to catch her in his arms, was more than he thought he could bear. Armand was right in one thing—he was not made of stone.

A few days later he insisted on going to the library to set his work in some sort of order for his successor. Gaston de la Rouelle looked slightly doubtful but at last agreed to a few hours spent at his desk.

He was busy writing when a footman came in to announce that a gentleman had called to see him. Donald straightened his back, conscious still of a dragging sensation in his right side; he imagined the visitor must be some acquaintance of Armand's who wished to use the not inconsiderable library, but he sprang to his feet in pleased surprise when he saw that his visitor was Neil MacEachain.

"Neil! Come in. I had no idea you would ride out to see me." He held out his hand warmly. "Sit down and tell me what brings you here."

MacEachain took the hand in a firm grasp, surveying Donald. "My sorrow!" he exclaimed in Gaelic. "What have you done to yourself?"

"Oh, I had an encounter with a pair of thieving fellows a few weeks ago and had the ill-luck to crack my head open on a mounting block."

Neil waited while Donald poured wine for him and then sat down in a chair near the desk.

"M. de la Rouelle told me of your accident as I came in and that you are leaving shortly—for England."

Donald put his own glass down and sat twisting the stem in his hands. "Yes, I am going to London. Bab has married and as, through this wretched accident, her letter to me was lost, I feel obliged to visit and meet her husband—" he broke off momentarily, "—a Major in the Life Guards."

"Good God!"

"As you say," Donald agreed rather tartly. "I cannot think how it came about. I must see her if only to try to understand."

"An extremely difficult task, I should imagine," Neil answered drily, and getting up he walked over to the window where he stood looking out into the garden, his dark face intent and brooding. There was a light summer rain falling and the garden was deserted, the distant trees and the lake lost in the mist. When he turned round again Donald saw that his black eyes were burning with an eager light.

"What is it? I thought you must have come here for some purpose."

Neil came back across the room and leaned his hands on the desk, facing Donald; even though they were speaking in their native tongue he lowered his voice.

"Not so long ago, Duidre, I asked you if you would be willing to serve the Prince again, and you answered that you would. Is that still true?"

"In any way I can, you know that. Only tell me how."

"His Highness thinks, indeed we all think, that it is just possible that a political move might succeed—I told you when we last met of the unrest there is. Anyhow he is determined to find out for himself how matters really stand—he is planning a visit to London."

If Neil had said he was preparing to visit the moon Donald could not have been more astonished. "He is going to London himself! But he must be mad, and you must be mad to condone his attempting such a thing."

MacEachain's eyes flashed. "He is not mad. He is full of courage and a bold stroke may succeed where caution fails."

"Have you forgotten Derby already?" Donald asked, aware that a bitter note had crept into his voice. In his mind there was a clear picture of that disastrous day when, almost in the hour of victory, a retreat was ordered—a retreat which Donald's father had resolutely opposed and over which the Prince had quarrelled violently with his commander-in-chief, Lord George Murray. But he had given in, turned his back on England, and Donald did not see how, at this present moment, that situation was to be reversed. "The English Jacobites failed us then," he reminded his visitor, "you cannot have forgotten how few came to join us. Is it likely they will do any more now that the Prince has no army at his back?"

"We are not planning in military terms. There are other ways, you know. You do not think that he can carry out such a stroke?"

"It is quite immaterial what I think—especially as I do not know yet what the plan is."

Neil removed his hands from the desk and stood upright facing Donald. "And I am not sure that I should tell you. It seems your loyalty has faded with the years, but then I forgot—the Frasers were slow to come forward last time."

Donald got to his feet, his arms folded tightly across his chest as if to hold in the angry indignation that rose up inside him. "I had not thought you, of all people, could say that to me. Maybe MacShimmi did not call the clan out at first but the Frasers of Duirdre were with His Highness from the beginning and by all the Saints we were there at the end and we shed enough blood for him."

"I beg your pardon," Neil said. "I was unjust. Yet your reluctance—"

"I am not reluctant, I am merely trying to see the thing fairly. You know, you *must* know that I would give my life for him."

At once MacEachain came round the desk and laid both hands on his arms. "I do, *laochan*. Perhaps it is just that you have grown weary of waiting—as we all have. But the Prince is determined now on action and if he meets a few of the leading Jacobites in London, think what that might achieve."

"I'm thinking of what it might do to him! And surely such work is for lesser men whose faces are not so well known. I know his presence may inspire greater confidence among our supporters there, but it seems an extremely rash idea." He broke off as Neil burst out, "Duirdre, if you could only see him now. Ever since we escaped from Scotland he has been oppressed and wretched, with no place to call his own, but now he has hope again. He is eager to go, to try his fate once more, and I would not dream of trying to prevent him."

"I still think it far too dangerous." Donald sat down again and picking up a quill began to smoothe the feather, a heavy frown on his brows. "If he was caught the Elector would never let him go. Even if he did not take the Prince's life, he would certainly take away his freedom."

"I know that," Neil said with a touch of impatience, "and that is why it will be so important to be well prepared for his visit and to guard him carefully while he is there. He does not intend to stay long, a week perhaps, and Colonel Brett is going with him. I don't suppose you know the Colonel? No, I thought not. Of course I wanted to go with him myself, but I am so well known to be his constant companion that he thinks it might be better for me to remain in Paris and show myself openly to allay any doubts concerning his whereabouts. Everyone will presume he is where I am." Neil paused that his next words might have their full effect. "But what we do need is another agent in London—a man we can trust, to go ahead and make preparations, lodgings to be in readiness and to sound out the general support we may count on."

Donald glanced up, half in disbelief. "You cannot mean—me?"

"Yes, if you will go. We have only one man there who knows the secret. There are plenty who profess to support our cause, but none we would trust to this extent."

"And His Highness would trust me?"

Neil smiled for the first time. "On my recommendation and his own recollections of you, yes. And now that you tell me you are indeed going to London for a perfectly acceptable reason, who better?"

Donald nodded. He was trying to assimilate all that this would mean.

Neil went on, "You could operate perfectly from such a secure address and no one would suspect a different motive for your being there. This is even better than I hoped—"

Donald interrupted him sharply. "You realize what you are asking me to do. I am going—against my inclinations, I grant you—to accept Major Astley's hospitality and then work from under his roof to overthrow the Government he serves. And whether I like it or not he is Bab's husband."

Neil fingered his chin, looking intently at his companion. "You do not think the end justifies the means?"

"I think anything justifiable if it is to bring the Prince into his own, but I shall be eating the man's bread and virtually betraying him." Suddenly the quill snapped between Donald's fingers and he threw it down. "It puts me in mind of Glencoe—am I to behave like a damned Campbell?"

MacEachain perched on the edge of the desk. "It is merely a matter of getting your values right and I am surprised that I should have to remind you of it. Who is more important—this English major or His Highness?"

"You know the answer to that—and I do not need reminding. But I cannot be expected to like it."

A shadow crossed Neil's face. "I do not like many of the things I have had to do during the past few years, but I would do the same again, and more, for him. However if you are going to be squeamish, MacDomhnull Ard, you will not make a good plotter." He had chosen the right moment to use that Highland title and he watched its owner carefully, as he stared down at the broken quill.

At last Donald raised his head. "I doubt if I'm cut out for intrigue, but if His Highness wants me to do it, there's no more to be said. What exactly does he want?"

Neil leaned forward eagerly, his point won. "You would have to contact our other agent in London and make arrangements for the Prince's stay—possibly in September. You would also have to interview all the people on a list we shall give you, and this must be done with great caution, sounding each man out before committing yourself in any way."

"Yes, I understand that."

"And of course, when the Prince arrives, you and our other man will act as his bodyguard as discreetly as possible. Anyway we can go into the final details later."

"Who is this agent I have to contact?"

Neil smiled again, the intense look fading a little. "I have kept that trump card until last. It is Fergus MacKenzie."

For the first time during their conversation Donald's face lit with spontaneous eagerness. "Fergus! I had no idea where he was, in fact I thought he had been killed on Drumossie Moor."

"No, he is in London now and he will be more than glad to have you with him. You are related, are you not?"

"Yes, my grandmother was a MacKenzie and he is my cousin." Donald got up and handed Neil his glass again, for neither of them had touched their wine. Then he said, half smiling. "I can't deny that the fact that Fergus is involved in this makes it a great deal more palatable. Don't think I would not give my right arm to serve His Highness, but I still think the whole plan is rash. Well," he paused and his face grew grave again, "perhaps in a situation like ours the improbable is more likely to succeed than the possible. But what sort of stroke is it that His Highness believes might pull down the Elector?"

"Politics, my dear Donald. Pressures from within the Government, an agreement maybe with the Elector's son who has no cause to love him—the possibilities are endless."

"I think I would rather do it with a sword in my hand."

"What do the means matter? We can none of us rest until the House of Stuart is restored—and do we not long to avenge our dead on Culloden Moor?"

Such an appeal could not fail to touch any Highlander and Donald lifted his glass, a surge of eagerness rising in him. "We have something to drink to again! Tell His Highness, Neil, that he may command me as he chooses."

"I knew that," MacEachain said, "before ever I entered this room."

After he had gone Donald stood for a long time by the window which he had thrust open, feeling the sudden need for air, for the coolness of the garden after the recent shower. It was hard to know whether elation or doubt had been the stronger emotion during his interview with Neil, but now, as the full realization of what was required of him came over him, he felt nothing but that it was a miracle, after these barren years, to be able to serve his Prince again, however distasteful one part of the affair might be. And he could only admire the courage that would venture right into the heart of the Elector's capital. Charles Edward had always had that kind of courage and to be part of this new adventure filled him with that excitement he had felt so long ago at Edinburgh when they marched out for England and the capital and the crown. Foolhardy it might be—he could not deny that—but in the end, who knew but that it might mean a new crowning in Westminster Abbey.

He came back to the desk and picked up the purse that Neil had insisted on leaving him for his expenses. The English Jacobites had not long ago sent the Prince a handsome sum and he would, Neil said firmly, use some of it to defray the cost of this scheme. At the thought of the trust thus placed in him Donald stuffed the purse into his pocket and began to calculate how soon he might leave. The opposing thought of the unknown English major, whose hospitality he was going to accept now for a double reason, faded into the background.

Exactly five days later he was stuffing the last of his few personal possessions into his valise. It was now six in the evening and early in the morning Armand was to drive him to meet the stage for Calais. When he closed the bag he stood looking round the room that had been his for nearly five months. Mentonnay had given him so much. Above all it was Marthe's home and he would never see her other than against the setting of this turreted house, the beautiful gardens, the lake and the park beyond.

He had waited all day, knowing he should not do so yet hoping, for a chance to say goodbye to her alone, but no opportunity presented itself and in the end he was forced to make his farewells in company with Tante Julie and Tante Clothilde who both wished him a safe journey. He kissed Marthe's hand and felt it tremble in his. She seemed pale but she smiled at him and expressed the hope that he would bring his sister to Mentonnay as they had planned. Then she was gone upstairs with her aunts.

He was desperately disappointed. Even Gaston de la Rouelle's blessing, which he asked if he might bestow on the parting guest when he came to take one final look at his wound, did nothing to relieve that. And then the priest said a surprising thing.

"Monsieur Fraser, if you will forgive me I will take advantage of my office and say something which you may consider I have no right to say. It is merely this—at present I see no way for you out of your unhappy situation, but if at any time I may do anything to solve that difficulty I shall be most willing to do so."

Donald stared at him. And then as the full meaning of the Curé's words became clear a slow flush mounted into his face. His first reaction was one of annoyance, mingled with embarrassment. "I did not think Armand would—"

"He did not need to tell me. I have acquired a fair understanding of people, my son, and it was not hard to see what had happened." He glanced at Donald and added, "I can see you do not wish to discuss it."

"No," Donald said and he added jerkily, "but even if everything else were favourable you would not wish to see—there is the matter of our different faiths—"

"True," the priest agreed gravely, "for me it is the main consideration, but there are other things. And I meant what I said.

Now may my blessing go with you, I shall pray for you."

He went out, leaving Donald even more surprised. Lying in bed in the darkness of his room he went over the short conversation; it seemed as if the priest had tried to give hope, had wished him to have a gleam of that transient thing, and yet—surely Gaston de la Rouelle could not wish to see his delicate cousin wed to an impoverished exile of a different faith, a different culture? Tormented by these thoughts, by dreams of what might be confronted by the harsh reality of what was, he tossed restlessly, unable to sleep. Knowing that he should put her from his mind it was the last thing he seemed able to do. It was better to think of her with pain than not to think of her at all. Some time in the small hours he dozed off and was awakened by one of the footmen bearing a tray of coffee and hot rolls, and at exactly a quarter to seven he went down into the hall.

There was no one in sight and thinking that Armand might be in the library he crossed the hall and entered the room where he had spent so many hours during the last few months. At first he thought it was empty and was about to go out again when a movement by one of the windows revealed, not Armand but Marthe sitting on the seat there.

He closed the door behind him and crossed the room to stand beside her. "Mademoiselle," he said quietly, "I did not think to have the pleasure of seeing you this morning."

She looked up at him, more colour than usual in her cheeks, and she seemed a little confused as she answered, "I was awake early so I came down to see you go. I hope you have a safe journey, monsieur."

He sat down beside her. "Thank you. I am very sorry to be leaving you all."

She looked out into the garden where the dew still lay on the sweeping lawn, the distant trees hazy in the early sunlight. "We are sorry too. I wonder if we shall meet again?"

There was such unexpected sadness in her voice that his resolve was shaken, but he said rather formally, "Of course we will. Your brother has urged me to visit Mentonnay when I return to Paris and I hope to avail myself of that invitation."

She gave him a faint smile. "I wonder if you say that because it is the polite thing to do?"

"No indeed. You once told me that politeness was not my strong point, so you cannot accuse me of it now."

But his joke went awry and instead of laughing she turned her head away, her face almost hidden in a fold of the thick curtains.

"Forgive me," he said, though he was not sure for what he wanted to be forgiven. He saw that her eyes had filled with tears, and at once he knew that this parting was as hard for her as it was for him. And this time he yielded impulsively to temptation, all his warm Celtic blood defeating his resolution. He caught her hands in his. "There is so much I have wanted to say to you—yet I think you must know why I have not said it."

She looked down at her imprisoned fingers, unable to speak, and his grip tightened. "I must go in a few moments—it is too late—but this cannot be the end for us. Believe that it is not."

She raised her head at that, a tremulous smile lighting her face. "You will not forget me then?"

"Forget you! I will never forget you." With sudden intensity he lifted her hands, pressing his mouth to each palm. "There will be a way, there must be, now that I know that you—" he broke off, shaken by the expression on her face, her eyes bright with the unshed tears.

"Whatever way you bid me take, I will take it," she said simply. "I came down this morning because I hoped—because I wanted you to know—"

"But I did know—I was sure!" he said in a moment of joy, the parting forgotten. "My heart's darling, I've no right to speak to you as I have, and against Armand's wishes—yet I am not sorry. I think perhaps after all he would understand." And he leaned forward, her hands still in his, to put his mouth to hers in a kiss that was gentle, all passion restrained, for this was not the moment for it. In the silence they heard Armand calling out that it was time to go. He released her and for the first time they looked at each with love given and received in equal measure.

"You are mine now," he said in a low voice. "Whatever any one may say you have given me the right. Only trust me."

"Always—always." She laid his hand against her cheek and then as Armand called again he bent his head for one last swift kiss. "I will come back," he said in a low urgent voice. "I will come back, my little love," and rising, left her sitting there. He wondered how he was going to make normal conversation to Armand in the carriage.

Chapter 7

When Bab Astley received her brother's letter announcing the day of his arrival she took it straight to her father-in-law's room. He still spent the morning in bed, rising only in the afternoon to dine with her, and this morning she found him sitting propped by pillows, a tray on his knee and sipping coffee which he held between long skeletal fingers. She had grown very fond of him and bent to kiss the wrinkled cheek under the white nightcap.

"Good morning, sir, I hope you slept well."

"Tolerably," he answered, smiling up at her. "I am the better for a sight of you. You look very pretty this morning, my dear. That shade of green becomes you very well. Are you going to ride?"

"I have already been out with Rupert. It is a beautiful day."

"Ah, if I were only twenty years younger." He gave a little sigh. "You are never still, either of you. What is that you have in your hand?"

"A letter from my brother. He will be here tomorrow."

"I am delighted to hear it, but I fear he may be displeased with me for hurrying your wedding and depriving him of the pleasure of attending it."

"He will understand," Bab said cheerfully. "If it had not been for his meeting with that horrid accident, he would have been here."

Lord Rawdon put down his empty cup and lay back on his pillows. "You were very gracious to indulge an old man. But," a glimmer of a smile crossed his face, "that fool of a surgeon told me I'd no more than a week or two to live and I wanted to see my only son married. Now here I am a great deal better, a fraud, when I should be under the sod in Rawdon churchyard."

"Indeed you should not," she retorted with spirit, "for I can't spare you. And," a little extra colour came into her face, "it may not have been proper in me, but I was not exactly reluctant to be married, was I?"

He laughed and reaching out took one of her hands in his. "Dearest child, I cannot tell you how comfortable it makes me to see you and

94

Rupert happy together. I thought at first when he told me—but never mind that. He is more fortunate than he deserves."

"And so am I. You have been so good to me."

"You have brought life back into this house," he answered affectionately. "I married late, you know, and Rupert's mother died when he was a child—so I did not have many years of content myself. When I am well enough we will go to Rawdon. You will like it there and when Rupert is away we will sit under the trees and I shall flirt with you myself."

"You are a wicked old man!" She shook her head at him. "But I am looking forward to seeing Rawdon. I don't know how long my brother will stay—perhaps he might care to come with us." The smile faded a little from her face. "You said you would speak to Mr. Pelham on his behalf, when he came yesterday—did you have the opportunity to do so? I did not like to disturb you last night, we came in so late from the Duchess of Grafton's ball."

"You have nothing to worry about. Your brother is covered by the general pardon and Mr. Pelham assures me that providing he is not concerned in any way in Jacobite affairs, he may come and go as he pleases."

"Of course he will not be," she said swiftly, "you know it is only a visit to see me. I am so grateful to you, and Rupert and I have so many plans for his stay that I wanted to be sure—" she broke off. It would have been more correct to say she had plans in which her husband acquiesced, but in her eagerness wanting for them to like each other she already saw them as brothers.

Her father-in-law was watching her closely, for he had grown extremely fond of her. He had been somewhat taken aback last winter by Rupert's sudden request that he should meet Sir Laurence Everard—a man of whom his son had only spoken in terms of the utmost contempt—but once he had seen Miss Fraser and discovered her to be the granddaughter of his old acquaintance, Lord Harlesdon, he did not hesitate to forward the match. And some weeks later, thinking himself a dying man, speed seemed essential. Yet here he was enjoying this delightful child's company and might yet live to see a grandson, a dream he had long and vainly cherished.

This girl, Lord Rawdon thought, would be the making of his son, to whose faults he had never been blind; she would soften the boy, take the cynicism from his mouth, restrain his gambling perhaps, and he wanted to see them with a growing family, living more at Rawdon than here in this London square.

He smiled at her. "Now go and make your arrangements and send Samuel to me in half an hour. I will dress this morning, I think." He surveyed her with the air of one who had been something of connoisseur. "Perhaps you will wear that yellow gown for dinner—to please me."

She bent to kiss him again. "I don't know why I give in to your whims, sir, but I will do so." She gave him his glasses and the latest news sheet and went away to find his valet. From the first they had been on excellent terms and even had she not been most happily wed, the change from living under Sir Laurence Everard's roof to that of Lord Rawdon would have been a pleasure in itself.

She sent Samuel to his master and calling for her maid Susan changed from her riding dress into the requested yellow gown. She wore her black hair unpowdered during the day and when Susan had finished the effect was very pleasing. She took one last glance in the mirror and then went to the guest room she had set aside for Donald's use. Rupert's man, Harper, was there supervising the laying of fresh brushes on the dressing table, lavender in the drawers for his linen, and the placing of a wig stand, that everything might be as a gentleman would wish.

"Thank you, Harper," she said. "My brother will be very comfortable here."

He bowed and withdrew, summoning the lackey to follow him, and left alone Bab sat down on the edge of the bed, looking about her. It was a richly furnished room, the four-poster bed hung with crimson curtains, a crimson silk coverlet laid over it, far more sumptuous than anything at Duirdre, and she wondered if Donald would like it, until she remembered his stay at Mentonnay. He would have got used to such finery there, she supposed. It did not seem possible that he was coming, would be here tomorrow, for her last memory of him was of that November day when he had marched beside their father under the Fraser banner out of Edinburgh for the assault on England, her white cockade in his bonnet, the piper playing Lovat's March. It was a sight she had never forgotten, the cheering crowds, the marching men full of confidence; Donald waving towards the window where she stood with her mother and her aunt never guessing, she thought sadly, that she would never see her father again, nor Donald himself for so many years. Would he have changed? She had changed so much herself, life at Duirdre long in the past, belonging to her childhood.

Now she was Lady Astley, the King having conferred a knighthood on Rupert on the eve of their wedding, with a large London house which, though it still belonged to Lord Rawdon, he had turned over entirely to her management. She moved in the highest circles, and Whig circles at that. The Duke of Newcastle and his brother Mr. Pelham, the most influential Government ministers, were visitors at the house, both being old friends of Lord Rawdon, and Rupert took her often to Court. She had been presented to the King, whom she found a kindly man, to Queen Caroline who was condescending and inclined to be waspish, and to the Duke of Cumberland who, it seemed, had little interest in anything but horse racing and the new course he was having constructed at Ascot. She looked at the fat overbearing young man with his high-pitched voice and tried to realize he was the victor of Culloden, the man who had brought death and torture and destruction to the Highlands, but she had no personal memories of that.

Now her life was bound up with Rupert's, with London and their friends, and because she was so happy the past remained the past.

But sitting here on this bed, thinking of Donald, she was aware of a tinge of nervousness. Would he think her heartless, disloyal, caring nothing for their father's memory, for Duirdre? No, surely he would understand, would know that living in England with their English mother and English relations, she could not help but become part of their world. And she wanted him to come, to share something of it. There had never been any deep affection between herself and her mother, and it was Donald whom she had loved most dearly—until Rupert came. It was important to her that they should like each other. But they were so very different—and how would Donald react to seeing that scarlet uniform every day? Fear rose and clutched at her. Knowing her brother's temperament, his passionate loyalty, how would it be? She twisted her hands together—nothing, *nothing* must spoil this meeting, for she loved them both, but how could she be unaware of the tensions that might arise? For one moment she almost wished he was not coming. Then, chiding herself for imagining difficulties where there might be none, she went down the stairs, ordered the carriage and went to call on Georgiana, where she spent a satisfying hour inspecting that young lady's marriage clothes.

It was not until late afternoon that Rupert returned home and hearing his voice in the hall she came in from the garden to find him in the withdrawing room, a note in his hand.

He came to her quickly, kissing her cheek. "My dearest, here is a note from Colonel Anderson asking us to accompany him tonight to a reception at St. James's. Brooks was going but he has a vicious new stallion who threw him today and apparently he is worse hurt than we thought."

"Oh, poor Captain Brooks, I must call on his wife. How soon must we go?"

"In about an hour." Major Astley laid down the note and put an arm about his wife's waist. "I cannot recall if I have told you today that I love you?"

She laughed and lifted her mouth. "You may prove it, sir."

His kiss was long and passionate. When he raised his head, he said, "I fear I shall receive the rough edge of Colonel Anderson's tongue one of these days for hurrying through my duties in order to come home—which I never did before."

"As to that, do you not think we shall grow so used to each other that I shall be sitting with my embroidery and you will come in apologising for being late and I shall say I had not even noticed?"

His smile widened. "Never! By the way, we shall probably be very late tonight, but will you still ride with me before I go on duty tomorrow? I want to see how you handle the mare."

"Of course," she answered, still standing within the circle of his arms. "She is the most beautiful creature I ever set eyes on and no one but you would have thought of such a birthday gift for me."

His arms tightened. "Nineteen!" he said. "You are still a child, but what would I not give you?" Rupert Astley was still surprised at himself, at the rapidity with which he had set about making this girl his wife. Some devil had prompted him, on the night of his affray with Everard, to prove his ability to take her from under the noses of all the other fortune hunters, to force Everard's hand and, it must be admitted, claim the enormous sum he had won, and yet after that first dance with her, after the next morning's ride, he knew himself to be snared. The tale of his winnings went round the town of course, but he had revealed to no one except Simon Ravenslow the manner in which that debt had been settled. Harry Cavendish of course had been there but could be trusted to keep his mouth shut and Sir Laurence was hardly likely to blab their bargain to polite society, in fact silence over the matter had been part of the arrangement between them. Yet despite all that, Rupert's desire for Barbara Fraser was no cool affair but conducted with the intensity he gave to anything that absorbed him. His courtship was swift and uncompromising—it was to be all or nothing—and Bab herself was swept away by the tide of feeling that engulfed them both. It was typical of her, he thought, that she talked no maidenly nonsense about being surprised at his suit or needing time to think. Their wedding at St. James's had been quieter than it might have been owing to Lord Rawdon's illness—it was an ill wind, Rupert told Harry, that did not blow some good, which speech caused even Harry to raise his eyebrows—and his lordship's recovery soon afterwards his son attributed to the care and affection lavished on him by his new daughter. The present harmony at Astley House gratified Rupert who had so often been at odds with his father, and he hoped it would not be interrupted by the arrival of his brother-in-law. He loosened his hold of his wife to ask when she expected him.

"Not until the afternoon," she told him. "He is coming by stage from Dover. Now let me go—I must change if we are to go out so soon."

He kissed her briefly and released her. "I think I must only dance with you once. It is most unfashionable to be in love with one's own wife."

She paused at the door, giving him a swift smile. "As to that, sir, are you so sure I shall have even one to spare for you?"

The reception was crowded, the evening very warm and for once Bab danced less than usual. Her mind was taken up with the thought of Donald's arrival, of the explanations which would have to be made, and she was not so naive as to be unaware of the divergence of their lives—a difference accentuated by this evening's royal affair. Somehow this great gap must be bridged and their old affection must do it. She only half listened to Harry's latest gossip, danced with several officers whose names she did not even catch, and was apologetic to young Lieutenant Chambers's complaint that she had quite forgotten her promise to go into supper with him.

Rupert spent most of the evening in attendance on the King. George II was now in his late sixties, a plain but well built man, only grown a little overweight, unlike his third son, the Duke of Cumberland, and he enjoyed the company of young officers from his Life Guards; he told scandalous stories when the Queen was out of earshot, laughed a great deal in a good-hearted way at any gossip with which they regaled him, and only grew ill-tempered when Mr. Pitt entered the gallery. He did not like clever Mr. Pitt. After supper he settled to a game of hazard and as Rupert was not required to play he wandered off to find Harry Cavendish.

Lord Harry was still in the supper room, sprawled on a couch with a glass of punch in his hand. He waved to Rupert and moved along the couch to make room for him. "It's devilish warm tonight. Do you want a glass of this brew? It's not half bad."

Rupert signalled to a footman to serve him. "You are right—tolerable. You have not forgotten you are to dine with us tomorrow?"

"Tomorrow? Oh yes, I remember—your brother-in-law is arriving and you want moral support."

Rupert gave him a scathing look. "Hardly. I merely thought it might ease us over the initial acquaintance if there was company at dinner. Mr. Fraser was 'out' in '45 and has lived abroad since—which tells me that his visit may not be a pleasure to me."

Harry glanced curiously at his friend. "By the way, do you know that Captain Harding is here tonight?"

Rupert sat up, instantly alert. "No, I have not seen him. I thought Barrell's regiment was still in Scotland?"

"So it is, but Harding's brother is gone out to America and he has put in a request to be transferred to the same regiment."

A heavy frown had settled on Rupert's brows. "How long will he be in London?"

"Only a few days, I think. Cumberland has signed the order."

Rupert let out his breath and Harry added, "You are playing a dangerous game, Rupert. Would it not be wiser to tell your wife—"

"Good God, do you think I want to rake up all that? And what would she think then? You must be more dense than I took you for, Harry, if you do not see that it would be foolish in the extreme. Anyway it is all in the past." He got up, set his glass down, and walked away, leaving Harry staring after him in some concern.

In the darkness of their carriage on the way home Rupert asked his wife if she had spoken to a certain Captain Harding during the evening. "A short fellow with blue facings on his uniform and a sash from the right shoulder."

"No—at least I don't think so," she answered vaguely. "Why, did you want me to meet him?"

"Not particularly," he said and leaned back against the cushions.

She had the odd idea that he seemed relieved, but she was tired and the name of the unknown captain was forgotten until the day came when it was to be sharply and unpleasantly recalled.

All cities were much the same and equally to be disliked, Donald thought, only London appeared larger and dirtier than most. He had spent the night at a modest inn at Dover and had arrived in London some two hours ago. He decided to walk from the inn where the stage had set him down, partly to look at the city and partly because he had to purchase some new clothes, so after a meal of cold beef and beer, he set out down Fleet Street.

There had been a storm after the heat of the day before but now the pools of water were drying in the sunshine and he walked along watching the crowds, looking up at the buildings to either side of him and presently went into an unpretentious shop for gentlemen's clothing where he ordered himself a suit of dark green satin—if he was going to stay with the Astleys for some time, he was not going to disgrace his sister. The tailor persuaded him to an elegant flowered waistcoat, which he was assured was the rage at the moment; he also bought several pairs of white stockings and a shirt that seemed to have an excessive amount of lace at the throat and wrists. Then he escaped before he could be persuaded to buy more. He was wearing today the coat of mulberry cloth that Armand had had made for him and a plain cream waistcoat; despite the fashion for wigs he still wore his own dark hair tied with a ribbon at the nape of the neck and it looked well enough beneath a black hat; he carried a long black cloak as well as his valise, and was sufficiently respectable, he thought, to present himself at Astley House.

And then before he realized it he was at Temple Bar. There he paused, looking up. The long poles above the arch all had skulls on them—there were no fresh heads, no recent executions for high treason having taken place, and grimly he wondered if one of those grinning relics was all that was left of his own Chief, Simon Fraser. He removed his hat and passed underneath before replacing it.

He walked on, less aware of his surroundings. Beggars swarmed everywhere, asking for alms, and at almost every step he was besieged by street-sellers imploring him to buy their wares, but ignoring their importuning he eventually reached the end of the Strand and came to a halt, uncertain of his way. After inquiring the direction, he crossed over to the Royal Mews and took a smaller, dirtier street where he had to tread carefully, for the kennel running down the centre was so choked with filth that it was overflowing on either side. He began to think he had been misdirected, but eventually he emerged into a wider street that led directly into a pleasant tree lined Square and a few minutes later he mounted the steps of a fine-looking mansion and rang the bell.

A lackey in a green uniform, white wig and gloves, opened the door and he was shown upstairs into a large elegantly furnished room, rich with china ornaments, portraits hanging round the pale blue walls. He stopped short in front of one. Could that really be Bab, that stiffly posed lady in a riding habit with a background of trees and a lake? He was still staring at it when a door opened behind him and a soft voice said, "Have I changed so much?"

He turned, and then she was in his arms and brother and sister were clinging together, aware of nothing but that the years between had vanished as if they had never been. Then he released her and stepped back, holding her at arms' length. "Let me look at you." Yes, she had changed. Gone indeed was the girl he remembered, who had waded the cold Highland burns with him, her shoes in her hand, who had scrambled up the mountain side, who had danced many a reel with him, the last in Edinburgh in that autumn of '45. Gone was the ardent girl who, with a tartan shawl about her, had waved goodbye to him on that final November morning, on fire to be marching with him, and he remembered that odd moment of premonition that they would indeed meet in London, yet not as they had dreamed it would be. Here instead was an elegant lady in primrose satin, the skirt drawn aside to reveal a white petticoat sprigged with yellow flowers, her dark hair piled high on her head, one long curl falling to her left shoulder; here was the lady of the portrait, the wife of an English gentleman, lovely indeed, he thought with a sudden pang, for it was still, to him at least, Highland loveliness and far from its natural setting.

"I would hardly have known you," he said at last. "You look well, *m'eudail,* and happy."

"I am," she took hold of both his hands, "happier than I ever dreamed I could be, and even more so now that you are here. Oh, but you are changed too." She released one hand to touch the long-healed scar on his cheek. "I did not know about that."

"A memento of Culloden. Others have worse."

"And you are so thin. Are you really well again?" Too concerned with the present moment she had scarcely heeded his words. "My dearest, when I heard of your accident I was so concerned."

"I am perfectly recovered now," he assured her, but she was still studying him, taking in every detail and because of the happiness, the emotion of the moment, she took refuge in somewhat breathless trivialities.

"No, perhaps you have not changed so much after all. You do not look like a London beau. And you still wear your own hair—that is not thought at all fashionable here."

"When did I ever care for fashion?" he asked, smiling down at her. "A shaven head and a wig seem to me to be the height of nonsense, apart from being extremely hot and uncomfortable."

"Well, Rupert has arranged for his valet's brother to attend you and he will see you curled and powdered for the evening."

Donald's amusement grew. "I will make every effort not to disgrace you. You look remarkably pretty. Marriage must agree with you."

She laughed delightedly. "Oh, it does. Now, come and sit down and I will get you some refreshment."

He followed her to a long satin-covered sofa, but refused to release her hand. "I don't want any refreshment at the moment, my dear, I want to talk to you."

"Very well." She sat down, spreading her skirts carefully. "There is so much I want to know—all about Mentonnay and M.de la Rouelle and—"

"There is a great deal I want to know too," he broke in rather gravely and her smile faded a little.

"Donald—please don't be angry. I knew you would be hurt, but I thought if I could explain, make you understand how it was."

He shook his head. "I am not angry, only surprised."

"Because Rupert is—what he is?"

"What do you think?" he countered. "You see, to me this has all come about so strangely, and so quickly. I cannot help it if everything English is alien to me."

"But not to me. Oh, do not think I have forgotten Duirdre, but I have lived here for nearly five years—and I was a child when we came." She had his hand in both hers now, urgent in her desire that he should understand. "I know it must have come as a shock to you to find that I was married—indeed I wanted to wait until I heard from you, I wanted you to come, and if Lord Rawdon had not been so ill, I would have insisted. Except that I did wonder if—" she broke off, staring down at their clasped fingers.

"—If I disapproved too much to come, or even to answer your letter? You should have known me better than that."

"I did—I do! But I could see how it would look to you. I had no thought of marriage, though our step-father had spoken of several possible suitors—he wanted to be rid of me, of course—and all Mama thinks of is that a girl should be settled as quickly as possible."

"So it seems," he said and his voice was harsh. "I did not think our poor mother would so soon fill my father's place."

"Don't judge her too harshly. She is not a strong person, Donald, you know that. She could not face life alone, I think, and although I do believe Everard took her because she was our grandfather's daughter and as he thought at the time an heiress——"

"He must have been soon disillusioned about that."

"Yes, I know. But grandfather left her with an adequate income even if his fortune came to Philip and me. Oh Donald," she caught her breath suddenly. "I was so sorry—so sorry you quarrelled with grandfather. You needed his help more than I."

He smiled ironically. "My dear, he never forgave me for being 'out' in '45. Should I journey to St. Albans to see our mother?"

"No, Everard is bringing her to town at the end of next week. It will be more pleasant to have Mama here and Everard is less offensive when he is under our roof."

"He sounds singularly unpleasant." Donald glanced at her. "Do you dislike him so much?"

Bab shrugged her shoulders. "I seldom exchanged two civil words with him, but really Mama seems content enough."

"Well, I suppose we must be grateful for that. I'm sure you were glad to be out of his house."

A flush stole into her face. "You do not think I married for that reason?"

"No, no," he said hastily. "I did not mean that. Only I still find it hard to accept the fact that the man you chose—and it seems you did choose him—should be a *saighdear dearg,* wear a fine scarlet uniform," a tinge of bitterness had crept into his voice, "to remind us every day of what happened four years ago."

"I knew you would not like it, but it is so long ago now and we cannot go on hating the English for ever. Don't you see how it has been for me? I know it is harder for you with Duirdre gone——"

He got up and walked away from her to the empty hearth. This conversation had been inevitable from the moment he had decided to come but it was more distressing than he had expected. "I think perhaps, after all, you feared to tell me what manner of man you were marrying, that you did not wish me to know of it until it was too late."

The colour flared in her face. "That is unjust. The haste was purely on account of Lord Rawdon's being so ill."

"Very convenient of him. Especially as I understand he is now much recovered. Major Astley must have been in a considerable hurry to secure your hand and your inheritance. Surely it would have been enough for Lord Rawdon to know that his son was betrothed?"

Bab got up and came to him. She was trying not to weep from

sheer disappointment that this beloved brother should be seemingly so far from understanding. "It was not like that. You are misjudging Rupert if you think him a fortune hunter. How can you when," she swept a hand out to indicate the room, "you can see that Lord Rawdon lives in this style?"

"Suppose then you tell me how it was."

She turned away and sat down in a chair rather suddenly. "I think we loved each other from the very first. I don't know how soon Rupert approached Everard, but it was not long after our meeting, or so he told me afterwards. It was not one of those cold arranged marriages—surely you must realize that?"

"All very romantic, my dear," he said drily, "but I do not imagine such considerations would weigh with Everard nor with Lord Rawdon for all I know. Clearly you were too carried away to consider—"

"What should I consider but that I love Rupert?"

"So much that no thought of what he was, of what he must seem to me, to every Fraser who knows you, could weigh against it?"

"Yes," she said almost defiantly.

He gave a deep sigh and turned away from the window, his arms folded, looking down at her. "I see you have changed after all," he said slowly. "I did not think the White Rose would die so quickly in your heart."

At the mention of that Jacobite flower, the colour heightened in her face. "You think I am disloyal? But what was I to do? I have had to live in England and it is not my fault that I fell in love with an Englishman—nor that he has a commission in the army," she added with spirit. "But I can see you think I should have refused him on that score, whatever feelings I had towards him."

He thought of his own love, whom he might not have, with whom he dared not contemplate marriage—knowing that he would go to almost any lengths to make that possible. Yet, as he had said to Armand, even if Marthe were his wife he would answer any call from his prince, any chance to fight for the Jacobite cause, and he had expected the same loyalty from Bab.

On an impulse he knelt beside her chair. "Dry your tears, my dearest. It was not your fault—I know that. You are a woman, and you have been long away from Scotland—and from me. And if you are happy, I will try to be glad."

She slid her arms round his neck. "That is all I want—and that you should like Rupert."

"I will try to do that too—though you must understand that of all people, a Hanoverian officer is naturally the last man I should have chosen for you. I presume he has worn that uniform for some time?"

"Since he was eighteen. He told me he was at Fontenoy and Dettingen."

"The troops at Dettingen were brought home to face us, that I know. Was he in Scotland?" He caught her wrist in a hard grasp. "Was he, Bab?"

"Yes, but—"

"When? Where? Was he at Culloden? Good God, if I thought—" he broke off. "If he was, then he has blood on his hands, maybe even Fraser blood."

"Donald, Donald!" she cried out as much at his words as in pain from his grip on her fingers, the ring he wore digging into her flesh, and looking down at it, recognizing it, she gave a little gasp. "Oh! Did you—did you take it from Father—afterwards?"

"Yes. Do you remember why he died, Bab?"

At the inflexible note in his voice she stiffened a little, but she did not flinch. "Of course I do. But that was nothing to do with Rupert, and we cannot live all our lives in the past. Father would have understood—he would, Donald! Rupert is a soldier and soldiers must shed blood in war—as you did yourself. The Life Guards did not reach England until May and though Rupert was in Scotland for a while, it could not have been until after Drumossie Moor."

He released her hand and got to his feet. "Did you ask him what he did while he was there?"

"He told me it was only in an administrative capacity—in Inverness. And I did not pursue it any further."

"But I would like to know exactly how he was involved," he said sternly.

She gave a little sigh. "What would be the good? It is all so long ago now and men have fought on opposing sides before and lived in peace afterwards. I could not bear it that you should quarrel with him over what happened four years ago. It is my marriage, now, that matters to me."

He bent and took her hands, drawing her into his arms. "I am sorry, *m'eudail,*" he said. "God forbid, if you are truly happy with him, that I should do anything to spoil your happiness. I am a brute to have distressed you so."

She laid her head against his chest. "I understand. Indeed I did know how you would feel, but for my sake you will try to like Rupert, will you not?"

"I cannot promise to do so, but I will try—for your sake."

She raised her head and looked up at him, her natural spirits reviving. "Dearest brother, I have dreamed of having you here. This is my home and I love it, and to have you with me is all I wanted. You will see Lord Rawdon at supper and Rupert has invited several people to join us, especially to meet you."

"I would rather have spent the evening quietly with you."

"Yes, I know," she said regretfully, "but he wanted to welcome you. His aunt and uncle, Sir Peter and Lady Cynthia Milne, are coming and Georgy will be here and our cousin Philip who wants so much to see you again. Isn't it odd that our cousin should be betrothed to Rupert's cousin? And Lord Harry Cavendish—no one can help liking him, he is so good-natured—and there will be Mr. Ravenslow, of course."

"Who is Mr. Ravenslow? And why 'of course'?"

"He is Rupert's closest friend. His estates border Rawdon," she explained. "He is a strange man in some ways, always very courteous to me, but he has never married and must be nearing forty now and is very reserved. Rupert says Simon is the elder brother he never had." She glanced across at the clock on the mantleshelf. "He promised to be home by four today and it is nearly that now. Oh," as a door banged, "how punctual! I do believe he is come."

She left her brother and hurried across the room but before she reached the door it opened and Rupert came in. He bent to kiss his wife's cheek. "Here I am, my love, as I promised."

She turned back to Donald, her face radiant, her hand in Rupert's as she made the introductions. The Major bowed. "You are most welcome, Mr. Fraser," he said formally.

Donald came forward and for a moment they stood facing each other. Dislike was instant and mutual.

Chapter 8

For his part, at that first meeting, Donald was aware of little but the hated scarlet uniform that he had last seen despoiling Duirdre—the actual wearer of it of less importance. Rupert saw a tall rather stiff figure lacking the polished ease of his contemporaries, a dark face wearing an expression that could hardly be termed friendly, and yet despite all that a likeness to Bab. For her sake he pushed his immediate reaction to the back of his mind, merely asking if his guest had had a good journey.

"As well as any journey, sir" was the rather short reply, and Rupert turned away to busy himself pouring wine.

"Bab tells me this is your first visit to London," he said, "but I believe you have been to England before?"

"Once," Donald accepted the glass, "to visit my grandfather. But that was many years ago."

"Then the town is a pleasure in store for you—at least I trust you will find it so. We have many fine buildings and there is a great deal of entertainment to be had."

"I cannot profess to like cities but, as you say, I do not yet know London. Paris is tolerable—in the winter."

Rupert indicated a chair for his guest and then sat down beside Bab on the sofa. Seeing them thus, the scarlet coat beside Bab's yellow gown Donald was conscious of the revulsion he had expected and which he must repress, but throbbing in his head was all the accumulated bitterness of the days after Culloden when those vivid coats splashed against the green of the glens were heralds of terror and death. And to see his own sister sitting so happily beside one was barely tolerable. He began to wonder how he was to get through the visit at all.

"Doctor Johnson," Rupert was saying, the words hardly penetrating his guest's attention, "our eminent man of letters, says that if a man is tired of London he is tired of life." He gave a slight laugh and added, "I shall, if you will permit me, take you to his Ivy Leaf club—the talk there is always amusing."

Donald, who knew nothing of this Doctor Johnson, merely inclined his head, and he was glad when Bab confessed she had not yet shown her brother his room and that it was time they were changing for supper.

"I imagine you have had plenty to talk about," was Rupert's comment and Donald glanced sharply at him but there was nothing to be learned from the soldier's countenance.

A few minutes later he stood alone in the guest chamber, drying his hands on a towel that smelled of lavender and staring thoughtfully out into the square. His valise had been unpacked and his sparse wardrobe disposed in drawers, his roquelaure hanging in rather solitary state in the large cupboard. A little smile of irony crossed his face as he imagined what the valet who unpacked it must have thought and was probably saying below stairs.

He threw down the towel and sat on the edge of the bed, looking round the luxuriously appointed room. There was no doubt in his mind that Bab was happy and he determined that he would do nothing further to distress her. Their first hour together had been clouded by the past, but, the explanations over, he must be glad that she had a husband who openly adored her. Nevertheless it was going to be hard to see that despised scarlet coat day after day and be pleasant to its wearer. And there was something about his brother-in-law that he actively disliked—an arrogance, a cynical expression on the well-moulded mouth, an air of mastery that was probably habitual but that did not sit well between Whig and Jacobite. No, he did not like the man, but for Bab's sake he would have to try not to show it.

At supper it became a little easier in that Major Astley had changed out of uniform and into a rich purple satin coat with a wealth of lace at the throat and wrists. He was an excellent host, for although Lord Rawdon sat at the head of the table, it was his son who saw that the guests were well served.

At first most of the conversation was directed towards the new arrival with a courtesy that Donald strove to emulate and it was not until Lady Cynthia began to talk of a water pageant to be given by the Duchess of Devonshire that he was able to study his recently acquired connections.

He himself was sitting on Bab's left with Georgiana Milne on his other side. Georgy talked to him happily of her friendship with his sister and presently he found himself complimenting his cousin Philip on their forthcoming marriage. Philip Denby had grown into just the kind of man his boyhood promised, quiet, sensible, staid perhaps as

Rupert had once said, but nevertheless not without a certain strength of character that made Donald sure that Miss Georgiana would not have her own way in all things.

As Bab had predicted Donald liked Lord Rawdon immediately. He found him pleasant to talk to, with a fund of anecdotes that were witty without being malicious, and his affection for his daughter-in-law could not help but endear him to her brother. It was Simon Ravenslow whom Donald found more difficult to assess and who, for that reason, interested him. Several times he was aware of Ravenslow's keen dark eyes fixed on him and he met that stare with one equally steady.

Presently Bab rose and took the ladies into the drawing room while the men sat over their port. Harry Cavendish, whose open manner made conversation easy, was talking of the theatre, asking Donald if he would not like to see Mr. Garrick and offering to escort him to a performance, an invitation given in so friendly a tone that Donald was unable to refuse it. The conversation turned on a recent meeting at Newmarket and Harry made some remark about the Duke of Cumberland. Rupert, who had moved up the table to sit in the empty seat beside his brother-in-law, noticed that he stiffened involuntarily.

"He's a good enough commander," Lord Harry was saying, "but poor old Fat Willie isn't inspired and a general should be. I swear he's turned to horse-racing to try for better fortune there."

"I thought," Philip Denby said in his serious way, "that at Dettingen the Duke distinguished himself."

"Oh lord, yes," Harry agreed, "but that was the King's victory. D'you remember, Rupert, how His Majesty dismounted and fought on foot with the rest of us? By Gad, that was something to have shared! It was different at Fontenoy—though we were outnumbered two to one. I don't suppose, Mr. Fraser, you ever heard how Charlie Hay—I expect you'll meet him sooner or later, Colonel Lord Hay—when we were facing the French near Fontenoy, stepped right out of the front rank to toast the enemy. He had a flask on him, of course, and he raised it to the Frenchies and told them that he hoped they would stand and fight and not run away and swim the river as they had done at Dettingen. Isn't that so, Rupert? And didn't the French Guards cheer as much as our own fellows?"

The corners of Rupert's mouth lifted. "I seem to recall that they did."

"Well, surely it wasn't they who retreated?" Philip asked, "Marshal Saxe was too much for the Duke that day, wasn't he?"

"Maybe so," Harry agreed, "but Fat Willie is a master of retreat. We stood until darkness fell—and we'd have won, I swear it, if it hadn't been for the Irish Brigade of the French army. Then the Duke brought us off, and came away with more men than one could have expected. I suppose the only victory he's won on his own was in Scotland—though we in the Guards missed that scrap—but then he had the advantage of numbers and disciplined troops set against a ragtail army that relied on the noise they could make rather than on—" Suddenly aware of the silence that had fallen, of what he himself had said, Harry broke off. A flush ran up under his fair skin.

"You talk too much, Harry," Rupert said and passed the decanter to his guest.

"Damme, I beg your pardon," Harry said awkwardly. He glanced at Donald. "My tongue runs away with me. I had forgot you must have been 'out' in that affair."

Donald lifted his head. "That affair, sir, as you call it, was for us Jacobites a justified attempt to put our rightful King on the throne. We failed, but there can be honour in failure as well as in victory."

The words fell into an even more uncomfortable silence, and Donald, aware that he too had said too much, looked directly towards Lord Rawdon. "If, however, you think, sir, you are harbouring a listed man in your house, let me assure you I was not attainted."

"I did not think it for a moment," Lord Rawdon said calmly. "Your sister has already explained the situation to us and I myself received that assurance from the Government list." He saw the surprise in Donald's face and went on, easing the talk away from such dangerous ground, "I believe you took service abroad afterwards?"

"I did, my lord. I served in the Régiment D'Albanie for two years."

Simon Ravenslow's penetrating glance was on him again. "You did not care for the military life, Mr. Fraser?"

"It was well enough," Donald said, "but I did not care to serve any longer under the flag of a King whose actions I despised."

As this unfortunate remark left no doubt in the minds of his hearers that he referred to the French King's treaty with the English, there was another awkward pause. Lord Rawdon looked down at his glass, the corners of his eyes crinkling a little, as if he was half amused at such bluntness. Harry, still in confusion, fumbled over the cracking of a walnut and Rupert glanced at Simon Ravenslow, one eyebrow raised. It was the latter who smoothly changed the subject to talk of the season's hunting and the stallion he had recently bought at Newmarket.

Donald sat silent, his mind only half on the talk. He wished he had spoken more guardedly; having always found it hard to dissemble he began to doubt his capabilities as a plotter, but it was too late now to turn back, and even had he been able to do so, he knew in his heart that he would not.

That night after the guests had gone and both Bab and her brother had retired Rupert was left alone with his father in the withdrawing room.

"It is very late," he said. "I'll ring for Samuel. I'm sure you should be in bed."

"Your concern is most touching," Lord Rawdon answered, "but I believe I am still the best judge of what I may do." He regarded his son with a close scrutiny. "You will have to watch your step with your brother-in-law—but I suppose you know that."

Rupert Astley made an impatient gesture. "Because he is so obviously a Jacobite? I knew that before he came."

"Maybe, but you could not have known what an uncompromising nature he possesses."

"You think he is actively concerned?" Rupert asked in surprise.

"Not necessarily. In fact, I hope he is not so foolish as to imagine his cause anything but lost, but it is evident to me that his loyalties are very much alive."

"He is certainly very prickly on the subject."

"That is what I mean. The conversation at supper took an awkward turn and you would be wise to keep off the subject of the Rebellion."

Rupert shrugged. "As to that, it was Harry who broached it but I'm afraid Mr. Fraser, however high-flown the language he uses, must learn that to us in England it was indeed a matter of dealing with rebels."

Lord Rawdon gave a little sigh. "Sometimes you are very obtuse, my son. Of course he was a rebel, but have you thought in what terms he may think of us? It is a more difficult situation than I expected because until he came we did not know what manner of man he was." He shifted his feet on the embroidered footstool. It had been a long evening and he was tired, but there were things he felt must be said. "And," he went on, "what if he asks you directly about your part in that unhappy campaign? What will you tell him?"

Rupert frowned, his fingers toying with a china shepherdess on the mantlepiece. "If he does, he will get a half truth. He is not likely to go about London asking questions in that direction and Barrell's regiment is still in Scotland".

"Singularly fortunately for you," his father commented drily. "Well, perhaps the air has been cleared a little, but I would advise you to be careful with Mr. Fraser."

"Of course," Rupert said. He glanced down at his father. "You do not like him either?"

"On the contrary," Lord Rawdon retorted . "I find him an extremely interesting young man. He has a kind of honesty, an inborn integrity that I may say I do not find among the rakes and gambling friends you consort with."

"In that case," Rupert retorted, "I am sure you must have been grateful that before my marriage I spent less time here than elsewhere—and may do so again if need be. I presume, however, you do not include Simon in that diatribe?"

"There are times," his father said in a cold voice, "when I wish I had taken a strap to you more often in your youth. Are you saying you are tired of your wife's company already? If so, you will have me to deal with."

"No, I am not," Rupert was angry now. His father's sarcasm never failed to rouse him. "But I reserve the right to choose my own friends."

"Yes," Lord Rawdon agreed thoughtfully. "I can only trust that Bab may have some influence in improving that choice."

"You seem to be suggesting, sir, that it has been a very one-sided affair. I am constrained to point out that she too has gained from our marriage."

"That," said his lordship, "remains to be seen."

"My dear father! Harlesden's heiress she may have been, but bred in a wilderness and with some unfortunate connections! I think you must agree I had something to offer her, quite apart from—" he broke off abruptly.

Lord Rawdon looked keenly at his son. "I often wondered what drew you to her. She seems to me to have qualities I would not have expected you to look for."

"Perhaps I have a predilection for black hair and green eyes," Rupert retorted and then seeing his father's expression he added, "Do I have to put it in so many words?"

Lord Rawdon sighed, "My dear boy, I know that you love her, but it is in your own fashion and I wonder how much you would be prepared to sacrifice for her."

"Sacrifice? I don't know what you are suggesting, and I am beginning to think we should not have started this conversation."

Rupert set the shepherdess down with a bang and turned his back on the empty hearth to face his father.

Lord Rawdon rose. "Then I shall go to bed." He walked slowly to the door and waited. Rupert was still standing by the mantlepiece, a stormy expression on his face, and then aware that his father was waiting by the door, he came across the room to open it.

"Thank you," Lord Rawdon said. "I had begun to think that your manners had gone out of the window—with a number of other things."

"Good night sir," Rupert said stiffly. "I have long been aware of your opinion of me, of my past behaviour—but I would do nothing to hurt her, you know."

His father paused by the open door. "In that lies my hope. One last thing—I think you should respect Mr. Fraser's difficult position in this house. You will earn your wife's gratitude if you contrive that his stay should be a pleasant one."

Rupert made a little grimace. "As to that I will do my best, but I don't think it will be easy. He is somewhat—unbending. And I doubt if he likes me overmuch." A faint smile crossed his face. "In fact, sir, relations can be the very devil, can they not?"

Lord Rawdon laughed and with a shake of his head went out into the hall where Samuel was waiting to give him an arm up the stairs.

In the days that followed Rupert did indeed put himself out to be hospitable to his guest. He took Donald down to his stables, suggesting that he might care to choose a mount to be at his disposal for the duration of his stay, and Donald selected a big roan that would be well up to his weight.

"You must let me show you something of the town," Rupert said. "Bab tells me she is promised to my cousin Georgiana this afternoon, a visit to the mantua-makers I believe, so we might ride out together and then spend the evening at White's."

"As to seeing the town," Donald answered, "I should like that but," he paused, his hand on the roan's smooth neck, "I am afraid that neither my tastes nor my circumstances are such that I would find any pleasure at the gaming tables."

Despite his conversation with his father the night before Rupert was nevertheless slightly taken aback. "Then we will dine there— they serve a very fair meal—and I'll get Simon and perhaps Harry Cavendish to join us. You must not mind Harry's chatter, he is not the most tactful of men."

Donald still had his back half turned to his companion, his attention seemingly on the horse. "Major Astley, do not think I am unaware of the totally opposite opinions of your acquaintances and your family to my own. I believe I owe you an apology for my bluntness at your dinner table last night."

A faintly amused smile lifted the corners of Rupert's mouth to be instantly repressed. "Oh, that was no matter, I do assure you. Now, if that animal suits you, shall we go? You will find White's entertaining enough even if you do not wish to play."

In the face of such an invitation Donald could only accept and they set off together in the direction of the city, a noisy dirty city as he had first observed, but full of life and vigour. Rupert took him first to the Tower. It looked grim and massive and impregnable and Donald sat his big roan, gazing at the grey walls, the iron-studded gates, the river smell borne towards them on a soft breeze.

"Would you care to go inside?" Rupert was asking. "The Lieutenant is an acquaintance of my father and I am sure he would be only too pleased to show us round."

Donald did not answer for a moment. He was thinking that if they had not turned back at Derby, if the Prince had marched on to London, might it not be King James III who would now be master of this great fortress? Instead, his own Chief, MacShimmi, had lain here before his execution, the lords Kilmarnock and Balmerino had gone from those gates to their beheading not far from the spot where he now sat his horse. "No," he said slowly, "I do not think I wish to go inside."

"No doubt you once expected to see it from a very different point of view," Rupert said flippantly, "and God knows what your skirted Highlanders would have made of London." But the moment the words were spoken he regretted them for he saw his companion's face darken with a justifiable anger. His own face somewhat coloured, he added, before Donald could speak, "That was unpardonable of me. Pray forget it, if you can."

Donald looked at him and beyond him to the shimmering river, the numerous boats, the busy wharf. If Major Astley was going to make such remarks, stir such warring emotions in him, then his visit to London was going to be far worse than he had imagined. Yet his brother-in-law's repentance seemed genuine. "You are right," he spoke at last, "it would have been better left unsaid, but you are also right in that you read my thought."

That was honest, at any rate, and handsome of him to acknowledge it, Rupert reflected, but he wondered how he was to follow his father's injunction and keep their companionship free of controversial matters, especially if he could not guard his own quick tongue. For the first time perhaps, he saw that he was capable not only of wounding, but of what was far worse in his eyes, tasteless behaviour. "Perhaps we can leave it at that," he said, entirely without his usual abrasive tone of voice. "I shall not offend in that way again. Perhaps you would like to take a turn in Paul's Walk?"

None too sure what Paul's Walk might be, Donald agreed and they rode somewhat silently back the way they had come, pausing only to mount the Monument for a view of the City. There Rupert pointed out famous landmarks, in particular the new stone bridge thrust across the Thames, not far from the crumbling, crowded old London bridge. The new structure had no houses upon it and was a wide thoroughfare better able to accommodate the amount of traffic needing to cross and it would soon be opened. Anxious to efface the recent unhappy exchange he then took his guest up Gracechurch Street with its busy shops and banking houses to St. Paul's Cathedral where they left their horses in charge of an urchin and entered through the great west porch. Once inside Donald was struck by the soaring beauty of the place but shocked to find it appeared to be the meeting ground for all the young bucks of the town, for ladies and gentlemen of quality who strolled up and down as if they were in a coffee-house. Somewhere he could hear a choir of boys practising but he could not see them and fine though the building was it did not seem to him to have the character of a place of worship.

"Paul's Walk," Rupert said, with a return to his normal manner. "One is always bound to meet acquaintances here whether one wants to or not!" He paused to make a group of young officers known to the Highlander and the light conversation that ensued grated on Donald, still smarting from the moment by the Tower. Was it his fault, he wondered, that life seemed to him a more serious business than it appeared to be to Rupert and his circle? Yet some of them must have been at Culloden, some of them as acquainted with blood and death as he was.

He tried to respond as pleasantly as he could to their talk but he was glad to be out in the sunshine again.

Rupert pointed out the high walls and gates of Newgate prison and even in the street the heavy unpleasant odour of the jail hung on the warm air.

"Visitors are allowed inside," Rupert explained, "but I would not advise it as I hear there is an outbreak of jail fever among the prisoners."

"In any case," Donald said, "I doubt I would find the state of the poor wretches in there in the least edifying. It has never seemed entertaining to me to take pleasure in the misery of others."

"Nor to me," Rupert answered, this time in complete agreement.

About noon he suggested they should stop for refreshment at a tavern and over their wine began to talk easily of making the Grand Tour in his youth, telling Donald with humour of the strictness of his tutor and his attempts to escape the inevitable round of museums and churches for the more exciting side of Paris. For the first time Donald glimpsed the charm that had captivated his sister and sensing that Rupert did indeed wish to redeem his unfortunate words of earlier in the day, joined him willingly on this neutral ground.

Presently they rode west along the Oxford Road and came to Tyburn turnpike where they were to turn south, and while Rupert paid the turnpike keeper, Donald sat his horse looking up at the great triangular gallows which stood, a permanent erection, ready for use. The gaunt structure was, it seemed to him, waiting to embrace its next victim and as he thought of the many whose last sight of life had been suspended from those beams, he felt a cold chill seize him, a horror that he had never felt before, even on Culloden field. There was something deliberate about Tyburn tree.

Hardly realizing what he was doing he dug in his spurs and cantered ahead so briskly that it took Rupert several minutes to catch him up. The Major said nothing, beyond giving him one curious look, and they galloped through the park as far as Knight's bridge where they turned back towards St. James's. It was Donald who spoke first, merely commenting on the roan's excellence.

"You have him well in hand," Rupert said frankly. "He is not an easy horse to ride."

Leaving their mounts at the Astley stables, he suggested they should walk the short distance to St. James's Street and there he conducted his guest through the pillared doorway of White's Club. In the hall a footman informed them that Lord Harry Cavendish and Mr. Ravenslow were waiting for them with Lieutenant Chambers and Rupert led the way up the thickly carpeted stairs.

It was Donald's first experience of a London club, and the garish decorations, the richness everywhere, the fashionably dressed men, many of them patched and painted and wearing what seemed to Donald an excess of jewels and lace, the young officers, all seemed to further the impression he had gained in Paul's Walk, of a world of exaggeration. Listening to the conversation, watching the scene as they ate the elaborate and well served meal he felt remote from these men, so utterly unlike the company he had kept either at home at Duirdre or in Paris. Only Simon Ravenslow held himself apart from the surface gaiety and talked quietly with Donald, much interested in his work as a librarian and inviting him to visit his own house, Blaydon Court, to see the fine collection of books there. Afterwards they went up to the gaming rooms and stood watching for a while until Rupert was hailed by an officer at one of the tables. He was a handsome man in his thirties with a striking personality that made him, wherever he might be, impossible to overlook; he had a brilliant smile and called out to Rupert to join his table for Hazard. Rupert glanced at Donald who begged him not to hesitate on his account if he wished to play and Rupert accordingly strolled off with Simon to two vacant seats, leaving Harry to look after his guest.

"Let us sit down over there," Harry suggested and called to a waiter to bring them a bottle of wine.

"Is this place always so crowded?" Donald asked for the atmosphere in the room seemed to him oppressive.

"Usually. This club and the Cocoa Tree are the best in town, you know. You can meet everyone of any importance at one or the other. For instance, that was Colonel Lord Hay who called Rupert over— he'll have his own brigade before long. You remember I told you about him the other night? And d'you see that raffish-looking fellow in black? That's Colley Cibber the actor, and sitting opposite him is Horace Walpole. He frightens the life out of me—too damned clever is Horry, what with sitting in the House and writing stuff I can't understand, *and* being something of an architect! Now over there by the door, that is Lord Chesterfield in the pale blue coat. He's talking to our commanding officer, Colonel Anderson, that big fellow in uniform—a martinet on duty but well enough off it, though he don't like to see his officers taking too much wine."

He glanced at Rupert and Donald asked in surprise, "Do you mean that Major Astley—"

"Lord no, Rupert's not one to sink too many bottles, never has been. No, I was just noticing he is having his usual good fortune."

"He plays well?"

Harry grinned. "Either that or he has the devil's own luck. Very few people have ever fleeced Reckless Rupert."

A slight frown crossed his companion's face. "Is that how he is called?"

"Oh, he's had that nickname for years, earned it in more ways than one too. At one time Lord Rawdon despaired of—" Harry stopped abruptly and then added hastily, "Not but what he hasn't settled down since he married your sister. We don't see him as often as before." Anxious to make his point, he blundered on, "He used to spend half the night here, but he don't do that any more—who would with such a bride at home?"

His clumsy compliment did not remove the frown and when another seat became vacant and Lord Hay suggested Harry should join them he was glad to be relieved of his charge and beckoned Lieutenant Chambers to show their guest round the rest of the club. Donald went with the young subaltern who, knowing something of his history, looked curiously at this man who had fought at Culloden. The lieutenant had heard tales enough of the wild Highlanders to arouse his interest, and he asked some rather impertinent questions but in so naive a manner that Donald was more amused than annoyed.

Presently they returned to the gaming room. "The Major has won again," Chambers remarked. "I don't play at his table, the stakes are too high. I see Colonel Hay has had no luck tonight. They say the Major won a fortune last winter—from Sir Laurence Everard, I think it was."

Donald repeated the name in surprise. "Are you sure?"

"Well, I'd gone home before the end, but the tale went round the next day. Oh, I forgot, Everard is some relation of yours, isn't he?"

"By marriage only," Donald said coldly. "When exactly was this?"

"Let me think—it must have been in January, because it was the day before my father went to Ireland—he's in the army too, you see—and that was why I left early. I heard they went on until after six in the morning! But no doubt as it was all in the family Rupert settled the matter with Sir Laurence with no harm done." Thus Lieutenant Chambers unwittingly finished what Lord Harry had equally inadvertently begun.

Donald had his eyes fixed on the table and the players and on his brother-in-law in particular. "Perhaps," he said briefly. It occurred to him that at that time Bab was not betrothed to Rupert and therefore the young lieutenant's assumption that the matter of the debt was 'all in the family' was a little previous. He was now seeing Major Astley in a new light and a certain sense of unease, though he could hardly have pin-pointed it, began to disturb him. Many men gambled—there was little harm in that, though he had no taste for it himself—but the connection with Everard was odd. Later, walking home with Rupert, attended by two link-boys, he asked him if he had known Laurence Everard for long. Rupert replied casually that they had been members of the same club for some years but that their acquaintance had been of the slightest until he had met Bab at Lady Denby's ball. They walked the last hundred yards in silence. Donald could not, after all, ask about that particular night in January and from what he had seen so far of Rupert Astley, he did not imagine he would take kindly to being questioned about what he might rightly regard as his private affairs—although, Donald thought, a tale repeated by young subalterns was not so private after all. Yet he had no grounds for thinking it was anything more than the kind of occurrence that must be frequent enought at any London club. He dismissed the matter as they entered Astley House, but when he went to bed he was unable to sleep, the day a confused jumble of impressions, emotions and a sense of uneasiness that kept him awake until dawn.

Chapter 9

The White Cock tavern was in a little alleyway off the Strand, a small building with low ceilings and a clientele composed almost entirely of Jacobites. It was well known to be their meeting place in London, but as all that seemed to emerge from its low doorway was hot air, the authorities chose to ignore it. The talk there was indeed inflammatory but, as Mr. Pelham wisely said to his brother, mere talk seldom set anything on fire.

On this pleasant June afternoon Donald had some difficulty in finding the place, however at last he ducked his head to enter the tap-room. The alley was enclosed and airless and consequently it was stiflingly hot inside, the tavern being fairly full at this time of day. He pushed his way past a knot of men arguing fiercely by the door and saw his cousin sitting at a table at the far end of the room, a tankard in his hand. Fergus glanced up and then leapt to his feet. He was a lean, raw-boned man with sandy hair and a freckled complexion and he held out a strong hand to grip Donald's, greeting him in their native tongue. It was the first time they had met since the day before Culloden and there was so much to say that an hour passed before they realized it. To Donald, after several days at Astley House and in company with his brother-in-law, it was sheer relief to be with one of his own countrymen, and a cousin at that, that he was able to forget for a while the place and the circumstances under which they were meeting. But presently he had to explain where he was staying and why—Neil MacEachain having omitted to put anything in his letter to Fergus other than Donald's imminent arrival.

Fergus was astonished, though he tried to hide his surprise under cover of a number of questions about Bab.

"You need not trouble to disguise what you think," Donald said in a low voice. "I assure you, my feelings were—are—the same. If I had been here, if my mother had not married again—but what is the use of talking of it? It seems it is a love match and Bab is happy, so what can I do? It is hard enough for me to be under Major Astley's roof without quarrelling with him, and I must think of Bab."

"It's done," Fergus agreed, "and I do not envy you. I am only surprised, remembering Bab as she was——"

"——a child then!" Donald broke in. "I have to remind myself how young she still is and, as you say, the thing is done and cannot be undone. I can only hope he will be good to her. His reputation does not seem to be all it might."

"Oh? Have you any reason to think——"

"None, but he has been something of a rake, I gather, and certainly a heavy gambler but apparently with luck on his side. It is his arrogance I don't like."

"Was he in Scotland? Did he serve under the Butcher?"

Donald frowned, staring down at his pewter tankard, the ale in it rather poor stuff in his opinion. "Yes, briefly, but not I gather until after Culloden. I intend to find out more."

Fergus was silent for a moment. Then he said slowly, "I am thinking you would be wiser not to do so. Oh, I know how you must feel, but Bab is married to the man and it is better to let the past lie. We have to think about what may be done now and from the point of view of the task you and I are here to carry out, it could not be better. You will be above suspicion staying at Astley House."

"I know," Donald said and then added in a burst of confidence, "I don't like it, Fergus—that part of it, I mean. He *is* my brother-in-law, whatever I think of him. Neil thought I was being squeamish."

Fergus rubbed his chin. "In a way I suppose he is right—we are not in any position to indulge in scruples—though I should feel as you do. Major Astley may be a *saighdear dearg* but you are eating the man's bread."

Donald let out a sigh. It was a relief to talk to someone as Highland as himself. "Thank God you are here. We can be meeting often in this place, I suppose?"

"Possibly," Fergus said, "but it might be better if you come to my lodgings when we go into details. No doubt the Government has its spies here, for it knows the White Cock well enough; those of us in the innermost circles greet each other by the sign of the blackbird." He beckoned to the serving man to refill their tankards. "At least this swill quenches one's thirst on a hot day, not but what I wouldn't prefer a bowl of usquebaugh. I might tell you, Duirdre, it would be easier if we could proceed with our work of preparing the ground and watching for the right time to strike, without this hazardous visit we are expecting."

"You think it foolish?" Donald queried. "I have thought so too, although one can't help but admire the courage behind it. As you know, whatever a certain person wishes, that Neil will contrive somehow. Where do you lodge? Perhaps I had best come there and we can talk more freely."

Fergus nodded, glancing round the room. "Even speaking Erse and in here, one is never sure there are not eavesdroppers. I live in St. Martin's Lane. It is only a step away, and my wife will be after making you very welcome."

"Your wife? I had no idea you were married and Neil did not mention it."

Fergus smiled and pushed away his empty tankard. "Our friend Neil has no time for such irrelevant details. I was wed last Christmas to Jane Grant, kinswoman to Grant of Glenmoristan. I think you may have met her when we were last in Edinburgh, at Holyrood House?"

"I remember her well, but," Donald paused, "is it wise for her to be here?"

"Oh, I am nobody," Fergus said cheerfully. "I cannot imagine that anyone should be interested in my activities. And she wanted to be with me as we are expecting a bairn in November."

Donald held out his hand. "My good wishes to you both. I shall look forward to meeting Mistress Mackenzie."

"You must come to St. Martin's Lane tomorrow, if you can. By the way *mo caraid* I have one piece of good news for you. Your Chief has been released."

"The Master?" Donald exclaimed. "Lord Lovat, I mean—when?"

"Only a week or two ago. I imagine he is back at Kirkhall, or what is left of it."

Donald leaned back in his seat. "Thank God for that." He and Simon Fraser the younger had always been friends; they had spent many hours together with rods by Beauly river or riding in the gentle countryside around Kirkhall, so very different from the wildness of Duirdre. Simon had come there often and stalked a deer with him in the heather, and it was good to know that Clan Frisealaich had a Macshimmi again. "So little has gone well," he said at last. "That is good news indeed. I thought at one time, when Bab was older, he might ask for her."

"Aye," Fergus agreed, "I remember you saying it. Well, it is all different now. But Jane and I would be so pleased if she would come with you to visit us."

Donald shook his head. "The situation is too delicate for that. I

123

must keep Major Astley from being curious as to my acquaintances in London. I have admitted to having one or two exiled friends here, but I don't want Bab involved. Fortunately he is on duty a great deal of the time so we may be able to arrange something later on."

Fergus nodded. "You are right, of course. And you know that as far as Jane and I are concerned you are welcome at any hour."

They parted near the church of St. Martin-in-the-fields, but as he walked back to Astley House Donald was aware of an uneasy wish that Neil had never come to Mentonnay. He did not like this cat-and-mouse work, he did not like to have to lie—even though it was all done for the man who might have his life if he needed it—and he did not want to embroil Bab in deception.

Something, however, must be said to her and preferring that it should not be under the Major's roof, he was glad to find, a few mornings later, that Rupert was not to accompany them on their early ride. He was to be absent for a day or two on a military affair taking place away from London, and Donald was glad to be relieved of his presence, though he had to admit that since the incident at the Tower his brother-in-law's behaviour had been impeccable. If Rupert felt the antipathy that he did, it was not visible. And he hoped his own loathing of that scarlet uniform was no longer so overt.

It was a fine morning and by now he had thoroughly mastered his big roan. As they rode out towards the park he watched his sister on her mare. "You had a horse of that colour once before," he said. "Father bought it in Maryburgh, I think."

Bab nodded, her eyes bright. "Yes, I remember—and how I loved to ride her with you. If I shut my eyes I can smell the stables at Duirdre and hear how the barn door creaked and how Angus Coll used to stand by my stirrup and tell you to mind me! Do you remember?"

"I remember everything about Duirdre."

"Oh—" the sparkle went out of her eyes, "I wonder what happened to that little mare."

"Some Campbell lady will be riding her, no doubt," Donald said. They were in the park now and Bab, in sudden distress, was gathering up her reins for a gallop. How often, he thought, had he seen her do that—in any moment of emotion, happy or sad, Bab found relief on horseback. "No," he said. "Bab, wait, I want to talk to you. Let us go slowly for a while."

Obediently she dropped the reins. "Very well. I wish I had not spoken of Duirdre. It hurts you so."

"It is not that. I have something to tell you." He paused, choosing his words with care. "My visit to you has coincided with something else, in fact I would probably have come to London anyway. Your letter provided me with just the invitation I needed."

"I don't understand."

"Be patient, *mo chridhe,* and you will. There are, even here thank God, many who still believe King James to be their rightful sovereign."

"Yes, I know that," she said slowly, "but now it is no more than an old loyalty."

"Do you think so? There are others of us who are convinced there may yet be a way to restore him."

Her eyes widened. "How?"

He rode in silence for a moment and Bab inclined her head as an officer, riding in the opposite direction, bowed to her and called out a greeting. But she did not smile, her eyes fixed on her brother, aware of how grave his face was. "How?" she repeated.

"That is not for me to say at the moment, but we must prepare for any possibility—or give up hope altogether and that we cannot do, as you must realize. And you, Bab," he glanced keenly at her, "how would you feel if there proved to be a chance still?"

The reins lay quite slack now and her mare, unaccustomed to so little demand on her, shook her head and rattled her harness as if to remind her rider that she did expect a gallop in the morning. But she was not to be obliged at the moment. Bab sat very still, her eyes on the distant trees. "I do not know. Once I would have said I would do anything for the White Rose, but now—"

"Now you are Lady Astley and mistress of a fine Whig house, and Duirdre, despite what you said just now, is only a memory."

She looked as if he had struck her. "Donald! You do not understand—indeed, I think you live on dreams. The Government is too strong—you must have seen since you came how firm the Whigs are. Everything has changed and—and I have had to change too."

"Yes," he said, a hint of bitterness creeping into his voice, "I see that you have. You can no longer be with us, Bab."

For a moment brother and sister stared at each other, the horses moving slowly forward together. He thought how lovely she was, sitting so gracefully in the saddle, her long green riding habit falling about the mare's pale coat, a little tricorne hat decorated with a green ostrich feather set on her dark hair, a silver topped whip in one hand. The two feet between them seemed to have become a vast distance. At last he said, "Even though you feel as you do, can I still trust you, Bab? I wonder what you would do if our Tearlach was to strike once more?"

She was gazing at him in horror. "If he was to—Oh God, is it to begin all over again? Isn't Scotland ruined enough? Hasn't enough blood been shed?" She shivered suddenly although they were in full sunlight. "It is too terrible to contemplate. If it came to that, if you— and Rupert—"

"Don't distress yourself," he said urgently. "No one is contemplating another rising. We know that is not feasible, but there are other possibilities." He leaned over and caught at her reins, bringing both horses to a halt. "You have not answered my question, Bab."

"Did you need to ask it?"

"Yes," he said steadily, "I think I did."

"Donald!" Her eyes filled and she who seldom wept found herself on the verge of it. "Of course I will keep your confidence. You are dearer to me than anyone in the world except—" she stopped abruptly.

"Except your husband—" he finished the sentence. He let the reins go and the horses moved forward again. "I know, child. Don't think I don't understand that. It was not, as you told me, your fault that you fell in love."

She put up a gloved hand and brushed away the tears with an impatient gesture. "No, but you are still my brother and you know I would never betray you—or the cause. What is it you are trying to tell me?"

"That I have work to do in London." He saw the surprise in her face and went on, "It is useful for the Prince to know who are his friends—whatever may or may not happen in the future, and I am here to find out."

Now her gaze was riveted on him. "You? But surely that is dangerous?"

"Not in the least—I am very careful, I promise you. But I tell you this to explain why I must be out sometimes and why I do not want to account for my movements to anyone."

"You mean to Rupert?"

"Yes, I mean exactly that. I have let him know there are one or two exiled friends of mine in London, but that must be enough, if he should ask—and that is true because the man I am working with is our cousin Fergus, wed these six months to Jane Grant."

"Fergus!" she cried. "We thought he had died on Drumossie Moor. He is really here in London, and married? Oh, I should very much like to see him, and Jane—they must come and dine with us."

Donald shook his head. "You are not thinking, *m'eudail*. If you will pause to reflect you will agree I must keep my connection with Fergus away from Astley House. We are involved in more than I can reveal to you."

"Oh—" she looked suddenly rather desolate, "I see. But I would have liked—"

"Of course. Perhaps we might go together to see them at their lodgings in St. Martin's Lane—later, when my work is done. Dearest," he leaned over and laid his hand on hers where it rested on the saddle bow, "dearest Bab, I would do nothing to involve you in any way that might compromise you, and I do not like asking you to keep anything from your husband, but on this occasion I am trusting you with far more lives than my own."

She raised her head. "Donald! You are in danger, I know it."

"No, I am not—I can promise you that. But it is a serious matter—for all Jacobites."

"Then," she said with equal gravity, "you can trust me, Mac Domhnull Àrd—with this and more."

"I never doubted it," he answered and smiled for the first time. "My darling, under the beautiful gowns of Lady Astley, you are still a little of a Fraser."

She managed to smile back at him, despite the shock of all he had told her. "Perhaps more than I realized," she said and gathered up the reins. "At least we are together again, that is all that matters to me. I won't ask any more questions and I will not speak of what you have told me—I don't want to think about it." She forced a laugh. "Can you still race me, I wonder?" and, digging in her spurs, was away across the turf.

Donald galloped after her and for a moment he too forgot the problems that loomed so large, seeing only her flying figure, admiring her superb horsemanship. No wonder, he thought, that Rupert was proud to ride here in the park with his wife every morning, and when he caught her up her eyes were sparkling, her cheeks bright, and she began to speak of her eagerness to see the famous Rawdon stud.

Nothing more was said and when, on the following morning, he announced his intention of going out, she only asked quietly whether he would return for dinner. He left the house aware of a deepening sadness, and castigated himself for not realizing before he came that he and Bab could never again be as they had been at Duirdre.

Fergus and his wife made him very welcome and for a while their hospitality, reminding him so much of home, eased the now familiar loneliness. Presently Fergus told him that he had sent a note to Lady Primrose, asking if they might visit her and that he had received a reply bidding them call this afternoon. It seemed a very prompt invitation and when they arrived at her house in Essex Street they found out why.

This elderly Jacobite lady, widow of Viscount Primrose, was small and dignified and utterly frank concerning her allegiance. A portrait of Prince Charles Edward hung prominently in her parlour and a letter he had once written her lay, framed in red velvet, inside a glass cabinet. The authorities blinked at her Jacobitism, her age and her sex seemingly rendering her beyond threat.

She rose to greet the two young men, elegantly gowned in black, her white hair perfectly dressed beneath a white lace head-dress. They both bowed over her hand and then she said, smiling, "Gentlemen, you see that I have another guest. Dr. King, may I present Mr. Fraser and Mr. Mackenzie."

Both Donald and Fergus turned in astonishment, Dr. King well known to them both by name and high on their list of people to be contacted—and here he was in Lady Primrose's drawing room and not in Oxford where they had expected to find him.

Seeing their surprise, he smiled. "I am in London for a few days," he said in the somewhat fruity voice that he used to full effect when preaching or addressing his students, "and I would not lose an opportunity to meet two gentlemen who are bound upon the same cause as myself."

"We are extremely glad to see you, sir," Donald said. "The Prince has heard much of your efforts on his behalf and has spoken warmly of you."

"And I of him, I think," the Doctor said. He stood beside Lady Primrose's chair, his hands behind his back, his large stomach placing some stress on his waistcoat buttons, a few stains of snuff decorating it. His eyes were small and set in a rather puffy face but they were lively and intelligent and he had an air about him that commanded attention. "I believe something more than shared loyalty brings you to London? Mr MacEachain wrote to her ladyship apprising her of it."

"Yes, sir," Donald answered at once. "We are here at His Highness's command, to number his friends, to find out who will stand for him if a political coup might be brought off."

"A great many," Lady Primrose said quietly but with deliberation. "The so-called Prince of Wales was here last night, supping with me. As you know, he is on the worst possible terms with his father the Elector, and he would be only too pleased, I think, to come to some arrangement with his cousin—" she glanced at the portrait hanging above her. "Of course, he cannot be seen to do so, but after a *fait accompli*, it would be a very easy matter."

"That is even better than we hoped for," Fergus said. "And your ladyship must be acquainted with many gentlemen who would follow his lead."

"There are some," she nodded, "the Duke of Beaufort, the Earl of Westmorland—"

"And I know of others," Dr. King went on. "I am, gentlemen, on my way to the Midlands, to Lichfield races to be precise, where, it seemed to me, I might well have the opportunity to search out our friends in that area without arousing checks, "my pleasure in that sport is well known."

"I understood," Donald hesitated for a moment, "that you, sir, are also well known for your sympathies. Are your movements not watched?"

"Possibly, possibly, but," the Doctor seemed quite unperturbed, "perhaps they think I am an old wind-bag and dismiss me as such. At any rate, my freedom has never been in any way curtailed—either of speech or of movement—so I shall go on as before, and await the day when the House of Stuart is restored. If my efforts hasten that day, that is all I could wish for."

"It may be nearer than we all think," Fergus said eagerly. "His Highness has plans—" he caught Donald's eye, and finished, "plans that are as yet without any set form or date, but firm nonetheless. Our work in London is to help them forward."

"Then you may count on me," Lady Primrose said, "and upon Dr. King, as you see." She rang a little bell at her side. "You will take some refreshment with me? We must drink a toast together—and in this company we do not need to hold our glasses over the water when we drink to the King."

Later, emerging into the sunshine, Fergus said, "Well, that was more than satisfactory. I was not going to say anything in front of Dr. King—though I am convinced he is wholly with us—but I think Neil is right, don't you? Lady Primrose's house would be the perfect lodging for the Prince and she would not hesitate to receive him."

Donald smiled. "She would consider it the honour of a lifetime, if I'm any judge. What a remarkable old lady!"

"She is indeed. What now, Duirdre? It is not much past two o'clock."

"We could call on Sir William Chandler, perhaps? He lives in Holborn—if that is not too far."

Fergus shook his head. "I can find the way—I am beginning to know this town. But I think we need to be wary with Sir William. He has estates in Lancashire but he never came out when we marched into England."

He had little difficulty in leading Donald to the right house, a rather shabby building, but on enquiring for Sir William they were shown into a comfortable room lined with books and fine panelling and a footman informed them that his master would be with them shortly. Donald noticed a bookshelf filled with works on astronomy and scientific discoveries and concluded that their owner must be something of a scholar. He was inspecting the titles of these volumes when Sir William came into the room. He was a tall, gangling man with a languid manner, and he greeted them with a slightly puzzled air until Fergus handed him the note of introduction with which Neil had furnished them. It was brief but there was a seal at the end bearing the shape of a blackbird.

Sir William read it through twice and then folded it carefully and handed it back to Fergus. "Well, gentlemen," he said and waved them to seats. "I am very pleased to make your acquaintance but I do not see what it is that you want of me at the moment."

"Nothing more than a few words, sir," Fergus said carefully. "We are merely here as representatives to talk with others of the same mind. We know that you stand for the true King—you may be able to help us to meet others in order that when the time comes for another attempt to restore His Majesty we shall know whose help can be counted on."

Sir William's eyebrows shot into his hair. "Mr.—Mackenzie, is it? Well then, Mr. Mackenzie, my family always upheld the Stuart cause and I shall continue to do so, but I do not see the likelihood of any circumstances arising in the immediate future in which my assistance might be of any possible use."

"Perhaps not now, sir, but I can assure you the Prince has not given up hope of achieving what we failed to do in '45."

"If he is making plans along the same lines as before then he must be a singularly foolish young man," their host said drily.

For some reason Donald had not felt at ease since they had entered this room. Now he sat up and retorted tartly, "Sir, you have no cause whatever to pass such judgement upon His Highness—seeing that you do not know what plans he has in mind."

Sir William leaned back in his chair and regarded Donald with what seemed to be faint amusement. "I am old enough to be able to speak my mind without having a young hothead jump down my throat. Pray take a glass of wine, Mr—er—" he appeared to have forgotten Donald's name, and leaned forward to pour out three glasses from a decanter that stood on the table by his chair. "As I see it," he went on, passing the glasses without rising, "we must be realists. Ill-judged enthusiasm will not serve King James. There are too many young men who would risk anything for the sake of adventure and we do not want a repetition of what happened before."

"His Highness," Fergus said, "has no intention of trying a further campaign from Scotland."

"I should think not. The folly with which that affair was conducted precludes any idea that another attempt should be launched by the Highlanders."

His tone was still languid, but both young men opposite him sat rigid. Fergus's face was grim and Donald set down his wine glass with a snap, barely able to control his resentment.

"Your pardon, sir," he said sharply, "but before you presume to criticize our countrymen, you would do well to remember that precious few English Jacobites rose to join us."

Sir William bestirred himself to remove his feet from a footstool and sat up. "If you mean that remark to be personal I may tell you that at no time could I give my support to so rash and ill-timed a rising. Nor did your army persevere far enough south to give us any reason to suppose that your unruly troops either could or would carry the enterprise as far as London."

"In other words," Donald answered bitingly, "you would only have joined us had you seen a victorious army enter the capital."

Sir William had the grace to look discomposed. "You are an exceedingly impertinent young man."

"I may be impertinent but I think we were misinformed when we were told this was a loyal house."

"Gentlemen!" Fergus leaned forward. "We shall gain nothing by arguing. Duidre, I am sure you did not intend to call Sir William's allegiance in doubt?"

Donald had intended just that, but he was aware of the futility of antagonizing what support they had, and Sir William, for all he would clearly never be an active participant, was still a man of standing, such as they needed. He swallowed his indignation and turned to his host. "If I have given offence, I ask your pardon. But you will understand, that to us who fought through the last campaign—" he broke off.

"Well, well," Sir William answered rather testily, "we will say no more about our differences, Mr. Fraser. I will only point out that if you are to raise support here in London you must realize that we see matters somewhat differently. Any move must be, to my mind, a purely political one."

"That is indeed what we think, sir," Fergus said eagerly. "We have heard much of the discord between members of the Elector's family. Is it not likely they will precipitate a crisis of which we may take advantage?"

"I can't deny that," their host agreed. "Rest assured that if I may serve the House of Stuart I will do so, but I must make it clear I cannot give my support to any scheme but one which is based upon a reasonable chance of success."

Donald opened his mouth to speak, encountered a warning glance from Fergus, and shut it again. Perhaps fortunately for him the door opened at that moment and a slighter, shorter edition of Sir William entered the room. The newcomer's pale eyes flickered from one to the other of the guests and then he bowed. "Your pardon, William, I did not know you had visitors calling upon you this afternoon."

"Come in, come in, my dear James. Gentlemen, this is my brother who, I can assure you, shares my opinions." He waved a vague hand. "May I present Mr. Mackenzie and Mr.—er—Fraser, I believe."

Donald rose and answered James Chandler's bow, but he added, "You will forgive me, Sir William, if I point out that in Jacobite circles I am still Fraser of Duirdre."

Again his host shot him that slightly amused look, the expression on his face clearly reflecting what he thought of the obstinacy of Highland gentlemen who with homes burned and lands confiscated still claimed their hereditary titles. "Forgive me," he said with exaggerated courtesy, "James, may I present Mr. Fraser of Duirdre."

James Chandler's thin face bore no expression at all. He was entirely without his brother's lazy manner and as he sat down opposite the two Highlanders he looked keenly from one to the other, listening as Sir William explained the reason for their visit. He made little comment except to endorse his brother's profession of loyalty and as there seemed to be no more to be said, Fergus rose, thanking Sir William for his time and hospitality.

James Chandler accompanied them to the door and there seemed inclined to be more expansive. "My brother is given to caution," he said in a low voice, "whereas I—let me have your direction, gentlemen, for I may be of more service to you."

Fergus thanked him and complied, but outside in the street he turned to Donald. "You know, *laochan*," he said with a half smile, "we shall not get very far if you do battle with every man who does not see eye to eye with you."

"Possibly not," Donald retorted. He was still smarting from the encounter. "But it seems to me we would do better without such men as Sir William. *Mo thruagh!* I would not have the gall to declare myself so openly a fair weather Jacobite!"

"We cannot do without him and others like him. Sir William won't move unless we are within sight of success, I know that—perhaps not until we have achieved it—but don't you see that we will need such men to show themselves then?"

Donald sighed. "I am sure you are right. It is not the way I had thought it would be done."

"I know." Fergus tucked his arm through his cousin's. "But you did not expect it to be easy, did you? The only way the King will come to Whitehall now will be by one swift stroke, made at exactly the right moment—or so I think. By the way, what did you make of the brother? He is obviously more prepared to bestir himself."

"Possibly, but I would judge him to be a doubtful friend—and a dangerous enemy."

"What makes you say that?" Fergus asked in surprise.

"I don't know." Donald frowned. "Perhaps," a faint smile crossed his face, dispelling the gravity, "perhaps I have the 'seeing'—or maybe I am just over suspicious. I think I need a glass of your wife's delicious punch to wash the taste of that meeting out of my mouth."

"*Slainte!*" his cousin said and led him in the direction of St. Martin's Lane.

Chapter 10

Thomson's, the glove-makers in the Strand, was reputed to be the best in London, and certainly the middle-aged lady emerging from their fine establishment seemed satisfied. She turned to speak to the gentleman accompanying her as the door closed behind them.

"Just fancy, the very shade of grey that I wanted. They will match my new gown perfectly."

"They were deucedly expensive," her companion grumbled. "I hope you have finished your shopping now."

"Yes, I think that is all. You would not have me disgrace Bab on our first visit, would you? Where is our carriage?" She glanced across the street and then with a little gasp caught at her husband's arm. "Laurence, look—there across the road—surely, yes, yes it is! You see that tall man, there? That is Donald, my son." She would have hurried across despite the passing coaches and horsemen, but Laurence Everard caught her arm and held it firmly.

"Caroline, wait. Are you sure?"

"Of course I am sure. Do you think I don't know my own son, even though he does look different? Let me go."

"One moment, if you please." He was still staring in the direction she had pointed, to where two young men who had emerged from a narrow passage stood talking to a gentleman who was leaning out of his carriage window.

"Let me go," the lady begged. "Laurence, please—that is my son that I've not set eyes on for nearly five years."

He continued to hold her, an odd expression on his once handsome face. "Not yet. The arms on that coach, I swear I know them—of course, it must be Westmorland, and outside the White Cock too. Well, well!"

The next moment the two young men climbed into the coach and drove off and she turned to her husband, almost in tears. "There now, they have gone, and I could almost swear that was my nephew, Fergus Mackenzie, with Donald. How could you be so cruel as to keep me from him?"

"Calm yourself, my dear," her husband said. "You will be seeing your son soon enough at Astley House, though I cannot answer for the other gentleman. Nor for Lord Westmorland—that was extremely interesting."

"I don't understand you," Caroline Everard said. She took her hand from his arm and fumbled in her reticule for a handkerchief. "You are behaving very oddly."

"Do you think so?" he queried drily. "I am not the only one whose behaviour is odd. The Earl of Westmorland is known to have Jacobite sympathies—and the White Cock is a nest of Jacobites. I wonder what your precious son is up to."

"Well, I don't see anything strange in that. How should he not meet men of his own way of thinking in London?" she asked with unaccustomed defiance. "I don't suppose he is so changed, and where is the harm in that?"

"Oh, no harm," he agreed, "as long as that is all it is. But he has wasted no time in finding them out, has he?"

"No, perhaps not, but—Laurence," she looked up at him with an appeal in her face, and she was still a very pretty woman, "I do not want anything to spoil my first meeting with him, nor to upset Bab or Rupert. Pray don't—don't mention what we have seen."

He paused for a moment, glancing down at his wife. Then he said slowly, "Very well, my dear, if that is what you wish," but he said it with the manner of one who had no intention of banishing it from his mind.

An hour later they were at Astley House and Lady Caroline was in her son's arms. She cried a little and laughed, was upset by the scar on his face but so thankful to see him that even his changed appearance mattered less than the fact that he was here at last. Donald for his part could not help but be pleased with his mother. She was a little plumper than before and she seemed perfectly content with her rather overbearing husband. Bab had prepared him as to Sir Laurence Everard's character and the greeting between them was cool, but as it seemed to Donald that they were unlikely to meet very often he made an effort to make polite conversation to his stepfather.

After dinner, Sir Laurence took himself off to Almack's Assembly Rooms, Rupert tactfully found business to transact with his father who had retired to the library, thus leaving Lady Caroline to enjoy her son and daughter alone in the withdrawing room.

It seemed strange to Donald that their reunion should be in a London house, so very far removed from Duirdre and from that last meeting in Edinburgh with no conception of the tragedy that lay before them. Now both were married to Englishmen and he could see little likelihood of there being frequent contact between him and them. His own future stretched bleakly before him and something of his thoughts must have shown in his face for his mother wanted to know his plans.

"Tell me about this Chevalier who employed you to catalogue his library. Do you return to him?"

Donald shook his head. "It is not very likely. I shall probably go back to France in September and seek a post as a tutor."

"I see." She looked at him rather wistfully. "I wish you did not have to live abroad. Could you not settle in England so that Bab and I could see you sometimes?"

"No," he said abruptly. "I could never live in this country while it is ruled by the Elector—and if he was no longer on the throne, no doubt I should be able to go home."

"But times have changed. Surely now you could—"

"It is no use talking to him about it, Mama," Bab broke in with a faint, unhappy smile. "I have tried, but he will go his own way."

"My father's way," Donald said. "Nothing can make me abandon that."

Lady Caroline leaned forward and set her hand on his arm. "Surely he would not want you to waste your life in exile?"

"I do not think, my dear Mother, that you can know what he would wish me to do." He saw the ready tears spring into her rather faded blue eyes. "Forgive me, but I cannot expect that you should understand how it is with me. I do not like our separation either, but I see no alternative at the moment."

She sighed, found a wisp of lace and wiped away her tears, another idea distracting her. "If you must live abroad, perhaps it would be better if you could settle down to a more comfortable way of living. Is there no French lady you might like to wed? If you were married I should not worry so much about you."

He felt the colour deepen in his face and hoped that Bab was not observing it. "You forget," he said shortly, "that there is no Duirdre now. I have nowhere to take a wife and no means to support one in France—at the moment, at any rate. If—if I married I would want my father's spirit to see his grandsons walk beneath Lurg Mhòr."

His mother looked at him. Sometimes he was really incomprehensible, she thought. She had never in her twenty-five years with John Fraser understood the Highland way of life, nor their attitude toward clan and family, their passionate adherence to Celtish tradition and beliefs, but because she loved this son of hers her eyes filled again. "My poor boy, you have lost so much."

At once he put both arms round her. "Dearest Mother, don't distress yourself. I promise you, I manage very well, and if Bab will have me I will come to visit you as often as I can." He held her close, while Bab fetched her vinaigrette, aware of the faint scent of lavender that emanated from her gown. It took him back to his childhood, reminding him of the times when she had soothed his ailments or bent over his bed at night. She might be foolish and not very perceptive but she had a quality of sweetness about her that had been strong enough to attract a man of such high intellectual abilities and sterling worth as John Fraser of Duirdre, and her son felt a swift rise of affection for her, mingled with the familiar aching desire for the past, for the Duirdre of his boyhood.

He dropped a swift kiss on her hair and wanting to dispel the poignancy of the moment he looked up over her head towards Bab, saying in a lighter tone, "Let us try to forget our sorrows and be glad we are together again for a little while. I gather Rupert and Bab have waited until your visit to give their first ball."

"Why yes," Bab said at once, "you must wear your prettiest gown for us tomorrow night, Mama."

Lady Caroline sat up, dried her tears once more and was soon lost in a discussion with her daughter over the merits of a blue gown as against a confection of pink satin. Donald left them to it and going to his room sat down to write to Armand. He had had a letter from him yesterday, containing news and messages from the family at Mentonnay. He said little of Marthe but that apart from a slight cold she was well. "Your company is much missed," he ended. "I have not engaged another librarian to finish your work, and your return is awaited eagerly by us all."

Donald was not sure what to make of that sentence and taking a quill sat for a long while, hesitating over his answer. In the end he said merely that he expected to return to France in the autumn and would apprise Armand of that event in due time. He longed to write to his little love, but he was not sure how Armand would take this; after their conversation on the matter and Armand's more generous attitude he did not feel inclined to do anything that might offend the Chevalier. He must wait—wait until the autumn, and some optimism, to which he was not usually susceptible, rose in him, giving him a wholly unfounded sense of hope. Surely he was not so little of a man that he could not find some way to make their marriage possible! He bent over the paper, telling Armand of his doings in London, knowing that all he said would be relayed to Marthe and the rest of the family, and ended by reiterating that he looked forward to seeing them all in the autumn.

Gazing out of the window into the busy square, it occurred to him that he was more at home at Mentonnay than here in London, despite the presence of Bab and his mother. They were now so much less of Duirdre than he—and as far as his mother was concerned she was merely back among her own. He sighed, sealed his letter, and went up to bed.

He was in his shirt and breeches when there was a tap at the door and Bab came in. "I just wanted to say goodnight," she said, "and ask you what you think of our stepfather."

"That man!" he broke in. "How could she? After our father!"

Bab sat down on the edge of his bed. She was wearing a patterned silk dressing robe and her maid had undressed and combed her long dark hair and she looked more like the Bab of their childhood. "I don't know," she answered after a moment. His coat lay on the bed beside her and she began to twist a beaten silver button in her fingers. "When he first came to St. Albans he was very masterful, and to Mama at least, still handsome—and he was determined to have her. He thought—" she changed her mind and finished rather lamely, "he seemed to get on well with Grandfather."

Donald opened a drawer to put away his cravat and stood for a moment staring at something within. Then he took it out and showed it to his sister. "Do you remember this?"

She took it in her hand. "Oh! your white cockade!" She turned it over, looking at her imperfect stitches. "It seems such a long time since I made it. And you have kept it all this while!"

"It is all I have left from the last day I wore the tartan," he said. "I buried our father with my own hands, Bab—and when I think what he was, and I look at Sir Laurence, can you blame me for what I feel?"

She shook her head. "Now you know why I found life at St. Albans so hard. Fortunately he used to go to Newmarket, to the races and often to London, without Mama and me—and I was glad. But Mama was happy and I had to hide my feelings."

"Well, you need see very little of him now, thank God." Donald took the cockade from her fingers and put it back in the drawer. Then he went to her and kissed her forehead. "*M'eudail*, I will help you to make our mother's visit a happy one and when they are gone back to

St. Albans we shall have a little longer together before I need return to France."

She caught hold of his hand. "Stay as long as you can, Donald."

He smiled. "My dearest Bab, I know you are pleased to see me, but you have a husband and a new life here in London—and if you do not go to bed you will not be at your best for your ball tomorrow."

She rose, smiling back at him, and went away, but it was some time before he followed his own advice and went to bed himself.

On the following evening he dressed in his new green satin suit with its flowered waistcoat and it amused him that the valet whom Rupert had put at his disposal seemed satisfied that his master's guest would not disgrace his efforts with powder and curling tongs and pounce box. When Donald surveyed himself in the mirror he realized he had not been dressed thus since the Prince's ball in Edinburgh and then he had worn the red of the Fraser tartan from his shoulder.

Recalling that occasion he went slowly down the stair and it was with a shock that he found Bab, in the hall, dressed entirely in white, with a white rose in the bosom of her ball gown. "Rupert is talking to Harper in the dining room," she said in a low voice. "Donald, I wore this for you—he will not notice, I have worn roses before, though not a white one."

He bent and kissed her. "*M'eudail*, I thank you, and this is the picture of you that I shall take back to France when I go."

"Oh, do not talk again of going," she said, and held his hand tightly. "I am not going to let you leave us for a long while. Ah, here is Rupert—is everything in readiness?"

He came to her and lifting her hand put it to his lips. "My love, you look radiant. Does she not, Fraser?"

"Indeed," Donald said. His eyes rested affectionately on his sister. He had never seen her look more beautiful, her hair powdered, enhancing the green of her eyes, her gown sewn with little white rosettes, the white rose itself in her breast, the leaves the only spot of colour, green as her eyes. "You will break some hearts tonight," he said mainly for the sake of saying something light.

Rupert drew her hand through his arm. "You may trust me to care for what is mine," he said, a proud smile hovering about his mouth, and led the way into the ballroom where they were to receive their guests, the significance of his remark not lost on his brother-in-law.

Socially, the evening was a great success. Donald could see that Bab, young as she was, seemed to have a natural aptitude for playing the hostess, that she said the right things to the right people, that because she was enjoying herself she made other people enjoy her hospitality. She was entirely taken up with her guests and Donald wandered away to spend some time with his cousin Philip Denby, whom he liked very well as their acquaintance deepened. Philip was totally unperturbed by the rather hectic pace of London society, and even managed to keep the flighty Georgy in hand without in any way clipping her butterfly wings. He talked to Donald of Wilde End, their grandfather's home, almost apologizing that he should be the heir.

"My dear Philip," Donald said smiling, "what should I do with an English estate? I presume it is entailed?"

Philip nodded. "Yes, I am bound by that, not that I mind, I love the place. Do you recall it?"

"I do indeed. I remember riding in the fine park. I wish you joy there with your charming bride."

"She is, isn't she?" Philip said simply. "I am the luckiest of men."

Why, Donald wondered, did every conversation have to remind him of what he had either lost or could not have? Presently Philip went to dance with his betrothed and Donald stood in the doorway of the ballroom, watching the dancers. He saw Bab standing up with Colonel Lord Hay, he smiling his vivid smile and she laughing at something he had said, while Harry Cavendish had Donald's mother on his arm and was pretending to flirt with her in a manner that made her forget she had a son of twenty-eight.

Just before supper Rupert, resplendent in pale blue satin with a flowered waistcoat, red heels to his shoes and elaborate clocks embroidered on his stockings, took the floor with his wife and Donald was watching them when a deep voice beside him said, "They look well together, do they not?"

He turned to find Simon Ravenslow standing beside him. "White has always become Bab," he answered rather absently. "She does look very pretty tonight."

"Very," Simon agreed, "but I think happiness has achieved more than the mantua-maker could do."

"I hope so," Donald answered before he was aware of what he had said.

His companion shot him a quick look. "I know how you must view this marriage, Mr. Fraser. I think you wish it had not taken place."

Startled, Donald nevertheless returned his glance frankly. "I trust I did not make it so obvious when I came."

Simon shrugged his big shoulders. "You did not show it markedly,

I assure you, but it was easy enough for me to deduce, knowing a little of your circumstances. I hope your stay here is convincing you of your sister's contentment with her choice."

"You seem concerned that I should be."

Simon answered rather abruptly. "I have known Rupert all his life. Perhaps I care as deeply for him as you do for your sister." He paused, considering his words. "You think him hard, careless, maybe worse—I do not know. You need not trouble to deny it," he added as Donald made a slight gesture. "I imagine you and I prefer plain speaking."

"You are quite right," Donald said, abandoning politeness to honesty. "I admit I have thought him less than worthy of her, but then perhaps that is because naturally I always hoped she would marry a man of our own race in our own country."

Simon leaned against a small table, his arms folded across his chest. "I understand Rupert better than most people. After his mother died he was a very lonely child. I taught him to ride and to fence and to shoot—he and his father never got on well, you know though that is something your sister seems to be mending. I believe his cynicism, his arrogance, is a veneer, a defence if you like, but when you hear a story or two about him, as I'm sure you will, don't think that is all there is to Rupert Astley."

"Oh? His manner does not lead one to think—"

Simon waved an impatient hand. "He seems to relish giving the worst impression of himself—God knows why—but of this I am sure. He will endeavour in his own way to make your sister happy. I am glad to have had this opportunity of putting in a word on his behalf."

"Did you think he needed it?"

"Yes," Simon answered directly. "I was not mistaken?"

"No."

"Then I am glad I have been frank with you, because I believe your sister will be the making of him."

Donald glanced across the ballroom. The dance had ended and Bab was now talking to a middle-aged gentleman in heavy full-bottomed wig. "I should be glad to think so," he said at last, and then aware of what those words implied he added, "I am more concerned with what he will make of Bab."

Ravenslow gave his curious crooked smile. "You are not very complimentary, Mr. Fraser. I see you think that might not be for the best."

"I am sorry," Donald said stiffly. "I did not mean what you may have thought—only that I have lost my Highland sister to a London hostess and must make the best of it." Donald gave Simon an apologetic smile and as Bab herself came at that moment to claim him for their dance, suffered himself to be led on to the floor. He protested that it was a long while since he had danced, but she took his hand firmly, promising to guide him through the steps, and Donald, who had forgotten what it was like to be young and carefree, found himself swept into the measure with a sense of pleasure long forgotten.

Lord Rawdon, leaning on a stick, came to the doorway with his son. "I think, my boy, you may congratulate your wife on this evening. It seems half London is here."

"All I can hope," Rupert said with feeling, "is that we are not forced to do this too often. An hour at any ball is usually enough for me, but the host can hardly slip away to White's, can he?"

"Certainly not," his father agreed, smiling. "Your brother-in-law's visit seems to be passing better than you expected."

"Oh, well enough. I have had several days showing him the town and his reactions have been somewhat odd, to say the least. He can be deucedly uncomfortable company."

"Yes," his father agreed drily, "I did not think he would suit the manners you and your set appear to cultivate."

Rupert opened his mouth to speak and then wisely closed it again. His father regarded him for a moment and then said, "You are blinder than I imagine if you do not see that London society is hardly to his taste but I think," he added shrewdly, "that you are coming to like him better than you anticipated."

Rupert shrugged, but he did not answer, only when his father requested a glass of wine, there was an unusually affectionate look on his face as he said, "I am sure you should not. The doctor said it aggravated your gout."

"For the time that is left to me," Lord Rawdon retorted, "I intend to please myself. If my gout is worse tomorrow I shall not blame you."

"Very well—on your own head be it."

His father regarded him with some amusement. "That is not precisely where my gout is situated." His eyes rested for a moment on the white figure of his daughter-in-law. "I will say this, my son—there are some things it has been worth surviving for."

Just before supper a late arrival was announced and the Duke of Argyll came slowly up the stairs. He was a tall, extremely dignified man over seventy years of age, dressed in purple satin with a quantity of lace at throat and wrists, an amethyst sparkling on one finger, and his whole air reflected his high standing both as the Chief of Clan Campbell and as the virtual authority and representative of the Government in Scotland.

Lord Rawdon greeted him and was presently joined by his son. After a short conversation, Rupert said he would find Lady Astley in order that he might present her, and went in search of his wife. He found her sitting on a sofa with her brother, sipping a glass of madeira and nibbling at an iced biscuit.

"My love," he said, "another guest has arrived. I want you to come and greet His Grace of Argyll."

Both brother and sister stiffened, and he saw the startled glance that passed between them. Then Bab said slowly, "I did not know he was coming."

"My father invited him and I forgot to tell you. Come, we are keeping him waiting."

She still hesitated, her hand on her brother's arm, and it was Donald who said, "You had better go, my dear—to meet MaCaileen Mor."

"I beg your pardon," Rupert said stiffly, "I was under the impression I had asked her to meet His Grace of Argyll. Are you coming, Bab?"

She was still looking at Donald, but in response to a slight squeeze of her hand she rose. "I wish Lord Rawdon had not asked him."

"I presume," Rupert answered in a tone she had never yet heard from him, "that my father may ask whom he wishes to his own house. He and the Duke have long been friends." He held out his hand, "Come, Bab—and I suppose, Fraser, you will accompany us?"

Donald rose and stood facing his brother-in-law, his hands clasped behind his back. "Pray excuse me. The Duke is not a man we—I— would ever willingly meet. Bab may be constrained to do so tonight, but I am not."

"For God's sake, lower your voice," Rupert snapped. He drew them both into an alcove. "I've never heard anything so absurd. Just because you were on opposing sides five years ago—"

"Five years ago!" Donald exclaimed in a voice lowered indeed but vibrating with passion. "Clan Diarmaid has been our enemy for more like four hundred years. It would be an affront to my father's memory if I took the hand of MaCaileen Mor."

"Good God, I am asking you to do no more than greet him as a guest under my roof! You Highlanders have the most ridiculous notions. But you may do as you wish—Bab at least will behave as my wife should."

"I am Highland too," she said quietly. "Nothing can alter that."

Donald glanced down at her. "I am afraid you altered that by your marriage into a Whig family, my dear. You had better do as your husband wishes."

Rupert rounded on him, "My wife will do my bidding without your interference, Fraser." He held out his arm once more. "If you please, Bab—and you will not meet the Duke wearing that!" He reached out, took the rose from the front of her gown and crushed it in his fingers. "Did you think I did not know the significance of it?"

She gave a little gasp and glanced at Donald. Then, with a helpless gesture she laid her hand on her husband's arm. But the quick exchange of glances, as if of permission sought and granted, had not escaped him.

"I think we can dispense with your company," he said in a voice of ice directed at his brother-in-law. "You have made your feelings abundantly clear."

Donald met his stare with one equally challenging. "I would naturally prefer to be excused the—honour—of meeting the head of Clan Campbell. As the Duke administers my sequestered property and as I would insist on being presented as Fraser of Duirdre, you must be aware that it could hardly be a pleasant meeting."

Rupert gave him one explicit glance and then, throwing the broken petals on the floor, led Bab away towards the top of the wide staircase. Donald turned and went out into the garden. It was intolerable to be under the same roof as the Campbell and he escaped to a secluded part of the garden. It was a warm night and he stood for a while by a little fountain, the water playing into a stone bowl, the scent of roses all about him. This house, these people, London itself, were all wholly alien; Bab was lost to him, and he would be a fool if he did not see that, and as for Marthe, was he not also a fool to dream she might ever be his? If only he could go home—with honour—lose himself in the mountains, lie in the heather, and shut his mind to anything but the sound of the burn tumbling down the hillside and the cry of an eagle in the empty sky above!

His hands clenched on the rim of the bowl, the water splashing over his fingers, and he lifted them to cool his face. He supposed some time he must go back into the house, but no one would miss him for a while and he began to pace up and down, wishing for the time to pass.

But it seemed someone did miss him, for Georgiana Milne had seen him go out and she came to look for him.

"Mr. Fraser!" She shook her head at him. "You are very ungallant, sir. I think I shall ask Phil to call you out." "Why?" he asked in surprise, looking down at her small frame in rose coloured silk. "What have I done?"

"You have forgotten I am promised to you for this set. Will you not come?"

She held out her hand, smiling, and unable to resist either the smile or her invitation, he crooked his arm and led her into the ballroom. There was no sign of the Duke and for that at least he was thankful.

But towards the end of the evening, unavoidably, they chanced to pass each other in the supper room and for a moment MaCaileen Mor stared coolly at Mac Domhnull Àrd. To the Duke, however, Donald was merely a tall gentleman in a dark green coat. He bowed and passed on, leaving Donald motionless, and a prey to what he knew to be a most primitive emotion.

It was not until past three o'clock that the last guest left Astley House. Lord Rawdon had long since retired, the Everards had gone to their room and Donald to his when Bab climbed the stairs to her own chamber. There she submitted silently to her maid undressing her and brushing the powder from her hair. She was tired and all the early enjoyment of her first ball had gone from her, dispelled by the short unhappy scene in the alcove. If only the Duke had not come, or if only Rupert had told her so that she might have prepared Donald. Yet she could not blame Rupert. The little he understood of her background could hardly explain with what loathing Donald thought of the Chief of Clan Diarmaid. She sighed, and when Susan had finished dismissed her, but instead of getting into bed, sat on by her dressing table. She was still there when the adjoining door opened and Rupert came in in his dressing gown. One glance at his face told her that he had not forgotten that exchange either.

"You are still angry?" she asked quietly.

For a moment, without his wig, his hair clipped very short, he looked like a sulky boy. "What do you expect? To bring up a feud between two half-civilized clans, here in our house——"

Her eyes clouded. "I thought perhaps you might have understood. There are more than half-civilized men who share that feud. We grew up despising the name of MaCaileen Mor. And he despises us— old hatreds die hard, Rupert."

"Your brother made that only too clear."

"He could not do otherwise. Yet I think I greeted the Duke as you wished."

"Your manner left nothing to be desired," he admitted grudgingly. He came to stand beside her dressing table and began to finger one of her brushes, turning it over in his hand.

"Then I am forgiven?"

He remained silent for a while. Then he leaned down and pulled her to her feet. "You are my wife," he said with sudden fierceness. "You must forget old sores." He held her wrists hard, staring into her face. "I think," he said abruptly, "that I am jealous."

"Jealous?" she asked wonderingly. "Of what?"

"Of so much in your past that I cannot share. Your brother—"

"Oh," she cried out. "Don't reproach me for being glad to see my own brother."

"I want you," he said, "all of you—with nothing—no one—between us."

"Donald would never come between us." Yet despite her vigorous denial she sensed that he felt, as she did, the rising of a small hitherto unnoticed barrier between them. Catching desperately at something to dispel it, she said, "Remember how long it is since I saw him, and he is here for so short a time. You will not quarrel with him about the Duke, will you?"

Rupert released her hands and moved a little away from her. "He was extremely rude."

"Perhaps, yet I think it was understandable—with Duirdre in the Duke's hands."

"I suppose so," he agreed rather wearily. He was beginning to grow extremely bored with His Grace of Argyll and at one with his brother-in-law in wishing that the Duke had not come tonight. "But Argyll did not burn his house, nor were the soldiers who did so Campbells, were they?"

"No," she answered, "but I did not know you knew that."

His face seemed to close up. "I expect you told me. Anyway I suggest we forget the whole tiresome incident."

"Tiresome?" She sat down again rather suddenly on her dressing stool. "Perhaps it seems so to you, but you must remember what the loss of Duirdre was, and still is, to Donald. He was there, he saw it all—"

"What?" Rupert's attention was riveted now. "He was *there*? You never told me that. I understood he came back afterwards."

"After the soldiers had gone, yes." She was trembling now with a

146

mixture of weariness and misery that she and Rupert should be quarrelling over something that in her first flush of love for him she had refused to consider, had banished to the back of her mind. "But he was there, a long way off, up on the mountain—he saw our father shot. And even if there were no Campbells present then, MaCaileen Mor holds Duirdre now."

"Good God," he said slowly. "No doubt he would like to run me through every time he sees my uniform."

"Oh no, no—well, perhaps he hates the uniform, but not you, Rupert. I told him—I told him you were not in Scotland until after Culloden, and then only for a short time. That is true, isn't it?"

"Of course," he said mechanically. "I am glad you made that clear."

"I did, and indeed Donald has tried to put the past behind him. It was only seeing MaCaileen Mor—"

"Bab!" he said so sharply that she jumped. "You may be right but I must ask you to refer to His Grace by his proper title."

"To a Highlander it is MaCaileen Mor."

"And to my wife, the Duke of Argyll!"

They faced each other, tense, pride on both sides, and then, without knowing who made the first move, she was in his arms again.

"To hell with the Duke!" he muttered and set his lips hard on hers. Passion rose in him, so that he was shaking with it and his demanding mouth, his skilled hands finally drove the tall powerful figure of MaCaileen Mor, Duke of Argyll, from both their minds.

Chapter 11

On the morning after the ball Donald came downstairs to an empty
breakfast room. Sir Rupert and Lady Astley were not yet down,
Thomas the footman told him, and Sir Laurence and Lady Everard
were breakfasting in their own room. Lord Rawdon seldom appeared
before noon so Donald, refusing sliced cold beef, sat down to a solitary
roll and coffee. The footman brought him the latest news-sheet and he
was turning the page idly when an item of information caught his
attention. It seemed that a certain Alexander Murray was in trouble
with the House of Commons for refusing to kneel and ask pardon for
a disturbance he had caused during the recent elections. Donald gave
an exclamation and read on, for Alexander Murray was on his list of
people to be visited. Mr. Murray was the brother of Lord Elibank,
both Jacobites but inclined to stay on the fence, and Neil MacEachain
had specifically mentioned them as two who might be firmly pushed
to come down on the Prince's side. The report however was brief and
merely said that Mr. Murray had protested that a candidate of his own
political leanings had been forced out of his place, and the writer
trusted that such disturbers of the peace would soon see the error of
their ways.

Donald laid the paper down. How far, he wondered, would such
men as the Murray brothers and Sir William and James Chandler be
prepared to go? It was difficult to say—and he was still brooding on
these thoughts when the door opened and Samuel appeared to say that
his master would be grateful if, when Mr. Fraser had finished his
breakfast, he would be kind enough to spare him a few moments.
Surprised, Donald drank down the last of his coffee and followed the
valet upstairs. He had not been in Lord Rawdon's bedroom before and
for a moment it seemed that the room was in darkness, but it was
merely that the curtains were drawn against the morning light. The
large bed seemed to occupy half the room and his lordship, leaning
against a mountain of pillows, was wearing, in a somewhat bizarre
fashion, a white turban on his bald head. Donald wondered what he
could possibly want. Had he heard of the difference of opinion last

night? But the face beneath the white nightcap betrayed nothing but a pleasant smile.

"It is very kind of you to come up to me," Lord Rawdon said. "I trust you will forgive me for receiving you thus, but I found last night somewhat tiring and my doctor has laid strict injunctions upon me as to the hours I must spend in bed."

"Of course, my lord. Is there anything I may do for you?"

"I hope it is the other way about. Pray sit down, Mr. Fraser—there in that chair beside me—I cannot conduct our talk while breaking my neck to look up at you."

Donald smiled a little and sat down as he was bidden. He liked the courteous old man and was never inclined to be on the defensive as he was in his son's more astringent company.

Lord Rawdon surveyed him for a moment. Then he said, "Your sister told me some while ago what happened to your home—Duirdre? I trust I pronounced the name correctly? It occurs to me," he paused aware of the change of expression wrought on the face opposite by the mention of that name, "it occurs to me that I might be of some service to you concerning it."

"Of service?" Donald queried, aware how his voice had sharpened. "In what way, sir?"

Lord Rawdon smoothed the rich tapestry quilt over his knees. His gout was extremely painful this morning, though he would not for one moment have admitted it. "I have no desire," he went on, "to interfere in your private affairs, but I have become extremely fond of my daughter-in-law and that emboldens me to broach the subject." He glanced briefly at the still figure before him and went on, "I don't know whether you chanced to meet him last night, but no doubt you saw the Duke of Argyll during the evening. He is an old acquaintance of mine and I might speak to him about the restoration of your home, or perhaps Mr. Pelham would—" He stopped, for a deep flush had flooded the cheeks of Bab's brother. "What is it, Mr. Fraser? I had the impression that you were deeply attached to your home, that you wanted it back."

"I did—I do." Unable to remain sitting still Donald got up and walked to the window where he stood with arms folded, looking out through the narrow space where the curtains did not quite meet. It was cloudy today, the air heavy, the garden still and windless, and someone had turned off the little fountain.

He was too dumbfounded to say anything. To be offered the chance to have Duirdre back, even if it meant receiving it at the hands of the

Campbell was something he had never dreamed of when he first came to this house, and for a few moments his mind refused to function.

"Of course I realize," Lord Rawdon was saying to his back, "that such a restoration brings its price. I am not entirely unacquainted with Scottish affairs and I know that you would have to swear a distasteful oath, that if you went back it would have to be without that sword at your side, that there would be other burdensome restrictions—but would it not be worth it?"

Donald stood so rigid that Lord Rawdon began to think him greatly offended, but the truth was that he was facing what was perhaps the hardest decision he had ever had to make. If it had come before he loved Marthe and knew that she loved him, then he would have refused it—such was his pride, he thought bitterly. But now—of course he wanted Duirdre back, even on the most humiliating terms, and he thought he could even stomach receiving it at the hands of the Campbell if it meant he could ask Marthe to be his wife. For one instant joy shot through him, and then was gone as rapidly. How in God's name could he do it at the moment? He was under Lord Rawdon's roof, yet he was plotting to overthrow that very ministry his lordship would approach on his behalf; he was plotting to dethrone the King whom Rupert served so closely, far more personally than he had realized. He was deeply committed to rousing sleeping Jacobites and doing it as a spy—a word he loathed and yet was forced to apply to himself, for anything useful that he heard in this house he would report to the Prince when he came. If he believed in his cause, he must do so, and he did believe in it. My God! he thought desperately, Neil had not known what he was doing when he sent him here—yet, even if he had known, Neil would have brushed his scruples aside. Take Duirdre, he would have said, and use it for His Highness when the time comes. But he was not Neil—he liked this old man who was waiting for an answer, this Whig house was his sister's home and her happiness was involved. On one side there was Duirdre held out to him—or the possibility of it and many Highlanders had now been allowed to return to their estates—and briefly he was back there, in the beloved place, seeing the mountain, the loch and the rowan tree. His house was burned but what joy to rebuild it if Marthe was to be its mistress! Yet on the other side of the coin there was honour—or what was left of that once prized commodity. Could he destroy the last shreds of it? Fighting this silent battle he was hardly aware that he had put both hands before his face in a wordless prayer for help. After a moment he heard the quiet voice again.

"Mr. Fraser, I trust I have not upset you by making the suggestion. Is it so hard a choice?"

Donald turned back to the bed. "My lord," he began hoarsely, "my lord, it is very good of you—I cannot express my gratitude but—there are things I have to consider. If—if I might have time—"

Lord Rawdon was shocked by a face so inexplicably ravaged. "My dear boy," he said gently, all formality gone. "I see I have inadvertently trodden upon ground I know nothing of. Believe me, I only wished to help you."

"I know, I know—and do not think me ungrateful." Hardly aware what he was doing Donald sat down again, his hands clasped tightly between his knees. "Would you think me very churlish if I waited a little while before deciding whether to avail myself of your generous offer?"

"Of course not. Take as much time as you wish." Lord Rawdon paused, his ready sympathy going out to this troubled young man. "Would you care to tell me about it?"

For the second time Donald was bereft of speech. If his lordship only knew what he was asking! And his need for advice, for that very sympathy, was such that he wished above all men he had met here in London that it was Lord Rawdon he could confide in. Yet Rupert's father was the last person to whom he could unburden himself. "You are very kind," he said at last in such a wretched tone that Lord Rawdon began to wish he had never broached the subject. "Believe me, my lord, when I say that if I could I would. No man could be more in need of guidance than I am, but I am not free—" he broke off. In a moment he would be saying too much. Somehow he got to his feet. "I will not forget that you offered me Duirdre," he went on in a low voice, "and if the time comes when I may accept it, I will trust that I have not been so thankless today that the door will no longer be open."

"It will be open," Lord Rawdon said. He was much moved. "I do not advise you, however, to wait too long. I am indeed a great deal better but I have the suspicion that my days are numbered and," he smiled a little, "my son has not the influence that I have, nor perhaps the tact to use it if he had." He had meant the remark to be encouraging, to help the young man to make up his mind, but to his distress, he saw another wave of scarlet colour those pale cheeks. He gave a heavy sigh. The young were so vulnerable, he thought, passing through vicissitudes he had long left behind and despite his gout and his sickness he did not envy them. He wondered what had caused that deep flush. Had his son fallen out with Bab's brother? He would not be surprised if he had, for Donald Fraser was hardly the cast of man to fit into Rupert's way of life. Yet he had hoped—he sighed again and said, "Think it over, Mr. Fraser, at your leisure."

Donald bowed. For the life of him he could say no more. He left the room and went to his bedroom where he sat on the edge of his bed for nearly an hour, clenching and unclenching his hands on the rich silk coverlet.

At last he went downstairs, meaning to go out, out of this house, anywhere where he might think more freely. He was tempted to go to Fergus, talk the thing out with him, but that would entail speaking of Marthe and this he did not want to do. He had not even spoken of her to Bab.

He had just made up his mind to walk in the park and had his hand on the knob of the front door when to his annoyance his brother-in-law came down into the hall. Rupert was in uniform and pulling on one glove, his hat under his arm.

"Good morning," he said abruptly, and then as Donald answered his greeting with equal brevity he paused on the bottom step. "I think I owe you another apology," he went on in a tone that revealed how distasteful he found that operation. "I said some harsh things last night—or so I understand."

Donald stood where he was. Even in his preoccupation he too was aware that this had not been an easy speech and wondered if Bab had urged her husband to it. He regarded this man she had married for a moment before answering. Then he said, "Perhaps the fault was mine. I had no right to refuse to meet a guest of yours—whatever my personal feelings."

"If I had considered the matter, I would not have put you in such a position," Rupert answered frankly. "I must admit that at the time it did not enter my head."

"I think it is I who put you in an awkward situation," Donald spoke with equal honesty. "I should not have come here."

"Should not have come?" Rupert repeated. "My dear Fraser, Bab wanted to see you more than anything in the world. She wanted you to know—" he broke off and a half smile crossed his face. "Whatever we may have felt privately we were both thinking of her, were we not?" On an impulse he held out his hand. "And I am glad you came. You may not believe it, but this morning I am inclined to admire your candour of last night."

The Highlander hesitated, but only for a moment. Then he came across the hall and took the outstretched hand. "You are generous, Major."

Slightly embarrassed, Rupert began to pull on his second glove. "I must go or I shall be late. I have to walk with His Majesty in the park—did you know that was one of the duties of a Guards officer? Probably not—but it is a very boring one, I assure you. I'm afraid Bab is tired after last night, you won't see her before noon. Were you going out?"

"Yes—I was also about to walk in the park."

Rupert gave him a keen glance. "Of course, to think over what my father has suggested. Yes, I have just seen him and he has told me what he proposed to you."

Donald gave him a sharp glance and was suddenly sure that Lord Rawdon had indeed said no more than that, had not spoken of the distress he had betrayed.

Rupert opened the door and held it for his guest to pass through. "I beg you to accept, Fraser—for many reasons." He gave him a sudden smile, bowed and was gone down the steps to where a groom held his horse, leaving Donald staring at his scarlet back.

The day passed, with his mind in such a state of turmoil that he was hardly able to attend to the afternoon's business with Fergus. They called on Lord Elibank and were received courteously but to little advantage. "If we achieve our aim he will say he was always for the Prince, and if we do not, why, he will assure Mr. Pelham he never committed himself," Donald said with rare bitterness. "His brother is a hothead and may be more trouble than he is worth. I am beginning to wonder, *mo caraid,* if we are wasting our time and the Prince's slender funds."

Fergus shrugged. "You may be right, but until we receive other directions what else can we do? At least, if His Highness does come, he will be comfortably lodged with Lady Primrose. I swear she would withstand a troop of the Guards if they came knocking at her door!"

A wry smile crossed Donald's face. "Led by my brother-in-law, no doubt. She is a very great lady." But the stout heart of one old lady was not going to further their cause, and in a lightning shaft of self-perception, he wondered whether, in the knowledge of Lord Rawdon's offer, he had sunk so low as to want it to fail. In a state of distraction he left Fergus and walked for some hours round the city, losing himself in the crowds, now in a wide street of fine houses, now in a squalid alley where dirty children and scrawny dogs scrambled together in the filth. At last, having walked himself into a state of exhaustion in which he could no longer think, he returned to Astley House, to fall so deeply asleep that his valet had to shake him awake to warn him it was near the supper hour.

For a week he was racked with indecision. He spent much of his time with his mother and Bab, rode with Rupert in the park, attended a concert and a play, but his mind was only half upon what his body was doing. Even the fact that he dined with Lady Primrose and her guest of honour turned out to be none other than the present Prince of Wales impinged on him less than it would have done otherwise.

Frederick of Hanover made himself pleasant to the exiled Scot, was gallant to his elderly hostess and talked in general terms of his favour towards the Tories. But neither Donald nor Fergus believed that Cumberland's brother had any intention of doing more than annoy his family by flirting with the Jacobite cause.

Georgiana's wedding at the end of this week was a sumptuous affair and she was a radiant bride, Philip quietly happy. Another love match, Donald thought, as his sister's was—although in Georgiana's case it had long been arranged. He listened to the words of the marriage service and lost himself in thoughts of Marthe. Here in this London church she seemed far away and elusive and the sight of Georgiana coming down the aisle on his cousin's arm only heightened his sense of his own burden.

The decision, finally, was taken out of his hands. On the following morning after a breakfast at which, with the exception of Lord Rawdon, they were all present, Laurence Everard followed Rupert into the hall, requesting a few moments of his time in the library. Donald sat on, drinking his coffee and only half listening to his mother and Bab chattering about the proposed visit this evening to Vauxhall Gardens.

"I used to go there in my girlhood," Lady Caroline was saying, happily reminiscing, "always so pretty with the lanterns in the trees and one was certain of meeting acquaintances there. Your grandfather knew so many people and he used to say——" She broke off, startled by the sudden sound of angry voices raised in the hall, the slamming of a door, and a moment later her husband came into the room. He was even redder in the face than usual and his expression was one of smouldering fury.

"Madam," he addressed himself to his wife, "you will please see that our clothes are packed immediately. We are leaving for St. Albans at once."

Lady Caroline gaped at him. "But—but we were to stay until next week."

"Please do not argue," he said sharply. "Have the goodness to do as I bid you."

She rose uncertainly. "I don't understand. Nor do I wish to go home yet."

Everard held the door open. "If you please, madam—your wishes have nothing to do with it."

Donald got to his feet. "My mother's wishes have a great deal to do with it," he said coldly. "Permit me to tell you I find your tone offensive."

Everard glared at him. "I shall use any tone I choose to my wife, and you, young man, can mind your own business. It occurs to me it would have been very much better if you had remained in France."

"I have no doubt you think so, but if you imagine you can ride roughshod over my mother while I am here—"

Bab also had risen from her chair and came round to stand beside her mother. "Mama, you do not have to go because he wants to leave. Surely you at least can stay until next week as we planned. I'm sure Rupert or Donald would escort you home."

Sir Laurence barely glanced at her. "Your mother is not remaining for one more moment under this roof. Caroline, pray tell your maid to pack your gew-gaws this instant."

She made as if to obey, but Donald caught and held her arm. "No, my dear Mother, wait if you please. You, sir, are, as I am, a guest in this house and my sister is entitled to some sort of explanation."

Sir Laurence folded his arms. "Do you think so? Well, if you insist on knowing why we are leaving, my girl, I suggest you ask your precious skin-flinty husband."

"Oh!" Bab gasped angrily. "Rupert is the most generous of men. How can you—"

"Generous?" he interrupted. "He'd rather see me in the Clink than make me a loan. I've got to get out of town in consequence. Caroline!" He indicated the door, but Donald who by now had grasped what must have happened, came to stand between his mother and her furious husband.

"Do I understand that you are so much in debt that you have the Runners after you?"

"A few paltry thousand," Everard snorted, his indignation getting the better of what discretion he had, "but the devil is in it, I haven't got it and I've been hard pressed. However Major Astley seems to have no objection to his father-in-law being clapped up in a debtors' prison."

"You mean you asked Rupert for the money?" Bab queried. "To pay your gambling debts?"

"Yes, and he turned me down, curse him. Since he married you, miss, he has had a great deal more than that at his disposal and it would not have hurt him to put his hand in his pocket for me, considering—" he broke off, eyeing her malevolently. "Well, it will no doubt take them some time to catch up with me if I'm out of town and I'll have to find a way—"

Donald gave him one disgusted look. "Had you no thought for the distress you would cause my mother? Surely you owe it to her not to get involved in such folly?"

Everard turned on him. "I'm surprised you are so dense. It is owing to her father's meanness—crazy old man that he was—that I am in this position at all. He left your mother a pittance and all that wealth to this chit and that dull cousin of yours who will have no idea how to use it." He gave a harsh laugh. "You and I are in the same boat, young man, and I wonder that you do not find it as intolerable a craft as I do."

"By God!" Donald could scarcely contain himself. "You are beyond everything, sir. I suppose my grandfather had a right to do as he wished with his own property?"

"Oh, a right maybe, but what of his duty? He led me to think when I married your mother—"

It was Donald's turn to be sarcastic. "Whatever he may have led you to think he must have very soon realized what you would do with a fortune had you laid hands on one."

"No worse than Major Astley," Sir Laurence retorted, "except that he has too much damned luck: he plays the cards and the horses as much as I do. And why that wench there—"

With surprising deliberation, Lady Caroline rose. "I think, Laurence, we will not go into all that again. We really have quite enough for our needs, you know, if you would but restrain your pleasure at the tables." She laid a hand on her son's arm, pressing it a little. "Pray don't say any more, Donald, not now. It is obviously better for us to go." And as Sir Laurence opened the door once more for her, she added in a low voice, "I know him, my dear, and I can manage him quite easily. Very well, Laurence, I am coming. Will you have the goodness to order the carriage? Bab, dearest, perhaps you will help me?"

Bab exchanged one astonished glance with her brother. They had both expected tears and recriminations during this interview, however, Bab had not lived in Sir Laurence's house for two years without knowing that her mother did indeed seem to have the knack of handling him, and she followed her out of the room while Sir Laurence went into the hall, shouting for his carriage to be brought round at once, leaving Donald alone in the dining room.

He paced up and down, seething inwardly, the silence only broken by the steady rhythmic ticking of the pretty china clock on the mantleshelf. He wondered how his mother could tolerate such a man, how she could be seemingly unperturbed by his tempers, his debts, even the prospect of Bow Street Runners arriving on her doorstep. Remembering Duirdre and his father, he found it inexplicable. Never for one moment did it occur to him that, much as she had loved her first husband, she had never liked the Highlands, that she was not sorry to be back where she felt she belonged, that she would rather have such a husband as Laurence Everard than no husband at all.

It was twenty minutes later that Bab and her mother came back into the room. Through the open door Donald could see two footmen carrying out a trunk under the direction of its owner, and he came forward to take his mother in his arms, his indignation rising again.

"Are you sure you wish to go?"

"Quite sure," she reassured him. "It is for the best. Perhaps Major Astley was right to refuse him—and Bab thinks so, do you not, my dear?"

"Mama," she said in a low distressed voice, "Rupert must have had good reason. I shall ask him later, and then write and tell you—"

Her mother gave a little sigh. "Perhaps another time your stepfather will not be so foolish. I have told him so often that his gambling will ruin us and maybe now he will heed me." She broke off with a bright smile. "Well, never mind. This is not the first time he has been in such trouble and we shall no doubt come out of it. You will come and see me before you return to France, will you not, Donald?" And when he promised he would try to do so, she smiled up at him and patted his hand. He kissed her gently and Bab leaned forward to tie the strings of her cloak. There seemed to be no more to be said.

At that moment Rupert came into the room followed by his father-in-law. "I very much regret, madam," he said stiffly, "that you should be leaving us like this. I would not have had it happen for the world." He ignored a sound like a snort from Everard, and went on,

"Pray allow me to hand you to your carriage." He held out his arm and Lady Caroline took it. She gave her son and daughter one last reassuring smile and then left the room with him.

Sir Laurence regarded Donald and Bab, left standing side by side. "I'm quite sure you are more than pleased to be relieved of my company," he remarked sarcastically, "and let me add the feeling is mutual."

"You had better go," Donald said. "I hope we shall not have to meet again, but as far as my mother is concerned, I warn you——"

"No, sir! I warn you." Everard had moved to the door but at that he came back to face them. "You're a precious pair," he added viciously. "You, miss, have the impertinence to put on that self-righteous air and defend your husband's meanness—especially after all the money he's had out of me. He has a strange way of collecting debts, has the Major."

Bab was staring at him. With cool dignity she said, "You have caused a hateful scene in my house and I shall be happy to see you leave, sir, but before you do I would like to know what you mean by that."

"Yes," Donald agreed grimly. "No doubt you have owed money at one time or another to most gentlemen in this town but pray tell us how Major Astley differs from your other creditors."

"It would be much better not," said a cold voice from the doorway and they turned to see Rupert standing there, his face dark with anger. "Sir, your lady is in your carriage and I believe it is better not to keep the horses standing."

Everard flushed at the supercilious tone and then as his eyes darted from one to the other he rocked back on his heels, stuck his hands in his pockets, and a malevolent smile crossed his florid face. "Well, my young friends! You stand there looking at me as if I were something off a midden, but you had better not start throwing mud at me—no, by God, or I shall have something to say!"

Rupert stepped forward. "Go," he said between tight lips, "go or I will have you thrown out."

"Oh no, you won't." Everard shook his head. "Not until I've had my say. We made a bargain, yes, but since you chose to treat me more like a beggar than a gentleman this morning, I hold that I am absolved from it. I think it is time you all heard a few truths."

"No! Damn you, I forbid it." Rupert's voice cracked across the room so sharply that Donald looked at him in surprise.

"What is all this?" he demanded.

"You may well ask," Sir Laurence agreed. He was beginning to enjoy himself. "Tell your sister to ask that high and mighty husband of hers just how he acquired her hand."

Bab gave a start but before she could speak Rupert said, a little too loudly, "Take no notice of him, he is talking nonsense. If you please, Sir Laurence—" he indicated the door.

"Nonsense, is it?" Everard queried and made no move towards it. "When her dowry was won over a Hazard table?"

"*What!*" Hardly able to believe what he had heard, Donald instinctively put his arm about his sister as she gasped, every vestige of colour receding from her face, and he turned to see what Rupert would say to such an astonishing accusation.

But Rupert it seemed was not going to answer or explain. He too had gone very pale. "Damn your soul to hell," he said in a low voice. "Is this all your word was worth?"

Everard looked from one angry young man to the other and laughed. "A forced bond, Major. And before that wench's brother flies at your throat you might as well know that if you have lied so, by God, has he! Ask him what he does at the White Cock, ask him why he visits such people as Lord Elibank, ask him why he rides in the Earl of Westmorland's coach."

Donald loosened his hold on Bab. "Have you been spying on me?" he demanded furiously.

"I am not the spy," Sir Laurence answered cryptically. "In fact I hardly think Astley will want you in his house when he inquires more closely into your political activities. He should have kept his eyes open—as I did."

"What in God's name are you talking about?" Rupert asked sharply. His eyes, a sharp flinty blue now, flickered from one to the other.

"Oh, I am sure Fraser will explain." Sir Laurence swung his cloak about his shoulders and swaggered to the door, well pleased with the effect his words had produced—it was almost, he thought, worth having the Runners after him to have achieved this. "You need not fear I shall enter this house again," he said pompously, and glancing at the brother and sister added, "As for that pretty pair, you're welcome to them."

"Get out!" Rupert snapped. "Get out, curse you, before I lose my temper."

"My pleasure, sir," Everard retorted mockingly. He clapped his hat on his head. "Neither of you *gentlemen* need show me out. And by the way, Fraser, you might on your side ask him what he was doing with a troop of Barrell's regiment in '46." And with that parting shot he went out and they heard the street door close behind him.

Chapter 12

For a moment the three left in the dining room neither moved nor spoke. In the silence that followed they heard a carriage drive away. Rupert walked over to the hearth and stood with his arms folded, his face white. The clock ticked on and it seemed as if no one was willing to break the silence, but at last Bab spoke in a dry, almost toneless voice.

"Was that true—what he said—about my dowry? It could not be—it must have been a lie. Yet why should he say it? Rupert—"

"I think we would do much better to ignore all his accusations," Rupert said with a not very convincing attempt to sound casual. "You must know him better than I do, and even I can see his bluster seldom amounts to anything." He leaned his shoulders against the mantleshelf, but he looked uneasy, or so it seemed to Donald.

He had not moved from his place beside Bab. "I do not think we can dismiss it as lightly as that." An instinctive feeling that whatever was now coming to light was going to be unpleasant made him add, "Would it not be better, *m'eudail*, if you went to your room and left us to discuss this?"

She shook her head. "No. It is very much my affair. Rupert," she looked straightly at her husabnd, "if it is just bluster and malicious bluster at that, why did he make up such a ridiculous lie? He must have had some reason. Can you not tell me?"

He shrugged his shoulders. "There is nothing to tell, Bab, I can assure you."

"I think there must be," she said quietly. "What did he mean about the Hazard table? Rupert, don't you see? If you don't explain I shall always have this uncertainty on my mind."

He turned away, leaned one arm on the mantelshelf, one foot on the fender, his back half towards them. Then he gave a little laugh. "It seems Harry was right after all. Perhaps I should have told you. Very well, you shall have the truth—though it would have been better not. Please try to believe me."

"I will try."

He began to speak, staring down at his booted foot on the bright brass of the fender. "It is perfectly true that I won a great deal from your stepfather and on that particular night the game developed into a sort of duel between us. I admit I had always disliked the man and I thought if I could drive him in too deep maybe it would rid us of his company at White's. It was the night of Lady Denby's ball—you remember, Bab?"

"I remember," she said but there was an expression of growing fear and anxiety on her face. "How could I forget that evening?"

"Nor I," he said. "I admit I asked Georgy to present me to you because," he paused, the colour deepening in his face," because I told her I was looking for an heiress who might be beautiful as well." He saw the expression on both their faces. "Oh, it was partly a joke, but perhaps I did mean it. Only when I danced with you and we talked I knew I must see you again. I came riding with you the next day, didn't I?"

"Dear God!" Donald said. "Because she came up to your requirements?"

"If you like, yes!" Rupert retorted violently. He raised his head and his mouth was set in a hard line. If they wanted the truth they should have it and he—he would stand or fall by it and by what had happened since. But beneath that defiance, he too was afraid. Who was it who was foolish enough to say the truth never hurt anyone? He folded his arms across his chest and faced them, recounting every detail of that night and the game of Hazard and his own outrageous idea that Bab's inheritance might cancel out Sir Laurence Everard's debt.

Donald was staring at him in shocked consternation. "And while all this was going on, was White's as crowded as I've seen it? Do half the men in London know the shameful way in which my sister's marriage was arranged?" He broke off, imagining the ribald laughter that such a scene would evoke at the club. Bab gave a little cry and put both hands to her face.

Rupert took one step towards her and then restrained himself. "No," he said, "I swear it. Nearly everyone had gone by the end, and anyway they only knew that I had found a way to settle the affair other than by calling the man out. The fact that we were betrothed some time later was quite another matter. At least," he raised his head, "no one had the impertinence to suggest otherwise to me."

"How can we believe you?" Donald asked slowly. "I can well imagine—"

"I do not lie."

"Do you not? A few minutes ago you assured Bab there was nothing to tell and yet here you are giving us a preposterous tale that, if Bab had known of it, would have convinced her never to speak with you again."

"Damn you," Rupert said. "Everard understood me well enough but we did not discuss it at the time, not until we were private. Only Harry knew, and Simon—I never told my father how it all began."

Bab's hands fell. "Then it has all been a sham, you took me to pay a debt."

"And if that is true," Donald began, "by God, if that is true——"

"It is not!" Rupert flung the words at them. "Allow me to finish. Bab," he looked directly at her, his defences gone, "Bab, it was true at the beginning that I was not going to let Everard slide out of his debt to me, that I suggested your handsome dowry would more than cancel it but even then I knew I wanted you—for other reasons. And by the time we had met in the park on several mornings and once, I think, at Georgy's house, I knew that I would have no other woman for my wife. You must believe that—Bab," he gave her a look charged with meaning, "you cannot doubt that."

Her face was still and cold. "Perhaps you do love me now—I know that you desire me, but I also know you took me in payment of a gambling debt, because you did not want to lose your money. It's horrible." She shivered suddenly, "And at least two of your friends know, but you never told me, you never trusted me enough for that."

"I did not want to risk losing you. Now I wish to God I had told you."

"I wish you had too," she said with a catch in her voice. She was quite calm still, but her hands were twisted together. "I don't think I shall ever be able to trust you again."

"Bab," he cried out, "for the love of heaven, don't throw away our happiness because of this—and we have been happy, you know that. You can't deny it." She shook her head mutely. "And if you had never found out——"

"But she does know," Donald put in. "She does know, and nothing can alter that. I had begun to think your reputation perhaps less than deserved, but now I see that you must have more than earned it."

Rupert swung round on him angrily. "My past, such as it was, has nothing to do with this. I admit the whole affair at White's sounds crassly stupid and irresponsible but afterwards, when I came to know

Bab, I would have married her had your grandfather treated her as he treated you!"

"That is easy to say now," Donald retorted. "If she had been a penniless exile I doubt if you would have asked Miss Milne to present you."

"I am not interested in what you think. Bab?"

She turned towards him, clutching at anything that might save the brief happiness she saw crumbling away. "However it began," she said slowly, "I do believe that, Rupert."

"Nevertheless," her brother said inexorably, "he built your marriage on a lie. Can you imagine that our father would have given you to such a man?"

"If it comes to lying," Rupert turned on him, "I think you owe me an explanation. Of what was Everard accusing you? You told me you had one or two exiled friends in London but not that they included Lord Elibank and the Earl of Westmorland." His eyes narrowed as he remembered something. "And Harry said he had seen you on the steps of Lady Primrose's house. I told him he must have been mistaken—though it is not easy I suppose to mistake a man of your height—and now I see that he was probably right."

Donald inclined his head. "I have the honour to be acquainted with Lady Primrose, though I cannot conceive that it is any business of yours."

"And the Earl of Westmorland, and the rest?"

Donald nodded again but he said nothing, and Rupert began to stride up and down, flinging questions at him. "And you visit the White Cock frequently? Oh, don't trouble to deny it, I'm sure you have many *friends* there—but what the devil do you do in that iniquitous haunt? You told me you spent your time seeing the town, but it seems you have spent it in the most notorious Jacobite society. I am very sure it is you who owe me an explanation."

Bab's hand tightened on Donald's arm but he gave no sign of noticing it. "What else did you expect?" he asked calmly. "I have never denied I am a Jacobite."

"No," Rupert retorted, "but while you were our guest I would have expected you to restrain yourself from doing what you must know would cause deep offence to both my father and myself."

"You can hardly be surprised that I have resorted to those who share my political opinions. I cannot see that that is so offensive."

"You make it sound very innocent, but you know very well that these people are suspect. I consider, sir, that you have abused our hospitality and my father will do so too. In fact I think it likely that his offer of assistance concerning your Scottish acres will be withdrawn."

Donald's face was dyed scarlet. "As to that, Major, it is for Lord Rawdon to say, and I think I would rather trust myself to his judgement than to yours." For a moment he paused, looking out into the street beyond. People were passing about their business, unaware of the crisis being enacted behind these windows. He heard a girl calling out "Sweet lavender for sale. Fresh cherries—who'll buy?" and he saw her rosy face briefly as she passed. Why in God's name had he ever come to this city to be involved in subterfuge and lying? And lie he must. At last he said, "Believe me, I had no wish to abuse your hospitality."

"No? If it were merely a few impoverished Scottish gentlemen haunting the White Cock I suppose it would be tolerable, but Westmorland and Elibank! There is more here than meets the eye. Everard called you a spy—was he right?"

"You may choose to insult me in your own house," Donald retorted, "but I will not tolerate that epithet."

"Why not? It is well known that Lady Primrose gathers at her house men and women who would be glad to see the Pretender restored, and I suppose it is not all mere talk."

At the sound of that derogatory name Donald gave up all hope that the present intolerable situation between them might be healed. He saw Bab give him one anguished glance and shook his head imperceptibly. "No, child," he said, "I cannot deny my King. You may as well know, Major, that as long as there is breath in me I shall live and work and pray for the restoration of His Majesty King James III who is the rightful sovereign of your country and mine."

"The rightful king is on the throne," Rupert flared.

"As far as I am concerned," Donald said, "the throne is occupied by the Elector of Hanover."

Rupert gasped. "How dare you use that name in this house? You will withdraw it, or leave at once."

"Stop—stop, both of you!" Bab stepped between them as if she feared swords might be drawn there and then. "I will not have you quarrel—I cannot bear it."

"I have no intention of quarrelling," Rupert said bitingly, "but your brother will either apologize for the way in which he referred to His Majesty or else he will go. No traitor is going to stay under my roof."

"Can't you understand?" his wife cried out. "He fought for the Prince, he has sacrificed everything for his sake—how can you expect him to deny that loyalty? Rupert—"

Donald caught hold of her arm. "You need not beg for me, Bab. Obviously, like Sir Laurence, I am no longer welcome in this house. I am sorry, *m'eudail*, but this was inevitable from the beginning. You must have known it when you chose a man who was not only a Whig but a *saighdear dearg*, an officer in the Elector's Guards, and apparently a liar as well."

"Be silent," Rupert broke in furiously, "or it is I who will forget the laws of hospitality that I understood, mistakenly it seems, you Highlanders set such store by. I wonder how much of your activities your sister knew of—she was bred up in the same school as yourself."

Bab gave a little sharp cry and Donald put his arm once more about her. "You damned dog! Leave her out of this, she knows nothing."

Rupert glanced from one to the other. "Then," he said in a voice heavy with meaning, "I was right in assuming there was something to know. But as I presume you will not tell me we will leave that for the moment—I will talk to Bab later. As for you, Fraser, do you apologize or do you leave?"

"You surely did not expect an apology?" Donald enquired mockingly. "You will not get one, I assure you." He glanced down at his sister, seeing her white face, the utter misery in her eyes. It was as if all the radiance, all the gaiety of spirit that had been one of the things he had so loved about her, had been crushed out of her. But whatever he thought of Rupert Astley the man was her husband and though he would dearly have liked to have suggested he and Rupert settle their score wherever London's duels were fought, he must give them at least a chance to mend what had been broken. He turned back to his brother-in-law. "It seems to me it should be the other way about, it is you who should be on your knees to Bab. Perhaps if I go you will get into that uncomfortable posture—figuratively anyway."

He laid his hand on Bab's shoulder, pressing it briefly and then went out, closing the door behind him. Bab sat down suddenly in her chair by the table, amid the remains of their breakfast, staring at the empty coffee cups, the crumbs on her plate, and it seemed to her that the shambles of that meal was an expression of what had been done in this room to her happiness. She was trembling, her lace handkerchief twisted between her fingers but she was dry-eyed, the horror of this morning's revelations taking her beyond tears.

Rupert stood silent. When a little shiver went through her he made a movement as if to go to her, to take her in his arms, but he did not cross the space between them. For the first time in his life he was faced by a direct result of his own arrogance and self-assurance and it was a situation he was not familiar with. Furthermore he was confronted by emotions he did not know he possessed. At last, knowing the silence must be broken, he said, "Bab, will you listen to me? I am sorry matters have turned out as they have between your brother and myself—I see now it must have been inevitable—but at the moment it is you and I that I am concerned with. Will you hear me out?"

"Very well." She nodded and sat waiting for him to speak.

He stayed where he was, his hands clasped behind his back in his familiar attitude. "This is not easy to say and forgive me if I say it badly. I have been no better than most men—my father would say a great deal worse than some—but as far as you are concerned, I am telling the truth when I say that I knew almost at once that I loved you. But by then I had made the proposal to Everard—some devil was in me that I wanted to see him brought down and once it was started I could not—or would not—go back. And I wanted you more than I have ever wanted anything in my life."

"And the means were immaterial?"

He was stung. "If it had been distasteful to you I'd not have forced myself on you, but you know it wasn't so. Bab!"

She raised her head to look at him. "Oh, I know I made no secret of how I felt. Perhaps I seemed very young and foolish."

"No, no." He was across the space between them and kneeling beside her. "My darling, don't you know me a little now? If I kept some things from you it was only because I loved you, because I didn't want you hurt."

"It wasn't just that you wanted Everard brought down, as you said—or my fortune and," her mouth trembled, "what beauty I have?"

For answer he took her hands and put them both to his lips. "No, I swear it," he said tensely, "though you are beautiful, Bab. I'll not deny that was what made me notice you in the ballroom above all the others—that and, if we are being so honest, what Georgy told me of your being an heiress. My love, all I can do now is to ask you to forgive a piece of mad folly. I can't say that I am sorry, for it gave you to me for my wife and for that I shall never cease to be thankful. I did not deserve you, but I shall spend the rest of my life trying to mend that deficiency."

"I wish you had trusted me," she said wistfully, "but then you were not to know that I shared your feelings about Sir Laurence. Only if I had been aware from the beginning—"

"I know—I know. I regret it more than I can say. Bab—can you forgive?"

How could she not forgive, she wondered, when he knelt by her chair, looking at her with just that expression on his face. She leaned forward towards his arms, but at that moment the door opened and Rupert sprang up, cursing under his breath as his brother-in-law came back into the room.

Donald put his valise, cloak and hat on a chair. He saw the colour in his sister's face and the closeness of husband and wife as he entered the room had not escaped him. Yet he must ask this one last question. "Astley, before I leave, there is one other matter we must clear up. Everard said I should ask you about a certain regiment—Barrell's, was it not? Why? I understood you had always been in the Life Guards."

"He has," Bab said, "haven't you, Rupert? Harry told me you had both served together in the Grenadiers since '41." She put one hand to the little bow at her breast, clutching at the silk. Surely there was not more to come?

Her husband stood back from her chair, all the tenderness gone. "So we have. Anyway this is of no importance now."

Donald remained by the door, a curious certainty growing in his mind, a perception of something that was to be even more terrible than he could imagine . "I don't think it is of no importance. Sir Laurence must have had some reason for making that remark and it would be much better if we knew what had prompted him."

Rupert went back to the hearth, resting both hands on the mantelshelf, his eyes on the little clock. He noticed that the shepherdess painted on it had hair like Bab's. There was a silence and he stood hesitating until at length, without turning his head, he said, "Well, if you will pursue it, you may as well have it all."

"It would be as well," Donald answered in level tones. He sat down by Bab, and took her hand in his.

Rupert let out a long breath before he began. "There was a time when I was away from my regiment. I was—I was involved in a mild scandal that for some reason annoyed my father, so much so that he requested my Colonel to send me out of town for a while. General Blakeney was an old friend of his and then in command at Inverness, so Colonel Anderson agreed to second me temporarily to the General's staff as an aide-de-camp."

"When was this?"

"In '46, not long after we came back from the French campaign. I told you I had been in Scotland for a while."

"So you did," Donald agreed, "but not until after Culloden. I wonder if that is true or false. It is hard to know."

The veiled contempt in his tone made Rupert retort angrily, "That at least you do not have to take my word for. Any officer will tell you when we were recalled and when we landed. I could not have got there in time."

"Very well, we will accept that. What about your service with Barrell's? Why should Everard make such a point of speaking of it."

"I remember," Bab said suddenly. "One night, you mentioned that name, you asked me if I had spoken to an officer of Barrell's. I don't remember the name—"

"Captain Harding," Rupert said automatically, but she went on as if she had not heard.

"You were concerned whether I had talked with him—I see that now. Why? What was there between you? What could he have said to me that I should not hear?"

"Naught but a mouthful of spite." Rupert turned round to face them, a grim look on his face. "I had a slight disagreement with him, that's all, and Everard must have heard of it."

"What sort of disagreement? It must have been something of some moment to cause Everard to think we should know of it. And how did he connect it with what you had been doing in Scotland?"

Rupert himself had been searching for this key in his own mind and in a flash it came to him—he had seen Sir Laurence at White's one night talking to a certain Mr. Harding who was related to the Captain. He bit his lip—so that was it! Captain Harding had told his cousin of that day when Major Astley had relieved him of his command—rightly—but he must have elaborated on it and given Mr. Harding information that had eventually been recounted to Sir Laurence Everard. God in heaven, he thought, how could he have guessed that the tale of one incident, enacted far away in a remote area, could reach the very man to put it to such spiteful and destructive use? With an effort he said, "There was war between us then, Fraser. Let us not revive it in this dining room."

But it seemed it was too late. He could see his brother-in-law was not going to let the matter rest there.

"Nevertheless, Major, there are one or two things that are not clear. You say you were aide-de-camp to General Blakeney, of whom I know of course, but how did you come to be connected with Colonel Barrell? His name was linked with Hawley's and Scott's for brutality—oh, not personally perhaps, but he allowed his soldiers to murder and burn and plunder at will."

"It was war," Rupert said again. "There are aspects of it that even I do not like and I can find no excuse for what some of our soldiers did—beyond the plunder they were entitled to. But they were murdered too, out in the heather, and I myself found a man under my command with one of those hideous black knives in his back."

Like lightning Donald leapt on his words. "In the heather! But we understood you to say you were at Inverness, on General Blakeney's staff. What were you doing out in the heather?"

Too late Rupert realized his mistake. He let his hands fall to his sides, and giving up all attempt to circumvent the truth, he said, "General Blakeney was visiting the Earl of Albemarle at Fort William and I was on my way to join him when I came upon a company of Barrell's which had got out of hand. They had sacked a house, their captain was drunk and he had indulged in—well, I'll not go into that. I made use of my rank and took over his company and his orders. I knew I was not urgently needed and I saw that his orders were carried out before I took the men on to Fort William with me. And that is the full extent of my so-called action in Scotland."

"If that is true," Bab asked in a broken voice, "why was Everard so anxious that we should know of it?"

Rupert shrugged as casually as he could. "God knows how that man's mind works. Let us leave it at that."

"Not quite." Some instinct urged Donald on, to probe further, for that there was more to know he was certain. A fool his stepfather might be but not so stupid that he would have sown so deadly a seed if there was no fruit to come of it. "Where did this incident take place? Between Inverness and Fort William is a fairly extensive area."

Rupert did not answer immediately and Bab trembled suddenly so that she knocked over a cup and the dregs of coffee trickled slowly on to the white tablecloth. "Rupert—" she gave him one imploring glance, "for pity's sake, tell us all of it. I know what happened to our people after the battle—you say you prevented that officer from what he was doing, but did my stepfather confuse the report, think it was you who were in charge of that troop?"

"No," Rupert answered. At least he was not going to take that route of escape. He stared at brother and sister facing him. That Bab was his wife seemed to have been forgotten—now they were two

Highlanders confronting him, an alien, an Englishman. His resentment rose, "It happened as I have told you—what more do you want?"

Donald leaned both arms on the table, his chin on his fists, "I want to know what orders you carried out when you had arrested this drunken officer?"

"They were looking for your fugitive leader, as every troop was, and I would have been as glad as any to be the one to take him." Rupert lifted his head defiantly. "Captain Harding was following a certain rumour that the Pretend—" he changed the name hastily, "that Charles Stuart was in the hills to the west of the Great Glen and I had no choice but to pursue that possibility. And there were others we were looking for, Locheil, Cluny Macpherson. Oh," he saw the expression on their faces, "I know you did not think I had any part in the harrying that followed the battle, and God knows I did little enough, so why should I distress you, Bab, by telling you of the only incident I was involved in? But when I found myself in command of that troop, having put their officer under arrest, I could do no other than carry out their commission."

"And you turned west from Loch Ness?" Donald asked. "Did you go down Glen Urquhart or was it Glen Moriston, or further south still?"

"We started off down Glen Urquhart. After that—I can't remember. There were just tracks and streams and godforsaken mountains, all with unpronounceable names."

Donald ignored this attempt at lightness. "Try to remember. Astley, I must know."

"Why?" Rupert demanded. "What does it matter where it was? Haven't we gone into what was a singularly insignificant affair quite enough?"

Donald shook his head. He did not know what drove him on, but some instinctive urge was there and would not be satisfied. "Did you come upon a forest? And where was your man slain?"

His voice had grown sharp and in sudden terror Bab put both hands before her face.

"My dear Fraser," Rupert retorted sarcastically, "do you want a geography lesson? I'm afraid I can't give it to you. I spent a few fruitless days searching in wild country I'd never seen before and trust never to see again—and all to no purpose."

"To no purpose? Did you find no fugitives, take no prisoners?"

Rupert shook his head. "None. I told you one of my men picketing our camp was stabbed one night. We caught a rebel an hour later and shot him—that was all."

"And you found no one else, none of the men you were searching for?"

"You know the Prince was not taken, nor Locheil, nor his brother Dr. Cameron. Great God!" Rupert added in a blaze of anger. "Why will you go on and on?" His voice shook. "Do you think I liked any of it? Oh, we burned a croft or two, chased a few men up into a barbarous mountain and got nothing for our trouble but to be lost and wet and dirty. I am a soldier and I am trained to fight but I suppose I need not enjoy such a bloody aftermath. And but for those damned orders I would never have gone to—" he stopped abruptly and his breath hissed as he turned his back on them, both hands once again on the mantleshelf.

There was a frozen silence. Donald rose. He strode across to the hearth and caught his brother-in-law by the shoulders, swinging him round. "Look at me," he said in a voice stiff with horror. "My God, it can't be true! But I can see it in your face."

Terrified, Bab gasped, "What is it? What is it?"

"He burned Duirdre! I know it—Astley, for God's sake! It is true, isn't it?"

Rupert made no attempt to deny it, conscious of little but the iron pressure of Donald's fingers on his shoulders, the dark anger in the face confronting him. There was nothing left to say now.

"You burned Duirdre," Donald repeated in the same stupefied tone, and he did not even hear the stricken cry his sister gave for he was seeing again what had been done that hot afternoon four years before, the burning house, the troop of soldiers, the officer on horseback dismounting to see if the owner of the house was quite dead. And that officer was his brother-in-law, Rupert Astley, standing here before him, mute and white-faced.

"It was you—*you*! God in heaven!" The blood rushed to his head and a wild rage seized him. At last! At last he was confronting the man who had taken his father's life, and his hands leapt from Rupert's shoulders to his throat.

Half choking, Rupert tore at the fingers closing round his neck, but he could not loosen them and it was Bab who sprang up and in an endeavour to fling herself between them forced Donald to release him. "Stop, stop," she cried, "Donald, let him go—you'll kill him."

"I mean to," he said between clenched teeth. "I swore on my father's *biodag* to kill his murderer." But with his grip relaxed for a moment, Rupert had wrenched himself free, his hands at his bruised throat.

"I did not murder him—I swear I did not," he said hoarsely. "You were there—Bab said so—you saw it. One of the troopers fired and not by my order. If he had surrendered sooner—"

"Surrendered! You damned *sasunnach*, no Fraser of Duirdre would surrender. You killed him as surely as if you had fired at him yourself. And all this time you have known! All this time while I have been here—and you knew when you married Bab—"

In the last few moments neither had looked at her but now with eyes dilated in a white face she gave a little cry. "Oh no, no—I cannot bear it—" she whispered and slid to the floor.

Donald was at her side in a flash and lifting her into his arms, but when Rupert came to help he turned on him. "Keep away from her," he said with such ferocity that involuntarily Rupert stepped backwards. Donald laid her on a couch under the window and chafed her hands, but she had barely lost consciousness and almost at once struggled to sit up.

"Donald—" she clung to him, "is it true?"

He caught her hands and held them firmly. "It is all too true," he said and then began to speak rapidly in Gaelic. "Listen, *m'eudail*, I cannot stay here. I'll kill him if I do." She gave a quivering sob, but he went on, "I must go, I have work to do. Afterwards I'll deal with him. But as for you—"

She leaned against him, trembling, afraid to look up to where Rupert stood as though turned to stone. "What am I to do?" she asked, still in their native tongue. "What am I to do?"

"I don't know," he said helplessly. "I can't advise you or tell you what to do—he is your husband—but send to me at Fergus's lodgings if you need me."

He got slowly to his feet and as he did so, Rupert came forwrad uncertainly. "Bab—"

She shrank back, stricken. "Don't come near me—don't touch me. He was my father too." And then unable to control her weeping, she pressed her handkerchief to her mouth and ran from the room. A few seconds later a door banged upstairs.

Neither of the two men spoke. Donald put a hand to his forehead and, surprised to find it wet with sweat, wiped it impatiently. He was still shaking with the shock of discovery, with the desire for that revenge he had dreamed of in the years of exile. The instinctive loathing he had felt for Rupert's uniform at their first meeting became a blind, unreasoning fury, exacerbated by the sudden recollection that only a few days ago he had taken the man's hand in friendship. He dared not trust himself one more moment in this house and turning abruptly he crossed the room to snatch up his hat, cloak and valise. Then, without another word, he hurried out of the house and into the square where, with the door closed behind him, he stood by the iron railings drawing in deep breaths of fresh air. He looked so strange that a passing hackney coachman hailed him and asked if he wanted a ride. He shook his head and set off for St. Martin's Lane. He did not know where else to go.

Left alone in the dining room, Rupert went back to the hearth where he stood, his head bent, beating his fist again and again against the mantelshelf. Then he went up the stairs to his wife's room. What he was going to say he did not know, but though he knocked and called quietly to her she did not reply, and when he turned the handle of the door it did not yield. He came away down the stairs, his face ashen. It occurred to him that he was long overdue at the Palace. He took up his hat and he too left the house.

Chapter 13

Lord Rawdon considered that his doctor was a fool. He felt well this morning and apart from the permanent pain of his gout he came slowly down the stairs, determined to ask his daughter-in-law if she and her mother would care to drive out with him, perhaps as far as Kensington. However meeting Harper in the hall and enquiring for the Everards he was astonished to learn that they had gone.

"When was this?"

"About ten o'clock, my lord, Sir Laurence had his trunks packed and gave the coachman orders, I believe, for St. Albans."

"I see. And Mr. Fraser? Perhaps you would see if he is at home and request him to—"

"Mr. Fraser is gone too, my lord. He took his valise and left about an hour later."

Lord Rawdon raised one eyebrow, but showing no other sign of surprise repaired to the library. He waited in vain for his daughter-in-law and when the dinner hour came her maid Susan brought him the message that her mistress had a headache and would not come down today. He left instructions that his son was to be asked to come to the library immediately upon his return, but it was not until after five o'clock that he heard Rupert's voice in the hall. He came in at once and Lord Rawdon saw that he had a heavy frown on his face and was unusually pale.

"Ah," he said, and went on without preamble, "I should be glad, Rupert, if you would tell me why my house is entirely denuded of people. It seems that the Everards and Mr. Fraser are all gone and without the courtesy of informing me. It is still the custom, is it not, for guests to take farewell of their host?"

Rupert came across the book-lined room, pausing to pour himself a glass of brandy before answering. He had had a long and wearing day, unable to concentrate on his duties, which included a dress parade in the hot sun for the benefit of His Majesty; he had snapped at his men, been less than co-operative with Colonel Anderson, snubbed Harry Cavendish for mildly enquiring if he was not well, and used his whip viciously on his horse—the last act troubling his conscience more than the rest. His mind went over and over the scene in the dining room; he cursed his father-in-law until he ran out of words with which to do it, he cursed himself for his folly in trying to hide from Bab what was bad enough but had been made to sound even worse, and wondered why in the name of the Good Being his brother-in-law had to be so ardent a Jacobite. Plenty of men had gone quietly back to their homes and their occupations determined to put the upheaval of the Rising behind them—but not Donald Fraser, and he did not at this moment want to give any explanations to his father. He wondered how much he knew of this morning's quarrel. It was possible he had heard nothing, but perhaps Bab might have spoken to him. He asked if his father had seen her.

Lord Rawdon shook his head. "She sent her maid to say she was indisposed and would have a tray in her room. I dined alone. It was Harper who informed me of the departures. Perhaps now you will explain."

Rupert sat down, sipping his brandy with what he hoped was an unconcerned manner. "My father-in-law took it into his head to return home in a hurry—no doubt there is some particular race meeting he wishes to attend—and naturally he did not wish to disturb you so early."

"A very sudden decision. Nothing was said last night."

"Yes, it was sudden." Rupert hoped no further elaboration was necessary, but he was soon to be disillusioned.

"And Mr. Fraser? I had come to think he had better manners than most."

Rupert shrugged. "He merely said he must be on his way today. Quite why I can't say."

"I'm very sure you can," his father said shrewdly. "Whether you will or not is another matter." He saw his son's face take on a little colour. "My dear boy, do you take me for a fool? Bab's mother and brother leave the house without a word of warning or a farewell to me, Bab shuts herself in her room all day, and you expect me to believe none of that signifies? I am not in my dotage yet. Come, let us have the truth."

How many more times today, Rupert thought wearily, was that to be demanded of him? But he was not going to reveal it all and he sought hastily for a mixture of fact and fiction that might satisfy. "If you must know, sir," he said with an attempt at nonchalance, "it was merely that Everard had got himself deep into debt and I refused him a loan."

"Very wise," Lord Rawdon commented. "You would not have seen your money back."

"So I thought. But he took it very ill. Anyway he thought the Runners might be after him so he left."

"Well, if there is no more to it than that I cannot see why your mother-in-law who is always aware of the courtesies, did not at least send to inform me of her departure. And young Fraser—what sent him off?"

Rupert shrugged. "God knows. He has behaved rather oddly since your suggestion of last week. Perhaps he has gone north to pursue some business of his own."

"I do not believe," his lordship said emphatically "that he would do so, if that is the reason, without telling me. He seemed more than grateful for the proposal I made even if he did not feel able to accept it at once." He broke off and sat looking at his son until Rupert began to fidget as he had done as a small boy facing him over some misdemeanour. "Of course there is more to it than that. Bab has not had a headache nor shut herself in her room in all the months since she has been your wife. She is not the sort of woman to indulge in the vapours. Rupert!" his tone grew sharp. "You may not wish to tell me what has happened, but you will at least admit that something contrary occurred this morning."

"Very well. If you must have it, yes, there was a quarrel—a damned nonsensical quarrel begun by that fool Everard."

"And the subject of it? More than the loan, I imagine, to have involved Mr. Fraser as well." And as Rupert remained silent he added, "I am constrained to remind you that this is still my house. I think I am entitled to an explanation."

Rupert raised his head. "As far as Sir Laurence is concerned I have told you the cause of his argument with me—that it led to something further I'll not insult you by denying. I should have known it would be obvious."

"You should indeed. My main thought, however, is for your wife. I have not seen her today, though she had the politeness to send Susan to me. What have you done that she should lock herself away for the entire day?"

"I?" Rupert's mouth was twisted. "You assume it was I who was the cause of it."

"It seems likely," his father retorted coolly. "I know you fairly well, my son."

"You are not very complimentary—and never inclined to give me the benefit of the doubt," Rupert told him with a flash of bitterness.

"Past experience has led to that. While you were single and consorting with your gambling friends, I interfered very little. I even ignored your several duels, conducted I will admit with some discretion. However, I always drew the line at open scandal, and you will recall I had to request your Colonel to allow you to withdraw from London when you were involved in that reprehensible affair with—a Mrs. Alenby, was it not? A pretty woman but a devil of a husband and a connection of Sir George Carteret's into the bargain. How you could contrive to cause a scandal within two weeks of returning from the Continent, I cannot imagine, and you were fortunate that there was a war in Scotland where you could be sent with a minimum amount of fuss."

"Fortunate!" Rupert exclaimed under his breath. "If only you knew!" He had listened to this account of his character with growing irritation and now in a sudden flare of exasperation he flung his glass into the hearth. "Oh, enough, sir, if you please."

Lord Rawdon regarded the smashed pieces without having so much jumped at this startling action. "I see that you still cannot control your temper. A pity—that was one of a rather fine set of Dublin glass." He shifted his gouty leg so that he might sit more upright in his high-backed chair. "Now attend to me, Rupert. What I have said has been intended to indicate to you that though I tolerated a great deal from you in the past, your situation is very different now and I will not allow you to distress your wife. You have—God knows how—persuaded a girl of great character and charm to take you and I cannot believe you so lost to what is best in this world that you do not know that."

"I know it, but perhaps she did not know enough about me when she wed me. You have summed me up most accurately!"

"My boy, do you not see that it is because I do not want you to waste your life as you have done so far. A young man is allowed his wild days. You have had them and if I may allow myself rare latitude," his lordship smiled a little, looking up at the angry figure opposite him, "you have done much to redeem your excesses by your military career. There I have no complaint. Colonel Hay has told me many things which have made me proud that you are my son. I only wish you could extend such behaviour to your private life."

Rupert had flushed, all his normal self-confidence missing. He saw his father smile for the first time during this awkward interview, and at last he said, his own voice sounding strange to him, "All you say about me is true. Oh, I don't mean about the army. I don't know what Charlie Hay said but he always exaggerates, and anyway soldiering is different. It comes easily."

"Does it? All men do not find it so."

Rupert gave a little shrug. He was entirely without vanity in the field, finding a satisfaction among his brother officers and his men, and the worse the conditions the more he responded to them. It did not occur to him to see any virtue in it, only an outlet for something he did not recognize for what it was. At last he said, "You will admit, sir, that since I married, you have had no cause to complain of my private life."

"None," Lord Rawdon agreed readily, "until today. Well?"

"I can't deny I quarrelled, first with Everard and then with Fraser, and that was about his Jacobite loyalties. He was—extremely rude— and it seemed better that he should leave."

"No doubt you were less than polite yourself."

"Perhaps—but I'll not tolerate His Majesty being called the Elector in this house."

"Did he do that? Well, I suppose we should have known." Lord Rawdon sighed. "I had hoped to help him. So many have made their peace and only the most obstinate still hold to that lost cause." He glanced up at his son. "I am very sorry. It was a pity you could not have kept the whole subject from coming to light."

"My dear father, do not assume it was I who brought it up. I had come near to liking him, God help me, and I would rather his visit had passed amicably."

"You surprise me. Who then?"

His son glanced down at the hearth. "I am sorry about the glass," he said inconsequentially. "It was something Everard said that sparked the whole thing off. It blew up out of nothing and should be as easily forgotten."

"If it was out of nothing it had surprising consequences—that both Sir Laurence and Mr. Fraser immediately left the house. Rupert! I suspect you are being less than honest."

"I would rather not," his son said shortly, "go into the whole wretched business again."

There was a silence. Lord Rawdon stretched his other leg. "Very well," he said and his voice was cold. "But what of your wife? How did she take this quarrelling of yours? To have her mother and brother leave in such a fashion cannot have been pleasant. No wonder she has a headache."

Rupert's mouth tightened, but he said nothing and his father went on, "I have told you I will not tolerate any ill behaviour towards her. Come," Lord Rawdon paused, "you had best tell me. What else did you and Fraser say to each other to cause her such distress?"

Rupert flung away from his father and crossed the room to the door, his eyes blazing. "You may say what you like about my past, and as for Everard I'm sure you will not weep over his departure. Fraser is damned near a traitor and I'm glad he's gone. But as far as my wife is concerned that is my own affair, and I will not discuss it with you, nor anyone else for that matter."

Lord Rawdon sat very still. "You are quite right, of course. It is your affair. Well, I think I shall relieve you of my presence also and then perhaps you will mend matters. I shall go down to Rawdon tomorrow. Pray have the goodness to ring for Samuel. I shall take supper in my own room."

Rupert strode across to the bell rope and pulled it savagely. Then he went out and with surprising restraint did not slam the door—which said something for the respect in which he still held his father. The prospect of a solitary supper in the dining room, the scene of this morning's drama, was not appealing however and he went upstairs to his dressing room, pausing for one moment outside Bab's locked door. Then he walked past it, flung off his uniform, put on the coat Harper held out to him and departed to White's, where he spent the evening playing cards with his usual good fortune and getting very drunk.

"Reckless Rupert is back with us," some wit remarked, "perhaps the sweet bed of matrimony is beginning to lose its charms," but he received only an icy stare that effectively prevented any further such observations.

It was late when Rupert returned home and Astley House was in darkness. A sleepy footman opened the door to him and led the way up the wide curving staircase carrying a branched candlestick. In his dressing room he sat on his bed in silence while Harper pulled off his boots. His valet seldom spoke unless addressed but tonight he said, looking up at his master, "Sir—forgive me, but you do not seem quite yourself. Shall I prepare you a hot posset?"

"No," Rupert said. "I am perfectly well. Get on with it, Harper," and he held out his left foot. When he was undressed, Harper flung his nightshirt over his head and held out his flowered dressing gown; he was aware that the fumes of wine lay heavy on his breath, but he must go to Bab, he could not sleep in this lonely bed. He must go to her, tell her—something! Would she understand that he had not known until after their betrothal, that she had not mentioned the name of Duirdre until he was so deep in love with her that he dared not tell her the truth? He had taken a risk, and he knew it, but the possibility of her ever finding out that he had briefly taken command of a company of Barrell's, that it had led him into the hills around her home, was so remote that it was hardly worth considering. He had shut the past behind him, and it seemed to him that she had done the same. Not until her brother came had the old memories revived. His hands clenched. She must listen to him—it was the future that concerned them, not what had in that wild and mountainous country he had so disliked.

Harper began to fold away his clothes, and he went to their adjoining door without it occurring to him that it might also be locked. When it did not yield to him a wave of furious colour rose in his face. By God, she had locked him out, her own husband! She had bolted the door against him, and the shame of this discovery—in front of Harper—sent what sense he had left after the night's drinking out of his head.

"Get out, Harper," he said thickly. "Damn you, get out!" His valet bowed and withdrew, expressionless and Rupert stood where he was until the passage door closed, one hand against the jamb of the connecting door. Then he raised the other fist and banged loudly on it. He was greeted only by silence and at that, angry, jealous, bitterly resentful, he lost the remaining shreds of his temper. He launched his shoulder against the woodwork, remembering there was only a small bolt on the far side, and at his second attempt it splintered. The door opened wide to crash against a small gilt chair inside and then he was in the room.

There a candle was still burning and Bab was sitting up in bed, her dark hair about her shoulders, a small white night cap tied beneath her chin. Her eyes, wide and a little afraid, were fixed on the door, but with her hands clasped tightly about her knees, she said as calmly as she could, "What are you about, Rupert? Could you not see that I did not want to be disturbed tonight?"

He came, none too steadily, towards the bed. "That's rich!" he said and his speech was slurred. "You may not have wished to be disturbed, madam, but by what right do you bolt the door against me?"

She saw him clearly now. "You are drunk!" she exclaimed in astonishment. "Rupert! I've never seen you so. You had better go back to your dressing room. We can talk in the morning." But she had lain here for hours, going over and over that terrible scene in the dining room, and what was there to talk about? She had married the man responsible for her father's death, for the ruin of her home, and that stark fact had faced her all through this long and dreary day. Now she felt drained, exhausted, wanting only to be alone. But it seemed he was not going to leave for he did not move from the bed, his arm round one of the posts. "Talk?" he queried, his eyes glinting in a fashion that sent a little shoot of fear through her, dispelling the apathy that had taken possession of her. "Do you think I have come to talk? I am your husband and by God this is the last time you will ever bolt a door against me."

He flung back the bed clothes and she gave a sharp cry. "Rupert— no, no!"

"Yes," he said between his teeth and caught her long hair in his hand, forcing her head back. His mouth came down hard on hers. She could taste the stale wine and in sudden horror she fought him, her hands against his chest, for this was a stranger, this was not Rupert, her husband whom she loved, who was a passionate lover yet gentle, who had taught her the art of loving and turned their nights into ecstasy. She had never dreamed he could become this brutal man whose mouth was bruising hers, whose hands were tearing at her nightrail.

She managed to free her lips momentarily. "Oh God, Rupert, don't! You are hurting me."

"I mean to," he muttered. "I mean to! By Christ, you will learn tonight whose you are!" He forced her down among the pillows, his hands at her breasts, her thighs, his mouth stifling her protests. She gave a moan and it seemed to her that she was being raped by a man she did not know. She could no longer fight him, his soldier's body was too strong for her, and half fainting from fear and shock and exhaustion she went down into what seemed to be a terrifying darkness.

When it was over he dragged himself from her. The candle was still burning and with one swift movement he extinguished it between thumb and finger before he stumbled away to his own room.

That night Donald dreamed he was in the heather again. It was the same dream he had had before—he was escaping across a moor in the rain, running headlong though he seemed to cover no ground. He was vainly trying to reach his father, the distance between them never lessening, but this time a figure rose out of the heather and he saw that it was Rupert, only the odd thing was that Rupert was wearing the tartan. He sprang at him and they struggled, rolling locked together down the hillside; he clutched at some heather to stay their fall but it eluded him and he awoke, sweating, in the darkness. For a moment he could not remember where he was, only that he was very uncomfortable and not in the luxurious bed where he had slept for the last few weeks. Then he realized he was on a couch that was too short and too narrow for him in Fergus Mackenzie's sitting room. His makeshift bed seemed to have come to pieces and with all drowsiness banished by the sharp reality of his dream, he got up, disentangling himself from the blankets, and groped his way across to the window. After fumbling for a few moments in the unfamiliar room, he found the curtains and drew them back.

Already it was growing light and in the east across the rooftops of London the sky was glowing with crimson and gold. He stood watching the dawn come up, oppressed by the strangeness of his dream, and then as the memory of it began to fade, its place was taken by the recollection of the events that had led to his sleeping on the couch in this shabby little room. He had told Fergus briefly what had happened and Jane had insisted on making up a bed for him, urging him to stay as long as he wished.

He had lain awake for a long time, reliving the scene in the dining room of Astley House, until at last he fell asleep, only to be disturbed by the dream. He could still hardly credit it—that Bab was married to the man he had seen in the distance that day, ordering the destruction of Duirdre. How, he wondered, could a man with any honour at all do what Rupert had done, marry on a lie, continue the lie, live it as Rupert had? And all the time he had made love to his wife, entertained her brother, he had known he had the blood of their father on his hands. It was incredible! The arrogance, the insensitivity of the man, Donald thought, was passing all things. But it was the stark truth and he had to come to terms with it—as did Bab.

He began to pace the room, struggling to suppress his desire for vengeance, the desire to have Rupert at the receiving end of his sword. It was Bab he had to consider, and he wondered if he had been right to leave her as he had done yesterday, but he had rushed out of Astley House, unable to stay one moment longer in the presence of his father's murderer, so nauseated, so shaken with revulsion that he was hardly aware of what he was doing. But he had left Bab in an intolerable situation and something must be done about it—yet he could hardly go round to Astley House. He must wait until she came to him or sent him a message, but he chafed at the thought that he could do nothing to help her.

At last, weary and confused by conflicting emotions, he went to his valise and brought out the little Gaelic Testament he always carried with him, thinking to calm his mind. Flinging open the casement he sat down by the window in the golden light of the sunrise, opening the book at random, but after one sentence he laid the book down, leaning his arms on the windowsill, his hands gripped together. He knew without reading the words what his faith, the faith by which he had lived all his life, would command him to do, yet generations of his ancestors seemed to rise and bid him do another—and no Highlander could lightly ignore the cry of the dead for vengeance. And he had cause to hate Rupert. Surely no man could have more justification for such hatred? All these years he had thought of meeting the man responsible for that June day at Duirdre, and now that he had done so—he laid his head on his clenched fists and could hardly keep himself from groaning aloud. Oh God, what was he to do?

He rose and began to pace again, caged and distraught, and no answer came to his desperate pleading.

An hour later he was shaving himself with the aid of Mistress Mackenzie's little hand mirror when his cousin came in.

"Duirdre," he said, "your sister is downstairs and asking for you."

"At this hour?" Donald rubbed his chin dry with a towel. "May she come up, Fergus?"

"Of course." His cousin ran back down the stairs and returned with Bab, ushering her in and then closing the door behind her.

Donald took one look at her face and then seizing her hand led her to the sofa, sitting down beside her amidst the jumble of blankets. "My dearest child! What are you doing here so early? Tell me—"

She looked at him out of dark eyes, purple shadowed, her face without colour, and as if she found it hard to focus on him. "I could not stay after—" she stopped and glanced down at her hand held firmly in his. With an effort she went on, "—after yesterday."

"What happened when I had gone?"

"Rupert went out." Her mouth felt dry and her head throbbed. Last night was a nightmare from which she thought she would never awake, for unlike most nightmares it had not faded with the morning. But she could not speak of that. At last she said, "I want to be—away—for a little while."

"Does Astley know you've gone? Or Lord Rawdon?"

She shook her head. "Lord Rawdon will not think it odd that

I am gone out so early, he is used to me riding at this hour. As for Rupert—" she gave a little shudder, "I did not want to see him. I don't know—" her voice trailed off.

"But what do you wish to do? There is no room here. As you can see, I slept on this couch and though it might be best for you to be with our mother, St. Albans is out of the question, I imagine."

"I hope I may never see Everard again," she said in the same toneless voice. "I thought of Wilde End and Georgy and Phil, but that is the first place Rupert would look for me and I won't see him—not just now."

"Then I don't know what to suggest," he said. "I cannot keep you with me, m'eudial. You know I have work to do, and apart from that I am being financed by Jacobite funds."

"I know, but I wondered," her hand tightened in his, "I wondered whether I might go to your friends at Mentonnay. They did invite me, didn't they? And Rupert would not find me there."

He had not thought of that possibility but it seemed the obvious answer and one that, since he must escort her there, would give him the opportunity to see his little love even if only for a few hours. He felt his face grow warm. "Of course Armand would welcome you, and Mlle Marthe. But are you quite sure?"

"I must think," she answered, "I must think. I don't know what to do, but if I am so far away—out of reach—perhaps when you come back—"

"I will write to Armand at once," he said, "and I think we may safely follow the letter in a few days."

"You can be spared for the time it will take?"

"I think so. I will talk to Fergus, but I must not be gone long. However there is no news yet of—" he broke off. She was so still, so pale, so lifeless and there seemed to be nothing he could say to comfort her. "In the meantime," he said gently, "we must find you somewhere to stay."

Without looking up she said, "My maid Susan is below with my valise. She says her mother will give me lodging for a day or two. I have brought what money I had, enough for our journey but nothing—nothing that Rupert gave me."

Suddenly her calm broke and she cast herself into her brother's arms, sobbing, "Oh, Donald, I did not think he could hurt me so much."

Chapter 14

The château of Mentonnay was even more striking in the summer than it had been in the spring. Below the terrace roses were massed in long beds and the lake was fringed with purple and yellow flowers, swallows and swifts diving over the water. The long avenue of lime trees opened on to a spectacular view of the house and Bab was stirred out of her misery to remark on the beauty of the place.

The family welcomed them warmly and the introductions in the drawing room passed off without any awkward questions, Armand merely saying how delighted they all were that Madame Astley had found herself able to come in response to their invitation. There was more colour in Marthe's cheeks than usual and Donald suspected that his arrival had brought it there; when he took her hand, pressing her fingers to his lips he felt a brief response. Then she carried Bab away to her room and Donald watched, the French girl's slight figure in white muslin barely reaching to Bab's shoulder, and he was certain that Bab would confide in her, that it would be Marthe who would comfort her more than he could.

As soon as he could do so he requested a few words with Armand in the library and when they were alone there Armand indicated a chair and sat down himself, waving a hand round the room.

"You have been greatly missed here, as you can see. Nothing has been done since you left. Even Picot only makes the appalling noise that greeted you for those he considers friends. Now tell me what brings you to Mentonnay, with your charming sister. We are of course delighted to see you but your letter had a note of urgency."

Trusting entirely to Armand's discretion and as briefly as he could, Donald explained the circumstances, leaving out nothing, and though he did not realize it he told it so baldly without mitigating any of the facts, that Armand was profoundly shocked.

"I do not know what to say," he said when Donald had finished. "*Bon Dieu*, what a story! I am more sorry for your sister that I can express. I begin to see what you feared when you first heard of the

186

marriage, though even you cannot have known how disastrous it was to be. What will she do now?"

Donald leaned forward, his hands clasped between his knees. "She does not know—and neither do I. I don't want her to make any hasty decision she may regret, and I cannot leave London for a few weeks yet. You understand that I am there on Jacobite affairs? I cannot be more explicit than that." The Frenchman nodded and Donald went on, "When my work is done I must make some arrangement for her, but in the meantime," he hesitated and then looked directly at the Chevalier, "I trust I am not trespassing on your kindness if I ask that she may stay here?"

"She is very welcome for as long as she wishes to do so."

"Thank you," Donald said warmly. "I wish I could have given you more warning, but she wanted to be out of London and quickly. Poor Bab," he added, "she is so very unhappy."

"That is understandable, but do not fret, *mon ami. Monsieur le mari* will not find her here," Armand told him with Gallic commonsense. "And Marthe will be glad of her company. Perhaps she will be able to cheer your sister a little, *hein?* As for yourself, how long can you stay?"

"I must be gone in the morning, I'm afraid. I shall have to catch the stage to Calais." He leaned back in his chair. "I wish I might stay longer. Nothing seems to have changed."

"Ah," Armand said smiling, "but there is one change to take place shortly. I was about to write to you when I received your letter—to tell you that I am betrothed to Mademoiselle Solange d'Espallier and we shall be wed in November."

"My best wishes to you both," Donald said at once. "I trust you will be very happy."

Armand shrugged his shoulders. "It is a '*marriage de convenance*', you understand. Solange and I have known each other since we were children and our parents arranged the marriage. She is a great-niece of the Duc de Château-Fermay, I believe you met him here once. Solange is pretty and amiable and I think we shall do very well together—and Mentonnay must have an heir." He glanced across at Donald, "It will be good for Marthe to have a sister, until—" he stopped, looking across at Donald, seemed about to go on and then changed his mind. "I have been thinking, *mon cher*, surely there is no need for you to leave on the stage in the morning? I myself will drive you to Calais. If we leave about three o'clock we should reach the coast before dark, and I know a tolerably good inn where we can stay the night. I can see you on to the morning packet before I drive back and you should be in London by the following afternoon."

"If you can spare the time there is nothing I should like better," Donald agreed warmly. This would give him the best part of the day here and the chance to be with Marthe, even if only for a little while—did Armand mean that? Was there some reason why he should? He looked across at his companion but though the Frenchman met his gaze it was with a blank expression that betrayed nothing. There was, however, one other thing that he wanted to say and he wrenched his thoughts back to his sister's predicament. "I have been entirely open with you, Armand, about the reason for our visit, but there is no need, is there, for the rest of the household to be aware of it—though Bab herself may choose to confide in Mlle Marthe?"

"None in the world," Armand answered promptly. "I shall say nothing. As for yourself—" his calm hazel eyes were fixed on Donald, "but no—it is for the good Gaston to speak with you. Come, *mon ami*, your old room is awaiting you."

Upstairs, amid those familiar surroundings, Donald wondered what Armand meant, but with so many more pressing anxieties on his mind, he was too preoccupied to speculate for long. He felt, most of all, an overwhelming sense of relief from the burden of the last few days. Here at least he could put aside that anxiety for a short while, knowing Bab was in safe hands, and stronger than all else was the joy of seeing Marthe again. When they had parted in the library two months ago their love had become acknowledged between them and the pressure of her fingers this afternoon had told him that she had not changed. She would understand he could say nothing of the future, but a few words of love to keep hope alive—surely there could be no harm in that? Only there was so little time.

At supper that evening the atmosphere was relaxed and pleasant. Bab's paleness and weary looks were explained away as the effects of travel. Tante Clothilde promised that the air of Mentonnay would put colour back into her cheeks, while Tante Julie launched into a long and lurid account of a journey she had once made to Italy. The Curé said little, but Donald had the feeling that with his usual perception, he guessed that something might lie behind this unexpected visit. He enquired after Major Astley and though Bab was prepared for such a question and replied calmly that her husband was much occupied at the moment with his duties, the priest's eyes rested on her with a thoughtful expression.

Donald found it hard to keep his own eyes from Marthe's face, and after a while it occurred to him that she looked even less well, for under the slight flush of excitement he thought he detected a physical languor which she tried to hide with eager talk, and in her evening gown it was easy to see that little flesh covered her shoulders.

That night, when everyone had retired, he went to his sister's room and knocked at the door; she bade him come in and he found her in a dressing robe seated by the open window, her head resting against the curtain.

She looked up at him out of eyes that seemed to him to have acquired a lifetime of sadness in a few short days. "I hoped you would come," she said.

He sat down on the window seat beside her. "Do you think you will be content here for the time I must leave you?"

"They are all very kind," she said slowly, "and it is a beautiful place. I trust I will not be too dull a guest. It is hard to speak normally. But M. de la Rouelle is very considerate, I think."

"He is the most generous of men," Donald said. "But I want to talk to you about something else. Bab, I am going to trust you with a secret, though I really have no right to do so."

"You know that you can trust me."

"With my own affairs, yes, but this concerns His Highness directly. And I am only telling you of it because I deem it to be absolutely necessary."

"You can trust me," she repeated a little wearily, "whatever you may have thought to the contrary."

"I know that, *m'eudail*. You are Highland, and a Fraser and a Jacobite born, despite everything."

"If I were not I should not be here," she said with a catch in her voice. "What is it that I should know?"

Briefly he told her of the Prince's planned visit and his own part in it. "So now you understand," he finished, "why I must go back to London at once. Fergus and I must be ready when he comes."

She was staring at him now, her attention distracted from her own unhappiness and riveted on him. "But it is very dangerous. Suppose he is recognized?"

"I think it is a great risk myself, but he is determined to come—*incognito*. He has great courage, Bab."

"I know—I know." She paused and took his hand, twisting the heavy signet ring he wore, the ring that all through her childhood she had seen on her father's finger. "But I am thinking of you—oh, Donald, if you were caught! What would happen if the plan was discovered, what would happen to you?"

"I hope we shall not be discovered. Belive me, we shall take every care."

"Yes, but if anything were to go wrong, if you were arrested," she persisted.

"My dear, you know as well as I do." He turned his head to look out into the darkness. "Death, or," he got up to snuff a guttering candle, "or transportation at the least."

"Oh!" She gripped her hands tightly together. His tall shadow suddenly seemed gigantic on the ceiling, like something dark hanging over them both, and she shivered.

He came back to sit beside her. "It serves no purpose to hide the truth," he said quietly. "You asked me and I have told you, but I have no intention of delivering myself up to the authorities." He put a finger under her chin and tilted it so that he could look into her face. "Come, Bab. You have never been afraid to face facts."

"No, but—" she twisted her face away from his clear, penetrating gaze, "I have no one left now, except you. I wish you had not to go back."

"My child, what are you saying? You would not have me play the coward? Nor desert my Prince?"

She lifted her head at that. "No, of course not. Forget that I said it."

"I shall be back here in a few weeks," he said lightly, "and you will wonder why you were so anxious. And then perhaps His Highness will have firmer plans and who knows what the future will hold for us then?"

"And if nothing comes of all this?" He did not answer and she gave a little sigh. "I think it is a hard and thankless life you have. Exile, working in secret for a restoration that seems to be less and less likely as time goes on, and all the while you are in London there is a risk. Oh Donald, it is not what I would wish for you."

"Nevertheless, it *is* my life," he said. He took her hand again. "And that brings me to what I want to say to you. Should anything go wrong, should I be prevented from coming for you, I want you to promise you will go back to England, not perhaps to St. Albans but at least to Philip. I know his wife is Astley's cousin but Philip is ours and at least you will be able to see our mother there and—" he paused. He did not in the least wish to go on, but it had to be said. "My dear, your future is in your own hands. I cannot tell you what is right for you, but indeed I don't think you can remain estranged from your husband indefinitely. Some arrangement will have to be made." He saw an extraordinary expression cross her face. Hurt he had seen, and anger, and misery, but now he thought he detected a momentary shaft of fear, followed almost at once by so great a look of longing that he caught her in his arms.

"*M'eudail*, forgive me. We will not talk of it now. But you had to know the risks I run in order to be prepared, to know what I would have you do should——should the need arise." Her head was against his chest and he stroked the dark hair, a deep pity for her consuming all other feelings at the moment. He had a sharp conviction then that the quarrel with Rupert was more his than hers. She was as much their father's daughter, but she was still Rupert's wife and nothing could change that.

At last, with a heavy sigh he said, "Write to me at Fergus's address and I will let you know mine as soon as I have found lodgings."

Slowly she raised herself, calmer now. "I have been thinking, Donald, I wrote no letter when I left Astley House——"

His mouth was set. "It will not hurt Astley to suffer a little as he has made others suffer. Let him know what it is to lose for a change."

She shook her head. "I was thinking of Lord Rawdon. He has always been so kind to me, and to you too. Could you take a note to him? Rupert will have told him something, I suppose, but I begin to see perhaps I should not have been so hasty——it will have been so awkward for them. If I could at least write to Lord Rawdon——"

"Of course," he said. "We have had no thought for him. Write your letter, Bab, and I will take it to Astley House."

She nodded, twisting her hands together. "But I do not want you to see——Rupert." And to her own surprise she found herself saying, "That day——you were so angry, I thought you would kill him."

"Bab!" He took those twisted fingers into his. "Child, do you still care so much for him?"

She looked beyond her brother into the dark recesses of the room, remembering the night that had followed that day when momentarily, after he had forced himself on her, she had seen his face in the candle flame, sobered, stripped of the rage, the jealousy that had driven him. She felt suddenly very weary. "I am beginning to think love does not die so easily," she said. "I have thought and thought and despite everything he has done——more than you know——I do not want him hurt."

He released her and got up once more. "I shall strive not to meet him, but if I do I cannot guarantee what may or may not come of it." He could not, after all, tell her that he meant to keep that oath sworn at Duirdre with his father's dead body in his arms, and though she might think she still cared for Rupert, might she not be better off rid of such a husband? Abruptly he bent and kissed her. "It is late. Try to sleep, my dearest, and while you are here rest and enjoy Mlle Marthe's company." He had thought a short while ago he might perhaps tell her of his own seemingly hopeless love, but she was too distraught to bear more trouble now. Instead he said, "When I come back we will talk of the future. Try not to fear for me—it is very unlikely that in the circles I shall move in now, I shall meet Astley."

He bade her goodnight and left her; there was no more comfort he could give her—and none for himself.

In the morning, after breakfast, Armand insisted on carrying Bab off to ride through the park. He had heard, he said, that Madame Astley was a fine horsewoman and if she would come with him to the stables he would find her a mount to her liking. She hesitated, with a glance at her brother, and Donald thought she might be too tired to accept but it seemed that Armand would brook no refusal.

Gaston de la Rouelle did not look up during this conversation, but the moment they had gone quietly asked Donald if he would come into his study.

Donald had not often been in this small book-lined room with its table covered with papers, its prie-dieu and large crucifix on the wall above. An austere room, yet when he was seated in a chair facing the Curé he was conscious of an unhurried atmosphere of quiet.

"You are well?" Gaston asked first. "Your wound is quite healed?"

"Quite," Donald said, "and as you see, the damage inflicted on my head is no longer visible. I'm afraid my sister's London friends think it quite out of fashion that I do not wear a wig."

The Curé smiled. "And did you care for London society?"

"No! I met some agreeable people, but God forbid that I should ever live there."

The force of this denial amused the priest. "I must admit that I did not think you would like it." His face grew more serious and he looked down at his hands, clasped together in his habitual manner, the attitude for prayer so common to him that his fingers could not help but interlace themselves. He began to speak quietly—the warmth of his affection for this young man who had come to Mentonnay, an exile, poor and proud, becoming apparent with every word.

Half an hour later Donald emerged from the study, a dazed expression on his face. As if from a long way off he heard himself asking a footman where Mlle Marthe had gone and on being told that she was in the garden he went out on to the terrace. But she was not on the terrace nor in the rose garden and some instinct took him along the path to the lake.

She was there, sitting on the log where they had sat together before, a shady hat tied over her brown hair, her pink muslin skirts falling about her to the grass. She looked up as he came and seeing his face she gave a little exclamation. "Oh! Monsieur, what is it? You look—" and then she stopped, not knowing what to say.

"My heart's darling," he began and then he too paused. He was still throbbing from the onset of such emotion, such happiness that he did not know how to contain it. He could not have believed that joy could so possess a man, body and soul, that he was aware of nothing else. Yet there was grief too, and fear—but that he must not let her see. "I have just been with your cousin, the Curé—" How to tell her? How to begin? He drew a deep breath and sat down beside her, possessing himself of her hands. "Marthe—tell me. You have not changed? You—you love me?"

"I love you," she answered without hesitation and looked searchingly at him. "What has happened? I've never seen you look—so!"

He drew a deep breath. "M. de la Rouelle told me—do you remember a relative of some sort, of his mother's, I believe, who died a short while ago and left him an estate in the south, in Vendée?" She nodded and he went on, "I understand it is not large, but there is a comfortable house and several farms, that it is good land and would be enough for—oh my heart, he says he does not want it, he proposes to make it over to you, for your wedding gift!" He saw colour flood into her cheeks and she seemed suddenly breathless.

"My—my wedding gift? You—you cannot mean—"

"Yes, beloved, yes! And it is with Armand's consent. He began to tell me something last night and then changed his mind and said M. de la Rouelle should do it. At first—at first I did not think I should accept, for it is not mine and I—" a note of sadness crept into his voice, "I still have nothing to offer you. There was a time in London when I thought I might, but that opportunity was lost. And now—"

"Oh," she cried out, "you will not let that keep us apart? What do I want you to offer but your love? And what does it matter how it is made possible if only we can be together?" "It doesn't matter," he said quickly, "though it is not the way I should wish it. I would feel happier if it were my inheritance. But M. de la Rouelle reminded me that if there was no one to receive, we could none of us give. What could I do but thank him? And we have Armand's blessing too. That is if you—will you marry me, my little love?"

She gave a sob of joy. "Oh yes, yes—I did not know—I did not guess—Armand said nothing to me."

"Your brother," Donald said, "is a most perceptive man. He knew that I should want to be the one to tell you." He put up one hand and untied the ribbons of her hat, letting it fall behind her to the ground. And this time it was no stolen kiss, with no hope of fulfilment, but as of right, long and deep.

At last he raised his head to look down into her face. "You know that I must go back to London for a short while?" She nodded and he realized how hard, now, it would be to leave her this afternoon. Holding her hands tightly, he said, "I understand that our betrothal cannot be announced until after the matter of the dispensation has been settled. M. le Curé says he will write at once to the Bishop. Will you marry a heretic, my heart?"

A little smile curved her mouth in response. "I think perhaps I will convert you." Then she asked more gravely, "Did Gaston say how long he thought the dispensation might take?"

"No, but some time, I think. He will put our case to the Bishop as strongly as he can, and in the meantime there is the business of La Verulai to be settled. It will be warmer there and perhaps suit you very well, my heart." He paused, looking down at her hands entwined in his, her fingers small and slender. There was more that he could not say to her, that the Curé had revealed to him. Both Marthe's cousin the priest and her brother were seriously concerned for her health and it was only because she had made it clear to Armand that if she could not marry the man she wished she would not marry at all— though she would in no way go against his express wishes—that they had considered how the situation might be resolved. Their concern had made them feel that any happiness she might be given could only be for her good, and the fortuitous death of Gaston's relative had brought them both to feel that a betrothal at least could be allowed. The priest had said that it might be that their marriage would never take place, that her strength might fail. He believed she had a lung disease that might not heal, whatever the doctors in Paris said. The only thing he and Armand asked of Donald was that if they were able to settle at La Verulai he would put his care for his wife above all else, the implication of that condition quite clear.

And he had given his word. Was that weakness in him, he wondered? If the Prince called would he refuse to go? Yet it seemed so remote a possibility, as Bab had rightly said, and here was this frail French girl whom he loved, needing him as he needed her. It might even be, as Gaston forced him to understand, that he might not have her for very long. Yet as he looked across the lake at the quiet beauty of the garden he felt a rising confidence in the healing power of love. Surely now that they were free to marry, now that the way had opened up before them, surely he could give her some of his own strength, let his love flow over her and give her the will to be well again? He believed it, she must believe it too, and he held her hands in his own warm ones, wishing that his strength might indeed be hers.

She was sitting quite still, watching him, and he thought suddenly that whatever she might lack in physical strength she more than made up for by an air of well-being, of content that must come from the spirit. She seemed to him to be enveloped in quiet joy, in equal confidence in him.

And then all his determination to keep only happiness between them on this day, to betray nothing of his own fears, to talk only in practical terms of their future, broke down. He slid to his knees beside her, his head in her lap. "My darling, my heart's treasure, I don't know how to tear myself from you. There's been no joy in me for so long, and none—ever—to touch what we have now. I cannot bear to be away from you now that I am to have you for my own."

She leaned forward, putting both arms about him, cradling his head against her, and now it was she who was the stronger. "It is only for a little while. I shall be waiting for you and I will have your sister to talk with. She will tell me about your home and when you were a boy—all the things a woman wants to know." She paused, her face glowing. "I still cannot believe it is true. Gaston is so good—God is so good. We will not be so ungrateful as to grumble about such a little parting, will we?"

"No," he said with an effort. He did not move. It was bliss to be in her arms, to be held thus. "No, we must not do that. And you will look after my poor Bab for me."

"Indeed I will. Already I can see that we shall be friends. She is very lovely, your sister, but she looks so sad."

"She is," he said, "but she will tell you about that, I am sure. I am going to be selfish enough to want all your attention for the little time we have left."

She bent over him, her lips against his hair. "You said yourself you will not be away for very long."

"No," he raised himself that he might look into her face. "It will not be long, and if it were my own choice I'd not go at all, but I am bound on a task for my Prince. You understand that?"

"Of course, Donald," she said his name for the first time slowly and caressingly, a little flush in her cheeks, "I would never keep you from your duty to him. I do not know a great deal about it—you will tell me more—but I wish he may succeed one day. Then you will be able to take me to your country that I wish so much to see. When we are married it will be my country too, and your home will be ours as well as La Verulai." She saw the sudden bleak look in his face. "You do not think I would hold you back from anything that might aid your Prince or give you back your home? *Cheri*, I am only a woman but I understand a little of what is in your heart."

"You understand—too much," he said in a shaken voice. A solitary bird flew across the lake with a strange haunting cry and he turned from her kiss to watch its flight, a sudden chill striking him and with it a premonition that he would remember this moment and her words.

As if she sensed what he felt she set her hands about his face. "However happy we may be," she said in a low voice, "nothing could ever be quite as perfect as this first hour. Whatever may come we have had this."

They fell silent, their arms about each other, the precious moments slipping away until in the distance they heard a bell ringing to announce *déjeuner*. Slowly he rose and drew her into the circle of his arms. "It is only goodbye for a little while."

"And I shall pray every day for you, that the Blessed Virgin will bring you safely back to me—she is a woman and she will understand."

He dropped a kiss on her hair. "And your prayers will be heard, my heart—I know it." He found her mouth, passion rising in him as she clung to him, and he thought he would never bring himself to end this last embrace. A moment later, however, he felt her body stiffen and her hand catch at his shoulder; startled, he loosened his arms and raised his head to see that her face was very pale and that she was breathing in agitated gasps.

"What is it?" he asked urgently. "My darling, are you ill?"

She shook her head, but she could not speak and only stood trying to take a deep breath, her hand pressed against her breast. Very gently he made her sit down again; he did not know what to do to ease her distress and could only sit by her, his arm about her shoulders as she was shaken by a spasm of coughing.

"Have I hurt you?" he asked remorsefully. "I should not have—"

"No, no—" she said as soon as she could speak. "It was not your fault." Slowly the spasm passed and her breathing grew normal again, but he could see she was exhausted and he held her against him, her head resting against his shoulder. He was thinking of what Gaston de la Rouelle had said, of what both the priest and Armand feared and which he had refused to believe. Now he sat staring over her head, his face grim. When she was quieter he said gently, "I would not hurt you for anything in the world. Is there anything I can fetch you? Shall I call your maid?"

She raised herself a little. She was still pale but she was able to smile up at her lover and assure him she was better, that she needed nothing but his arm about her. "It was foolish of me," she added. "Sometimes I am a little breathless, but it soon passes."

"You will see this doctor in Paris? Armand mentioned him and maybe he will—"

"Oh, I will do as Armand wishes, but really I am not ill."

He took her face in his hands, looking closely down at her. "You are more precious to me than life itself. You must take care of yourself for my sake. Do you feel well enough to walk back to the house now?"

"Of course." And she got to her feet without hesitation.

To his relief she did seem recovered and with his arm supporting her they began to walk slowly back along the path. At the gate they turned as if by common consent to look at the place that had witnessed their first happiness.

"When you are gone," she said, "I shall come here and think of you. I have always loved it and now it will have a magic it never had before."

"And I shall carry the memory of it with me to the London streets," he told her, smiling a little. But he was holding her as if he could not let her go, his eyes on her face as if to learn every detail of it. He kissed her again, very gently this time, and then swung open the wicket gate. As she walked through the bird that had flown across came winging back, making its mournful cry, and Donald stood still, his gaze sweeping round the clearing, confronting the birch wood, those trees of ill omen for him that he had hitherto so carefully avoided. They now seemed, in different sunlight, hauntingly beautiful.

And in another moment of that strange Highland intuition, he was possessed by a terrible conviction that he would never come here nor hold her in his arms again.

He took her hand firmly. "Let us go by the copse," he said. "The shade will be better for you," and as if walking deliberately to meet whatever fate that moment presaged, he led her under the interlaced green of the silver birches.

Chapter 15

Simon Ravenslow was walking up the stairs at White's Club with his usual unhurried step; dressed in mulberry satin with cream small clothes, the finest lace at his throat and wrists he was as always an impressive figure. It was very late and a sultry evening, thunder rolling about in the distance, and he thought perhaps he would have been both cooler and more comfortable if he had returned to his rooms in Jermyn Street after his supper engagement. However he had not seen Rupert for a while and had decided to stroll round to the club on the chance of finding him there. He was half way up when he heard his name called and saw Harry Cavendish leaning over the balustrade, his usually placid face wearing a puzzled expression.

"Simon! I was never more glad to see anyone. Come up, will you?"

Simon appeared only mildly interested. "As you see, I am on my way to the card room. What is it this time? Do you want a loan? If so, I had better warn you that I have only a few guineas in my pocket."

"No, no," Harry said impatiently. "It is Rupert. D'you know what's the matter with him?"

"I've not seen him for several days," Simon answered, and his tone was more alert. "Why—what's amiss?"

Harry leaned forward and spoke confidentially. "Well, he came in about nine with a face as white as a sheet. I asked him what was wrong and he near bit my head off. And you know how neat he is— tonight he looks as if he's been in the saddle all day, or else slept in his clothes, though come to think of it, he doesn't look as if he has slept at all." Harry paused for breath as a heavy frown gathered on the older man's face.

"Go on," Simon said, certain that this was not all. He had reached the top of the stairs and stood looking down at Harry. "Was he not on duty today?"

"No, he asked for a few days leave, when was it? Wednesday or Thursday, I forget which. Anyway I've not seen him since then. You know what Rupert is, he can usually hold his liquor and he seldom goes beyond a second bottle, but tonight he's taken more than most men can stomach, and he's in a damned ugly mood." He broke off as a burst of laughter came from the card room. In these hard drinking days it did not seem to him that the quantity was of any importance, only the way in which one disposed of it.

Simon took his arm and together they walked into the gilt and candle-lit room where most of the tables were now deserted and a crowd of men gathered round one in the centre.

Simon stalked across the room, took two elegant gentlemen by their shoulders and twisted them out of the way, ignoring their protests. At the table, which was littered with bottles and glasses, half a dozen members were playing cards and opposite to where Simon stood Rupert was leaning back in his chair. His wig had slipped slightly to one side, his coat and waistcoat were undone and his cravat, untidy and bedraggled, was hanging loose, but it was at his face that Simon was looking. As Harry had said, he did indeed give the appearance of a man who had not seen his bed for several nights; his blue eyes glinted in a white face and before him on the table was a small gold-mounted pistol. There was considerable noise and argument but Simon's deep voice cut across the hubbub.

"May I enquire what is going on that is providing you all with so much entertainment?"

A momentary hush fell and then half a dozen voices began to speak at once. Simon held up his hand. "If you please—Captain Brooks, perhaps you will explain?"

The captain shifted uncomfortably in his chair. Since his fall from his horse he was very stiff and this perhaps was why he did not look directly at Simon Ravenslow. Before he had a chance to speak however, Rupert leaned forward.

"Do you want to play, Simon? Pull up a chair—but there's no limit, and anyone who can't stay the course is likely to get a bullet through his coat."

"He's done it too," Harry whispered to Simon. "Ludlow had an argument with him earlier and Rupert put a bullet through the shoulder of it without even scratching his skin. He went off home in a mighty sulk, I can tell you, and threatened to send Rupert his tailor's bill."

Rupert gave a sudden harsh laugh and glanced across at Simon. "Don't you think I can do it?" he enquired tauntingly and there was only a slight slur in his speech. "I may be drunk but I've not yet lost my skill." And picking up the pistol he fired it across the room at a sconce of candles, extinguishing the central flame.

"Dashed good!" Harry exclaimed admiringly. "I can't do that when I'm sober."

Simon, however, stalked round the table and seized the smoking pistol. "We can dispense with such boy's tricks," he said curtly, and when two waiters burst into the room he dismissed them, assuring them Major Astley would pay for the damage to the wall where the bullet had embedded itself.

Rupert slewed round in his chair. "God damn you, Simon, you interfere too much. If you wish to play, come and play, but if you're going to be sanctimonious you'd best leave us to our amusement and take your glum face elsewhere." He drained his glass and as he refilled it Harry muttered, "Lord knows where he puts it, must have a stomach like a wine-vat."

Several of the men eyed Simon with some misgiving for even Rupert did not normally address him in such a manner. Apart from being a crack shot and the best swordsman in the club, Simon Ravenslow also had the ability to dispose of the most offensive gentleman with a pithy phrase or two and few cared to cross him. Nor was he the man to take such remarks from anyone, but he merely pocketed the pistol and said, "Gentlemen, you may not be aware that a storm is about to break." As if to reinforce his words there was a crack of thunder almost over their heads and he added, "I believe we would all be wise to go home before the worst of it."

There was a general move towards the door and the party round the table broke up with considerable talk and scraping of chairs.

"What's the matter with you all," Rupert exploded. "Good God, are you afraid of a little thunder?"

"Not at all, dear boy," an exquisite opposite him was gathering up a few remaining guineas, "but I've a new coat made by Fotherby, y'know, and damned expensive, and as you've spared it your treatment I've no mind to have it spoilt by the rain."

"Aye, and you know what it's like trying to get a chair in such weather," Captain Brooks added. "There's never one of the wretched things in sight."

"My God," Rupert said, "what a lily-livered lot. Where's that damned footman? You there, fetch another bottle."

"Haven't you had enough?" Simon queried. He shook his head at the lackey, set a hand under Rupert's arm and heaved him to his feet. "Come, we'll go back to my rooms and you can recover yourself before you go home."

"Ah!" Rupert said and his mouth curled down at the corners. "Perhaps you are fortunate you have no wife waiting for you, eh Harry? And what about you, Brooks? Does Mrs. Brooks wait up to fry you if you've had a bottle too many? Perhaps we'd all be better off with the ladies of Drury Lane."

There was a ripple of laughter at this, but by this time most of the participants in the game had left and a few moments later only three were left in the card room. Rupert stood leaning the flat of his hands on the card table, his pile of guineas scattered, all the aggressiveness suddenly gone out of him. His face was a curious shade of green.

"You need air," Simon said and with a curt nod to Harry, piloted him out of the room and down the stairs to the street door. Harry made no attempt to follow. Simon, he thought, had handled the situation in his own expert manner and might be left to finish it.

In the street Simon turned on his companion. "If you choose to make a drunken spectacle of yourself, I suppose you are at liberty to do so," he said in a voice of ice, "but you will not return to Astley House until you are sober and if you cause another scene at the club I myself will call you out and teach you a lesson that, by God, you will not forget. Do you imagine there is not some tattling fool who will carry such tales as this evening's affair to your wife?"

Rupert swayed unsteadily and as a flash of lightning illuminated the street caught at a hitching post. "You need not concern yourself about Bab," he muttered. "Nothing I can do can cause her any more unhappiness—I've done enough already." And lurching away from Simon he was violently sick.

It was not until after the spasm had passed that he was aware of Simon's cool hands holding his head. Gasping a little, he pulled out a handkerchief and held it to his mouth. "My—my apologies. I thought I was better able to—"

"Come," Simon said and his voice was less harsh. "If you can manage it we'll walk to my rooms. The rain will come soon," he added as another clap of thunder rolled round them.

"We can go home—there's no one there but the servants."

If Simon was surprised he did not show it but merely took Rupert's arm again and it was not until they were in the library at Astley House and he had put Rupert into a chair that he said, "Now perhaps you will tell me what all these heroics are about?"

Rupert sat slumped in the chair, his hands hanging over the arms. Despite the closeness of the evening he was shivering. Outside the rain had begun to fall and it drove against the windows, lashing at the panes with all the violence of a summer storm. A lackey came in to draw the curtains, but at a brief "not now" from Mr. Ravenslow he retreated.

There was a short silence, during which Simon waited. Then Rupert put a hand to his forehead. "Bab has left me," he said baldly.

Simon gave him one astounded glance and then, going to a side table, poured some brandy into a glass. "Drink this," he ordered and watched as the shivering gradually subsided. "I presume she found out?"

"Everything—every damned thing. My God, what a fool I have been!"

"I will not say I told you so, but I did urge you to trust her. One could see from the start she was no flighty miss without a brain in her head."

"I know—I know," Rupert said wildly. "Do you think I've not told myself that over and over again since she went. But I thought I'd lose her if she knew."

"And now you have lost her because you didn't tell her. I presume you mean she knows not only about that foolish game of Hazard but about the business in Scotland as well. How did that come about?" At the end of the explanation he pursed his lips. "Singularly unfortunate for you. Did you try to talk to her afterwards?"

"Yes, but her door was locked. I went out for a while and—oh yes, I got drunk!" Rupert paused, staring into the empty hearth. Then he went on, speaking jerkily. "I came back—I don't know when—hours later, and her door was still locked. Harper saw and that infuriated me, so I—I forced the lock and—" he came to an abrupt stop.

Simon regarded him with cool dispassionate eyes. "You surprise me. No wonder she has shown a distaste for your company. But doubtless she will come back."

Rupert raised his head. "After—*that*?"

"My dear Rupert, your past philandering has only, it seems, given you experience of a certain sort of woman. I am to understand that you want her back?"

"Dear God!" Rupert said. He put the glass down. The brandy had done its work and the greenish hue had faded from his face. "I never thought that I—*I* would care so much."

"Where has she gone? Have you any idea?"

"No. At first I did not realize she had gone. I thought she would be back in the evening, but she didn't come. I waited a few days and then I couldn't stand it any more so I rode out to St. Albans—the day before yesterday, I think. She wasn't there, of course—I should have known that. Thank God, Everard was out or I think I'd have challenged the man, father-in-law or not. I told Lady Caroline there had been some muddle over our arrangements, and she seemed to believe me. Then I went to Wilde End but Bab wasn't there either and I had to tell Georgy we'd had a slight—disagreement. Philip, who's got more sense than I first credited him with, told me that if Bab came to them he would do his best to persuade her at least to see me. My God, if it was only a disagreement! Now, I don't know where else to look, for I've no idea where her brother is."

Simon glanced at the rumpled clothes, the hollow tired eyes, and asked Rupert when he last ate.

"I don't know—yesterday morning, I think. I haven't thought about food."

Simon rose and rang the bell and when a footman appeared ordered the man to bring a tray of cold meats for his master.

"I don't want it," Rupert said but was told briskly not to be foolish and when the tray was brought Simon stood over him until he had eaten a little of the mutton.

Then the older man said, "Obviously Bab has gone away with her brother."

Rupert nodded. "There's nowhere else she could be that I can think of. I wish I knew where he went when he left here."

"Have you thought he might have taken her to his friends in France? Do you remember one evening she spoke of such an invitation?"

Rupert laid down his knife and fork. "I believe you're right. I don't know why I didn't think of that, but I've been near beside myself with worry. What was the man's name—La Rouerie or La Rouelle? Something like that and I seem to remember his estate was beyond Versailles. I could go——"

"Wait a moment." Simon sat down astride a chair beside him, his arms folded along the back. "One thing at a time. Does your father know that Bab has gone?"

"No, he went to Rawdon that morning, and I don't propose to tell him—not yet anyway. I'm not in the mood for parental recriminations."

"They are doubtless due. I am bound to say you have handled the affair very badly from the start."

"You've never minced your words, have you?" Rupert countered bitterly. "Do you think I don't know it? Do you think I've not

204

blamed myself over and over again these last few days? I've not slept for wondering if I shall ever be able to put right the wrong I've done." He dropped his head on his clenched hands. "As for the business in Scotland, I thought it so unlikely that she would find out—there seemed no need ever to speak of it, and as for Fraser I never thought about him at all. Oh, I knew he might visit us, but he was in France and I did not know until he came what sort of man he was, nor how close he and Bab were. They were always talking together in that damned heathenish tongue of theirs and they would stop when I came into the room." Passion rose in his voice and he went on, "Nor did I suspect he was a damned spy."

"That seems a harsh word for a few hours with Lady Primrose or at the White Cock—yes, Harry told me about that. But what else did you expect?"

"He was our guest—and he said things to me that no man would stomach!"

Simon leaned his chin on his folded hands, regarding Rupert thoughtfully. "It seems neither of you was blameless but it serves no purpose now to try and apportion it. We must decide what to do."

Rupert pushed the tray from him and leaned back, giving a weary sigh. "What is there to do? Oh, I could go to France, try to find this M. de la Rouerie or whatever his name is, but if Bab is there I couldn't force her to come back. Even if I could, I don't want it to be that way. I want her to come of her own free will, Simon." With a sudden gesture of desperation he got up and went to the window where he stood staring blindly at the streaming panes, watching the raindrops chasing each other down the glass. "But I don't think she will find it easy to forgive what I have done."

"My dear boy," Simon said with a glimmer of a smile. "Don't you know there's nothing a woman enjoys so much as forgiving? Get a good night's sleep and we will talk again tomorrow."

When he had gone Rupert went slowly upstairs, so tired it was an effort to walk. Outside the door of the large bedchamber he had shared with Bab, he lit a taper from the sconce in the passage and went in, lighting the candles on the table by the door. The bed lay untouched, the covers turned back, the draperies tied at the head. The room had the appearance of waiting—waiting, he thought, for a mistress who would not come. He went over to the cupboard and opened the door. Most of her clothes were there. He could see the white dress she had worn for their ball and put out a hand to touch it. Then he crushed a fold of the skirt between his fingers before turning away to the dressing table where the silver-backed brushes he had given her for a wedding gift lay neatly in position. So she had not even taken those! He ran his finger over the back of one and then picked up the patch box. Inside lay several black velvet circles and one or two little stars. She had worn one of those, he remembered, on the night they went to the Devonshires' ball shortly after their marriage. With a convulsive movement he dropped the box and the patches scattered over the carpet.

He sat down on the edge of the bed, leaning his head against one of the posts that supported the canopy—and then, remembering what he had done here only a few nights ago he flung himself from it. Now it was empty and it was all his own fault. The whole house was empty without her—he felt empty himself, bereft of all the things he had so wantonly thrown away.

In his dressing room he threw off his clothes and lay down on the small bed. What sort of man was he that too much wine and rage and jealousy could drive him to such lengths? Before that terrible quarrel he would never have believed he could behave in such a manner and he looked at this picture of himself with sudden loathing. Now, somehow, he had to find the courage to ask Bab to let him try to make up for what he had done. But would she? Would she give him the chance? Was Simon right, that she would forgive, that this nightmare would end? At last, too exhausted to think any more, he slept.

In the morning when he had eaten breakfast he went into the library and was there glancing through a letter from his father when he heard a knock and voices in the hall. He turned his head, listening, in sudden painful anticipation but there were only men's voices and he turned back to the letter as hope died. Then he heard the footman, Thomas, say, "But, sir, the Major's in the library. Will you not step in?" And another voice answered, "No, thank you. Just hand this note to Lord Rawdon, if you please."

In two strides Rupert was across the library and into the hall. "You may go, Thomas," he said sharply. "Mr. Fraser will be staying."

Donald halted by the front door. He had felt certain that at this time of day Rupert would be out and it was no part of his plan to confront him at the moment, but short of causing a scene in the hall there was nothing else to do but hand Thomas his hat and follow his brother-in-law into the library.

When the door was closed Rupert turned on him. "I wonder you have the effrontery to come, but now that you are here, perhaps you will have the goodness to tell me where my wife is."

Donald laid his letter with great deliberation on the table that stood by the window. "I came to bring this for your father—from Bab."

Rupert flushed. "Damned good of you! I suppose it has not occurred to you that I've been near frantic the last few days, wondering where she was. And you come here with a note, not for me but for my father who, as Thomas may have told you, is at Rawdon. Now you will tell me where you have taken my wife."

"I have no intention of doing so. She wishes to be left alone, for the moment anyway."

"But I must talk to her." Rupert broke off, unwilling to plead his case before so unyielding a listener, but after a moment he added, his anger rising, "Good God, man, you'd no right to take her away. If it had not been for your interference, I might have made her understand." Yet her brother was in no way responsible for the final act that had driven her away and Rupert turned his back on him, his eyes on the square outside.

Donald stood still, his arms folded on his chest. "You mean you wish to persuade her to forget your lies, your deceit, that you married her knowing you had our father's death on your conscience. Have you any idea what you have done to her?"

"I have, God help me, I have," Rupert threw the words at him. "But she is still my wife and we cannot remain like this. If she would try to understand, let me make amends, somehow——"

"That is entirely for her to decide, of course," Donald answered coldly, "but I shall see that she is not forced into meeting you until she wishes to do so. Permit me to tell you that had I been in England I should not have allowed her to marry a man whose reputation was not one that a Fraser of Duirdre would tolerate—quite apart from your behaviour in Scotland," he added and had the satisfaction of seeing a furious colour dye his brother-in-law's face.

"Damn you, you go too far! I take insults from no one in my own house. You can name your seconds, sir."

Donald came forward so that they stood facing each other. "If you think you are injured let me tell you that it is nothing—*nothing* to what you have done to me and my family and to Duirdre. I will fight you willingly for taking my father's life and my sister's happiness, but I will not name seconds nor make a public matter out of it. I will fight you here and now or not at all. This room is big enough to serve."

For a brief moment they glared at each other and then Rupert nodded briefly. He crossed to the door and locked it while Donald pushed back some chairs. Then both men removed their coats and tucked back the lace ruffles at their wrists.

Donald drew his sword and stood weighing it in his hand; it was a new blade that Armand had given him when he left Mentonnay in June and the balance was perfect. He knew now that he had wanted to meet Rupert in this way, that it was what he hoped for when he returned to London—whatever he might have said to Bab—for only the shedding of blood could satisfy the hatred that lay between them.

Rupert stood waiting, the point of his sword resting lightly across his other hand; there was the briefest of salutes and the blades came together.

At first they both fenced warily, testing each other's methods and strength. Donald had the advantage in height and he was of larger build but, as he soon discovered, Rupert was astonishingly quick on his feet and had obviously learned the art of duelling from a master. He used several continental moves that caught Donald unawares and in the first five minutes he not only ripped Donald's shirt sleeve open but the tip of his blade whipped across his forearm. The cut was only slight but the blood flowed rather freely and the hilt of Donald's sword became sticky and less flexible in his hand. But he too had fenced abroad and he made a swift riposte that held his opponent at bay. And the fact that he was at last fighting to avenge something that had eaten the heart out of life for the last few years gave him a surge of strength and determination. Rupert, who had been equally confident of his own dexterity, found himself facing a man bent on final revenge; this was no polite duel between gentlemen to satisfy a point of honour—he was indeed fighting for his life. He tried every move he knew, every subtle thrust, but the Highlander's sword countered each and at last, forced to retreat step by step, he found his back against the shelves that lined the walls. His knees began to feel less than steady and he knew he was paying for last night's folly.

There was no sound in the room but their hard breathing and the ring of the blade. Donald was aware that he had his quarry cornered and waited for the chance to send home the final stroke—and in his mind there was only one thought, that his father's spirit would never now cry shame on him.

And then, as if across a wilderness of space, he seemed to hear Bab saying, "I do not want him hurt—" He was momentarily thrown off guard and Rupert lunged at him, but he quickly regained his control. He found that his ascendancy was now such that with part of his mind he could thrust and parry and with the other think clearly.

No, he could not after all take Rupert's life. Perhaps he had never intended to. Bab still cared enough for this man to want him spared and surely honour would be satisfied if he drew blood. Suddenly it was if a great burden had rolled from his shoulders and he thrust Rupert's guard aside, prepared to send his point home and finish it. But at that moment Rupert's legs seemed to buckle under him, and as he lurched sideways Donald's blade slid, not as he intended neatly into the arm, but into his breast.

With a horrified exclamation he wrenched it free and caught Rupert in his arms as he fell, both swords clattering to the floor. For one instant he thought that he was dead, but Rupert was only unconscious and the wound was to the right side of his chest, the blade having passed between two ribs. Fumbling a little with one hand, Donald managed to unlock the door and with Rupert's inert body in his arms, went out into the hall, shouting for Thomas. When the footman came running he said, "There's been an accident, send someone for a surgeon and find the Major's valet."

Thomas gasped in horror at his unconscious master and then calling for Harper, ran out himself to fetch the surgeon. Harper came hurrying down the stairs and when he saw Rupert's wig fallen off and his cropped head hanging limply over Mr. Fraser's arm he was stirred out of his normal self-effacing manner to give a startled exclamation. It was obvious that his master and one who had recently been a guest here had quarrelled to the point of duelling and he cried out, "Sir— sir, what have you done?"

"I don't know how bad it is," Donald said briefly. "If you will prepare his bed, I'll carry him up."

Harper asked no further questions but hurried up the stairs while Donald followed more slowly with his burden. Between them they stripped off the blood-stained shirt and when Harper brought water and linen Donald washed the wound himself, pressing a pad of linen over it and holding it tightly in place.

Quite suddenly he was aware of blue eyes staring up at him, the query in them plain enough. "I don't know," he said, "but I don't think it is mortal—for which I thank God."

A puzzled expression crossed the face on the pillow and as Harper carried away the bowl with its reddened water, Donald added, "Yes, I did mean to kill you—but that's over now. I've sent for the surgeon."

Rupert gave a little sigh. "Perhaps it might have been for the best." And then an odd gleam of humour lifted his mouth. "There's nothing like a little—blood-letting—to ease a situation. I—I am glad it was—

mine." His head rolled sideways and Donald, more than surprised by these disjointed words, saw to his relief that Rupert had only fainted.

At that moment the surgeon, having fortunately been at home, walked in and took charge. He commended Donald on his prompt method of dealing with the wound and proceeded to bandage it. Afterwards he turned to look at him, his quick eyes noting his coatless state. "An affair of honour, I presume?" he asked and then added, "You are wounded yourself, sir. Let me see that arm."

"It is nothing," Donald said, but the doctor insisted on washing and dressing the cut. As he tied the bandage he asked, "Is there anyone, apart from the servants, to look after Major Astley? His wife, perhaps?"

"No," Donald told him carefully. "She is in France and his father is in the country. Perhaps his friend, Mr. Ravenslow, should be sent for."

The surgeon nodded and now that Rupert was seemingly in good hands, Donald felt that his presence would no longer be wanted in this house, but before he left he took a last look at the still figure on the bed, the bandages about his chest, the blood on those white breeches. "You are sure he will recover?"

"I hope so." The surgeon sent him a sharp glance. "You may think yourself lucky, young man, that you did not kill him. From the look of things you were not far from it."

"I know it," Donald said soberly and went out of the room and down the stairs, pausing only to collect his coat and sword from the library. Outside the house, under the trees in the square, he drew a deep breath. So he might have done it, unintentionally! At the moment of deciding he could not do it he might have taken Rupert's life, and as he began to walk back to St. Martin's Lane, through the bright sunshine that had followed last night's storm, there was only one thought in his mind—thank God I did not do it, thank God I did not kill him.

Chapter 16

In August London was enveloped in a haze of heat. In the little room he had found high under the eaves of a house in George Street Donald sweated as he sat at the table under the window. This was wide open but there was no breeze to stir the air and the unpleasant stench that rose from the crowded streets and alleys lay heavily over the sweltering city. At night there was little respite and Donald lay on his narrow bed and longed with both body and spirit for the cool silver water of the loch beneath Lurg Mhór—but it was as far away as ever and even when he was free to leave it would be to France that he would return and La Verulai that would become his home. Unable to sleep he tried to imagine what this unknown place would be like, if there was a river winding through it, if it was wooded or open, and sometimes he dreamed of dark-haired children playing there.

This morning he had risen with the dawn and was sitting now, his shirt open to the waist, writing letters. He had written to Marthe, a letter that seemed to bring her into the room, even more than the dream of La Verulai and the thought of children that, sadly, might never be born. He tried to tell her of his love and yet when he had finished his words seemed utterly inadequate. Reluctantly he left her letter and began to write to Armand, thanking him for his hospitality to his sister, and then finally he began a letter to Bab—a difficult one this, for he did not know what to tell her. He laid down his pen, wiped the sweat from his forehead, and stared out of the window at the blue haze of early morning lying over the roof tops.

It was two weeks now since the duel and he could not rid his mind of the memory of it. Somehow the old hatred had died during those few moments when he had had Rupert at his mercy. Nor could he forget how his brother-in-law looked as he lay on his bed afterwards, nor the few words spoken during that brief return to consciousness, and he pondered on the enigma of this man whom he had begun to like against his will, a liking that had turned to loathing, and whom he had finally all but killed. Now, paradoxically, he knew he would have no peace until he was sure that Rupert was recovering from that wound—that he too did not have blood on his hands.

And then, if only the Prince would come, he could leave this hot, stinking town and never see it again.

The problem of Bab remained, but that he pushed for the moment to the back of his mind, for there were other and more pressing things to occupy it. Presently his landlady brought his breakfast and when he had eaten he put on the rest of his clothes, and within twenty minutes he was once more knocking on the door of Astley House.

When Thomas opened it he asked to see Harper, and Thomas, who was becoming used to odd occurrences, showed him into the library with wooden-faced civility. A few minutes later Rupert's valet came into the room.

"You wish to speak with me, sir?"

"Yes," Donald turned round. He had been looking at this room that, when he was last in it, had been the scene of their duel. Rupert had fought well, and yet, remembering it now, it seemed to him that his brother-in-law had tired quickly, far more quickly than he would have expected an active soldier to do, and he wondered why. "Yes," he repeated. "I wanted to enquire after Major Astley. Is the wound healing satisfactorily?"

Harper's face betrayed nothing. "Yes, sir. The doctor seems very pleased with Sir Rupert's progress and has allowed him up in his room today. Do you wish to see him?"

"No, I think not." Donald picked up his hat and Harper opened the door for him. "I merely wished to be sure he was recovering."

He came down the steps so deep in surprise at his own secret relief that he almost ran into Harry Cavendish who was standing, one foot on the bottom step, staring open-mouthed at him.

"My lord." Donald bowed stiffly and would have passed him had Harry not caught his arm.

"Mr. Fraser, one moment, if you please. I heard of the circumstances that put Rupert in his bed and I confess I am a little curious at seeing you here."

"I came to ask how he did," Donald answered abruptly. "Harper assures me there is no further cause for anxiety."

"No, thank God," Harry said with no sign of animosity. "I don't know a great deal about your side of the matter, Mr. Fraser, but I am glad to have this chance of speaking with you. Stay a moment," he added as Donald made as if to move away. "I want to say something I would have said the moment I heard Rupert had fought with you, that the truth had come out, if I could have found you."

"You? What is any of it to you?" Donald queried, with a lifted eyebrow.

"Rupert has been my friend since we were at Eton together and I wanted to tell you—" Harry paused and then plunged on with his eager vindication. "He's a damned good fellow really, though he does his best no one should see it. Why, God knows. And as for that business in Scotland, I wasn't with him then, but I can tell you this— he'd have done nothing an officer need be ashamed of."

"No? Well, you may be right. It depends on the point of view. In war there are other standards apparently of what a soldier may or may not do. My cousin was raped by four soldiers in front of her husband, and then, Lord Harry, forced to watch him hang."

"My God!" Harry said. "No wonder you hate us."

"I don't hate you. It is in the past now but nothing can erase the memory of what was done then."

"I suppose not, and maybe Fat Willie deserves to be called the Butcher for what he allowed his officers to do, but Rupert would have flogged any of his men who had behaved thus. I've served with him and I know. Ask anyone—Charlie Hay or Captain Brooks. His discipline may be hard, but he's fair, and his men think a deal of him. And another thing I know for certain—he cares for your sister as he has never cared for anyone in his life. Mr. Fraser," Harry added appealingly, "can I not make you believe that at least?"

Donald had stood quite still throughout this speech. After a pause he held out his hand. "Thank you, my lord, for what you have told me. Even if I had not begun to change my mind about Major Astley, the fact that he has such friends would be enough to tell me that I might have been mistaken in my view of his character."

Harry, looking slightly embarrassed, had stuck both hands deep in his pockets, but he brought one out and took Donald's in a firm grasp. "I hope you will bring Bab back to him. Believe me when I say it is he that needs her."

"As to that, my lord, my sister must make up her own mind," Donald pointed out, "but I will repeat what you have told me and I think it must weigh with her as it has with me." He made Lord Harry a slight bow and then walked away across the square. Yes, Harry thought, and I shall repeat to Rupert what you have said to me and that you came to ask after him. He ran up the steps and on up the stairs to Rupert's bedroom with a lighter heart than he had had since Simon Ravenslow had told him of the duel.

Donald walked on towards Cockspur Street and the Strand. The heat was intense, but at Mentonnay the fountains would be playing and there would be no stinking streets, no need to step over filth or be beset with importuning beggars. He wished he was there with Marthe's small hand on his arm; he would like to talk to her about Bab and about Rupert, for she had an odd little streak of wisdom, but for that he must wait, and he wished with all his heart that the projected visit was over.

A few more weeks dragged by. The heat lessened and two days of solid rain washed the streets clean, at least for a short while. He and Fergus had carried out all their instructions and now there was little left to do but wait. When September came in he began to feel restless and impatient. He had received a guarded letter from Armand saying that the doctor in Paris had told them little beyond the fact that Marthe needed rest and care; another letter from Bab spoke of her growing affection for the family at Mentonnay, and while she said little of her own troubles she let slip that when Marthe lay on her couch she wanted to hear always of the days when they had lived at Duirdre. He read the letter several times, his anxiety growing, for it seemed that his little love had become almost an invalid, and even her own letter, assuring him that she was well, did little to alleviate his concern for her.

He spent most of his evenings at the White Cock in company with other exiled Scots and it was something to be able to talk to his own countrymen and speak in his own tongue. One evening in September he was sitting only half listening to one of his companion's anecdotes when he glanced up and was startled and somewhat discomfited to see Rupert enter the tavern, look quickly round, and then walk across to his table. A rather odd hush had fallen and most eyes were on the newcomer wearing a uniform seldom seen in this place.

He inclined his head towards Donald's companions and said briefly, "Forgive me for disturbing you, gentlemen. Mr. Fraser, I would be grateful if you would favour me with a few words in private."

Donald was so astounded by his sudden and surprising entrance that for a moment he did not answer. Then he said coolly, "I cannot conceive that we have anything further to discuss, but if you insist I think we had better step round to my lodgings." He cast a quick glance round the tavern, but most of the men there had returned to their own conversations, with the exception of Sir William Chandler's brother James, who was eyeing the stranger thoughtfully.

Rupert too was aware of that look, of the lowered tones. "As you will," he said and followed Donald to the door. Outside they walked in silence along the Strand and a few moments later were climbing the ill-lit stairs of the house in George Street. In his room Donald turned to face his brother-in-law. He did not ask him to sit down.

"Now, Astley——" he said.

Rupert laid his black tricorne on the table before he spoke. "I understand I have to thank you for calling at my home to enquire for me. Harry said you probably wanted to be sure the Runners were not after you."

Donald gave one of his rare laughs. "The thought had not entered my head."

"I did not think it had." Rupert glanced round the room. It seemed poor and bare and stuffy and quite unlike anything he had had to experience except in inferior quarters on active service. He became aware that Donald was waiting for him to speak. "We have said some hard things to each other, and we have both had cause to do so," he began eventually, "but I want you to know that I bitterly regret what happened at Duirdre—and not only because you happened to find out that it was I who was there. It was only by the most damnable ill-luck that I was in Captain Harding's place. Surely you know that? And," he had his gloves in his hand and began to pull at the fingers, not looking at Donald, "you have been a soldier yourself. You must know that orders have to be obeyed, and I would have been less than human to have turned my back on the chance of being the one to apprehend Charles Stuart."

Donald turned away to light the candles, for the last of the daylight had gone. The justice of this appeal could hardly be denied. At last he said, "I suppose so. I will try to see it that way."

Rupert set his hands on the table and leaned across it to face him. "Is it so hard? And as far as your father was concerned, do you not think he would rather have died there than on the gallows? He was attainted, he would not have been pardoned. As it was he died quickly, defending his own home, not in some alien city and not a traitor's death."

Donald stood in silence, looking down at Rupert. Then he sat down at the table, his hands locked in front of him. It was true—he had thanked God often enough that his father had been spared the ghastly death reserved for those found guilty of treason. John Fraser might have got away to France before the arrival of the soldiers that afternoon, but Donald had never considered Rupert guilty of being there, only of what had been done when he was there. Now Rupert's words, spoken with a wholly new sincerity and without the arrogance that had so angered him in the past, made a deep impression.

He looked up after a long silence. "We have crossed swords on it," he said slowly. "I want no more than that."

"Thank you." Rupert inclined his head. "Now I must talk to you about Bab. I have said nothing to my father because he is at Rawdon, but he writes asking that we should go down there as planned and I shall have to tell him something which," he added honestly, "I don't wish to do." He saw the scepticism in the face opposite and added, "Oh, not for the reason you think. My father is so fond of Bab and I don't want to——" he broke off. "Fraser, I know I was crazed to lie to her as I did, but whatever has happened in the past, I want her back now because I'm very sure I can't do without her."

Donald subjected him to a long and searching look. "I think you are speaking the truth. What is it you want of me?"

"You can give me the chance to talk to her."

"I promised her I would not—not yet anyway. But if it is any comfort to you, she is in France with the lady I hope to marry and will receive nothing but kindness from her." A look of surprise crossed Rupert's face, but Donald ignored it and went on, "I have to be in London for another week or two, but when I return to France I will tell her what you have said. Then it is for her to decide."

"I suppose I must be grateful for that." Rupert straightened his back, his face in the candlelight seeming suddenly wan. "Would you—would you be so good as to take her a letter?"

Donald hesitated, but only for a moment. "That at least I will do."

Rupert picked up his hat. "Thank you. If she agrees to come back to me, I swear to you that she will never have cause to reproach me again. I will bring the letter in a few days."

He turned away to the door, but at that moment it burst open and Fergus Mackenzie precipitated himself into the room. His face was alight with excitement. "Duirdre, are you there! I have just heard——" He broke off at once. "I beg your pardon. I had no idea you had a guest."

Donald made the two men known to each and Fergus began to excuse himself, apologizing again for intruding, but Rupert said quickly that he had been about to leave, and with the briefest of farewells he went away down the stair.

"If I had known your brother-in-law was here——" Fergus was beginning, but Donald interrupted him.

"It does not matter. What has happened? Do not tell me that—at last—"

"Yes, yes!" Fergus seized his hands. "His Highness is here! He has come, as he said he would!"

Ten minutes later, having barely controlled the desire to run all the way to Essex Street, they were being ushered into Lady Primrose's elegant drawing room. She herself sat in a big winged chair, gowned as richly as she would have been for a court reception, a proud smile hovering about her mouth. By a table a rather military looking gentleman in middle age was pouring wine but it was at the young man who stood by the mantelshelf that Donald was looking. He was wearing pale blue satin and a black wig, and he seemed to have very dark eyebrows; for a moment Donald was startled into uncertainty and hesitated by the door.

Then the young man looked directly at him out of large and very beautiful brown eyes that were unmistakable. "Mr. Fraser, is it not? I remember you, sir, when you attended your Chief, my lord Lovat, but I see that my disguise is so effective that you do not remember me."

In a flash Donald was across the room and down on one knee, the Prince's hand to his lips. "Your Highness!" he exclaimed and the moment was such that he could say nothing more, aware only of the fingers that lay in his, the emerald ring that glittered on one on them.

"I am very pleased to see you again, and to be able to thank you for the preparations you have made for my visit," Charles Edward said. "Her ladyship tells me you have been most zealous. And this is Mr. Mackenzie—welcome, sir, and my thanks to you too."

Donald stood up as Fergus knelt in his turn, and it seemed to him that the years slid away and he was back in the ballroom at Holyrood House. Then they had youth and hope of victory before them and no knowledge of the black tragedy that lay only a few months away. He came back to the present and looked closely at the Prince. Years of exile and poverty, of wandering unwanted from one court to another throughout the length of Europe, of being too much in the hands of women, had taken their toll of him and His Royal Highness Prince Charles Edward Stuart, though he was still a young man just approaching thirty, looked tired and rather dissipated. The pale blue eyes had lost their former sparkle and the lids were puffy; the tall figure stooped a little, and there was more flesh on him than there had been in the days when he was skulking in the heather, but his smile still held the same charm that had endeared him to so many in the Highlands that not one man or woman was tempted to betray him for the thirty thousand pounds offered by the English Government.

He turned to Donald again. "I was extremely sorry to hear of your father's death. I counted him one of my most faithful friends—and so few are left," he added in a melancholy tone.

"I thank you for your sympathy, your highness," Donald answered. "My father counted it an honour to serve you in any way and risked his life gladly whether it ended on Drumossie Moor or on our own hearthstone."

"Ah, do not mention Culloden," the Prince said at once and his eyes filled with swift tears. "I cannot bear to speak of it. So many dead—and nothing won."

Donald remembered what Neil had said of the terrible remorse Charles suffered and he added quickly, "Sir, the cause itself is not lost. You still have friends left, as my cousin here and I have found during the time we have lived in this city."

"Yes, friends," Charles agreed and blinked back the moisture from his eyes, "I am surrounded by friends, and believe me, I am grateful. Colonel Brett, let me make you known to these gentlemen and then we will drink a toast together."

The Colonel bowed and passed the glasses round. Lady Primrose rose to her feet and the Prince raised his glass. "To His Majesty," he said and everyone in the room echoed his words, toasting the solitary exiled King in Rome.

For a while the talk was about the Prince's journey and he spoke eagerly of the places he wished to see in London. It was obvious he intended to spend a good deal of time viewing the town and he mentioned the Tower, the new bridge over the river, and St. Paul's church. Fergus and Donald exchanged anxious glances. The whole visit was hazardous enough without risking recognition in such public places but he seemed quite determined and full of hope.

"If there were four thousand men ready to follow me I would put myself at their head," he said enthusiastically. "I have twenty-six thousand muskets stored in readiness at Antwerp!"

It was plain to see he had no idea of the kind of Jacobite loyalty that existed in England and presently he suggested they should make some plans. For the next hour he sat round the table with them all, listening as Donald and Fergus reported on their work, named the few men who might be trusted to meet the Prince here in this house and it was past midnight before he said that he was weary.

His hostess rose and Donald and his cousin would merely have bowed and taken their leave, but he came forward at once and held out a hand to each of them.

"Gentlemen," he said warmly, "you have constituted yourselves my bodyguard while I am here and I cannot express to you what your loyalty, your friendship, means to me. God alone knows whether I shall ever be in a position to repay you."

"We want nothing," Fergus said in his clipped way, "nothing but to be of service to your highness."

Later as the cousins walked home, Fergus added, "He is very hopeful."

"I know," Donald sighed. "I wish we had not to disillusion him."

"You think we must?"

"My dear Fergus! You are a lawyer, you know how to weigh a case clearly and see both sides of it, and you cannot be deceived any more than I am. Our last, our only hope is to wait and see if an opportunity occurs for a move against the Government. Surely you must realize that."

He heard his cousin give a heavy sigh. "Aye, I do," Fergus agreed and they walked the rest of the way in silence.

Four days later Donald stood, a self-appointed guardian, outside the door of the drawing room in the house in Pall Mall where the Earl of Westmorland had been entertaining them all to dinner. Now the Prince sat in conference with his host, with Dr. King, the Duke of Beaufort and several other gentlemen. After the meal Fergus had gone to fetch some papers the Prince required and Donald waited in the hall for him to return. He would have been happier if the Prince had remained within doors at Lady Primrose's house instead of so much visiting about the town.

As he had expected Charles Edward was learning to his cost that there was little for him to hope for in London. There were people who talked eagerly of their desire to see the Stuarts reinstated, but it was soon obvious that no one was willing to do much else, and he was rapidly losing any faith he might have had in the active loyalty of English Jacobites. Dr. King told him plainly that though there were those such as himself who spoke openly and would continue to speak for the Jacobite cause, any thought of an armed rising was out of the question. The Duke of Beaufort expressed his delight in seeing him and in the same breath urged him to leave England as soon as possible, while the Earl of Westmorland, courteous and deeply respectful as he was, said in his blunt manner, "There's nothing here for you, sir."

Charles made in a gallant endeavour not to admit his disappointment, nor show that he recognized this second defeat, but it was a heart-breaking business and Donald pitied him, for he must know by now that he could do nothing but return to his barren life abroad.

However there were some lighter moments. The Prince wandered round the town without recognition, though Dr. King's manservant did remark to his master that the visitor who took tea with him was very like the busts of Prince Charles which were sold in Red Lion Street. He behaved much as any visitor from abroad might do and was so interested in the Tower that he visited it twice. He stared, fascinated, at the massive walls, the gates and drawbridges, and Donald wondered what his thoughts were on seeing the fortress that might have been the symbol of his father's sovereignty.

"A heavy cannon would soon have that main gate down," was his comment and Donald and Fergus gazed at each other in consternation. And when, on the wharf, one of the Tower ravens landed almost at his feet and hopped along beside him Charles remarked delightedly that the bird obviously recognized its master. Whereat his companions both urged him to lower his voice.

He also startled them all one morning by asking when he was to meet his cousin Frederick. They were in the dining room of Lady Primrose's house and the Prince had just finished his breakfast. She herself was not yet downstairs, but Colonel Brett looked up from the sliced beef he was consuming hungrily to exclaim with his mouth full, "Sir! That would be far too dangerous."

"But I hear he is much in favour of some sort of arrangement between us. It seems to me he is above all an ally that we need. Mr. Fraser, you yourself told me——"

"He did dine with Lady Primrose a few weeks ago," Donald agreed, "and it is true, sir, that he talked in those terms, though I would respectfully suggest that it is partly because he is at odds with his father and he knows the Elector is angered by his choice of friends. But that quarrel may be mended at any moment."

"And he is the Elector's heir," Fergus added. "He did not seem to me, your highness, to be the kind of man to throw material advantage away. In plain words, I think he plays with us to satisfy his own mood of pique."

Suddenly irritated, Charles threw his napkin down on the table. "Good God, gentlemen, have none of you any word of encouragement for me? Everything I have been led to expect, everything I wish to do, is frowned upon by my cautious followers. By God, I wish I had my Highlanders at my back now! I would show you how I would deal with such waverers."

Donald felt a deep flush rise in his face. "Sir, you misjudge us. I do not think you have cause to complain of our behaviour either in the past or at the present time. If we are careful now it is only because you entrusted us with your safety."

Fergus added stiffly, "And if your highness should ever again have an army at your back, can you doubt that we who fought at Culloden would be with it?"

At once Charles's irritation fled and his smile returned, though there was a bleakness about it now. "Forgive me, I should not have spoken thus. Of course I do not doubt you, my friends. I see it is that you doubt the present Prince of Wales. You think he might betray me?"

"I think it would be foolish to give him the chance," Donald said. "Surely your highness understands that?"

"I suppose so," Charles shrugged his shoulders. "But you in your turn must admit I have found less enthusiasm here than I had been led to expect."

"That at least is true," the Colonel agreed. "Your time here seems to have been spent to very little purpose, gentlemen."

Charles saw the indignation on the faces of the cousins and interposed, "You are too harsh, my dear Brett. It cannot have been easy and I think Mr. Mackenzie and Mr. Fraser have done all they could and I must appreciate their concern for me." And this time he gave them the old brilliant smile.

But there were many difficulties, the Prince himself at one moment like a boy on a visit to London, at another the frustrated leader of a defeated cause driven to desperation by the hopelessness of the situation.

Donald himself had one awkward moment. On the third morning he and Fergus with James Chandler accompanied the Prince on a walk through St. James's Park and the four of them were coming down a path near the lake and watching the wildfowl, the Prince talking of his great-uncle, King Charles II who had introduced the birds there, when Rupert Astley rode by.

He merely bowed in Donald's direction and passed on, but Chandler's mouth was drawn down and when the Prince enquired who the soldier was, Donald replied in some embarrassment that he was a connection by marriage.

"An unfortunate connection," Chandler remarked. "I cannot think there are many of us who can boast a redcoat in the family."

"Boast!" Donald exclaimed angrily. "Do you think I am pleased to own him?"

"My dear Mr. Fraser," Charles said in some amusement, "do not fret yourself. We cannot choose our relatives or, I promise you, I would have done without a great many of mine. And yours, indirectly, have been of service to us."

For a while Donald toyed with the idea of seeing Rupert and trying to find out whether his brother-in-law had any idea of the identity of his companion, but in the end he came to the conclusion that he might possibly only arouse curiosity where none existed before. Rupert certainly could never have seen Charles Edward in the flesh.

Now as he paced the hall in Westmorland's house he felt ill at ease over the whole visit, and as the door behind him opened and closed sharply, startling him, he turned to see James Chandler standing there, his face stormy and flushed. He glared at Donald.

"They do nothing but talk," he said irritably, "and now it seems they must send me to fetch Lord Appleton to talk some more. I trust you are not addicted to the vice of overmuch talking, Mr. Fraser."

He stalked out of the house, leaving Donald staring after him in some bewilderment. He had not the least idea what Chandler meant, but he gave a little sigh, wondering at how difficult it was for men to work agreeably together.

He knew what they must be discussing behind those doors. Two days ago Charles Edward had expressed his intention of abandoning his Catholic faith and accepting that of the Church of England. It would, he said, make him more acceptable to the English Jacobites. Donald listened to him doubtfully. There was some truth in what the Prince said, but remembering his Fraser cousins, most of them Catholic, the other Catholic clans, the staunch English families who had clung to the old faith, it seemed to him that there would be many to whom it would give a deep sense of betrayal, the death of their hopes of toleration. And he could not believe the Prince's intention came from any real conviction, nor did he see anything to change his mind when he accompanied Charles to a church in the Strand where the Vicar, though a known sympathizer, received his convert without having any idea of his true identity.

The affair caused a great deal of discussion at Lady Primrose's house, but to Donald and also to his cousin it seemed that the Prince had neither peace nor satisfaction in what he had done. And Donald told Fergus, with rare cynicism, that if it achieved nothing beyond annoying the Prince's brother Henry, Cardinal York, he expected his highness to revert to his old faith. Fergus was greatly troubled. To his straightforward mind it seemed that the Prince was playing a devious game with men's deepest feelings.

At eleven o'clock Fergus returned and handing over his papers came back into the hall. "You have been here two hours, Duirdre. Why don't you go into the dining room and have some refreshment?" He slid his hand into his pocket and pulled out a letter. "And take this with you. I found it waiting for you when I got home."

Donald took it, glancing at the superscription, hoping to see Marthe's delicate hand, but it was in Armand's writing, and disappointed, he crossed to the dining room where he poured himself a glass of wine and took an apple from the sideboard before he broke the seal on his letter. To his surprise he saw it was brief and he sensed at once that something was wrong, for Armand always wrote at length. Hastily he scanned the few sentences and then every vestige of colour fled from his face. He dropped the apple and it rolled away across the floor.

In a few words Armand told him that Marthe was desperately ill. She had collapsed one afternoon and the doctor who had been summoned immediately from Paris appeared able to do little for her. In his opinion both her lungs were now affected by the disease from which she had been suffering and there was little hope for her. It could only be a matter of weeks, perhaps less, before the end. He could of course be wrong, but he did not think so. Marthe was asking for Donald, and Armand begged him to come.

For a moment he could not think and he read the letter several times before the awful words took on any reality. Then he sprang to his feet, crushing the paper in his hand. He must go—go at once—and he flung open the door. At the same moment the street door opened to admit Chandler and another gentleman. They crossed the hall and as they opened the drawing room door Donald had a brief glimpse of the Prince standing by the hearth, a lonely and disconsolate figure. Then the door closed again and Donald in turn shut his door and leaned his back against it.

Slowly the full realization of his position dawned on him. If he went to Charles Edward and explained the situation, His Highness would undoubtedly tell him to leave immediately, but had he any right to ask? For months he had prepared for this visit, for months he had been employed in the Jacobite cause, serving that unhappy young man in there—could he now desert what he knew to be his duty, that of protecting a Prince who had little care for his own safety? He and Fergus were in a particular position with regard to him and there was no one else to whom in conscience he could hand over his share in the business. He had been financed by the Prince's slender funds and it seemed a point of honour to see the affair through to the end. Charles did not seem now to have much desire to prolong his visit and it could surely only mean a delay of a day or two at the most. If he went now and the Prince was taken he would never forgive himself. If he did not go—

He sat down suddenly, clenching and unclenching his hands on the table amid the litter of plates and glasses and, torn one way and then another, he did not know that an hour had passed. He thought of his little love at Mentonnay, remembering the premonition that had come to him when they had left the lake together on that last morning, when they had walked through the wood of silver birches. It seemed now that it was true. He would never make her his wife, they would never live together at La Verulai, and the thread of hope that had never been anything but slender had finally snapped. And somehow he had always known it would be so.

Now she was dying and he could not go to her. Yet why should he not? Was it not beyond reason to put duty to the Prince first in such a situation? In despair he leaned his head on his clenched fists and tried to think clearly. Only four days ago he had renewed his loyalty to Charles Edward, refuted indignantly the Prince's accusation that he might be a waverer—an accusation at once withdrawn in such a manner that now he could not for his part withdraw from the venture, and certainly not at this final hour. And had Marthe herself not said she did not wish to be the cause of his failing in his duty?

At last, across an ocean of mental stress, he heard voices in the hall and knew that the meeting was over. Footsteps came towards the dining room and he rose quickly, his decision made, so that when Fergus and Lord Appleton came in he was able to talk to them with no sign of his inward stress. Only Fergus, knowing him well, wondered what had been in the letter to bring that haggard look to his face. But also, knowing his cousin, he did not ask.

Late that night Donald wrote to Marthe, a long letter in which he told her he was detained by that duty which he had explained to her at their last meeting and he promised to come the moment he was free— in fact, he hoped to be with her almost as soon as his letter. Once that was said he was able to pour out his love for her and his longing to be with her. She would understand, he knew that, but he knew too that he was giving her whom he loved more dearly than anything on earth, a blow that might well do her final harm. What was a scrap of paper when she wanted him? Yet the doctor did not say hope was lost, and even if it was she might linger for a while yet. Oh God, surely that was not too much to ask? He bowed his head over his letter in desperate prayer that he might reach her before it was too late, and at last, too distraught to go to bed, he fell asleep at the table.

The next evening in a house in Holborn, two brothers faced each other across a candlelit table. The younger, with the hatchet face, said sullenly, "I tell you, William, it has gone too far."

Sir William Chandler appeared to be stirred from his usual indolent manner. "I know that. I disliked the whole project from the beginning. Did I not say so?"

"You did indeed, but did you imagine that would stop two young hotheads like Fraser and Mackenzie? Don't you see we're both likely to get our necks stretched if this business comes out? It is one thing to talk of the Stuart cause over a bottle of wine with a few friends, but this—! I tell you I never dreamed His Highness would want to go wandering all over London, exposing himself to public view, even if he is disguised. He is continually risking capture and putting us all in totally unnecessary danger." James Chandler's eyes flickered over his brother's face. "If we are not careful some of us will swing at Tyburn before the business is through."

Sir William put a hand involuntarily to his throat. "What can we do?"

The younger Chandler leaned forward in his chair, dropping his voice though there was no one else in the room. "I had better tell you I had a meeting with Mr. Pelham's secretary this afternoon."

This time the older man nearly choked and his face went grey. "James! What in God's name are you about?"

"Protecting our interests, my dear brother. He was kind enough to inform me that we are suspect. It seems you wrote a somewhat unguarded letter to Sir Henry Frere before he died, a letter which found its way to the Chief Minister."

"Good God! But surely there was nothing so very incriminating in it?"

"Perhaps not, but enough to throw suspicion on us. Something must be done, and at once."

Sir William grasped his wrist. "You cannot be meaning that we should betray His Highness? Even you could not be so cold-blooded?"

A faint smile lifted the thin mouth. "Of course not—and I thank you for the compliment. No, that would involve us too deeply for our own comfort. We can only thank God that rash young man will not be here for much longer—did you hear that he plans to leave tomorrow? No, I merely sounded out Mr. Pelham's man today and I tell you this, the Government is well aware that a great deal of plotting goes on—though of course they know nothing of the Prince's visit—and they are resolved to put a stop to it. They seem determined to make an example of someone and I am equally determined it shall not be either of us."

Sir William opened his mouth and closed it again and his brother went on, pressing home his advantage. "If you think it is any good continuing our allegiance to what is now a dead cause, then you are a bigger fool than I took you for. We had better make sure of our continued good health by assisting the authorities."

"How?"

James leaned back again, satisfied that he had made his point. "It is quite obvious that it is Fraser and his cousin who are not Englishmen and do not reside here, nor hold property, who are most likely to do something impulsive and pitchfork us all into Newgate. And they have less to lose. I know that Mackenzie is planning to leave London as soon as the Prince goes. Anyway he is not so dangerous, his wife is about to bear him a child and he is more concerned at the moment with getting her home to her family. It is Fraser who is the obvious choice, and he'd be better out of the way. A little information given to Mr. Pelham's man—after the Prince has gone, of course—and you and I may breathe again." The smile on the younger man's face widened. "Is it not simple, my dear William? Mr. Pelham will be grateful to us. He wants information and he wants a scapegoat, and I propose to give him both."

Sir William raised a drawn face. "You mean we buy our safety with Fraser's life? For it will mean his life, you know that."

James Chandler shrugged. "Maybe. But I am not so sure. I told you that he met a man whom I thought I knew in the White Cock? Well, that same man passed us in the park the other day and bowed to Fraser—and he was wearing the uniform of the Grenadiers."

"Great God!" Sir William was shocked. "Did His Highness see him?"

"Oh yes, but he made light of it. However, *I* have remembered—

the officer is Lord Rawdon's son. I've seen him at Almack's, though I believe he is usually to be found at White's. I have made it my business to find out."

Sir William gulped down his wine. "You—you think Mr. Fraser is in the Government's pay because of his acquaintance with Lord Rawdon's son?"

"Hardly that or we should have been seized by now, all of us," James pointed out emphatically. "But if he is taken it may save him. His sister is married to Rupert Astley."

Sir William collapsed in his chair. "If I had known all this I would never have—" he put a trembling hand to his brow.

"Of course you would not," his brother interrupted mockingly. "You've not the stuff of a martyr in you, William. Now I think Mr. Fraser has."

"But—but suppose he should turn informer—try to involve us to save himself?"

"You misjudge your man," the younger Chandler said shrewdly. "He would never do it. In any case it may not come to that. But what is disturbing is that the Prince knew of his connection with the Astleys apparently, even while Fraser was still in France—they decided to use it, yet no one considered that we should be told. Oh no," he made a derisive sound, "you and I, it seems, are not to be admitted to His Highness's most intimate circle. Yet we may suffer as much for our loyalty as anyone else."

Sir William was wringing his hands. "I don't like it. It's a horrible business and I want no more of it. Whatever the circumstances, to betray a man who has done us no harm—"

"Would you prefer to stand your trial for treason?" his brother queried mockingly. "Shall I describe to you the death reserved for traitors? Would you like to swing until you are half dead, have your bowels ripped out of you and burned before your eyes, your heart cut from your body while you still lived? Good God, William—think!"

Sir William had both hands over his ears. James was watching him through narrowed eyes; he saw with something like satisfaction the conflict on his brother's face, the revulsion, followed by a slow but inevitable capitulation to expediency.

Somehow Donald had lived through these two days. His whole heart and mind were at Mentonnay but with determination he saw the business out to the end and hoped he appeared normal. Finally he rode out with Fergus to see their charge on board a ship at Gravesend. It was a weary and disillusioned young man to whom they said farewell. Donald would have liked to bend the knee and kiss his hand, for this parting had a note of finality about it—not admitted but felt by all of them—but such a gesture was out of the question.

With genuine warmth the Prince thanked them both for their care of him but his eyes were, it seemed to Donald, haunted. He glanced at the sailors busy about the ship, at the indifferent crowds bustling about the quay and said sadly, "Do you think I shall come back, gentlemen?" And when Fergus would have made an encouraging answer he shook his head. "No, I doubt it. We shall go on making plans, but I think I need divine intervention—a miracle perhaps—to succeed now, and it does not seem to please Almighty God that I should do so."

Then he was gone, accompanied by the stolid Colonel Brett, and though the cousins stayed to see the ship weigh anchor, they had no more than one last brief glimpse of him.

Once back in his lodgings Donald packed the rest of his belongings and then finished a letter to Neil, giving him a detailed but guarded account of the Prince's visit and its negative results, for it was unlikely that His Highness would be back in Paris for some time, and he knew Neil would be hungry for news. He mentioned the store of muskets at Antwerp and pointed out that there were no hands to use them.

Then he went out to St. Martin's Lane. Fergus and Jane were leaving at once for the north, to stay with relatives on the border so that when the time came Jane might cross to a friendly house and their child be born on Scottish soil. He assisted Fergus with their baggage, and settled Jane in the stage coach. Then, waiting for the driver the cousins paced slowly up and down the yard together.

Fergus said, "Write to me, Duirdre. I should like to know how you go on."

"Of course." Donald took his arm. "Fergus, will you take some advice? Go home and make your peace with the authorities, then you can practise law again and give your wife and child a proper home. You are fortunate to have them—do not put them in unnecessary danger."

Fergus looked quickly at him. "You think I should do it? Take the oath, I mean?"

"Yes. Surely after this week you can see there is no further hope for us? Our loyalties remain, but there is no use spending our lives in plotting and planning. Nothing will ever come of it," he added bitterly.

"I've never heard you talk like this."

"I've never felt thus before. Can't you see it will be a bad thing for Scotland if all the loyal men spend their lives abroad? Scotland needs loyalty too. Go home, *mo caraid*, and bring your son up in the place where he belongs."

"Perhaps you are right," Fergus said slowly. "I will think about it. But what about you? Are you going to stay in France? Could you not try to get Duirdre back? It might be possible."

"I don't know—nor do I care very much just now. But you must go, the driver is getting up."

They shook hands. There seemed to be nothing more to say. But as the coach rumbled out of the yard, Donald stood for a moment feeling oddly desolate before he turned and hurried back to George Street. It was as if, in the person of Fergus, his last link with home had gone. But his one thought now was to get to Mentonnay as quickly as possible. He had hired a horse from a near-by livery stable and intended to ride all night in order to catch the first packet across the channel in the morning; he would, he *must* get there in time to give her some of his own strength, to hold her hands and help her to cling to life. He did not believe the French doctor's verdict—it was possible that he could be wrong, and Armand was always inclined to be less than hopeful where Marthe was concerned. She was young and they had so much to live for, and now that he was free to go to her it would be too hideous a trick of fate if she was snatched from him. He refused to believe it and as he went up his rickety stairs two steps at a time there was an incoherent prayer on his lips—oh God, let me get there in time—only let her live—

He flung open the door and then stood rooted to the spot. In the split second that he paused there he saw that his room had been ransacked; every drawer was open, his valise lay overturned on the bed, his neat packing pulled out, and his papers strewn all over the table.

Then a man stepped from the alcove by the window, the letter to Neil MacEachain in his hand. "Mr Donald Fraser? I am the Sheriff's officer and it is my duty to—"

Even as he spoke Donald was wrenching instinctively at his sword but he had it no more than half out of the scabbard when hands seized him from either side of the door, two men tearing the weapon from his grasp and pinning his arms behind his back.

An hour later he was thrust into the noise and filth and squalour of Newgate prison.

Chapter 17

"In 'ere," the keeper said. His name was Richard Ackerman and he was a large man with a mottled face and red hands, dressed in a coat that was too tight for him and which had once belonged to a prisoner of quality; it was smeared with stains and from the smell that exuded from his person it seemed that they were mainly of alcoholic origin. He carried a great bunch of keys and flung open the door of the small cell as if he were ushering its occupant into a palace. "In 'ere," he repeated, "as fine an apartment as any genelman could wish. Come on now, I 'aven't got all day."

Donald stood hesitantly in the doorway. "I don't understand. Why—"

"Don't 'ee ask too many questions," Ackerman admonished him. "It 'aint 'ealthy—not 'ere anyways. A genelman come and give me some gold, plenty of it, and 'e says 'you put Mr. Fraser in a cell by 'isself and look after 'im proper. Spare no expense,' 'e says, so 'ere you are. I thought you'd be glad to get away from them 'ell-cats down there. 'Urry up and get in." He gave the prisoner a shove and closed the door behind him.

Donald stood where he was, just inside the door, and looked round the room. It was no more than eight feet by six and furnished only with a chair, a table, and a narrow truckle bed on which there was a straw mattress and blanket. The floor was none too clean, but at least it was dry and there was a narrow barred window through which he could see rooftops and sky and, dominating all, the dome of St. Paul's cathedral. Still more surprising than his arrival in this room was the fact that on the table lay his valise and black cloak. He went to the valise and opened it. His few possessions lay neatly packed and on the top, in a folded handkerchief were the white cockade, the medal Neil had given him, and his little Gaelic testament. He picked up the cockade and held it in his hand for a moment. Then with a weary sigh he put it down and went to sit on the edge of the bed, his manacled hands clasped, the chain dangling between his knees.

A week of anguish—it seemed more like a timeless abyss to him—

separated him from the man who had been arrested on the afternoon of the Prince's departure, a nightmare from which he had not awakened. At first, half out of his mind, he had hardly been aware of what was happening to him. He was too stunned to think of anything but the awful fact that at that last moment he had been seized, prevented from riding to Dover, to the ship that was to take him to France and to Mentonnay. He seemed to remember appearing before some official and then he was taken to the prison, the manacles fastened, and he was pushed into the central courtyard to fend for himself.

He had stood there, blind to everything but his despair. Oh God, he had thought, what was he going to do, what *could* he do? If he had not waited that last half hour to see Fergus away he would have been gone before the Sheriff's men came, yet here he was in this hell-hole, this bear-pit—how, he was still not sure. He must get away, somehow— he had to reach Mentonnay, for nothing else mattered.

And then full realization dawned on him. He was not going to escape this awful place. He was chained, accused of the worst crime against the State, and aware only too clearly of the fate of his fellow Jacobites four years before, he could be under no illusion as to what probably awaited him.

Gradually he had begun to take in his surroundings. The Press yard, the central courtyard of the prison, was crowded with men, women and children, from all walks of life, in all stages of depravity—drinking, gambling, arguing, singing, fighting, a mass of suffering, stinking humanity. There were elegant gentlemen there for a debt, a highwayman or two, aging prostitutes and young girls, mingling with thieves and cut-throats, felons and murderers; there were ragged beggars, boys and old men degenerating together, and as soon as the motley crowd realized that a new inmate had arrived the dregs of it surrounded him. They fingered his clothes, the men urging him to come to the wine shop to spend his gold, the women offering to accommodate him for a few pence, until he flung them off in such a fury that, yelling abuse, they left him alone. It was not until much later that he realized that his purse, with his travelling expenses in it, was gone, filched by one of the ragged crew.

Visitors were allowed during the day provided they could pay their sixpence to enter and threepence to leave again and by the wine shop a party of street women were screaming with laughter at the antics of one young man as he imitated Keeper Ackerman's ponderous walk. One of them leered at Donald and made room for him on a seat beside her.

In instinctive revulsion he stumbled away, past the gaunt treadmill, turning his face from the prisoners fastened to it, the grinding of it in his ears, to a corner of the yard where he sat down on a stone ledge, his head in his hands. The walls were high, forming a well, and within the air was fetid. He felt stifled, and he remembered that when he and Rupert had ridden past this awful place the stench had spread into the street outside, and Rupert had told him of the highly contagious fever that had raged there since the spring, prisoners going up for trial infecting their judges and jury so that often those who tried them died before the condemned. Now he did not wonder at it. Inside it was even more repellant than he had imagined.

But all this and his own desperate situation were as nothing compared to the terrible numbing grief that now he would never see Marthe again, that she had asked for him and he had not gone to her, she wanted him and he was not there. He thought of that night in Lord Westmorland's dining room, with Armand's letter lying on the table before him. He had been mad, mad! He had thrown away everything for the Prince, sacrificed Marthe's happiness on the same altar, and it had all been for nothing. Why—why, in God's name, had he been such a fool as to put what he thought was his duty first, that duty which seemed now to have been given in vain? Tortured by remorse, stunned and incredulous, his agony of mind was such that he did not even wonder how he came to be here.

Darkness fell at last. The men and women were separated for the night and locked in cells and he was forced to lie on a stinking straw pallet, stiff with the sweat of the previous occupant, on the damp floor of a cell which housed nine other men, all accused of varying crimes, including one man who had murdered his wife. Donald lay next to him and though he buried his head in his hands he could not escape the man's complaining voice. Sleep eluded him and in the morning he was turned out with the rest to face a day in the courtyard. Discovering his purse was gone, he found a few loose coins in one pocket, enough to pay his "garnish" to the jailor, and received his allowance of bread and beer, but his stomach revolted against it, and though he forced down some of the bread he gave most of it to a boy with hollow cheeks and sores on his hand.

On the second morning a down-at-heel young man approached him and bade him good day. "And what, if one may ask, has cast you upon this dung-heap, sir?" he enquired. "I suppose, since you are a gentleman, it must be debt, as it is with the rest of us."

"No, sir, it is not," Donald answered shortly, "but I must warn you that my pockets are empty." He was becoming used to being approached by impoverished prisoners who obviously thought the newcomer might be worth the price of a drink

The young man flung up his hands in protest. "Indeed, I was not going to touch you, sir. 'Pon my soul, the thought never entered my head. I admit that debt is my crime and I could not conceive what other offence could have brought you here for you are not like them." He jerked his thumb towards several rough individuals who were watching a fight between two lads and yelling at them to punch or bite or tear each other's hair out.

"I am accused of treason," Donald said baldly, and walked away, leaving his companion staring after him. He pushed his way past the fight and across the yard to the gate where he stood leaning against the wall, his gaze fixed on the square of sky high above him. It was a grey day, a threat of rain in the air and he longed for it to fall, to wash away some of the filth and dispel the stink.

For the first time since his arrival he began to puzzle over his arrest. As far as he could see none of his companions was sharing his fate and he was thankful that Fergus had got safely away. Someone had obviously suggested to the authorities that his lodgings might be worth searching, but he could not believe one of his own Jacobite circle would have done such a thing. How then had he come under suspicion? Who could hate him enough to send him to almost certain death?

Suddenly he pressed his back against the wall, his body rigid, as the answer—or what seemed to be the answer—flashed upon him. It did not seem possible and yet, apart from his fellow plotters, there was only one man in this city who knew where he lodged and that man was Rupert Astley. Could he have chosen this way to revenge himself? And yet, as Donald thought of their last meeting and Rupert's apparently sincere desire to make amends, it seemed unlikely. But the more he thought of it, the more he became certain it was true—and the less he wanted it to be. He thought the hatred had been wiped out between them, he had envisaged Bab eventually returning to her husband, the past, if not forgotten, at least put behind them in a present that must be lived. He had, God help him, begun to trust Rupert—could Rupert then have done this thing?

He flung himself from the wall, the noise, the filth, the squalid struggle for survival becoming so intolerable that he did not know how to bear it—he wanted to tear his way out, leave this damnable city for good, never hear the name of Rupert Astley again. Trembling, he fought his way to the beer shop, thrusting men aside, not caring if they swore at him for spilling their drink, swearing back at them as he put his last coin on the counter and seized the bottle of wine it purchased. He drank it in great gulps—anything, anything, to deaden the horror that was enveloping him.

That night the murderer who generally lay next to him was sitting against the wall, shivering. His cheeks had become two bright red fever spots, his eyes were glazed and he had all the symptoms of a man in the grip of jail-fever. Donald brought him some water from a jug in the cell, but there was little he could do and he spent the night listening to the man's wild babbling as he lapsed into delirium. By dawn he was dead and Donald lay with his back to the corpse and his face to the wall, fighting the nausea that rose in him .

He was certain now that he would never leave here except for the scaffold or the grave of a fever victim. But it no longer mattered. He had failed Marthe and soon she too would be gone—if she were not already lying beneath a stone in the chapel at Mentonnay. He wanted to cry out "Marthe, forgive me." And in a moment of utter desolation such as he had never known, not even that night at Duirdre when he had held his father's body in his arms, he buried his head in his hands, his body seized by a shuddering he could not control.

"I beg you, sir," the voice beside him was that of a young man, his elbows out of his ragged coat, no shoes on his feet, but with a friendly expression on his pinched face, "don't give way. No doubt your friends will have you out of here before long."

Donald dragged himself up, away from the corpse, struggling to suppress the tremors that had shaken him. "I fear not. I have no one who knows I am here."

"Then we are in like case, sir. I walked down from Manchester to seek my fortune and all I found was this place—for taking a slice of bread when I was hungry. And now I cannot pay my debt." His fellow prisoner eyed Donald curiously. "But I am surprised that you, sir—"

"I live in France," Donald said by way of explanation, "and my friends are far away. Here I think I have only accusers—but I thank you for your kindness." A kindness all the more touching, he thought, in that it came from a ragged youth who knew nothing of his circumstances. And when the jailors came to remove the corpse and they were turned out of the cell, they went down into the yard together and later, when the dinner hour came, shared their meagre meal.

Over the next few days he was dimly aware that he was becoming as the other prisoners. Without money, with only the fourpence a day allowance by the authorities, a man in this hell became less than a man. He had no other clothes to wear, no means of washing; he lived on the bread and beer doled out to each prisoner, and sat for long hours fingering the heavy chains on his wrists. Marthe, he thought bitterly, would not have known her lover could she have seen him now. He had gone down into such a pit of misery that there was not, there could not be a God, only a black fathomless void into which human souls were flung to suffer without reason or hope.

After a while it occurred to him that he ought to make the request, apparently allowed if one could pay a messenger, to send news of his plight to someone. Philip Denby seemed to be the only possible person, though what his cousin could do to help him he did not know. But Philip could at least write to Bab and then she would certainly come back. She would bring tidings of Marthe and that was all he cared about—his own fate mattered not at all in his hunger for news of her. He turned out his pockets, searching for a last coin but he found none—even this small chance of contact denied him. And then, ten minutes ago, the jailor had fetched him and brought him to this cell. He could not understand why, nor who would pay for such privileges for him, pack his belongings and bring them here. Could it be Lady Primrose who had sent such help? Yet that was unlikely for the plotters were now split up and as far as she and the rest knew he was on his way to France. Like his arrest, it was a mystery and he did not even want to think about it. Sooner or later there would be an explanation, he would be tried and condemned and then it would all be over. But always into such thoughts came haunting memories of Marthe and the terrible desire to know if she still lived. Oh God, did she still wait for him? He leaned back against the wall, his eyes closed, desperately weary, the torment rising again. Would he ever be able to know dreamless sleep—until the long sleep from which there was no awakening?

Some time later, how long he did not know, the door opened. "In 'ere," the jailor said deferentially. "A visitor for you, Mr. Fraser, the genelman you're be'olden to." He set a basket down on the floor and the door closed behind him.

Donald opened his eyes. When he saw who his visitor was the colour rushed into his face. "You! I hardly thought even you would dare to come here."

Rupert stepped back involuntarily, appalled equally by the

contempt on the prisoner's face as by the unkept, shackled appearance of the fastidious man who had been his guest. Then in a voice of utter astonishment he said, "You don't mean—you can't think that I—"

The voice that interrupted him was deadly. "It seems obvious. Did I hear the jailor say that you were responsible for this?" Donald flung out an arm to indicate his cell, the chain jangling. "What are you trying to do?"

"Good God!" Rupert muttered half to himself, and then he came across to the table and faced the prisoner. "Fraser, how can you possibly think that I—I betrayed you?"

"No one else had cause to do so. No one apart from my own associates knew where I was lodged—and how else would you have known I was here at all?"

"I went to your room with a letter for Bab," Rupert said quickly. "Don't you remember? You said you would take it to her, and your landlady told me what had happened."

Donald looked up at him and then lowered his gaze again. "I would rather you went. I cannot leave and I do not see why I should be forced to listen to any more of your lies."

Rupert came and sat down on the bed, "I would be grateful nevertheless if you would listen to what I have to say."

Donald turned his head away and stared towards the window. "I suppose I am not in a position to make you leave but you need not force your presence so closely on me."

Rupert got up as if he had been stung and went to stand beneath the window which was as far as he could get from the bed. Then he swung round. "You shall listen to me, by God you shall! After our duel the doctor told me that your quick action in dealing with my wound saved my life. I owe you that and if that were not enough, don't you think for Bab's sake, I would not want you taken? I may be many of the things you have thought me, but I'm not a damned informer, and I'll not leave this room until I've persuaded you of that at least."

"Then your stay is likely to be a long one," Donald retorted but there was a weariness in his tone that made Rupert come back to the table and lean across it to face him.

"For God's sake, think!" he said forcibly. "If I had done it, why should I have had you brought to better quarters, why should I have sent Harper to fetch your clothes? Do you think I would have come to see you myself, if I had put you here?" He watched his brother-in-law intensely as he spoke. It had become of immense importance that

Donald should believe him. "I swear to you," he said slowly and clearly, "on my honour—though you think I have none—on my sword, if you like, that I did not betray you. Will you believe me now?"

There was a long silence. Donald sat staring at the floor. After what seemed an interminable time he raised his head. "Forgive me," he said with some effort. "I think I have misjudged you. In fact," he looked slowly round the cell, "it seems I am very much in your debt. Bab will be grateful to you."

Rupert shot him a swift, almost angry look. "That was not the reason I did it."

"Was it not? I do not know of any other reason why you should mind where I was lodged."

Rupert was silent again. Through the bars he could see only a small patch of sky and he became suddenly and sharply aware of what imprisonment must mean, especially to such a man as Donald Fraser.

"You owe me nothing," he said at last. "It is I who—" but there he broke off, not knowing how to explain any further.

Donald leaned back against the wall. "Whatever the reason I have to thank you for delivering me from the common cells. I think it was as near hell as I have been."

"I know." Rupert sat down on the edge of the table and for a moment their glances caught and held until he said in a matter of fact tone, "Thank God I found out. I have instructed the jailor you are to have everything you need—I have lined his pockets well enough to ensure that—and he tells me that though he cannot remove those," he indicated the manacles, the chafed wrists, "he will find lighter ones that will be easier to wear."

Donald opened his mouth to speak, and then with a helpless shrug he closed it again and Rupert went on hastily, "Now I think we ought to consider what is to be done. I understand your trial will be in about ten days' time. Forgive me if I ask you some questions, but if I am to be of use there are some things I must know. For instance, what evidence have the authorities against you? Were any incriminating papers found in your lodgings?"

Donald stared at him, rather taken aback by this obvious concern. "I don't know." He paused, trying to remember. "Yes, there must have been some." He got up and turned out his valise. There were a few papers there, but nothing of importance. "My diary is missing and one or two letters, one I had just finished writing, and several connected with my work in London—which was to further the Jacobite cause, as you must know."

Rupert stared down at his shining black top-boots. "Well, it looks bad, but I will procure the best advice that I can. Do you have any idea who might have betrayed you?"

"None, in fact I cannot imagine—" Donald broke off, a little colour rising in his face. "Now that I know it was not you, it must have been one of my own associates, which I find hard to credit and extremely unpleasant, but I can see no other alternative. Nor, I think, do I wish to know who would have done so vile a thing. Perhaps he will come forward at my trial to accuse me—though it makes no odds to me now."

"No odds? What do you mean? I should have thought it of the utmost importance to know."

"I mean that I shall be proved guilty," Donald told him plainly. "They have enough evidence from my private papers to prove I plotted against the Government. Nor will I deny my allegiance to King James. You said you would procure me advice—it is very kind of you, but you must know as well as I do that I shall not be allowed counsel to speak in my defence and must therefore conduct my own. And to do that will be no great difficulty for me, because my defence will be that I gave my loyalty to him whom I believe to have the right to it."

Rupert stared at him in some desperation. "Then you will be condemned out of your own mouth."

"Very likely."

"But you can't just make them a gift of your life! Fraser, I beg you to think of Bab and what it will mean to her, to your mother, to everyone who cares for you."

"I do not see that I have any choice."

Rupert said nothing, for he could think of nothing to say in answer to this. When at last he did speak it was in a halting manner. "Would you like me to arrange for Bab to come back? She must be told and she would want to be here."

"Yes, but I doubt whether—"

"Oh, do not concern yourself," Rupert interrupted, a bitter note creeping into his voice. "I know she would not welcome me, but I think Simon Ravenslow would go and escort her home." A thought struck him and he added, "Did you not say she was staying with the lady to whom you are betrothed? Would you like Simon to bring her also?"

It was a question he might have expected, but nevertheless it caught Donald unawares. "She—" he began and then he could not go on. Coming as it did after a week of such intense anguish, it was small wonder that Rupert's well-intended enquiry, added to his unconscious relief that Rupert was not what he had thought him, should be the means of breaking down his reserve. Hardly aware of what he did, except that here at last was someone who might understand what he had been enduring, he put his hand in his pocket and held out Armand's letter.

Rupert took it and read it rather hesitantly. Then he laid it down and walked away to the window.

In the silence that followed they heard the interminable hubbub from the Press Yard, and from the street outside the rumble of cartwheels, the sound of hooves, of vendors calling their wares—all the noise of London life. Somewhere a bell chimed the hour, and bells from other churches took up the call, reminding the citizens that time was passing.

After a long while Donald raised his head which he had lowered on to his clenched fists. "I was just leaving for France when I was arrested," he said in a barely audible voice. "Perhaps if Mr. Ravenslow would be kind enough to bring Bab she will have news—though I know it already," he added half to himself.

Rupert came back across the cell. "I am more sorry than I can say. It is damnable that you should have been taken just then but do not lose heart. Perhaps Bab will have better news."

The Highlander shook his head. "I dare not hope for it. I think—I think I knew Mlle. de la Rouelle was very ill when I took Bab there."

"There is always hope," Rupert said in a singularly gentle voice. Then he went on, "When Simon brings Bab where would you like her to stay? I think this is not the moment to ask her to come back to me, but Georgy and Philip are in town and would be glad to welcome her."

Donald nodded, thankful to be forced to turn his mind away from his own grief. He tore a piece of paper from Armand's letter and with a stub of pencil wrote the direction to Mentonnay on an unused portion. He handed it to Rupert and then, drawing a deep breath, he said, "There is one thing I should like to tell you. You have been frank with me and I would be the same with you. You think, I know, that I abused your hospitality and so I did, but do you not remember saying once that we all had to do things we did not want to do?" He saw his brother-in-law incline his head and went on, "I had already

239

decided to accept your invitation when my friends told me that there was work for an—agent—in London. They put it to me in such a manner that I could not refuse, but I want you to believe it was not the way I planned my visit, and when I arrived I liked it even less."

Rupert came round the table to sit down on the bed, and this time he was not rebuffed. "It is almost what I suspected, but I am grateful to you for telling me. We have both been placed in damnable positions and had things been otherwise, had I not worn this uniform—"

Donald laid a hand on his arm. "Don't concern yourself any more about that. We were not to know the circumstances that would bring the three of us together." He glanced up as the door opened. "Here is the turnkey for you."

Rupert got up. "I will ask Simon to leave for France at once. I know he will do it and Bab should be here in a few days. And your mother? Should we not—"

"Not yet," Donald said hastily. "She will be so distressed. If—when I am condemned—"

"But I imagine Everard takes in a news-sheet. He will have seen of your arrest."

"I had not thought of that." Donald felt suddenly desperately weary. "Very well. Perhaps Philip will go."

"Of course." Rupert looked round the cell. "And I will see that you get some more blankets. The nights are getting cold. Oh, and in that basket you will find a bottle of wine and a capon. I beg you will make use of them."

For the first time Donald smiled. "You seem to have thought of everything."

"That was Harper. I was about to leave when he appeared from below stairs and suggested you might be glad of them. Yes, yes, I'm coming," he said impatiently to the jailor who stood swinging his keys in the doorway. "By the way I have written to my father asking him to return to London at once. He has a great deal of influence."

"That was very good of you," Donald said warmly. "Lord Rawdon was always extremely kind to me and I only regret—" he clasped his arms across his chest, the chains rattling. "If I had been able to accept his offer, how different it might have been. Yet, at that precise moment, I could not."

"No," Rupert said, "I can see now that you could not, in honour, do so. But I too wish—"

Donald rose and this time it was he who held out his hand, remembering the only other occasion on which they had shaken hands, after the quarrel over the Duke of Argyll. "I cannot thank you enough, though why you should do all this for me, I don't know."

Rupert took his hand. He too remembered, but he ignored the last remark, merely asking if there was anything else his brother-in-law needed. And when Donald shook his head, he added, "I would like to come again—perhaps tomorrow, if you will allow me?"

Their hands still held. "I shall be very glad to see you," Donald said.

When the door had closed and he was alone again he began to pace slowly up and down the eight feet from the door to the window. He was thinking of his brother-in-law and the extraordinary change in his behaviour—so extraordinary that it had induced him to confide in him as he had done to no other man. It was a relief, so great that it was physical as well as mental, to know that he might speak of Marthe to someone, and he remembered Rupert's gentle tone, so surprising that he was greatly moved by it.

He paced up and down, thankful for his privacy, but presently he paused under the barred window, too high for him to see more than a few rooftops and that great dome surmounted by a cross which was catching the odd gleam of light as the clouds parted for a brief sunset. Even Rupert's ready sympathy could not really ease his state of mind; it was Simon Ravenslow who would go to Mentonnay, while he, who had lost his precious freedom, must wait here, locked and chained in a room he could cross in three strides.

He snatched up his cloak and wrapping it about him, flung himself down on the bed. Night came and the room was plunged into darkness, but it was no deeper than the darkness in his own heart.

Chapter 18

Georgiana Denby sat in the little salon of her house in Clarges Street and watched her cousin wear a path in her new carpet with his impatient pacing. She had some embroidery in her hand but she had not set a single stitch in it. Instead she watched him, thinking how trim he looked in his well cut blue coat with silver lacings, buff breeches and black top boots, the lace at his throat held in place by a diamond pin. However distraught he was Harper would never let him leave the house other than *point-device*.

At last she said, "Do seat yourself, Rupert. I can't bear to see you so restless."

He grimaced. "When was I ever restful?" Nevertheless he took a chair opposite her and began to drum his fingers on the arm of it.

"Dear Rupert, she will come no sooner for your impatience, and indeed I do not want you here when she does arrive."

"I don't mean to be—not in evidence anyway. I only want to know she is safely come."

"Well, I will take her straight to her bedchamber and then you can slip out. Anyway, they may be delayed, she may not come today at all."

"Simon will make all haste—it should be today."

Georgy sat silent for a moment, watching his face. He seemed utterly changed to her. Gone was the arrogance, the sarcasm that had withered her so often when she was a child visiting Rawdon in his supercilious Eton days. Instead here he was torn with anxiety, caring more for others than himself, for she could see that not only was he distraught over the rift with his wife, but the fate of the man in Newgate seemed to have become of paramount importance. Unhappily she said, "What will happen now? Will you go to Mr. Fraser's trial?"

"Of course, but I do not know what will happen. I count on my father to do something. The Duke of Newcastle has been his friend these twenty years—surely that must help?"

"Uncle William will know what is best," she agreed. "And I will talk to Bab, beg her to let you come here to see her. You want that, don't you?"

"Of course," Rupert said again but he added sharply, "Only I won't have her pressed—you understand that, Georgy? It is only to be when she wishes it."

"Yes, yes, I understand. Oh dear, it is all so distressing. I wish Phil was here, but he will be back with Lady Caroline tomorrow. He thinks—he thinks it looks very black for Mr. Fraser."

He gave a faint smile. "Philip was never one to be over-sanguine."

"Perhaps not." She gazed out of the window. "This is the first time he has been away from me since we wed and it has made me realize——" She broke off and Rupert turned his head away to gaze at the handsome fireback behind the hearth. It depicted two peacocks with tails spread and it reminded him of the peacocks at Rawdon. At the moment neither Georgy's own happiness nor Rawdon were subjects that brought him anything but added pain.

Seeing his expression she said, "That was thoughtless of me. I only want to—what was that?" She sat up, listening. "Yes, it is the street door, I think they are come." She saw how white his face had become and jumping up, bent over to kiss his forehead. "Dearest Rupert, it will all come right, you will see." And she hurried away, her embroidery fallen unheeded to the floor.

He rose involuntarily and went to stand by the half open door. Through it he heard voices below and then on the stairs; he thought he caught Bab's low tones but he could not hear what she said. Then a door closed above and he ran down and out into the street where Simon was already climbing back into his carriage. Rupert flung himself in and on to the maroon velvet seat beside him.

"Simon, tell me quickly. How is she? How did she take the news? Has she—has she spoken of me? For God's sake tell me."

"In a moment, boy, let me get my breath. I was about to drive round to Astley House anyway, in the hope of finding you." Simon tapped on the roof of the carriage with his cane for the driver to proceed. Then he turned to look full at Rupert. "She is well," he said at last, "but tired for we travelled as fast as we could. My arrival was a great shock to her, of course. She could see at once that I had brought grave news and for a moment I think she thought it concerned you——"

"Yes?" Rupert sat taut on the edge of the seat. "Go on——"

"She asked me what had happened to send me to Mentonnay. My dear boy, it is quite obvious that she still cares for you."

Rupert lowered his gaze to the floor. "Thank God," he said under his breath. "And then you told her it was her brother who——"

"Yes. She took it very bravely—she has great courage, Rupert. She packed at once and we were gone in an hour. I met the Chevalier for a few moments and he——"

"I want to hear about Bab," Rupert broke in. "You can tell me about La Rouelle later. You must have talked on the journey home."

"Not a great deal once I had told her the facts. Her concern was all for her brother, naturally. I did not think it either necessary or proper to tell her of your duel." Simon paused and looked briefly out of the window. They were already turning into St. James's Square. "I told her, however, some of the things you said that night when I learned she had left you."

Rupert's hands clenched on the red velvet. "And——"

Simon sighed. "She said she could not think of that now." He saw the eagerness die out of the face beside him and added, "You could hardly expect her to think of anything but her brother's plight, yet I believe she will remember what I said."

Rupert leaned back against the cushions. "Perhaps. I have to thank you for making this journey for me, Simon."

"I was glad to be able to do it, but it was most unfortunate that I had to arrive at Mentonnay when I did because M. de la Rouelle had just lost his sister, and I think Bab had grown very fond of her."

"What? She is dead?"

"Yes, she died two days before I arrived."

"Good God! And Bab will have to tell him." Rupert turned his face to the window. "Damn your coachman, doesn't he know where I live? He's gone past the house. Simon, will you come in and take supper with me? I don't think I can stand my empty table tonight."

But the telling of that news did not prove so hard after all, for one look at his sister's face only served to confirm what Donald already knew in his heart. They gazed at each other, oblivious of Ackerman's apologies for the behaviour of a woman in the court below who had screamed at Bab, asking if the lady was come from Drury Lane to see a highwayman who was to be hanged on the morrow. Bab had heard neither the abuse nor his apologies. She had not meant to weep but the sight of her brother manacled, in this awful place, and coming on top of all she had endured in the past week, unnerved her so completely that she threw herself towards him, sobbing. He could only hold her arms, the chains lying between them and for a while neither of them moved or spoke.

At last she controlled that desperate weeping and without looking up, she said, her voice shaking, "Donald—Donald—she understood, better than anyone. She never doubted you had done what was right. Even when you did not come, after your letter, and when M. de la Rouelle said—"

His face contracted. "I can imagine what Armand said."

"He—he did say some bitter things at first, but then I tried to explain—perhaps I said too much, but I was sure he was to be trusted and I told him why you could not come at once."

"You did quite rightly. And the Prince has gone so there is no more danger to him. You say she—she did understand?" A muscle moved at the corner of his mouth, but otherwise he gave no sign of the urgency of his desire to know it all, every word, every gesture that might ease the intolerable remorse.

Bab brushed away her tears. "Oh yes, yes. When your letter came she said she wanted to be alone to read it and later, when I went up, she told me you were—delayed. I was so upset—yes, I was, Donald, for I thought you could not know how much she wanted you—" she felt a convulsive movement shake his body, and she went on hastily, "I should not have said that—but Marthe knew better than I." She stopped, and her arms tightened about him. "Dearest, she was so—so strong. Although she was ill and frail and—and dying, she was so strong in spirit, far more than the rest of us. She never questioned your decision. Even at the very end—"

He drew in his breath. "Go on, Bab, I must hear it all."

"She said that if you did not come in time you were not to feel any regret, that she had known from the very beginning that you must put your duty to the Prince first, and that she would not like to be the cause of your failing in it." She paused and then burst out, "But I think I almost hate him! What good has his coming to London done? He asked too much! It has put you in this dreadful place when you should have been at Mentonnay—and all for a word."

He led his sister gently to the only chair and walked away to the window where he stood with his back to her, for the iron bars had become blurred and he could not trust himself to speak. At last he managed to say, "A word that meant something to me, Bab—then at any rate. And, it seems, to her."

Bab sat stiffly in the chair, her hands clasped, her eyes on his back. She did not say that when his letter had come, for the first time in her life she had felt him to be wrong, had rebelled against what seemed to be a harsh decision. Yet now, thinking of Marthe and seeing him in this miserable cell, she knew that she must not fail him at this moment. Calmly and dry-eyed now, she went on with what must be said. "Marthe thought only of you. She said she was glad you had had that hour together before you left. She even thanked me for—well, never mind that. She said she was so happy in the love you had for each other and she was only sorry for the distress you would feel. On the last morning—" Bab put a hand to her head, for the telling of it was proving so much harder than even she had expected, "she asked for pen and paper and wrote a note to you. I think it is very short, for she could not hold the pen for long, you see. I have it here." She reached in her reticule and took out the scrap of paper. He held out his hand for it and put it into his pocket but he did not turn round. "Thank you, Bab. But tell me the end."

"The doctor came that morning and he said there seemed to be a change. M. le Curé administered the last Sacraments. I didn't understand much of it, of course, but it seemed very beautiful—and comforting somehow. Afterwards she looked at me and said 'Tell him', and then she took Armand's hand and seemed to fall asleep. At first I didn't realize—I had grown so fond of her." Bab put her handkerchief to her lips and the jangling of the chain caused her to look up and see him brush his hand over his own eyes.

He came back to the table and knelt down beside her. "Don't cry, m'eudail," he said, lapsing into their own Highland tongue. "You have been so good telling it all to me, and I know it must have been very hard. I was sure, even before you came, that it was all over—I did not think La Verulai was ever more than a dream to give us a little strength for what was to come."

"I think she felt the same. She often used to speak of it but—as you say—more as if it was a happy dream. She never complained of what had happened to spoil it. She only thought of you—and of her brother. His distress was so painful to see."

"Poor Armand. I must write to him. He will miss her so much."

She leaned her head against his shoulder in utter wretchedness. "At first he seemed almost crazy with grief, but M. le Curé took him away for a long walk through the woods and after that he was himself again. I don't know what any of us would have done without the Curé."

"I had cause to know what he can do," her brother agreed. "I am thankful Armand is to be married. Tell me—are his feelings very bitter towards me? I would be very sad to think our friendship had ended that way."

"Oh no," she cried out. "When Mr. Ravenslow came it was all explained and M. de la Rouelle said to me himself that if his sister understood without knowing the circumstances, how much more should he when he did." She saw relief crossing her brother's face and added, "At one time I felt I should not have been there but I was able to help Tante Julie and Tante Clothilde, and Marthe was glad to have me. We talked of you when I sat with her and she knew I would tell you everything."

"I thought I had failed her," he said slowly as if speaking to himself, "but if she did not think so—at least I can keep one promise I made her." And when Bab looked questioningly at him, he went on in a quiet unhurried voice, "I promised her our parting would be a short one."

"No—no!" She threw her arms about his neck. "Donald, my darling, don't—don't speak of it. You will come out of this place— they cannot, *cannot* prove you guilty."

He got up and drew her to the bed that they might sit side by side. "Listen to me, my child. We have faced this before, we knew the risks I ran. We can't rail against fate now."

Fear clutched at her, but she tried desperately to keep it from becoming too evident. "Simon says there is not a great deal of evidence against you. Surely—"

"A few papers," he agreed with a faint smile, "but they are, I fear, more than enough to serve the Government's purpose. My trial is fixed for Thursday of next week and until then we can only wait."

"There must be something I can do," she said desperately. "I understand Lord Rawdon is coming and he knows so many people. They cannot condemn you! What harm have you done?"

He sighed. "You must understand, *m'eudail*, I am being tried for treason, and I cannot prove my innocence because from their point of view I am guilty. And I am in good company—our Chief counted it no loss to die for King James III."

"An old man of eighty!" she exclaimed. "You have more of life to lose than he did."

"There were many other men, some younger than I," he said gravely, "who died in the same cause. Shall I sink so low as to deny them? No, my dear, we must have no illusions. My informer saw that my rooms were searched and they found sufficient to furnish all the proof they need—they will not be too nice over a mere Jacobite."

"Oh!" she beat her hands together. "If I knew who had done such a thing to you."

"You must not think about it." He glanced down at her, hoping she had never considered the possibility that had driven him mad during those first days here in Newgate. But it seemed such a thought had not entered her head and he went on thankfully, "I have come to the conclusion that, unknown to us, we had an associate who was either a spy for the Government, or who became afraid for his own neck. And," he added candidly, "I would rather not know his identity. It is easier to forgive a man if one does not know who he is, and I must not die without forgiving my enemies, must I? But I fear he will appear at my trial and that will make it harder." His grip on her hands tightened as he saw her anguished expression. "Dearest, you must be brave for me. You know I cannot lie about my allegiance to the Prince and to the cause."

"Donald!" She gazed at him in despair. "Oh, think! You cannot just let them—" she broke off, unable to finish.

"I do not believe I shall have much choice. I cannot stand up in court and acknowledge George of Hanover, even if they would pardon me if I did so. Nor will I become another Murray of Broughton, buying my freedom at the expense of others. Surely you did not expect me to do that?"

"No, no—oh, I don't know. Your life is more precious to me than one king or another."

"But not to me," he broke in, his voice taking on a stern note. "Nor, I think, to you, if you will consider. You would not have me play the coward, would you, Bab? Nor beg my life on such conditions? I would be a most unworthy son of Duirdre if I did."

But she was trembling, terror in her face. "Donald, I can't bear it—I can't bear it for you. If—if they condemn you, I know—I know what that means—Tyburn and—" She could not go on for her teeth were chattering, her body rigid.

"Bab," he tightened his grip on her hands, "Bab, darling, I know—indeed I knew long ago I might have to face this. We have to find our courage together."

She straightened a little at that, but all her colour had vanished and she swayed sideways. He caught hold of her and put her gently back against the wall while he poured out some of Rupert's wine for her. She drank it obediently, her eyes wide in her ashen face, but after a moment she seemed to recover a little.

"Are you better?" he asked anxiously. "I did not mean to doubt your courage, child. Forgive me."

"I am so sorry," she said in a low voice. "It is not only that—but I've not been very well lately."

"My poor girl. It has all been too much for you."

She shook her head. "I think—I think I am going to have a child."

He stared at her. "Bab, are you sure?" She nodded dumbly and for a moment he did not speak. The news had taken him entirely by surprise, for it was one contingency he had not considered. "But, *m'eudail*," he said at length, "if this is true then you must tell Rupert and soon."

She glanced up in horror. "How can I—after what he has done?"

Her brother began to walk up and down the cell while he thought rapidly. He had never underestimated the influence he had over her and the future of both herself and her child might well rest on what he said now. When eventually he spoke it was in slow careful tones. "Did you know that Rupert has been here to see me every day during the past week? I have come to know him a great deal better and I think we have both been too willing to believe the worst of him. I know now that though he may have been extraordinarily thoughtless, and deceitful, yes, he never wanted to hurt you in any way—and as far as Duirdre is concerned he and I have settled our quarrel and I do not believe we should hold him responsible for our father's death. I want you to go back to him—for I'm sure you could be happy again."

She sat twisting her handkerchief between her fingers. "I don't know—I don't think I could face him yet."

Donald came back to sit beside her. "The child you carry is his, and if it is a son he will be heir to the Astley title and estates, and you cannot deny Rupert his heir. Nor can you go on living estranged from him. If I am not here—"

"Oh don't," she cried and turned her face into his shoulder. "When we were children at Duirdre, when you took me up the mountain or fishing in the loch, we never thought—never dreamed we would come to this."

"No," he said and looked grimly over her head at the bars. "It is as well that one's childhood is not marred by any such knowledge. We were happy, Bab. And now you must not deny your child his right to such a home. Believe me, I would not advise you to return to Rupert unless I was sure that he does indeed care very deeply for you. You will find him changed."

"How—why?" she asked wildly.

He hesitated, but only for an instant. "By many things. And I know that you have not lost your love for him, whatever you may think at this moment. If I am not here you will need him."

She pressed his hand against her cheek. "Oh, don't speak so. I will find a way to save you. Perhaps there is not enough evidence and they will pardon you, or—or only condemn you to transportation. If you were sent to America—"

"Somehow I do not think they will do that. I am the son of an attainted traitor—to them at any rate—and they will treat me as such. That is why I want to be sure you know my wishes for you."

"I understand," she said miserably, "only don't make me think of anything but you just now."

"Very well," he agreed. "We will talk of it again later. But remember this—not only do I owe Rupert this room and these candles and blankets as well as better food and writing materials, but more than that—an odd friendship perhaps, but friendship all the same."

"Friendship?" she echoed. "You and Rupert? Why, when you left Mentonnay I thought—"

He smiled a little. "Yes, it is strange, isn't it? But true nonetheless. I expect one day he will tell you how it all came about."

With an effort she said, "I am grateful for all he has done, but I cannot go back—yet."

She looked at him so piteously that he leaned forward to kiss her forehead. "I think your time is nearly up, *m'eudail*." And bending down he picked up a nosegay of flowers and herbs, a sweet smelling mixture of rosemary and thyme and sweet basil. "You dropped this when you came in. You had better have it when the jailor takes you out again."

His sister took it and sat looking down at the little posy. "Simon insisted I should bring it because of the fever." She shivered suddenly. "I am glad you are here, away from that terrible crowd down there."

"Oh, I am sent down to exercise every day," he said lightly, "but I have never taken a fever in my life and am not likely to get this one. I promise you I am very well, but you must walk through as quickly as you can. And don't be distressed over what you have had to tell me today. You have brought me, my darling, what I needed most."

Outside in the street she looked round for Simon's maroon carriage but the only one outside the prison gate was black and emblazoned with the Astley arms. Rupert sprang out and came across to her, his face tightening when he saw how she shrank back.

"Forgive me for coming," he said in a low voice. "Simon did not want me to take his place, but I had to see you, I promise I will not importune you in any way and I will take you straight back to Clarges Street, but we must talk about what is to be done for your brother."

She hesitated and then reluctantly allowed him to hand her to the carriage. Once seated there she found her heart pounding uncomfortably and she gave him a quick glance. She had not seen him since that last moment of revelation in the candlelight in her bedroom. Now there was a graver expression on his face than she had ever seen before—naturally perhaps under the circumstances—but there was also a new honesty in his eyes, and when he spoke it was in a low subdued tone.

"I deeply regret that I had to send for you—for this."

She turned away to look at the houses of Holborn sliding by the window. "It was good of Simon to come."

He went on, "I realize that this is not the time to talk of our affairs, but I want you to know that if I can be of any service to you or to Lady Caroline, you have only to send for me."

"Thank you," she said quietly. "I will remember."

"Simon or Philip will take you to Newgate again tomorrow. In the meantime we must think what is to be done, but my father should be here tonight and he will advise us."

"I am glad he is coming." She turned back, a pathetic hope in her face. "I thought of him too. He will be able to do something."

"I hope so, but I fear there is evidence against your brother that will be hard to refute. And from what he has said to me he is unlikely to prove the best advocate for himself."

"I know, I know! He says he will never take the oath and I am afraid that at his trial he will say things that will only make matters worse."

"We will have to try to persuade him to be as prudent as he can." Rupert stared down at his clasped hands. "I think that will not be easy."

"No," she said and at the distress in her voice, he put an impulsive hand out to touch hers. But almost as quickly he withdrew it and merely said, "We must try to find a way for him to refute the charges and if that is impossible, work for a commutation of sentence."

She did not meet his eyes. "You said 'we'. It matters to you?"

"Yes," he said firmly, "it does and not only because of you, Bab. I have come to know him a little and I believe our lives would be the poorer without him."

She raised her head. "That is true, but I did not think you would know it."

Before the clear, almost scornful look in her eyes he lowered his own. He had thought for one moment he had begun to break down the barrier between them, but it seemed it was there, as impregnable as before, and he sat silent, fighting an overwhelming desire to take her in his arms and comfort her and kiss away her sorrow and grief.

She too was aware of his closeness, of the need to feel his arms around her once more, and the knowledge that she carried his child, and that he did not know it, made the moment even more poignant. But she braced herself. She must not think of herself now, nor of him, only of Donald and remembering all her brother had said she went on, "He tells me you have been every day to the prison, that you and he——" she paused uncertainly. "And yet I thought, even before that day when Everard told us the truth, that you did not like him."

Rupert gave an odd laugh. "I told you once I was jealous of him. I see now that it was because he had something—a quality—I had never had. So I resented it, and your affection for him. Foolish, was it not? But that is long past." He changed the subject abruptly. "Simon has gone to fetch your mother from St. Albans." The carriage pulled up then by the house in Clarges Street and when the footman let down the step, he handed her out, and before she could stop him took her hand and pressed it to his lips. "One day I will ask you to forgive me, Bab. Not now, but soon."

She gave him one bewildered glance, as if she had endured all and more than she could bear today, and then without another word she ran hastily up the steps and into the house.

Georgiana was on the stairs and she came hurrying down, for the first time face to face with tragedy, her small face pale. She folded the taller Bab into her arms and tried to comfort her, but later, when Bab had been induced to rest on her bed, it was Georgy who sought comfort in her husband's arms.

"Oh, Phil, it is all so dreadful, and when I think of that ball last winter, when Rupert was being so hateful and he asked me to present him to her, I wonder, if I had not done so, if any of this would have happened."

Philip held his wife close to him, his hand stroking the fair head, regardless of its elaborate coiffure. "My dearest, who can tell? We cannot, thank God, see into the future and you must not blame yourself. Bab and Rupert were happy—they will be again, I'm sure, but differently, when all this is over."

She shuddered. "Do you—do you think he—Mr. Fraser—has any chance of being acquitted?"

"I don't know. I am not aware of the precise nature of the charges, but I well remember the executions of four years ago. I doubt the Government will look kindly on any one who wishes to revive that cause, and I do not think Mr. Fraser the sort of man to compromise."

She was weeping quietly now. "I cannot bear it. Although he was so reserved I liked him very much. I danced with him at their ball and I made him laugh. It can't happen—it *can't*. Poor, poor Bab! If only she would let Rupert take her home." Gently Philip lifted his wife's chin and looked down into her face. "I don't think she is ready for him yet. Since I have learned the facts, that it was more than a mere lover's quarrel, and it will take longer to mend. We must be patient for a little while and you must care for her."

"I will, I will—I love her dearly. Oh," she buried her face in his shoulder, "if it was you—or Rupert—in that terrible place, accused of treason, I don't know what I would do. And Bab is so brave. Hold me close, Phil."

He stared over her head, his grey eyes troubled. "There is still hope, my love," he said, but his arms tightened about her, for in truth he did not believe it.

After Bab had left him, Donald stood in the centre of the narrow room, fingering the letter in his pocket. He could feel the creases where it was folded and he still hesitated to read it, though he could hardly have said why he did so. Darkness fell and at last he lit a candle and sat down by the table. As he took the letter from his pocket he saw that it had been folded twice and when he broke the seal he smoothed out the creases before he looked at it. His mouth felt suddenly dry and he found it hard to hold the paper steady.

"Beloved," she had begun in the small spidery writing he had only recently come to know. "If it is not God's will that you should reach me before I am gone I leave this little note with Bab to tell you that I know you have done what is right. I believe in you, in our love and in His goodness to us both. We had our perfect hour and it will have to suffice us until we are together for all eternity. Having dearest Bab here has been like having a part of you. Don't grieve too much for me. I have been so happy in your love, and I pray always to Our Blessed Lady for you. M."

At the end the writing tailed off into a scrawl as if she had been too weary to do more than put her initial. The obvious weakness of the fingers that had held the pen caused him to put his head down on the scrap of paper, torn with grief and pity for her pain. But he had faced this before and it was only a momentary agony for he knew that her sufferings were over and he was only thankful that she had never known what danger he himself lay in at this present moment, that he had not added to her burden. And she had not thought he had failed her—she had understood.

For a long while he sat holding her letter in his hand, reading the few lines again and again. The jailor brought his supper and he ate it, hardly realizing what he did, for he was absorbed into a quiet stillness like that of a deep pool, where no disquiet could disturb the mirrored surface.

Then he went to stand under the window where he could look up at the sky, and very slowly the dark night through which his mind and spirit had passed began to give way. Everything, suddenly, became very clear and very simple. It fitted together, became a whole in his mind. What had seemed pointless suffering was no longer so, and it caught at his imagination—the whole desperate business of life, the ecstasy and the pain, the sorrow and the joy, and in the very centre of it a purpose, dimly perceived maybe but there nonetheless, and of which he was a part.

He leaned against the wall, his miserable surroundings no longer of any importance, his own danger forgotten. And all that he had believed and hoped and prayed came flooding back to fill the void that had yawned so pitilessly before him. How long he stood there he did not know, but when at last he lay down on his bed it was to sleep dreamlessly for the first time since the night when he had received Armand's letter.

Chapter 19

On the following Thursday afternoon, the second day of October, the gardeners were at work in St. James's Square, sweeping up piles of dead leaves, autumn on its way in London as elsewhere. A carriage, driven at speed, turned into the square, scattering one pile, to pull up at the steps of Astley House. Rupert sprang out and entering the house went straight to the library where he knew his father would be waiting.

Lord Rawdon sat by the fire, his gouty foot resting as usual on the stool in front of him, and he glanced up quickly as his son came in. "Well?"

Rupert flung himself down in a chair on the other side of the hearth. "It is all over."

"And the sentence?"

"Tyburn—on Monday." He leaned forward, both hands clasped tightly together. "Father, you've got to do something. He must be saved and you are the only one who can do anything now."

"I will try," his lordship answered slowly, "but I must tell you that since you went out this morning I have learned that the Privy Council summoned him to appear before them last night. They wished to question him, I gather, with regard to certain entries in his diary, but according to Earl Gower, the Lord Privy Seal, who did me the honour of calling on me, they got nothing out of Mr. Fraser. I'm afraid he made his case no better by his refusal to answer them."

Rupert got up and poured a glass of brandy which he drank off before he spoke. "He would never compromise—we saw that today."

"Tell me what happened."

Rupert refilled his glass, glanced at his father who shook his head, and then came to lean on the mantleshelf, one foot on the polished brass fender. "When I got to the court—it was at the King's Bench as you know—I found the place crowded. I suppose such a case would always excite attention, but even so I had to fight to get in. Philip and Simon must have got there much earlier with Bab and her mother, for I could see them sitting near the front. I don't know how they bore it what with the closeness of the crowd and the way things went." He swallowed the rest of his brandy. "Then he was brought in. Father, I have never seen anything like his bearing, everyone was talking of it afterwards. When I first saw him in Newgate he was—I don't know how to explain it—he was as you would expect a man in his situation to be. But since Bab came he has been quite calm and at times he has seemed almost happy, yet she had to give him news that—" he broke off abruptly. "To get back to this morning, he answered the court with a frankness and dignity that is beyond description. He said he had followed the dictates of his conscience and could therefore have no regrets. I remember he said," Rupert paused and then repeated, as if he was seeing that scene over again, "he said it was a thorough conviction of its being his duty to God, to his injured King and his oppressed country that brought him to work for that cause, and that if it was his fate to go to the scaffold he hoped he would do so as a Christian and a man of honour ought to do."

There was a short silence. Lord Rawdon stared into the fire, a melancholy expression on his lined face. Then he said, "He has a fine spirit. Tell me what evidence was brought against him."

"His accuser was called and swore his testimony, a rat-faced fellow named Chandler. Someone said he was brother to Sir William Chandler and I seem to think I've met him some time or other. Anyway, he said he had been led astray by the plotters but had seen the error of his ways and was turning King's evidence. A devious, mean-minded creature, but it is he who will go free, for the authorities will wink at his own implication with the Jacobites! If I could have got my hands on him—"

"I'm glad you could not. His evidence was damning enough, I imagine?"

"Yes, it was, and then the business of the muskets pretty well finished it."

"What muskets?"

"It seems that the Pretender bought some thousands of them and had them stored at Antwerp—ready for use against us, I suppose." Rupert gave a sudden, derisive laugh. "How sane men like Fraser could be so misguided as to—but that's neither here nor there. He was foolish enough though to mention them in a letter to a friend which he left unfinished in his room while he was out. The Sheriff found it, of course. It was read out and despite the fact that he had also said there were no hands to use the weapons, it was sufficient to show that had there been he would not have hesitated to join such an army against us—even to promote the whole project had he the chance to do so."

"I see. And then?"

"Oh," Rupert let out his breath slowly. "Even had the judge wanted him acquitted I doubt he could have persuaded the jury after that. But he relished passing the sentence—it was Judge Thomson and you know what he's like—I swear he enjoyed repeating all the details. He said the prisoner was condemned out of his own mouth, as he was, God help him. I warned Donald, I begged him to be careful what he said, but he didn't measure his words. In fact he made a point of asserting his loyalties."

"So then it was all over?"

"Yes. He bowed and did not speak again. I was trying to see Bab at that moment. Lady Caroline seemed to have fainted and Everard was getting her out—I forgot to tell you he was there too. Simon and Phil were with Bab. She—she did not give way."

"I did not imagine she would. She is made of the same stuff as her brother—though you may be thankful she does not share his opinions to the same degree."

Rupert was silent, hardly hearing his father's last words. For him perhaps the worst part of this terrible day was having to stand there at the back and do nothing while others cared for his wife. The fact that she had not wanted him, had not asked him to come, hurt most damnably. It seemed to him, despite what Donald had said, that if in this crisis she did not want him, then she would never need him again. And the secret knowledge of what he had done that last night shook his confidence in the hope he had clung to ever since she had returned. He had probably forfeited her love forever, his own life as nearly wrecked as that of the man in the dock.

He had had one glimpse of Bab, proudly erect, her dark head lifted, despite that death blow. And he had wanted to fight his way to her side, stand beside her, share her pride in the bearing of the condemned man, face with her the grisly horror of the sentence, but he said nothing of this to his father and went on, "Then they took him away and I came home. There is so little time left. What can we do?"

His lordship lowered his gouty foot to the ground. "I still have some influence, my son, and I liked that young man. But I had the impression that you and he were not the best of friends, and since you have told me why your wife is no longer living under our roof, I am at a loss to understand your change of heart, though I admit I am glad to see it. Frankly if I had known the details of your exploits in

Scotland I should have made sure you told Bab the truth before your marriage. What are you going to do about that situation?"

"She cannot think of me now," Rupert's tone was curt. "Later perhaps."

"I trust you will go carefully about mending the matter—but I imagine that by now you are fully aware of past mistakes."

"For pity's sake, sir! I have explained to you why I acted as I did. I know it was folly, but at least Donald no longer holds it against me."

His father inclined his head. "That is generous of him. No doubt your endeavours for her brother will help restore your wife's confidence in you."

Rupert slammed down his fist on the mantelshelf as if he was goaded beyond endurance. "God in heaven, will no one believe that is not my only motive? Listen to me, sir." He leaned forward, his face pale with the intensity of what he was trying to say. "I have only just begun to learn what sort of man Bab's brother is, and he does not deserve to die this kind of death. Oh, I know he has plotted against the King, harmlessly enough it seems, but so have others and he is being made to pay the price for them all."

Lord Rawdon lifted a thin hand and touched his son's sleeve. "Calm yourself, my child. You know as well as I do that no plotting against the State is harmless. A pardon is out of the question."'

"I know that," Rupert retorted edgily, "but there are only three days left. Must we stand by and do nothing while he—he is butchered?"

"Of course not. We can try to get the sentence commuted, though you understand it could only be to imprisonment or transportation—to be sold in the Colonies?"

"I know—I know, but at least he would be alive and we might eventually procure a pardon for him."

"It is possible. Order the carriage for me. I will go and see the Duke of Newcastle at once and if necessary request an audience with His Majesty." Lord Rawdon rose gingerly to his feet and with the aid of his stick walked slowly across the room while Rupert went into the hall, shouting for Thomas. A short while later his lordship was driven away and his son went back to the library to stand before the fire, staring down at the flames. He saw a log about to fall out and kicked savagely at it, sending the sparks flying up the chimney.

Friday came and went, and Saturday. On Saturday afternoon Armand de la Rouelle arrived unexpectedly, a disconsolate figure in black, and spent a couple of hours closeted with the prisoner in

Newgate. Then he was gone as unobtrusively as he had come and no one knew of his visit until Donald told his sister of it the next day.

Rupert went about the town like a man demented, enlisting the aid of any who would listen to him. He induced Colonel Hay to speak to his kinsman, old Queensbury, and Harry Cavendish to approach the Duke of Devonshire, while he himself interviewed anyone who might be thought sympathetic; even begging his father to approach the Duke of Argyll, until Simon thought he might well ruin his own career by his vehement desire to save a man convicted of high treason, quite apart from the fact that he made no secret of his daily visits to the prison. But Rupert was beyond reason. He had never been a man to take kindly to cautionary advice and he seemed now to be in so dangerous a mood that Simon began to wonder if his frantic attempt to save Donald Fraser's life, had become a kind of reparation for the past.

Lord Rawdon did what he could but the Secretary of State remained adamant. Finally he obtained an audience with the King and was to present himself at three of the clock on Sunday afternoon.

In all this activity the one man who remained quite unruffled was the prisoner himself. He seemed almost indifferent to the efforts being made on his behalf, though he was not ungrateful, and at last Rupert said in some desperation that it seemed as if he wanted to die.

At the same time that Lord Rawdon was due at the Palace, Simon took Bab and her mother to Newgate for the last time, and it was a heart-breaking task he would have given much to delegate, but Bab had not wished for her stepfather's company in the prison and Sir Laurence Everard had the grace to wait in the carriage outside. When Simon returned with the two women, Lady Caroline was on the verge of collapse. Bab was greatly concerned over her mother's state, and Simon thought her control beyond praise, but her white face and tense figure showed him at what cost that control had been achieved. Only when they reached Clarges Street and Georgy had taken Lady Caroline upstairs did he see her turn blindly to Philip and break into inconsolable weeping.

He left them and drove the short distance to Astley House, his dark face heavy with his sorrow for them all. Lord Rawdon's carriage drew up almost at the same time and he came forward to help his lordship alight, easing him down the step on to his good foot.

"It was of no use" the old man said wearily. "His Majesty said he saw no reason to interfere and he felt that justice should take its course. I did obtain one concession—but let us go inside. I must give the news to that boy of mine." He leaned heavily on Simon's arm as they mounted the step. "He's breaking his heart over this business—or is it over that pretty wife of his? I don't know."

"Both, I think," Simon told him. "But as far as she is concerned, my lord, I am certain their differences will soon be mended. I think her brother will at least have achieved that."

"Do you say so?" Lord Rawdon shot him a quick look. "I'm glad to hear it." He paused on the top step. "I'm too old for all this dashing about and it has been to no avail. That young man in Newgate will die tomorrow and for my part I'm sorry—very sorry." And still leaning on Simon's arm he went into the house.

At Donald's request his brother-in-law was to be the last to visit him and it was almost dusk when Rupert entered the prison. As always when the gates closed behind him he was stifled by the fetid air in the teeming, enclosed Press Yard, but this afternoon he felt his gorge rise as he passed the treadmill and the miserable victims mounted on it. Hot one moment and icy cold the next he had to support himself by the wall and as he entered a passage he was seized by such an attack of dizziness that he paused there, thankful that the turnkey took a moment or two to unlock the heavy door. What in God's name was the matter with him? Had he become so womanish that he could not conduct himself properly? He braced himself and went on. Donald was now in one of the condemned cells, a small dreary place, the stone walls lined with planks studded with nails. There was a barrack bed, a chair and a table, and this time no sky to be seen through the tiny barred window, only a blank wall and little of that. He found Donald, still fettered, sitting at the table, writing, a candle burning in front of him for it was already dark in there.

He sprang up as his visitor entered. "My dear Rupert, I've been expecting you. Let me offer you some of your excellent wine. It is odd, isn't it, once a man is in this part of the prison the jailor will bring in anything one may wish for—and thanks to your generosity to the fellow I have just dined off a most delicious salmon. Now sit down and we can talk."

The warmth and completely natural manner of his greeting eased something of the tension that was gripping Rupert and he sat down, accepting the mug and drinking off half its contents at one gulp. "I have brought the clean shirt you wanted," he said at last.

"Thank you." Donald took it and laid it on the bed. For a moment his face clouded. "Do you by any chance know how my mother is?

She was very distressed when she left me."

"Georgiana is caring for her and I understand Sir Laurence is to take her home tonight, or at least as far as the inn at Barnet. It seemed best she should be away as quickly as possible, but Bab—Bab will stay at Clarges Street. She has your cousin and mine to care for her," Rupert added and could not entirely keep the bitterness from his voice.

But Donald was not aware of it, and only by the tightening of his mouth did he betray how hard the partings had been, nor how they had unnerved him for a while. He did not know which had been worse, his mother's weeping and final fainting, or Bab's unnatural calm.

Rupert picked up his mug and drained it, glad of the warmth of the wine for he felt very cold again. "My father saw the King this afternoon. It was our last hope and he—" he came to an abrupt end.

Donald sat down on the bed, facing him. "You do not need to tell me. I never expected any other answer. After I realized it was Chandler who was going to testify I knew my case was hopeless. The fact that it was one of my own persuasion who betrayed me was hardly palatable," he added grimly. "And God knows how many others he may have named against whom the Government hasn't yet moved." He glanced at Rupert. "Surely you did not think the verdict would be changed?"

Rupert shook his head helplessly. "We had to try. I thought English justice might be tempered with some mercy, but I was wrong. My father did obtain one concession—" he broke off. Somehow he had to get the words out. "Afterwards there will be no—exposure on Temple Bar."

Donald let out a slow breath. "It will matter little to me, but I think you have spared Bab the final horror."

"We thought," Rupert went on, "we thought—afterwards—" he paused again. God, how hard this was! Many times in his military career he had dealt with the dead and dying, friends among them, met with anguished relatives, written painful letters, yet nothing, ever, had been as this was now. He gripped his hands hard together and went on, "Afterwards, if it is agreeable to you—and Bab—we will take you to Rawdon. I wish—I wish you had been able to see it. There is a path across to the church from the house, and great elm trees— and the rooks build there in the spring. It is not perhaps where you would want to rest, but—"

Donald gave him a little smile. "What! A Jacobite and a non-juror from Tyburn Tree! I doubt your parson will approve of that."

Rupert lifted his head in amazement but seeing the gentle humour on the Highlander's face and, moreover, the wish behind it to ease his difficult task, he responded gallantly. "My father still has some say with whom we choose to lie in our own ground. And in the end—" his voice trailed away.

"Thank you," Donald said. "No one could do more for me than you have done. I have caused a great deal of trouble and distress, but tomorrow will see an end to that."

There was so little personal anxiety in his voice that Rupert heard himself asking, "You are not afraid?" before he realized it was a question he should not have asked.

But Donald answered without hesitation. "I thank my God He has taken away my fear. I must admit," a brief shadow crossed his face, "that I could have wished to die more privately. Do you remember the day we rode together past the Tyburn turnpike? I had a presentiment then—Highland men sometimes have that kind of 'seeing', you know—but I think I have less to fear from the gallows than most men. I am tall and heavy and I pray I shall be all but gone before they—"

"Donald!" Rupert broke in, his voice shaking. "For Christ's sake—"

"Listen to me," his brother-in-law said quietly. "You are taking it to heart far more than I am. Death is but a door and they cannot take away my soul, nor keep it from passing through that door, whatever they may do to my body."

Rupert got up abruptly as if he could bear it no more, and walked away to the door where he stood leaning against it shivering. Donald watched him in silence and then he too got up. "Rupert, you are cold. I think you had better have some more wine. You do not look well to me."

Rupert roused himself and came back to the table, but he crashed on to the chair rather than sat on it. "It is nothing. I seem to have taken a chill, that is all—these damned October mists." He took the wine and drank it and after a moment the shivering ceased. He was aware of the prisoner looking anxiously at him, and in order to turn the conversation from himself he asked if there was anything further he could do.

"Yes," Donald answered at once. "I have several requests to make of you. I have written a number of letters and I would be glad if you would deal with them for me. I have very little to dispose of. What clothes I have I shall give to some of the men here who are in desperate need, but tell Bab that tomorrow I shall wear the white cockade she made me on my best coat." He put a hand in his pocket and brought out the gold medal Neil MacEachain had given him that April day in Paris seven months ago. He glanced at the word "Revirescat"—no, the cause would not flourish again, and the medal would become no more than a collector's piece. Better that it should buy freedom perhaps for that impoverished young man who had befriended him. With a little sigh he put it back in his pocket and went on, "I am most grateful to you for finding an Episcopal minister to attend me. Mr. MacPhee has been extremely kind and I am glad that it will be one of my own countrymen who will bring the Sacrament to me in the morning before I leave. This Gaelic testament," Donald picked up a small leather-bound book from the table, "I will keep with me until the end—it was a gift from my father—but I would like Bab to have it. And there will be a letter in it that I also want to keep with me, but I have asked her to burn it afterwards. Mr. MacPhee will no doubt be kind enough to bring these things and my letters to Astley House later tomorrow. There is one final matter." He paused and looked intently at his companion. "Rupert, you did not know, did you, that Bab is going to have a child?"

. If he had had any doubt about it, this question was fully answered by Rupert's reaction, for a look of utter astonishment crossed his face and he clutched at the edge of the table as the blood rushed to his cheeks.

"No—no, I did not. I have spoken to her only once since she came back. I—I did not guess. You are sure?"

"Bab was quite sure when she told me."

"But she did not see fit to tell me." He remembered how only a few days ago she had sat beside him in his coach, yet she had said nothing. Slowly the flush faded. "If anything was going to bring her back to me this would have done. Yet I have had no message—nothing—"

Donald sat down on the edge of the table. "I think she is not very much aware of it at the moment. You must forgive her if her thoughts are all for me just now—we were always very dear to each other. Only have patience. When I am gone and she has had a little time to grieve, you will fetch her home and, I pray, be happy as you were before. And you must be together when your child is born."

Rupert shook his head in bewilderment. "I can't take it in yet—Oh God, she *must* come back to me now."

"She will. I have told her it is my last request of her."

Rupert looked up. "You told her that?"

"Yes. And she will come, not only because I asked it, but because she wants to. And that brings me to another thing." Donald pulled the ring he wore from his left hand. "I want you to have this. I took it from my father's hand the night I buried him. You will see it bears the Fraser badge."

"But I can't take it," Rupert said. "Surely there is someone else, a Highlander perhaps, you would prefer should wear it."

Donald shook his head and held out the ring. When it lay in Rupert's palm he sat silent for a moment looking at it. It was of gold and heavy, and the embossed badge of the Duirdre Frasers, a sprig of yew, was surmounted by a few words in Gaelic.

"What does the writing mean?" he asked.

"Nothing without God," Donald said quietly, and then he added, "If you should have a son, I would be glad if you would give it to him. He will carry my father's blood."

Rupert slid it on to his own finger. "He shall have it. And I am more than honoured that you should entrust me with it." He paused for a moment and then went on in a swift burst of uncontrollable feeling, "I wish we had not wasted so much time in enmity. My God, if I could only get you out of here!"

Donald laid a hand on his shoulder. "I beg you not to distress yourself. You did all you could and one day perhaps you will come to see that this is the best, perhaps the only way for me. For a while now I have seen that—and *she* will be waiting for me, and my father," he added half to himself. "Oh," he saw the look on Rupert's face and went on, "I can't pretend that life has entirely lost its appeal, nor that I do not shrink from—tomorrow—but I believe I shall be given the courage to bear it. Rupert—Rupert, you are a soldier—you know it is not death that is frightening, only the manner of it."

"It is one thing on a battlefield, another to—" Rupert could not go on. Nausea rose, threatening his command of himself, but he fought it down, his head on his clenched fists.

"My dear fellow," Donald slid his hand further round Rupert's shoulders. "I am very sure you know that one does not fear for oneself as one might for one's friends, and you are suffering more for me than I am for myself. I assure you I am not being in the least heroic when I say that despite any natural feeling I may have about tomorrow, they cannot disrupt in any real way the peace I have been vouchsafed in my own mind. Rupert, you must believe that."

Slowly Rupert raised his head. He wished he did not feel so ill. "I see that you believe it," he said at last. "Forgive me, I did not mean to make it any worse for you."

Donald leaned over to pour out some of the wine. "There is nothing to forgive. I think you should drink this, you have been wearing yourself out for my sake." He watched Rupert drain the glass and as he did so they heard a clock striking somewhere. "We shall have that confounded jailor back for you in a moment. One last thing—where will you be tomorrow?"

A shiver passed through Rupert but he contrived to answer calmly. "Colonel Anderson has been good enough to give me leave until Friday. If—if you wish me to—"

"No—no," Donald interrupted. "I only wanted to be sure that you would not try to come. This is one journey I must make alone though I would be glad if you would pray for me. We leave here at nine but I don't know how long it will take to reach Tyburn." He looked at his brother-in-law, seeing two spots of colour in the pale cheeks, the strained expression. "My last wish is that you and Bab should be happy together. Be gentle with her, but don't let her grieve too much. I want her thoughts to be with the child that is coming, not with me."

The bolts of the door shot back and Ackerman appeared. "I must lock up now, Major—if you'd be so good as to come."

"In a minute. Wait for me outside."

"Well, it's gone five," the man grumbled, "and I've my duty to do."

Rupert turned on him. "Wait for me outside, curse you. Great God, you've had enough of my gold! Take your damned carcase outside for one more moment."

Ackerman made a grimace but the truth of this statement could not be denied so he withdrew, jangling his keys ominously.

As the door closed Rupert turned back. "I cannot keep Bab's thoughts from you," he said, "nor mine—nor will we wish to. But I will try to remember all you have said."

Donald held out both his hands. "Goodbye," he said and there was great warmth and affection in his voice and in his smile. "Our friendship may have been short, Rupert, but it is one of the things I would not have missed. I can never repay you now for all you have done for me since I was taken."

"I don't want any thanks." Rupert took his hands, searching vainly for words that would express what he wanted to say, but he could find none. He was only aware that the moment had come to tear himself away and he did not know how to do it. He felt a last pressure from Donald's fingers and then as Ackerman opened the door again he was released. Somehow he got to it. He meant to turn there for a last farewell, but he dared not trust himself to do it, for the floor seemed to be heaving under him and he stumbled outside as the bolts shot behind him.

Donald watched him with a great deal of compassion. Then as the door closed he sat down by the table. He had spoken the truth when he said that nothing could destroy his peace of mind, but he was nevertheless conscious of an almost overwhelming relief that the strain of the day's partings was over at last.

But he had letters to finish and drawing pen and paper towards him began one to Fergus. He hoped that no tidings of what had happened would reach his cousin until it was all over, but Fergus and Jane had gone to a remote enough place to be far from London news. He had already written a note to Simon Ravenslow expressing his gratitude for the latter's care of his mother and Bab. He had also written to his Chief, Simon Lord Lovat, and to his cousin, William Fraser, who, after tomorrow, would become the Fraser of Duirdre. Donald wrote to inform him of this in the hope that perhaps one day Duirdre would be returned to the family; William, he thought with wry humour, was far too cautious to press for it, but whether William liked it or not, the title for what it was worth would be his. Donald signed his hereditary name 'Mac Domhnull Ard' for the last time and sealed the letter.

Finally he intended to write to Gaston de la Rouelle. Armand's visit yesterday had been a complete surprise and one for which he was immensely grateful for he felt he was able to ease Armand's grief a little—grief that was, he knew, for himself as well as for Marthe. Poor Armand had been reproaching himself bitterly for his earlier attitude towards the love between his sister and the Highlander and Donald was at least able to set his mind at rest over that. He had brought a letter from the Curé and Donald received it almost with wonder, for it was as if the priest had known his need, that kind as Mr. MacPhee was and of his own faith, it was Gaston de la Rouelle to whom he could have opened his heart tonight. There had been a rare sympathy between them. But though he might not have Gaston's company at least he had his letter and as he read it it was as if the Curé was talking to him in some quiet room at Mentonnay, the words reaching out across the distance between them, saying the things he most needed to hear. And there was comfort in the thought that at Mentonnay they would all be praying for the repose of his soul as they did for Marthe's—a strange kind of union, but union nonetheless.

He took up his pen and began his reply. After half an hour the candle had burned away and he lit another and it was a full hour before he finished writing. But at last he sealed it and placed it with the rest in his valise.

Now that his affairs were finally in order he sat with his arms folded on the table, watching the flickering candle flame and the thought came to him that he would not again watch candlelight casting shadows on a wall. And he remembered as a boy watching another such point of light creating strange shapes on the wall of his room at home. His mind went back to that time, when the joy of life was on him. In the days before Bab was old enough to be his companion he had spent much of his time with Aileen Dru who had taught him the history of his clan, its ancient songs and poems, the traditions passed down from father to son. The bard had also taught him how to look for the tracks of a stag out on the mountain and where to be at the fishing, and he saw himself, a lanky boy in kilt and plaid, a flat blue bonnet on his long dark hair, standing barefoot in the icy stream, not caring for the cold, lost in the excitement of landing a salmon. He wondered if Aileen Dru's son had rebuilt his father's house, if Achnahoy had ever got home, if Morag was still in the glen. In those early years, as Mac Domhnull Og, 'Donald the younger', they had all watched over him, taught him every craft they knew, deeming that worth more than his tutor's lessons or his later years as a student in Paris, and he remembered all the familiar things of home, the kitchen at Duirdre, Morag's hands always busy, always ready to give the perpetually hungry boy a fresh-baked bannock and a bowl of milk. None of them had known, then, that he would end here, in this miserable place, far from the freedom of his own mountain.

And suddenly, the flesh he thought he had subdued rebelled against him. He was assailed by nightmarish visions of what was to happen tomorrow—the rope, the knife, the fire, his body torn and wrenched apart before a crowd of staring faces—and the horror, the indignity, the hideousness of it filled him with a blind terror. He twisted his hands together and for a moment he was oblivious of everything but his anguish, his palms pressed against his eyes as if to shut out what he saw, the fetters cold against his face.

It was short, that last urgent desire for life, the natural shrinking from such a death, but as he had told Rupert he had already fought and won this battle. And seemingly from out of the origins of his race, the familiar instinct born of the Celt in him came to his rescue, calling him to the realm of the half-seen that led to Tir nan Og, that Paradise awaiting the souls of men. He had felt it before, by the loch where the clear water lapped the stones, on the slopes of Lurg Mhór with the brisk wind in his face, and now it was here, filling the dark cell with its unnamable appeal, an appeal all the stronger now because of his profound belief that the two he loved most would be there, awaiting him.

Slowly the anguish died. Peace returned and with it a great weariness. Outside, beyond the walls, church clocks began to chime again. There were not many hours left until Mr. MacPhee would bring him his last Communion and he must make preparation for it. He got up and knelt down by the table and in trying to recollect his sins, it seemed to him that all his past life sped before him and short as it had been—as men measure time—there was much that he would not have wanted to change.

Chapter 20

The morning of the sixth of October heralded one of those clear days that sometimes come in early autumn when the air is keen but there is still enough warmth in the sun to dispel the night frost. The sky was blue and the crowds who began to make their way at an early hour down the Oxford Road towards Tyburn remarked cheerfully that there seemed to be no fear of rain. There would be a good view of the execution, all the fruit sellers and ballad-mongers would be out, and there would be plenty of side-shows to keep the waiting onlookers entertained. People began to line the route down which the procession would pass and whole families hurried for good positions near the gallows. Many had brought their breakfast with them and while they ate there was pleasure to be had from watching the milling crowds, and a man with a performing monkey did a profitable hour or two's business.

In his rooms Simon heard people passing under his window on their way and when two men paused to discuss where they would get the best view, he got up and slammed down the sash. A breakfast tray stood on the table but he found he wanted nothing more than the hot coffee. He paced up and down restlessly for another half hour and had just made up his mind to go to Astley House when there was a knock on the door and his manservant came in.

"I'm sorry to disturb you, sir, but Harper is here and wishes to speak to you."

"Harper?" Simon queried. "Send him in at once," and he waited impatiently for him to climb the stairs.

"I beg pardon for troubling you, Mr. Ravenslow," the valet began apologetically, "but his lordship is concerned about the Major and he sent me to fetch you."

"Why? What has happened? Out with it, man."

"Well, sir, as far as I could make out Sir Rupert never went to his bed last night, for it was only ruffled on the top, and I found him in the library this morning. He sent me for a change of clothes and the shirt he took off was soaked with sweat. I tried to persuade him to take some coffee at least but he would not, and he looked really ill, sir." Harper paused, his thin face reflecting his anxiety for his young master. "He said he had a cold, but I think it's something more than that."

"I'll come at once and see him," Simon interrupted. "Wait while I find my hat."

"Just a moment, sir," Harper stepped forward. "The Major's not at home. When he was changing his shirt he said to me, all of a sudden, 'It's no good, Harper, I've got to go. I can't stand it here.' And he went rushing out of the house. I went to his lordship and he's of the opinion the Major's gone to Tyburn. And he's not fit, sir—he's not fit for any of it."

"Good God!" Simon muttered and then he said aloud, "All right, Harper. I'll see if I can find him, but it's not going to be easy. Half London will be there."

"I know, sir," Harper said miserably. "I saw the crowds as I came along—there's more to it than the usual hanging, isn't there? And I liked that young man when he stayed with us. I can't believe it's going to happen to him."

"It's true enough," Simon said laconically. "Go home now and tell Lord Rawdon that I'll try to find the Major."

Ten minutes later, without waiting to have his own carriage brought out and the horses harnessed, he was walking along Piccadilly looking for a hackney coach but every one he hailed was occupied and it was not until he was half way along that he found an empty one and ordered the man to drive through the park as near the Tyburn turnpike as he could. The driver grumbled a little, muttering that the gentleman might as well walk, for a coach would never get anywhere near the gallows and if he wanted a good view he was too late.

"Drive on, damn you," Simon said between his teeth. "Hurry, and I'll double your fare."

"Do me best." The driver whipped up the horses, but progress was slow for there were other carriages going in the same direction and a good many horsemen obviously on their way to the spectacle. Crowds jostled each other in the road and wandered along enjoying the fine day and prospect of holiday entertainment—the fact that the entertainment consisted of seeing a man hanged and disembowelled deterred no one. To the London citizens it was a rare and stimulating event, for there had not been one since the executions of '46, and they saw nothing cold-blooded in their interest.

Several times lively groups slowed the coach to a standstill and once an impudent apprentice climbed on to the step asking for a lift. Simon struck out at him, cursing long and fluently. Eventually the driver leaned over and told him he could go no further.

"All right." Simon climbed down. "But wait here for me. I may need you."

He was now on the outskirts of a vast crowd and people were still wandering up to swell the sea of faces turned towards the gaunt gallows rising up above them some hundred yards away. Simon joined the throng and began to push his way through, using his height and broad shoulders to some advantage. Even in such a crowd as this his authoritative air stood him in good stead; he ignored the indignation of those he replaced and eventually found himself not far from Tyburn tree itself.

He looked up at it, the ladder resting against it. On the scaffold lay a long block, a large knife and an axe, and nearby burned a fire, its flame bright in the sunshine. Simon looked at them briefly, his mouth twisted.

There was as yet no sign of the procession, though from the distant shouts he guessed it was not far off. His eyes swept over the people to the right and left as far as he could see; Harper had mentioned that Rupert was not in uniform but wearing a dark blue coat and that he had gone without a hat and in a brown tie wig. If Rupert had been taller it might have been easier to find him, but in a dense crowd a man of average height was just one of a mass of heads. It was hopeless, Simon thought. Everywhere he looked he seemed to see a man in a blue coat and a brown wig and none of them was Rupert.

A sudden swelling roar made him turn his head and as everyone surged forward he found himself borne along by sheer weight of numbers. The procession had come into sight and he could see the four black horses, plumes waving on their heads, drawing the low wheel-less sledge on which the prisoner lay bound. In front of him sat the masked executioner while behind came the Sheriff and his escort and the carriage bringing the minister who was attending the condemned man. The procession came to a standstill by the scaffold and the Sheriff dismounted while two of the guards released the man on the sledge and helped him to his feet. Simon looked intently at him as he stood up, towering over the heads of the Sheriff's men, the manacles struck off, his arms pinioned above the elbows. He did not seem to have had too disorderly a journey. The London crowd was not known for its compassion and on such occasions found a use for rotten eggs and pigswill, and worse, but his coat, on which Simon

271

saw pinned a scrap of white ribbon, was only stained in one place and his breeches appeared to be muddied more from the sledge's contact with the dirt in the road than from any other source. Simon was aware of a sense of relief and as the noise of the spectators lowered to a hushed and expectant murmur, the prisoner turned and walked unbidden and unconcernedly up the steps and on to the scaffold. A couple of wags had clambered up and now sat astride the great beam above his head where the rope was fixed, but as both the Sheriff and the executioner had paused at the bottom of the steps to await Mr. MacPhee who was coming down from the carriage, for a brief moment the prisoner stood alone beneath the gallows. And there was in his bearing all the pride and dignity of the ancient race from which he was sprung.

A murmur ran round the crowd and then Simon heard a voice, a voice he knew, say sharply, "Oh God!" He swung round and to his astonishment found that no more than half a dozen people separated him from Rupert. As Harper had said, Rupert was hatless, the sweat running off his face. At once Simon tried to carve a way through to him, hardly noticing the curses or the snatches of conversation about him, but it seemed that the undulations of the crowd were only sweeping them further apart.

"What a shame," a girl's voice cried shrilly. "Such a handsome young fellow!"

A red-faced man laughed raucously. "'E don't look as lively as that Toby we 'ad 'ere last month."

"No," another man agreed, "but t'aint often we get a cull from those 'eathenish places up north, and on the Tree for treason too. Look, there's the parson."

"That baint no parson," the first man retorted. "Tis a popish priest more likely."

A fat woman giggled. "Ah, so 'e may be. Got any rotten eggs, John?"

"'E should be strung up too," the red-faced man said pugnaciously. "'Ere, let's push a bit closer."

Simon's temper flared and he almost threw the man aside. "Get out of my way, damn you. Rupert—Rupert!"

"Well, I like that!" the fellow grumbled. "We all want to see, don't we?"

Simon ignored him and struggled between the girl and the fat woman despite their protests, until at last he reached through to Rupert and caught him by the shoulder. "Thank God, I've found you. What possessed you to come?"

Rupert turned and looked at him dazedly. Quite apart from the sweat and his hectic colour, his eyes were glinting in an odd way and he seemed to find it hard to fix them on Simon. "How—how did you get here?" he asked in an uncertain voice.

"Never mind that." Simon put up a hand and touched his face. As he thought, it was burning. "You are ill," he said. "We must get out of here at once. Take my arm and I'll get you through."

"No—no!" Rupert flung off his arm. "I must be here. I can't do anything for him but if I'm here—" he broke off, staring in horror at the sea of faces, curious, interested, gloating, "at least it will be someone who is not come just to jeer or stare." He began to tremble violently. "Simon, look at him—look at him."

Despite his anxiety to get Rupert away before the end, Simon turned to look up at the scaffold. The Sheriff was there now and seemed to be asking the condemned man if he wished to address the crowd, but he shook his head, merely handing the Sheriff a brief statement which he wished to be read later. The Sheriff nodded and beckoned to Mr. MacPhee to mount the steps and begin his last office.

The crowd was a good deal quieter now but even so Simon could not hear what was being said, though he could see the dying man clearly, his lips moving in response to the prayers, his eyes fixed on some spot away in the distance, where the trees of the park were turning yellow and brown. It seemed to Simon that he had already gone beyond the reach of the men who surrounded him, ready to do their work, and for a moment he gazed up at the scaffold, profoundly stirred by what he saw.

Then he heard Rupert's teeth chattering in an alarming manner. "Come away," he said. "Come away, for pity's sake," but Rupert wrenched himself free, and striking off the restraining arm tried to push his way forward.

"I must be nearer—if he could see me—let me through—damn you—damn you—"

Simon caught hold of him again and this time Rupert put a hand to his head and swayed unsteadily. In complete bewilderment he looked at Simon and muttered, "What is it? Where—" and then he collapsed like a log against his friend.

Somehow Simon got an arm round his waist, supporting him as best he could, but the press was now so great that he was unable to progress at all and with Rupert's dead weight against him he despaired of getting out.

"What's happening?" the fat woman cried. "I can't see."

273

"He's praying with the minister," someone told her. "You oughter be nearer the front, mistress, you won't see nothin' 'ere." She was given a shove and the movement gave Simon the opening he needed.

"Make way there," he commanded, "can't you see this gentleman is ill? Make way, confound you."

The crowd shifted a little, obligingly good-humoured, and with much pushing and heaving Simon managed to make his way towards the outskirts of it, others only too pleased to take his place. Half carrying, half dragging Rupert he pressed on, the sick man's head lying limply against his shoulder, or rolling alarmingly as Simon lurched, and with no illusions about the gravity of his state, Simon ordered people out of their path with such ferocity that they gave way before him. But by the time he was clear of them all he was battered and breathless; Rupert had lost his wig and his coat was ripped, and though Simon did not know it, he no longer possessed either purse or silk kerchief.

When he came in sight of the spot where he had begun his search, to his relief the hackney carriage was still waiting for him, the driver standing on the box in order to see what was happening.

"Come down," Simon ordered. "This gentleman has been taken ill and I need your help to get him inside."

The man shrugged and climbed down, remarking that he couldn't see much anyway. He drew in his breath in a whistle when he saw Rupert and between them they lifted his inert body into the coach, laying him along the seat as comfortably as they could. Then the driver climbed back on to the box but as Simon was about to enter the coach himself he heard a strange sound, a long low swelling sound emitted by the crowd and it told him that the end had come. His dark face contracted and he had a sudden memory of Donald Fraser standing with him in the doorway of the Astleys' ball-room. He bowed his head for a brief moment and then, jumping in, he slammed the door and shouted to the driver to go as fast as he could to St. James's Square.

The rest of that day he and Lord Rawdon sat by Rupert's bed. For the most part he was unconscious and rambling in delirium, and the doctor who was summoned confirmed what Simon already suspected, that the patient had caught the jail-fever that was raging in Newgate prison. There was little to be done for him. The doctor bled him and told them to await the crisis. Night came and for much of it Rupert talked wildly, sometimes loudly and at other times in a low uneasy mutter; he talked of Bab and of Donald, of Duirdre, of a duel, of Newgate and the execution. He seemed to think that Bab was still in France and twice he spoke of a child and Simon and his lordship exchanged glances.

"We ought to fetch her," Simon said, and Lord Rawdon answered, "Poor child—poor child, she has borne enough today. Tomorrow—if he is no better."

Throughout the night his body was shaken by convulsive tremors and he tried to throw off the bed covers. Simon tucked them back and sponged his face and hands in an endeavour to cool the fever. Once he seemed to be sensible and spoke Simon's name, but he soon drifted off into a restless state between delirium and unconsciousness.

Lord Rawdon looked old and weary as he sat helplessly watching his son suffering. Once Simon persuaded him to lie down for a while, calling the housekeeper to take his place, but he was gone barely an hour before he came back to the bed. During the night he and Simon talked of the execution and Simon told him of what he had seen. The old man sighed deeply. "Ah, that young man had courage of a rare order."

Doctor Morgan returned early in the morning and by now it was obvious, not only to him but also to the watchers by the bed that the sick man was considerably weaker. He still rambled in a thin uneven tone, but there was no strength in his voice and when his eyes were open they glittered unseeingly, his breathing shallow and uneven, the fever spots vivid in an otherwise ashen face, his freckles dark blotches against that pallor.

The doctor said, "I will bleed him again and then perhaps he may rest a little, but he seems to be in great distress of mind over something and that is not helping him, my lord."

Lord Rawdon's own face was grey and haggard. "That young man who died so gallantly at Tyburn yesterday was his brother-in-law, sir, and I believe my son had become more attached to him than any of us realized."

"That explains a great deal. I imagine Major Astley was too much upset to pay attention to the first symptoms of this terrible fever."

"That is true," Simon agreed. "He said he had a cold."

"A cold!" Doctor Morgan exclaimed. "He must have been feeling considerably worse than that, if I am any judge."

"He was not concerned with himself," Simon said, and wondered if Rupert's new found selflessness was to cost him his life. He turned away from the face on the pillow to glance at Lord Rawdon. "I'll go for Bab," he said and left the room.

They had given her some laudanum drops last night and Bab had slept, only to waken afresh to misery. The shock of it as she came out of the mists of a drugged sleep was such that she could have wished she had not gone to bed at all but had sat on here by this window where she had spent all day yesterday. Georgy had begged her to rest, to take a little nourishment, but she had been unable to swallow anything but the few sips of brandy that Philip had insisted on giving her. Susan had come a little while ago to attend to her toilet and she had submitted to having her hair dressed. Now Susan had gone, saying she would fetch some hot coffee, and Bab sat down again in the same chair by the window. The fine weather of yesterday had given way to soft autumnal rain that fell steadily on the garden outside, the last of the summer fading from it.

She was quite numb. Yesterday the impossible had happened, such black horror enveloping her that nature had, mercifully, laid a pall over her mind. On Sunday night she had wept until she had no more tears, torn by hopes of a last minute reprieve, until hope died and exhaustion finally quietened her. Now there was nothing—only the chair in which she sat, the upholstery cream coloured with pink roses and green leaves and she traced the pattern with her finger.

Of herself, of Rupert, of their child she could not think. Life was a hideous nothingness, peopled by men who could perpetrate the thing that was done yesterday, and she did not think she could ever begin to live again. She tried to see Donald as he had been at their last meeting, in the dark cheerless cell, smiling at her with a serenity she could neither understand nor emulate. She wanted to see every line of his face, the dark hair drawn back from his forehead, the straight dark brows, the wide-set grey eyes, the scarred cheek, but the more she tried to see him, the more indistinct the picture grew until, still dazed from the laudanum, she wanted to cry out "Oh God, let me remember—don't let me forget". But there was only the rain at the window, the silence, a brain that could not think in a head that ached intolerably.

A quiet knock came at the door and thinking it was Susan with her coffee she did not answer. It opened and she heard footsteps, and then turning her head slightly she saw Simon Ravenslow, his cloak dripping with rain, his sodden hat under his arm.

She put a hand to her breast. "What—what is it?" Could he have come to tell her that the nightmare was not true, that there had been a pardon? But no—that was yesterday—and Philip would have told her. She gazed up at him in mute appeal as he stood looking down at her.

"Bab," he said gently, "I would not have disturbed you now for anything in the world, but Rupert is very ill. The doctor thinks he is dying." He heard her breath hiss between her teeth and he went on, his voice low but growing more urgent as he saw the dazed look on her face. "He caught the fever from that infernal prison and practically wrecked his chance of recovery by refusing to acknowledge he was ill. He was thinking only of your brother."

For a moment he thought she was going to faint, but she caught at the arms of her chair and said uncertainly, "What—what do you want me to do?"

"Come to him. He is half out of his mind but he has been calling for you and the doctor says he must be calmed if there is to be any hope of a recovery. He—" Simon hesitated for he had not meant to say this, but something made him go on, "he was in the crowd yesterday—I found him there. He collapsed before the end and I brought him home. Will you come?"

She caught her breath again and he wondered for one moment if she was too shocked to understand. But almost at once she rose. "Of course. Would you hand me my cloak from that cupboard there?"

She seemed to Simon at that moment to have found something of the same inner strength as her brother and in silent respect he handed her the cloak, draping it about her shoulders. Two minutes later they went out together and were driven through the rain to Astley House.

Lord Rawdon was waiting for them on the landing above and he came forward at once when he saw her. "My dear," he said gently and put her hand to his lips before he opened the door for her.

She stepped inside and stood still for a moment staring at the bed, stricken by Rupert's appearance. This was not the man she had quarrelled with, who had destroyed her trust, abused her body. Then he had been always in command, always sure of himself. This Rupert was sick and weak, and without hesitation she flung off her mantle and went to him, falling on her knees by the bed and reaching for the hand that lay plucking at the bed covers. And then she saw the ring on his finger. Donald had prized it above all things and now she saw in it the measure of his forgiveness. How then could she do less than he had done?

With a little cry she caught the hot, dry hand to her lips, kissing it and the ring together again and again.

Rupert stirred. "Bab," he murmured, "I wish—but I have been a fool—and she won't—Donald said—" his weak voice trailed away and she got to her feet to sit beside him on the bed, gathering him into her arms. It seemed to her that his whole body was on fire.

"Hush, my darling, hush," she said swiftly, "it is all right now. I am here."

His eyelids flickered and opened and for a moment he looked round uncertainly as if part of his troubled mind caught and held the familiar voice. Slowly full consciousness returned and he said, "I—I thought I heard—"

Tears were running down her face now as she pressed her lips against his damp forehead. "Dear love, you did. I am come home and I will never leave you again."

He turned his head to look up and when he saw it was really she who held him he clutched feebly at her. "Bab—Bab!" A tremor shook him. "I tried—I tried to save him—you do not know—"

She made an effort and controlled her tears. "But I do know. No one could have done more, and oh, my love, at what cost!"

He made a sound, his face pressed against her. "Bab," he said again. "Is it you or did I dream—something—I thought—"

Her arms tightened about him. "It is no dream. I am here, Rupert." She held him so that he rested more comfortably and though for a while the weak restless movements of his fingers, the tremors that racked his body continued, gradually they ceased, his breathing grew more regular. Presently he gave a long deep sigh and was silent for so long that she looked up at the doctor, terror in her face.

He put his hand on the sick man's wrist and then glanced reassuringly at Lord Rawdon and Simon who still stood by the door, before he smiled down at her.

"It is all right, my lady," he said, "he is sleeping. I think now he has a chance."

Epilogue

November 1750

By the first week in November autumn colours were dying in the countryside around Rawdon; the last few bronzed leaves clung to beeches and the hedgerows were bright with spindleberry and hawthorn, and wild rose hips. In the gardens at Rawdon Hall a few roses were still in bloom and the last of the Michaelmas daisies.

When Rupert was at last pronounced well enough to travel he and Bab, with Lord Rawdon, set out for Berkshire. They arrived in the evening after dusk and on the following morning as they sat at breakfast he talked of all he wanted to show her. They were not in the long formal dining room but in the small parlour which trapped the morning sun, and they were alone as Lord Rawdon was as usual breakfasting in his room.

"This afternoon I will drive you down to the village," Rupert said, "and then round by some of the outlying farms. My old nurse lives in one and I know she will want to meet you, my love. There is the house for you to see, of course, but I think we should take advantage of this fine day."

Bab looked out of the window at the sweeping lawns and the flower beds bearing the last vestiges of summer. "The sun is still warm," she agreed. "Are you sure you feel well enough to drive, Rupert?"

He put his hand over hers, smiling. "Thanks to you, my darling, I am a whole man again and I feel extremely well." Then the smile faded from his face and he said gravely, "I wondered whether you would like to walk across to the churchyard this morning? It is only a little way."

She was sitting very straight in her chair but she nodded calmly. "I hoped we could go today. I would have wished to come.when Philip and Simon brought him down here, but you were so ill and you could hardly bear me to leave the room. Nor could I have borne to leave you."

"I know," he said gently. "I remember very little about those first few days, but I do remember you coming—it is something I shall always remember." His grip tightened on her hand. "You are not too tired after the journey?"

"No, indeed. You must not treat me like an invalid, Rupert. I am really very strong and Dr. Morgan said there was nothing to worry about—only I wish I might ride. The park looks very fine."

"It is, and when the spring comes we will ride every morning as we used to do in London, but in the meantime, whatever Dr. Morgan says, I mean to take great care of you."

She gave him a warm smile and as she rose to her feet, laying down her napkin, he walked with her to the window. "The gardens must be beautiful, in the summer," she said. "It is very strange—I used to look forward to the time when we would come here. You remember how we planned that you and I and—and Donald would come together? I never thought it would be like this." She turned her head away and he put his arms about her.

"Don't, my darling," he said swiftly. "He did not want you to grieve. One of the last things he said to me was that I was not to let you grieve too much. He wanted your thoughts to be with the child that is coming."

She leaned her head against his shoulder. "It was like him not to think of himself. Sometimes I cannot believe he has gone."

"I know," Rupert said again, "but I think something of him will always be near us, maybe only memory—but enough." He looked over her head to the sunlight casting the shadow of a great cyprus tree across the lawn. "I think if we had not fought—" for by now he had told her of their duel, "I might not have come to know him so well, but in the short time that I did he taught me what it means to live, and to die, for what one believes in—whatever that may be. I shall never forget him," he added in a low voice, "never."

There were things he had hesitated to tell her while the wound was so recent, but some instinct told him that now was the moment to reveal a little of what he had seen, and he went on, "Simon had me away before the end, but I did see him on the scaffold and I don't think that anyone who was there that day will forget him either. It is odd, I have so clear a picture of him standing there, though everything else is hazy. It is the last thing I remember before waking up in bed at home. Simon said I was quite violent but I don't recall that, only seeing Donald there. He seemed to be—I don't know how to describe it—out of reach somehow, and I believe that what they did to him could not touch him."

For a little while Bab was silent but at last she said, "She was very like him, you know—Mlle de la Rouelle. There was something so akin in the way they took their misfortune. They had so little chance of happiness as we have it, and yet it did not seem the important thing to them. If—if they had lived I would have been glad to have had her for a sister and I used to think," she gave a sad little laugh, "that there could never be anyone good enough for him. But she was. And now they are together. I do believe that."

He was silent for a time, staring out across the gardens to the tall elms beyond. Then he said gravely, "I think we must believe it. But until I knew Donald I seldom thought about such things. Only to him it seemed quite natural."

She turned in his arms so that she could see into his face and they looked at each other in silence, both aware that they were united now in a way that they had never been in the early days of their marriage despite their ardent love. Then he bent his mouth to hers in a long gentle kiss that expressed without words what was in both their minds this morning.

Half an hour later they were walking along a path in the direction of a gate that led to a long walk between two rows of ancient elms. At the gate she paused to look back at the mellow red brick house. "It is a lovely place," she said slowly. "The house looks warm, and secure. I feel a part of it already."

Rupert paused, his hand on the gate and there was an eager look on his face. "Do you? I hoped that you would."

She nodded, picking a few of the Michaelmas daisies to tuck into the lace at her breast, while her eyes roamed over the house and the stables, the barns and gardens and to the woods beyond. "I should like to be here when our child is born," she said slowly. "It must be a happy place for children to grow up in."

"It should be," he agreed. "I was too lonely. But please God it will be different now."

"I wish we had not to go back to London. I would have liked to stay until the spring. There are so many memories in London."

Rupert stood very still, his hands thrust deep into the pockets of his coat. "You can stay here, my darling. There is no need for you to go back to town."

"But I could not be away from you, especially now."

"You need not, indeed I would not permit it. We will both stay here."

"But," she turned to look at him in astonishment, "surely you have to be in London? Or is your regiment to be moved? I thought the Guards were always—" she broke off. "Rupert! What has happened?"

He took the hand which she had laid on his arm. "You remember I went to see Colonel Anderson a few days ago? Well, I went to resign my commission."

"Resign your commission?" Her astonishment grew. "But why?"

He leaned against the gate and scuffed at the gravel with the toe of his shoe. "I have thought of it a great deal, in fact I thought of little else but our future while I lay in that confounded bed, and it seemed the best thing to do. It was," he stared down at the patterns his foot had made, "it was my being in the army that caused all the unhappiness between us and as long as I wear that uniform it will be a reminder. Once I felt proud of it, but one evening in Newgate Donald told me what had made his people come out, risk all they had, and I learned many things I did not know. I learned of the oppression they had suffered, how our authorities have for years tried to crush their way of life, destroy them by every possible restriction. I was in Scotland such a short time myself and I never thought it was worth while to find any of this out. I don't mean that I have changed my political views. Do you remember," he gave a faint smile, "how Donald taunted me once with being too staunch a Whig? But we didn't come out of that campaign very well, and I never liked Fat Willie's methods. Did you know he was nicknamed Butcher Cumberland? And it was justified." Rupert paused and then added, "I have done what seems to be best for us, Bab. Forgive me that I did not consult you, but I felt it had to be my decision alone."

She caught his hand to her cheek. "I know how much the army meant to you. And you have given it up for me, and in a way for Donald too."

He stared at her. "Yes—yes, that's true. I knew you would understand."

"Oh, my love," she said and the look on her face was enough reward for any sacrifice he had had to make. "What will you do now? I think you are not the man to be idle."

He shook his head. "No. I thought if you agreed we would spend most of our time here. There is a great deal to be done on the estate. My father has not been able to do much for a long time and our bailiff is getting old. I know, though he has not said so, that Father would like me to be more than an absentee landlord." He looked around him with some satisfaction. "I think I shall like it very well. I shall turn into a country squire. Will that please you, Bab?"

She laughed. "Very much. I was happy at Astley House, but after a childhood at Duirdre I often felt London very confining. But what of the things you used to enjoy, the clubs and all your friends?"

He answered without hesitation. "I've no regrets there, my dearest. And I was never one for the *"beau monde"* as you know. I think we shall settle down here very comfortably and I've a notion that if we are here Simon will spend a great deal of time at Blaydon Court, which is only about ten miles away. No doubt Harry will favour us with his enlivening company now and again, and Charlie Hay too. Georgy and my aunt and uncle always used to spend a month here in the summer as well as Christmas so expect Philip will fall in with that arrangement. And if I hanker for a visit to White's and you must needs visit your mantua maker we can always spend a week or two at Astley House. As for my father, he told me last night that this place will come alive again now that it has a mistress once more."

She gave a long sigh. "I am so very glad. It is so strange, looking back to Duirdre and then to those days in Edinburgh, that in the end my home should be here, at Rawdon." She paused, her hand on the gate. "I have just realized it is five years ago to this very day that I stood at the window of my aunt's house in Edinburgh and watched my father and Donald march away. It seems like another lifetime."

"I think it was," Rupert said, "for me too. We will try to remember only the best, Bab." He swung open the gate and then drew her hand through his arm. "Come, my love."

They walked down the path for the most part in silence. At the end of it lay the old grey Norman church with its squat tower over which ivy rambled in some profusion and against which the Rector waged a constant battle.

Dark yews surrounded the churchyard and its gravestones and there was a quiet beauty, a sense of peace there that did much to ease the ache in Bab's heart.

"Over here," Rupert said gently and took her to a corner that was separated from the rest by a small railing. "This belongs to my family. My mother lies there next to my grandfather."

There was no need to tell her where Donald lay for there was only one new grave in the small enclosure and she went forward to stand beside it, her head bent and her hands clasped tightly together.

Rupert stayed where he was. These first moments, he felt, belonged to her alone, and leaning on the iron railing he looked out over the low wall of the churchyard to the meadows that fell away to the left of

Rawdon Hall. As far as he could see, and beyond, the land belonged as it had for centuries to the Astleys of Rawdon, and he had told Bab the truth when he said he had no regrets about leaving either London or the army. Even in his most rakish days he had never lost his love for Rawdon, and it needed only a purpose to bring him back.

On this autumn morning the distant woods were a mass of russets mingled with the dark green of the conifers and there was a fresh smell of dead leaves and burning wood and damp earth. He drew a deep breath, remembering how on his last visit to Newgate he had described this place and he pondered once more on that strange fortnight of meetings in a prison cell.

Three weeks ago he had been very near death himself and as he slowly regained his hold on life and his strength came back he had found it was to perceptions sharpened and a mind more keenly alert than before, as if life—so nearly wrested from him also—could no longer be taken for granted but savoured in an entirely new manner because of the man whose mangled remains lay here.

His mind went further back, to a happening that seemed to belong to another age, the burning of Duirdre. He tried to remember John Fraser, but could only recall a tall, defiant figure coming out to meet death. His son was worthy of him, Rupert thought—and how strange were the twists of fate that had brought him and Bab and Donald together. He went to stand beside his wife, remembering Donald's words—that death was but a door—and he had no doubt that though the Highlander's body might rest in a small country churchyard his spirit had long since soared to that freedom it had so ardently desired.

Presently Bab bent down and taking the daisies from the bosom of her dress, she laid them on the grave. Then he led her away between the yews and old grey stones and they walked home under the tall elms where, as he had once told Donald, the rooks would build again in the spring.